STAY
WITH ME

Sheryl Wright

BELLA
B O O K S

2017

Bella Books, Inc.
P.O. Box 10543
Tallahassee, FL 32302

Printed in the United States of America on acid-free paper.

First Bella Books Edition 2017

Editor: Katherine V. Forrest
Cover Designer: Judith Fellows
Family Tree created by Sarah Lever

ISBN: 978-1-59493-549-7

Other Bella Books by Sheryl Wright

Don't Let Go

About the Author

Born and raise on Toronto's Urban Rez, Sheryl struck out at the tender age of sixteen to find her path. In those early days, she worked as a Militia Trooper completing several full-time postings with the Canadian Forces, plus a tour as a United Nations Peacekeeper. In between those postings, she tried her hand at several jobs with one goal: To save enough money for Fight School. *"I was determined to learn to fly, and I wouldn't let anything stop me."* By age 26 she had her tuition, studying aviation at the American Flyers Academy in Florida, while also completing an Electrical Engineering degree in her spare time. Her flight experience includes Canadian Airlines, Bearskin Airlines, and Her Majesty's Canadian Armed Forces, in which she served as both a member and an officer.

In mid-career, she suffered a serious health challenge, and on October 13, 1999, she was pronounced clinically dead. This would not be her only Near Death Experience. *"No one sees a life challenge coming. How you face these trials forge your character. An NDE is the ultimate wake-up call. In the aftermath, I awoke with a new desire…write, write for others, share the journey, and all the dreams whirling around in my head."*

Today, Sheryl is most proud of her first two lesbian contemporary romances from Bella Books: *Don't Let Go* and *Stay With Me*, and has work in the anthology *Happily Ever After*. Her entry into fiction begins with her award-winning military thriller trilogy: *Contrary Warriors: Opposite Sides of the Coin*, *Blood Legacy*, and *Carved in Ice*. Other books include the *Ground Rules for Writers*.

You can reach her by email at info@sherylwright.com. *Please don't be shy. I can't describe how much I enjoy connecting with readers and hearing your opinions and insights.*

Acknowledgments

Have you ever heard the spherical chicken joke? Being the egghead I am, I always LMAO, while my partner and friends give me that look. You know, the "you're being weird again" look. What that also means is I'm the type compelled to share milestones even some that may surprise you. Like my best rejection letter, and yes, if you're pondering the prospect of writing a book, you will get them. Consider them gold. The world is a busy place where someone will rarely take the time to help you learn from your mistakes. That rejection came from Karin Kallmaker, and I continually thank her for it every time we meet and will probably continue to do so for life. Yes, her advice resonated so deeply with me, it produced a remarkable change in my work and spurred me to continue learning and writing until I got it right.

Writing for Bella Books is so unlike my experience of working with my first publisher. First, there is always someone ready and willing to step-up with a level of kindness and professionalism I've not encountered before. From publisher Linda Hill, who when my wife couldn't attend GCLS 2016 Convention in Washington, DC, went out of her way to shield my extreme shyness and was vigilant in making sure I was enjoying myself and not hiding somewhere. Her partner and fellow Canuck Jessica, who translates my Big Smoke localisms and keeps me on point; to Tracie, patient and kind Tracie to whom I owe a Quart of Maple Syrup and a big bear hug. Bella is an extraordinary family in which I am honored to be included.

The best part of the Bella Family is the astronomical skill and quality of the editors and fellow authors. Can you imagine having peers like Pol Robinson, MB Panichi, and Lila Bruce take an interest in your work? And then they assign an editor. Holy *fracking gosa*, Batgirl, it's Katherine V. Forrest! And not once but twice. It's more than an honor; it was downright *Royal*! Oops, I'm showing my Canadianess again.

Much like Linda Hill, Katherine V. Forrest is a force of nature. As a Developmental Editor, she kicks my butt to deliver all the love and guts a story deserves while taming my inner engineer who tends to dream in numbers. Her skill, heart, and kindness come through in everything she says and does. And good *Gods* the woman knows lesbians! Bless 'er heart.

Finally, I want so much to thank everyone who read *Don't Let Go*. It's not your average lesfic romance, it's a complicated story of family and love. Right on! Or should that be Read on? Either way, thanks for being here and please enjoy the journey

Nia: wen; Sheryl

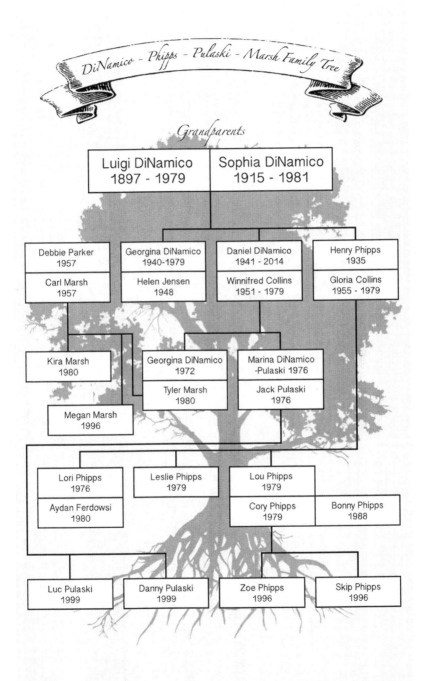

DiNamico - Phipps - Pulaski - Marsh Family Tree

Grandparents

Luigi DiNamico	Sophia DiNamico
1897 - 1979	1915 - 1981

Debbie Parker	Georgina DiNamico	Daniel DiNamico	Henry Phipps
1957	1940-1979	1941 - 2014	1935
Carl Marsh	Helen Jensen	Winnifred Collins	Gloria Collins
1957	1948	1951 - 1979	1955 - 1979

Kira Marsh	Georgina DiNamico	Marina DiNamico
1980	1972	-Pulaski 1976
	Tyler Marsh	Jack Pulaski
	1980	1976

Megan Marsh
1996

Lori Phipps	Leslie Phipps	Lou Phipps
1976	1979	1979
Aydan Ferdowsi		Cory Phipps	Bonny Phipps
1980		1979	1988

Luc Pulaski	Danny Pulaski	Zoe Phipps	Skip Phipps
1999	1999	1996	1996

Dedication

To Kandy and Geneviève

CHAPTER ONE

Georgie DiNamico had that pouty look she got whenever Tyler Marsh tried to convince her she should do something new, usually something she wouldn't like. Tonight the discussion centered on their chosen attire for their upcoming wedding. "Baby," Tyler said, "don't give me that look. You know very well how great you look in a dress."

"Uniform…skirt."

"No! You are not wearing that drab old thing to my wedding." That got a wide grin from Georgie. "*Your* wedding?"

Tyler had to laugh at herself and her stance. Tackling Georgie on the old leather couch, she snuggled in, savoring her scent and warmth. For Tyler, there was nothing as perfect as being held in Georgie DiNamico's arms.

It had been more than a year since that fateful January morning that had started Tyler on this path. When Georgie's cousin Lou Phipps had drawn all the stakeholders and company advisers together to challenge Georgie DiNamico's place in the family hierarchy. For years she had been the heir apparent to the DiNamico legacy but a surface to air missile had changed all that. A pilot with the Air National Guard, she had been nearing the end of her second tour in Afghanistan when her helicopter was hit. The only survivor of the crash, she had endured years of survivor's guilt on top of multiple physical wounds and a debilitating head injury. With the love and support of her family, she had recovered physically but it wasn't until Tyler came on the scene that she really started to live again.

Tyler had done that by simply seeing the woman for who she was instead of judging her by her deficits. And seeing Georgie as the capable woman she was, Tyler had just assumed she would still want to take the helm of the new division. She was just glad the new business plan included a position for someone with her skill set. It wasn't like there were a whole lot of companies out there looking for advice from an economic ethicist, certainly none in western New York.

As soft lips began to trace along Tyler's temple, she couldn't deny the woman loved her completely. That was the thing most people didn't appreciate. When Georgie committed, she was all in without reservation, and Tyler could only thank her stars she had taken a chance on her. Of course, that didn't mean Georgie was without her own opinions. Wedding planning, she was starting to realize, was going to be as challenging as last year's preparations to thwart the attempted hostile takeover of the family company.

While she had gotten Georgie through that and all the upheaval that followed, not everything had gone as planned. The biotech company Georgie had wanted to create had morphed into a leaner enterprise, concentrating on broader R&D challenges. After the company reorganization, Georgie had remained the chief innovation officer at DME and across the newly formed companies. She had named two of her engineers as directors to run the engineering change programs in the other divisions and report to her. Her feisty cousin Lori Phipps was now the president at DynaCraft Yachts. The legacy DiNamico Marine Engineering—or DME—now served as the parent company to both Georgie's new R&D enterprise and

DynaCraft. And a third new company was created to manage investments and real estate. Lou Phipps, now president of that new division, DPP Holdings, had been a bigger challenge to rein in. With her sister Marnie formally named President and CEO of DME, things had worked out exactly as everyone hoped. Even Lou was happier presiding over his own small division. At last there seemed to be accord among the family members and it radiated steadiness throughout the companies.

Everything had worked out as planned with only one real wrench. When the time came to name Georgie president of her new division, DynaTech Research, she had shied away, demurred. This after Marnie and Georgie had spent weeks negotiating the organization, plus sorting things like personnel to be transferred to the new company.

In view of all this, Marnie had taken Tyler out to lunch, just the two of them. Tyler had been perplexed by the invitation, even a little apprehensive. They hadn't gone far, just down to the Fleet Street Grill, and as usual, Marnie hadn't wasted any time. Sitting at the prime table in the restaurant's bullnose, she had ordered her lunch and sampled her CC & Coke before asking straight out, "If you and my sister break up, will you still want to work with her or would that be too hard?"

Tyler choked on a mouthful of too hot coffee, burning her lip in the process. "What? Oh my God! Did Georgie ask you to…no…no she wouldn't…"

Marnie rolled her eyes. Shaking her head, she told her, "Will you relax. Must I remind you, tact is not my strong suit?" Seeming to recognize how much she had startled her, she added, "I'm sorry, kiddo. I promise you, Georgie hasn't said anything to me. Well she has, but it's all slimy-lovee crap. I swear to you my sister is bat crap crazy mad in love with you. That's not what this is about."

Tyler fished an ice cube from her water glass. Wrapping it in the linen table napkin, she pressed it to her burned lip. "Marnie…I swear, you scare the *crap* out of me!"

That elicited a smile. "Sometimes you sound so much like Georgie…the old Georgie," she qualified. "Thanks for that."

She let out a long and somewhat showy sigh before taking another gulp of her cocktail. "But honestly, we need to have a hard conversation. It's the what-if talk and I promise, my sister has nothing to do with this. Am I clear?"

"Yes, I think...but why now?" It was a fair question or at least it looked like Marnie considered it so. Would she answer though? She was stubborn and could not be pushed to make any decision until she was good and ready.

Relinquishing her tumbler, Tyler watched as Marnie resorted to tapping her nails on the linen tablecloth. It was just her thing and everyone knew the more frantic the tapping or clicking, the more complex the information to come.

"You're wasting your time writing papers," Marnie said. "The work you did on the new business plans, the strategy sessions, and this whole innovation factory idea you have Georgie designing is outstanding. I think it's time you take on more, a lot more."

Still pressing the ice cube to her lip, Tyler slumped in her seat. "I appreciate the vote of confidence but honestly, I don't think I can handle another thing. Between the papers you want me to present in Miami, the ongoing strategy sessions, not to mention Georgie's special needs..."

Marnie's tapping fingers migrated from their relatively quiet drumming on the table to tapping on the rim of her drink. "It's time you hire a personal assistant for her. It's not right for you two to be dating or shacking up or whatever you want to call it, and you having to handle her personal shit too."

"Worried she'll start to think it's all part of my wifely duties?"

Marnie snorted at that. "I do love our knucklehead but her middle name is Oblivious!"

Now starting relax, Tyler admitted, "It does make it hard for her to surprise me with anything when I'm the one making all her calls and reservations."

Marnie tittered but then asked with concern, "Please tell me she's not being completely obtuse?"

Smiling, she reassured her, "Trust me, if there is one thing Georgie is not when she's with me, it's obtuse. I'll admit I don't know why, but she just seems so transparent to me. At least she has been. Do you think that might change?"

Marnie shook her head. "Honestly, when it comes to my sister, what you see is what you get. What I do know is her loyalty isn't just some knee-jerk thing the Air Force instilled. I kind of think the only thing she has ever truly craved is to be understood, respected, and to be part of something...*more*. You bring all those things but it's your understanding, your comprehension that matters most."

Finishing off the last of her cocktail, she signaled to the waiter for another. That, Tyler noted, was not usual. She was about to ask what was wrong when Marnie gave out a little giggle. "They're calling you the 'Georgie Whisperer' down in admin."

"Marnie, what's really going on?"

She waited while the waiter delivered their lunch and her second cocktail. "Christ kiddo, how do you always know? Never mind. Here's the thing. I had planned to bring you down here, learn if you could or would cope with a shake-up between you and my sister, even scare you a bit, read you the riot act then let you stew while I made a decision. But I can't do it. I already know what I want to do. The only issue is where you stand with Georgie if things don't work out. And don't do that...don't think something's wrong. This is just a manpower planning exercise, nothing more. Got it?"

Tyler sat up straighter. She was sure there was no reason to worry about her relationship with Georgie, at least ninety-nine percent sure. "Okay, I buy your premise and it is a valid question considering some of the new strategies being incorporated." She was quiet as she sampled her grilled chicken. "Normally, I would raise the issue of ethics in broaching such a conversation between employee and employer, but I'll let that rest. As far as I'm concerned, I'm having lunch with my girlfriend's sister, who is asking personal questions I am willing to answer. So, the easy answer is no. I could not continue on as Georgie's personal assistant if things were to fall apart. I want to believe that I'm mature enough to do so with the executive assistant duties but...

well…traveling with her would be really difficult, especially if she met someone. Then…I don't know…"

"Forget the assistant duties, all of it. You'll hire someone." Reading Tyler's confusion, she explained, "You're the one who has to. You know what she needs better than anyone. Hell, you've turned a crappy job into an art form. You're running a tight ship and you're a damn good judge of character. I'll send the job requisition and salary scale to you and Susan and leave it in your hands."

"And I'm just supposed to hire someone?"

"Well, I would like to meet the final candidate before you offer him or her the job but it's really just a rubber stamp kind of thing. I do it with all new hires, and of course you'll need Georgie's two thumbs up but I warn you now, keep her out of the loop until you have the final pool narrowed down to two or three." Marnie's grin edged into the mischievous as she warned with a wink, "Trust me on this. Do you want her up for three days straight writing heuristic algorithms to make the choice for you? You know that's what she'll do!"

Admitting she was right did make Tyler smile. "Oh God, you do know your sister." She sampled some of her salad, not really tasting anything as she considered Marnie's question. "If I'm allowed to be completely honest here, it would almost kill me to stay if things fell apart, but I love this job too. And I think we both know I would have to leave Buffalo if I wanted to continue working in my field. Frankly, it would suck to come to work every day and see her. It would hurt like hell, but without the assistant duties we wouldn't be working so closely. Under those conditions I would work hard to stay. So, easy answer, yes, I would continue working here if given the chance. Who knows, maybe in time we could be friends. Now, if you're asking me if I had to choose between Georgie and the job, I choose Georgie and I can't imagine a time when I wouldn't."

That drew a smile from Marnie. "Good to know. Although I can't imagine how you would ever be in that position. So, tell me, how much of your billable day is devoted to Georgie's shit? Oops, excuse the potty mouth, kiddo."

"I didn't want to say anything earlier, but you're a little out of character, at least for this early in the day. Is there something else going on?"

Marnie pushed back from the table. It was a distancing action. After a long silence she pulled herself back to the conversation. "Answer my question first. Give me a ballpark?"

"That's easy. Half my day is devoted to Georgie. She still sequesters herself until eleven thirty every day, but once she opens her office door, that's it, I'm needed at her side. Now answer my question please."

"Okay...where do I start?" Marnie asked rhetorically, while resuming her incessant tapping. "I want to offer you a new position, something newly created, but I have some...some family issues that would need to be handled discreetly before the offer could be finalized." She held up her hand to halt further query. "Before you ask, these are my issues that I need to cover with my sister's girlfriend, not an employee. Things I would feel better discussing sooner rather than later."

"Like me and Georgie breaking up?" She was getting upset again but there was no point in letting Marnie know how much. Still, Marnie seemed to waffle between distancing herself and just coming out and explaining what was going on.

Polishing off the second CC & Coke, she stared hard at the empty tumbler but instead of ordering another, she asked for coffee. They waited while their table was cleared and the fresh coffee served. It wasn't until Marnie had the first sip out of the way before she turned her complete focus on Tyler. "My sister loves you deeply. That much I know. What comes next with you two is a complete mystery for me. Not that I mind, but I need to be prepared for all contingencies."

"Such as?"

"Tyler don't do that. I'm not giving you a hard time. Just between you and me, I think you're the best thing that ever happened to her. She loves you and we all see how much you care for her. And everything's changed now. You guys can get married! Is that something you might consider?"

"Marnie, please, this is a conversation I should be having with Georgie, not you."

"Will you just humor me?"

"No, I won't. Honestly, I don't understand where you're going with this." It took everything she had to keep her seat, and the grin on Marnie's face said she damn well knew it.

"You're a pain in my backside but you're also a good egg. So here goes. We want to name you President of DynaTech Research. Now before you say squat, the offer comes with some conditions. Some are for my employee, Dr. Tyler Marsh, but most of these caveats are for my sister's girlfriend. Whom should I talk with first?"

With a rush of delight, Tyler gave her a sheepish grin, starting to comprehend Marnie's situation. "Since conveniently enough you're having lunch with your sister's girlfriend, now might be a good time to talk to her."

"I need you to sign a prenuptial."

Silenced by shock, she finally squeaked out her objection. "What's the issue?" she croaked. "You already have me managing her estate."

"No," Marnie corrected, "I have my employee Dr. Tyler Marsh managing my sister's holdings, not you, not her girlfriend."

The distinction wasn't lost on her but it did take a moment to consider everything she was hearing. "We've been playing with the idea but she hasn't actually asked. I do want to marry her but I also know that things have to happen in a certain order for her. When whatever it is she needs to see happens, if it happens, I know she'll ask and I think you know I have no issue signing anything you want as long as any kids we have are protected. Still, until then, can we shelve the conversation?"

"Sorry kiddo, no. I'm still stuck at the part where she hasn't asked and you aren't a hundred percent sure she will. What's up with that?"

Caught out, Tyler was uncharacteristically lost for words. She shrugged, fighting back tears. She knew in her heart Georgie loved her, wanted to spend her life with her, but she hadn't asked for her hand—or anything, really. She hadn't even asked her to move in, although Tyler had pretty much insinuated herself completely into Georgie's life. Maybe that was why. Maybe Georgie just assumed she was satisfied with that.

"Hey now, let's backup here," Marnie said. "You admitted you understand how she has to check all the boxes off before she can move on to the next step. I'm going to stick my nose in it and speculate that she's waiting for you and me to finalize your new position before she pops the question. Doesn't that sound like her, kiddo?"

Tyler nodded, wiping an errant tear away. "Is that what she's waiting for, for me to agree to a prenuptial?"

"Oh no-no-no, that's all me, kiddo. Georgie would kill me if she knew we were having this conversation but I have a corporation to run and a family legacy to protect. You can understand that, right?"

Finally settling down, Tyler tried to look at the situation from Marnie's point of view. "I'm starting to see a bigger picture. If I take the top job, which I'm not even sure I can handle but, good God, yes I want it! So, if I take the job, we will hire someone to assist Georgie but you don't want to pass all my responsibilities to the new person, things like managing her money. I get that and of course it would make sense to get a written agreement in place before handing that kind of thing off to the girlfriend. I get it, really Marnie I do. I just never considered the distinction. Still, I really think this is something I need to talk about with her, don't you?"

Marnie caved but didn't appear too dejected. "So, you want the job? If you do, I suggest you get your ass in gear and find her a new assistant."

Now feeling much better, she smiled. "You really think I can do it, you and Georgie?"

Offering up her trademark grin, Marnie nodded, finishing her coffee before explaining, "You, kiddo, are perfect for the job. You've been managing her department and leading this new strategy for all these months. Face it: your education and experience make you the perfect choice to lead a startup research firm. And as a bonus, you can manage and communicate with your chief innovation officer and VP of engineering. And…

before you ask, that is the title and job she wants. She was adamant that you be offered the spot as company president. Frankly, I'm a little miffed I didn't think of it myself."

Now, remembering back to that lunch a month ago, Tyler could still feel the roller coaster of emotions that conversation had been. That night, over dinner with Georgie, she had laid out the plan to hire a new assistant before Marnie announced her promotion. Georgie had been so excited, and pleased, and relieved—yet there was still no marriage proposal. As the days, then weeks passed by she started to wonder if she was wrong, even questioning if maybe Georgie was waiting for her to ask. No, she knew that wasn't it.

Almost a month to the day afterward, she was just finishing dinner at her parents' when Georgie sent her a text asking her over. As much as she loved spending her nights with Georgie, she had made some personal rules about spending time with her family, especially now that her sister had delivered a precious little girl. This was her family night. Besides, outside the rain was torrential. Still, Georgie did manage to lure her out. She arrived cranky and disheveled only to find a note from Georgie, "I'm on the roof, G." along with a raincoat and umbrella.

She stormed her way up the fire stairs pissed as all get-out at having to go back out into the storm when she could be home and toasty warm and making googly eyes at her little niece.

Pushing the fire door open she stopped in her tracks. Georgie, decked out in rain gear and wearing the peaked wool watch cap she preferred when sailing, stood in the bullnose much as she had almost a year earlier. Seeing her fearless in the center of a magnificent storm, Tyler had fallen in love with her again. Unlike that night, the weather now was unseasonably warm for snow, but it had deteriorated into a hard cold rain. Lightning, also a strange sight for so late in the season, illuminated the dramatic backdrop, while a dozen hurricane lamps lit a wide circle around Georgie. She reached out, taking Tyler's hand, leading her to the center of the circle, the center of her storm. Then she did something that truly warmed Tyler's heart. She closed her eyes to see the words, words Tyler now knew she had long since prepared.

"When I first read your résumé, I knew you were smart and accomplished and ready for a new direction...When you first entered my office, I knew you were poised and beautiful and prepared for any challenge...But it wasn't until you walked out here, into the storm, that I allowed myself to see something more. I wasn't sure, but I wanted to hope that what I saw was real." She closed her eyes again and Tyler was warmed by the effort it must have taken her to craft her words and commit them to heart. "You once said, you imagined that was the first time in a long time I had felt any attraction to a woman, but the truth is I have never felt for anyone what I feel for you...There is no doubt in my heart or my mind that you are brilliant and gorgeous, the whole world sees that, but you, the real inside you, took my heart and my breath in a way I hope to never comprehend...I love you Tyler Marsh and I want to build a life together, me and you."

Georgie closed her eyes again, opened them, and then, smiling, got down on one knee. Between Tyler almost tackling her on the spot and the pounding rain, Georgie had a hard time getting the rest of the words out, not to mention the ring.

CHAPTER TWO

When Lori Phipps decided to hire Tyler Marsh's baby sister to take over as security for the boatyard, she never imagined the kid would be so diligent much less observant. "You're sure about this?"

The look she got in return was answer enough.

"Hey, no offense kiddo! I know you're on your game. I just don't wanna chase anyone off if they have a legit reason to be down here."

Pulling out the seat at the opposite desk in the little cottage that served as the security shed and her unofficial office, Lori realized she needed more info. "Well, if it's a she, she's obviously not one of the creeps who thinks this is a good place to play whip-o-willie."

Megan smacked her hands over her mouth. "Oh boss! My dad's gonna laugh his ass off when I tell him that one."

Lori grinned. The Marsh family were all good people in her books, even junior here. She had gotten to know the kid during last year's family dustup, her own family that is. The DiNamico/Phipps clan had finally found peace, and a lot of credit was due to Megan's older sister Tyler and her budding relationship with cousin Georgie. *Budding relationship—yeah, right! Those two are madly in love and absolutely perfect for each other.* What she wouldn't give for something like that. Yes, she had made a good life for herself, even building her own craftsman home just steps from the beach. She had a life most people would give an arm for and she rarely lacked for company. Especially now. Since being officially named president of DynaCraft Yachts, it was as if the lesbians were coming out of the woodwork. Too bad she wasn't interested. Oh, she wanted someone, but seeing Georgie and Tyler together had convinced her of one thing. If it's not the real thing, then why the hell bother?

"I don't think she's a creep. I think she's in trouble," Megan said, almost as a confession.

"Trouble?" she asked, having to think that through. Turning her attention back to the parking report, she noted, "She leaves every morning and she's back at the same time every night."

"I checked the computer. I didn't watch through every single night but all the ones I checked, yeah."

"I trust your instincts."

"You do?"

"Yeah, I do. Don't be so surprised. Hell, I never would have even thought to check the computer for overnighters." Lori sighed, trying to decide what to do. "Okay kiddo, what would you do if you were me?"

As if sensing the importance of the question, Megan sat up straighter. Even Lori had to admit she looked the part of a cop in the uniform. Tough, smart, in control. "Well first off, she's not hurting anyone, so I don't really want to give her the heave if she has no place to go." She chewed on her knuckle for a moment then forged ahead. "I think she's in some sort of trouble, probably with her folks. I think maybe she's been kicked out and has no place to go."

"Okay, I'll buy that, but tell me what you're basing that on. More good intuition?"

Looking very much like the cop she wanted to be, Megan removed a memo pad from her pocket and folded it open on the desk. "She usually arrives at one of two times: six thirty or ten thirty p.m. She always has takeout with her. She parks by the spit to eat her meal then places her garbage in the public trash. She then takes a walk to the public restroom. If it's the early arrival, she then leaves the property for a long walk, usually about an hour. Afterward she returns and drives out for a short while. I followed her the other night."

Lori raised an eyebrow, but said nothing. She'd reserve her comments on driving the security truck off the property later.

"She just drove around. Eventually I thought she spotted me, so I just turned around and came back. She pulled back in less than five minutes after I did, so..."

"So, she's just driving around like she has nowhere to go, I get it. What else?"

"I think she's scared, at least at night. When she comes back from her drive or on the late nights, she always tries to park close to the main shed in the little alcove. It's pretty hidden there."

"But we have cameras up everywhere and a big honking Under Surveillance sign. Why there?"

"Honestly, if it were me, that's where I'd park. One, the surveillance signs would discourage any creeps and two, you can't see a car parked there at night unless you pull up right in front of it..."

"What about the security lights?"

"They're on a timer. Once she's in her car and settled in I doubt there's enough movement to trip the sensors."

That surprised her. "Wow, you did do your homework. I had totally forgotten about that. How long do you think it took her to figure that out?"

Megan smiled. "Two nights. She parked under the spotlights by the public washrooms for the first two nights. If I had to sleep in my car, I would pick a well-lit place too. That is if I couldn't find someplace that felt safer."

"And you think she's been parking in the slip because it's safer than out under the spotlights?"

"Here's what I'm thinking," Megan said. "I have to sleep in my car but I'm scared so I pick a place that's really busy twenty-four seven, but that comes with noise and nosy assholes. Next you find a quiet place but well-lit so people aren't too interested in your car but that has other risks."

"Like?"

"Like some asshole noticing you're in your car alone. Even though the parking around the washroom is really bright, there aren't a lot of people around and God knows how long it would take the cops to get out here…well, I'm just sayin', hiding sounds like the safer bet to me."

Lori nodded, agreeing with Megan's evaluation. "So how do we help her out? I mean, if we confront her, she's liable to take off and go hide some other place. I don't know how you feel about it but if we can help one person, then why not?"

"Agreed, but boss, how can we help? You said it yourself, if we try to approach her, we'll probably just scare her off."

Lori sat silently, tossing her lack of options around hoping something would stick. Finally, groaning, she picked up the report again. "So she leaves at six ten every day. Every day?" At Megan's nod, she asked, "Feel like going for a drive tomorrow morning, nice and early?"

"Oh man, don't you think she'd spot the truck?"

"Don't stress it, kiddo. We'll find you some inconspicuous wheels. How's that sound?"

"Maybe I should stick around tonight, you know, just to make sure she's okay."

Smiling, she had to admit the kid was committed to doing the right thing. One day she was going to be a damned good cop. "No worries. I've got the security app on my phone. I can walk over here faster than the cops can respond. I'll set the app to notify me every time the light sensor is activated. There!" She held up her cell phone as proof that she had just changed the settings. "Okay, head on home and say hi to the family and I'll see you bright and early."

Megan grabbed her uniform ski jacket off the chair. All bundled up for the cold, she grabbed the keys to her Chevy and headed out. At the door she stopped. "Boss, thanks for listening. See yah tomorrow."

Lori watched her breeze out, listening for the starter on the Chevy try to turn the engine over. She didn't relax until she heard the engine rumble to life. Well, that was one of her little flock sorted for the day.

As Lori walked from the boatyard to her house, she couldn't help but worry about the homeless woman Megan had noticed. Even for late March, it was still damn cold and the snow had been relentless. Tonight wouldn't be too bad, with temps expected to stay in the low forties. Still, she didn't envy the woman. Her mind had been running wild with all the possible scenarios that would drive a woman onto the street. Why was it always the women who had to run? It seemed women and kids, the most vulnerable, were always the ones to pay.

It was hard not to turn around and go out to the woman's car. She wanted to just ask her if she was okay and what she could do but Megan was probably right. The vulnerable had a way of shying from help. How could they not? Anyone desperate enough to live in her car might be feeling some measure of fear not to mention shame. People were proud. Besides, this was the evening Megan said she wouldn't return, if she returned, until late.

She was trying to decide if she should walk back over later on when she noticed all the lights in her place were on. For a moment she happily imagined that her sister Leslie had stopped by with something for her supper. She did so once or twice a month but she usually called first, teasing that she wouldn't risk popping into Lori's bachelorette pad unannounced. Smelling the sweet scent of a hardwood fire and spotting the corresponding smoke chugging from her chimney, she groaned, knowing for a fact that Leslie would never light a fire in the fireplace. That meant Peachy was here and had probably gone to some great effort to create the ultimate romantic evening. *Sweet baby Jesus...give me strength.*

Lori had made the ultimate mistake with this one, letting a casual hookup get too close. Oh sure, Sue Ellen Peach was a great gal and certainly fun to be with but Lori knew deep down she wasn't long-term relationship material, even if she was sexy as all get-out and had the sweetest ass! It wasn't that long ago she had given up on relationships, but seeing Georgie and Tyler

Marsh together had renewed her white picket fence dream. She was finally in the place where she could care for a family and have the time for a loving and intimate relationship. Too bad old Peachy wasn't the one.

It had been a banner year at work. The upset her brother had failed to orchestrate actually initiated some amazing changes. She was now leading her own company and with Georgie's help and Marnie's encouragement, she had revamped the entire line and rolled out their biggest and best yacht to date. They had debuted the DynaCraft Super 69 at the Miami International Boat Show after taking her for a three-week shakedown cruise. It had been amazing. The Super 69 was big, fast, and fun to sail. Not only did they take the top award for Best New Design, she had personally taken a dozen new orders. She was now in the enviable position of having more work than the boatyard could handle. In this economy it was more than fortunate, it was downright miraculous.

Hanging her coat in the mudroom, she kicked off her work boots and braced herself. It wasn't Peachy's fault she hadn't been clear about her intentions. She had been out with her only a few times before inviting her to come along on the shakedown cruise. To be perfectly honest, she had only asked because Peachy wasn't working and could afford the time away. Besides, the last thing she wanted to do was play third wheel to Georgie and Tyler's lovey-dovey adventure. Setting out from Baltimore in January had been a bit intimidating but seeing that old spark of challenge in Georgie's eyes was all the motivation she needed.

The first four days aboard had been hard on Tyler and Peachy. They had been forewarned that around the clock either she or Georgie would need to be at the helm. Both had offered to serve as watch but the reality of freezing temps, heaving swells, a pitching deck, and having to constantly break ice off the running lines and sheets had been shocking. She did give them credit; cold and miserable, they both stuck it out. By the time they reached the Bahamas, they were thawed and ready to have fun and Peachy had been all that and more. Still, as much fun as they had together, Lori knew there was no emotional connection between them.

"Hey Peachy, I wasn't expecting you."

"Oh, you're home," she said with what almost passed as surprise. "I was just dropping this off," she added, pointing to the casserole dish she was just putting in the oven. "I was in the mood to cook today. I guess I got carried away. When I couldn't find room for it in my fridge, I thought of you and brought it over. I hope you don't mind me letting myself in."

"I see you set a fire too. Feeling cold?" she asked without rancor or encouragement. She was aiming for neutral as she slid into a kitchen chair.

"You're mad?"

"No. It's very thoughtful, but…"

"But, I didn't call and I let myself in which would have been totally embarrassing if you had brought someone home, right?"

Lori tried to smile. "Thanks for remembering that little fact and I do appreciate the food and all but…Peachy, we talked about this."

Smiling and clearly not too bothered by Lori's reaction, Peachy swooped across the kitchen, quickly straddling Lori and wrapping her slender arms around her broad shoulders. "Hey, no worries, okay? I know the dealio! We're just casual, nothing more, and I know better than to just show up here but I just wanted to have a little fun tonight. You can't blame a girl for that, can you?"

Groaning, Lori couldn't help but grab her ass. Peachy was a vivacious redhead, and absolutely crazy in the sack, but she had to be sure. "It's just fun right?"

"I'm just here for a good time," she declared, clamping her lips on Lori's mouth and grinding her ass into her cradling palms. When she came up for air, she added with her lopsided grin, "The casserole will take forty minutes, any idea how we can pass the time?"

Lori knew exactly how they would spend the next forty minutes, and the forty after that, and the forty after that…

* * *

There were really only two ways out of the Cattaraugus Creek community. You could head out the west side on Hanford, or take Allegany. Megan was betting the mystery woman would be headed to Buffalo, and would take Allegany up to Main. Staking her bet, she was parked at the Sunset Bay Restaurant when she spotted the blue Ford. *Right on time.*

For once she was glad she and her dad had spent the evening working on her car. They had finally replaced the starter with one they were sure wouldn't burn out in a week. Since taking up the job as the boatyard's one and only security guard, she had surprised the Marsh clan with her dedication. Back when her boss Lori, Marnie, and her sister's girlfriend Georgie had been hiding out in her family room planning their strategy to fight cousin Lou's takeover attempt, with her sisters and mom lending a hand, she and her dad had spent their time cooking and yapping about stuff. It went a long way to repairing the damage her emotional spat had been causing.

Back then they were arguing about college. She had withdrawn from UB without their knowledge and there had been hell to pay when they figured it out. At the time she couldn't explain it to them. How could she make them understand? College was okay if you knew what you wanted to do. Only thing was, she didn't have a clue at the time. Then she'd overheard Lori complaining that she would probably have to hire some security company to cover the boatyard now that their nephew Ethan was leaving for the Marine Corps. That caught her attention. Not being a security guard but the idea of community policing.

Both Lori and Georgie had been against bringing in some outside security company. The boatyard was the center of a small and thriving community. Everyone knew to call the boatyard security cottage for help and often did because Ethan Phipps had been more than a site security guard; he was family and a welcome face when things were strained. Lori had seen to Ethan's training, sending him off to the Buffalo Police Academy for several courses. The academy commander had been one of the people to write a great recommendation for Ethan that got him into the marines for officer training. At the moment Ethan was in Pensacola learning to fly. How great was that? And Ethan was doing something else. Once he learned Tyler's sis would be taking his old job, he had connected with her on Facebook, offering insights and experience to smooth the way. Now, a year later, they were buddies and had hashed out all the things she was interested in learning and doing.

Following the mystery woman up Route Five, it was easy to see this was the work she wanted. Not following trespassers but making a difference in the community. Her dad was like that in his own way too. Fixing cars and helping your friends and neighbors was cool and all, but policing lit her fire. For the first six months on the job she was just happy to be employed but it wasn't until starting her part-time training at the police academy that she knew she truly belonged in uniform.

Back then she sat with her folks, trying to sort out her feelings and make them understand this boatyard thing wasn't just a sabbatical from university. Megan had assumed they would be concerned because she wasn't interested in some high up degrees and professions like her sisters. It was cool that Kira was a lawyer and Tyler was a…whatever it was she did, but that wasn't who Megan was. She wanted to be a cop. And not just any cop. She wanted to join the New York State Police. She wanted to chase bad guys down the highway and help lost kids get home and…and figure out what would cause a woman to live in her car?

Her parents' first concern had surprised her. They were worried that working for a statewide employer might take her away from them. Her dad got it, but Debbie Marsh had been scared for her little girl. Policing, especially at the community level, was rewarding and dangerous, but what if they wanted her to move way downstate? She had shown them everything on the New York State Police recruiting site, and all the research she had completed by herself. The NYSP would give her a choice of postings and even if she ended up a little farther away than she wanted, she would work her way back to the Greater Buffalo Area soon enough.

They had just hit the Seneca roundabout when mystery woman turned for Route 20. That surprised her but she followed along making sure to leave a car between her Chevy and the blue Ford. Her fourteen-year-old Cavalier was a very common vehicle for the region but she and Carl had invested a lot of time over the last year turning the old convertible into something special. Carl had picked it up at auction thinking it would make a great project for the car club. The front end was completely smashed in but Carl was the best at what he did and could tell the difference between salvage and garbage. While they worked on the frame and body, Georgie had offered a boat engine. It was a strange choice but the Dynamic Straight Six, the only operating prototype built, produced more than 340 horsepower on the Dyno. Even though she ran on diesel, she purred like a kitten and as a bonus, Megan hadn't spent a cent on gas. The boatyard had been turning out their own biodiesel for years. The old fryer grease from three of the local restaurants had been providing all the resource material needed to perk up their own fuel. Nothing was wasted at her work. She liked that, liked the attitude, and the people.

She hadn't really liked Georgie DiNamico when her sister first brought her home. She seemed weird and slow. She would come out with all these big convoluted questions then only utter a few words when you asked her something. It had been her mom, as usual, who had hauled her into the kitchen to give her grief. No one had told her Georgie's head was fucked up from getting shot up over there. Still, it was weird, but Georgie did try and it was obvious that she had it bad for Tyler. Megan hadn't thought much of that. Her only worry had been for how it would look if they got together. But she had been wrong about Georgie. She was good people and so was her family.

Proof positive was Lori's job offer. It had come when Georgie's family had been camped out with her mom and sisters, trying to figure out some business shit. Lori had slipped outside for a smoke and caught Megan sneaking a butt too. That's when she found out from Lori about the security job at the boatyard. It wasn't glamorous but it did come with some police training and a lot of responsibility. Lori said her nephew had done it for a year after graduating from the University of Buffalo while he applied to the marines.

She had spent half the night on Facebook with her academy friends and some state cops asking what they thought. Most considered working as a security guard beneath them and even detrimental to her future application to the state police, right up until someone asked which guard company she was considering. Opinions reversed immediately, when she explained it would be for the DiNamicos. Everyone who knew Buffalo knew the DiNamico family and how they treated their security people. They got their training at the police academy, they had great uniforms and all the best equipment, but better than that, she had learned that a recommendation from them was like a golden invitation to the police force. She'd have to work to earn that recommendation but she was up for the challenge and said as much to her parents when she told them the job required their joint endorsement. Without it, neither Georgie nor Lori would give her a chance. Respect, it turned out was the first rule if she wanted to work at the boatyard or for DME. Respect for family, respect for community, but most of all respect for her own efforts.

All of this was probably why she was following the blue Ford as they made their way along the Buffalo Skyway. It looked like they were headed downtown. That didn't mean anything except she was wondering why the woman had taken the route she had. I-90 would have been faster, so why...*The I-90's a toll road. That cost money.* Sure enough, she followed the blue Ford off the skyway at Church, staying a few cars behind. It was still early, even by downtown standards at just 7:05 as the mystery woman turned cautiously onto Pearl Street.

Megan was considering the irony of having someone camp way out at the boatyard only to spend an hour driving to within a block of their head office...on the same block as the head office. Then the blue Ford pulled into the parking lot for the DiNamico Building. Megan, a little more than confused, stopped her Z24 on Pearl Street and studied the young woman carefully. Sure enough, she parked her car, grabbed a knapsack, and headed for the side entrance with her covered head held low, eyes down, never looking around.

Huh? Mystery Woman works here?

Then why didn't Lori know her? She knew everyone, prided herself on knowing everyone who worked for the DiNamico and Phipps families. Maybe it was just a coincidence. Some of the offices were rented out and she could work at one of them? Still, why would she seek out shelter at the boatyard if she didn't work here? And if she did work here, work for the family, why hadn't someone stepped up to help her out? Megan had worked here for over a year and knew for a fact that the DiNamico/Phipps clan took care of its own and that included employees.

She now had a right to pursue the case, if for no other reason, she convinced herself, she needed to identify the woman in peril to her employers. Trying to decide her next move she jumped when someone knocked at her passenger window. Powering it down, she warned with a growl, "Geez Sanjit! What the hell… you trying to kill me?"

He grinned up a storm, leaning his lithe frame into the open window. "Hey Megan. I didn't mean to startle you. I just wanted you to know you can park in the lot. There's lots of room today. Are you here to see Marnie? Oh, don't tell me you got accepted to the academy before me? Does Lori know? Wait, maybe I should transfer out to the boatyard? What's it like out there in the winter? Hey, open the door, I'll ride into the lot with you and point out an open visitor spot. So, what's the deal, do you have paperwork to do?"

Megan popped the door locks and waited for a gap in his inquisition. "Sanjit! Come up for air, man. I swear, you ask more questions than my sisters put together."

"Kira and Tyler aren't here yet. You didn't come here to see them did you because I don't think Tyler will be here until eight and Kira doesn't come in until the day care opens at eight thirty. Of course you know all that, sorry," he apologized, pointing out the correct parking spot for her. "I was just so excited to see you. Please tell me you got in? That's why you're here, right?" he asked hopefully.

The truth was, they were both applying to the police academy and had hopes of being accepted in the same class. They had started their jobs on the same day, attending training together, and both looking forward to a career in law enforcement. Starting as a security guard at DME, or whatever they were now calling the family of companies operated by the DiNamico/Phipps family, was a good move for good reasons.

Way back during the Depression, old Luigi, the company founder, had needed some security to keep tabs on his building lot and the construction materials he'd been accumulating. Looking for a way to help unemployed veterans, he started hiring them, in time expanding his recruiting to include off-duty cops. Doing so fused a connection between the company and professional law enforcement that lasted to present day. Pretty much everyone working security for the DiNamico companies was a retired cop, an off-duty cop, or a soon-to-be cop. Still, both would-be police officers Sanjit and Megan would have to wait until a new academy class was called. You had to be a hired employee to attend the police academy and that wouldn't happen until the next state funding round or a lot more retirements took place. While they worked here at DME, they were both studying the fundamentals and talking about being cops. It was their thing.

"Dude, take a breath. I'm not here to see anybody. Well at least I didn't plan on it."

"A mystery!" His eyes were big and bright. "Tell me everything."

"Okay, but you can't say anything. Not till I tell Ms. Phipps what I found, okay?" She pinned him with a stern look, waiting for him to nod his acceptance. It was the only time he ever shut up. "That woman that pulled in, in the blue Ford, does she work here?"

He had to think for a minute, looking around the lot. Pointing to the car in question, he asked for confirmation before pulling his smartphone from his jacket and tabbed to the security app he used for parking access and visitor notifications. "Here we go…" The file didn't provide much information but he shared what was there. "Her name is Aydan Ferdowsi; she's an intern in engineering. Let's see who she works for…" He tabbed through another page before saying in confusion, "It says here she works for Tyler Marsh? Did you know, oh no, what's this about? Not Georgie, please tell me it's not like that?"

"It's not like that. Geez, will you chill already!" At least she hoped it wasn't like that. Shit, if Tyler broke up with Georgie… no, that couldn't be it. She waited for his incessant questioning to peter out. The minute he settled down, she told him the whole story of the mystery woman.

"What are we going to do?"

"I don't know yet. I guess I need to talk to Ms. Phipps."

"Not your sister? If the big bosses find out we knew this woman was in trouble and we didn't do anything…"

"We'll do something, I promise. Just keep it to yourself for now. Let me get back to the boatyard and talk to my boss. Seems as how that's where Miss Ferdowsi likes to hide out, it might be better to approach her out there."

"Maybe. March might signal spring to some but it's still darn cold out. We can't let her sleep out there for another night, can we?"

"No way, buddy. Don't worry. If Ms. Phipps can't think of something, I'll talk to Tyler. She's supposed to be a big boss now too. I bet she can help. At least I hope so."

"Me too." He climbed out of her car and opened the lift gate for her to head back out for her shift at the boatyard.

She had some of the answers Lori Phipps was looking for, she just wasn't sure if she'd be all that happy about them.

CHAPTER THREE

Aydan was quick to dress and cover her head, always concerned someone would walk in on her. She didn't think anyone would question her showering in the women's basement locker room. Everyone was welcome to use the mini-gym across from the machine shop, and she was sure the early morning security guard just assumed it was why she came in when she did. She wanted to believe she didn't care what he or anyone else thought, but she did. Stepping up to the mirror, she expected to see dark drooping bags under her eyes or deep creases along her forehead. She didn't. To her own eyes, Aydan Ferdowsi looked exactly as she had before, before her world came crashing down.

She sucked in a harsh breath, forcing herself not to cry. She had been weeping too much and for too long. If she had no place among her family, then she would banish all thoughts of them. As she adjusted her hijab she asked herself, quite unkindly, why she still wore it. This situation had forced her to forget her colorful silk scarf she loved to wear, opting instead for the drab and traditional hijab. Still, she had more to consider than whether her family would object. At the moment though, she bowed to the habit out of necessity. She would wait until her hair grew back then she'd worry about faith, modesty, and a million other things she could now choose for herself.

It was hard enough trying to find your place in the world without the people you love holding you back. All those years of walking on eggs, kowtowing to the views of others, and constantly trying to prove she was a good daughter had taken a toll. Today, she would turn thirty-seven. *Thirty-seven years old—and what?* She had been a docile child, an obedient young woman, even going so far as to turn down a full ride scholarship to Cornell. Instead, she had done her duty to family first, playing full-time nursemaid to her ailing grandparents. Enrolling at UB, she had been allowed to complete only one course at a time. It had taken all these years but she had finally completed her engineering degree. The only thing stopping her from pinning PEng to her name was her co-op time or lack thereof.

Two years ago, when her grandfather passed, she had assumed she would be allowed to take on an internship but her grandmother, who ruled the family with an iron fist, had vetoed the idea. Now she was gone too, but that didn't seem to matter to her mother. After completing all her course work, she sat with her mom, explaining the need for real-world experience. She wouldn't approve. It was time to marry. Aydan was a smart girl from a good family. There was no need for her to lower herself to work for strangers, or risk her reputation by working with men. Aydan had been prepared for that, explaining that her academic adviser had found a placement for her with a company run by women. Her mother sat stone-faced as her little brother and arch nemesis, searched the Internet for information on DME and DynaTech Research. He read to them of the recent company restructuring, the naming of Marnie Pulaski as CEO, the new R&D company, DynaTech Research, and its management including the Afghanistan veteran Georgina DiNamico, and her fiancée Dr. Tyler Marsh. They might have missed the significance of that announcement if her stupid brother hadn't shown the webpage to everyone. Of course

Ms. DiNamico and Dr. Marsh would have stupid engagement photos up and on the corporate website no less! She didn't have a chance.

Back at UB the next day, she had witnessed the look of both shock and revulsion when she had tried, badly, to explain why her mother forbade her to work at DME. Her academic adviser had clarified in no uncertain terms that she was free to accept any internship available. He couldn't, however, help her in finding one where she could set her own hours, work with other female engineers, have a woman boss, and be involved in cutting-edge R&D. DME was a unique company both in outlook and within the region. Under their new organization, they were only accepting two interns per year and every student in the engineering program had their name on the list. The only reason she was being offered the placement was her marks. As if to accentuate his point, he held up his cell phone, "I have the names of the next twelve students on the list right here. You say you want something else. Right now I can offer you an internship at a packing plant. Either that or there's a company that sells cardboard boxes. Say the word and I'll switch you to one of them and give the guys a shot at their number one pick."

Staring at the phone as if it might make the call all on its own, she tried not to panic. She'd been in this position before and knowing it made the moment so much worse. She didn't like people making decisions for her, never had, yet she had sat passively all her life as exactly that took place. The last time it felt this horrible, she was twenty-one and had just finished her first year at UB with marks that placed her at the top of the Chancellor's List. Sitting with her mother she was paralyzed as her grandfather explained to the recruiter from Cornell why she could not accept their scholarship. It all sounded like bullshit to her and judging by the look on the recruiter's face, he thought the same. Just like then, she was being warned that there were others, not as smart or as deserving, who would receive their offer. She had said she understood, standing firmly at her mother's side. Still, every night, she had lain in bed reliving that moment. And in time she had changed the outcome, practicing everything from compromise to outright defying her mother and grandparents. Still, here she was in the exact same situation and being offered a second chance and what was she doing but the very thing she hated herself for, over and over again... "Wait..."

He placed his smartphone back on his desk and gave her time to explain. When she remained silent, he offered kindly, "Aydan, I have been your adviser for almost ten years. You are my top ranking part-timer and my greatest concern. May we speak as friends?"

She nodded, but didn't look up.

He lumbered out of his tiny office and returned with a faculty member in tow, closing his office door behind them. It wasn't something he usually did with students, especially females, and never with her.

"Aydan, I would like to introduce you to Professor Winowski, she is the Dean of Applied Math."

Aydan stood, offering her hand to the older and taller woman. That didn't happen often, the taller part. At five-nine, she was used to being the tallest woman in the room, certainly the case at home. Dean Winowski took a seat.

Her adviser explained, "I have asked the dean to join us, so that you might get a woman's opinion on your situation and your options. I also thought you might like to ask her some questions about the internship at DME. She's the academic liaison for them and knows most everyone over there."

Unsure of what to say, she sat in embarrassed silence, watching the two faculty members exchange looks. Dean Winowski took the lead, edging forward in her seat. "Aydan, David has spoken at length with me about your academic achievements. Given your limited access and schedule, I can't help but think you must be a remarkable engineer."

"Thank you, Dean. I took your freshman class," she added shyly.

"I remember. You were quite a fan of Mandelbrot, if I recollect?"

That made Aydan grin, finally giving her the courage to look up. She was rewarded with an open and reassuring smile.

"I understand you're trying to choose a placement for your cooperative learning credits. May I ask what your options are?"

Nodding, she wanted to explain but caved under the woman's scrutiny. Instead she looked to her academic adviser for help.

He was long used to her reticence and jumped in. She half listened to him describe the opportunity at the packing plant. Just the idea of having to work in an office adjoining a meat factory made her ill. Still, she considered it as he droned on. She liked Dean Winowski, respected her, and knew as she watched her polite interest that the woman would never consider such a disgusting job. Maybe if she explained about her mother, about her concerns for her welfare, not to mention her morals…It wasn't until he moved onto the job at DynaTech Research that the dean took any real interest.

"DynaTech Research. Are we talking about one of the new companies to come out of last year's restructuring at DME?" At his nod, she qualified, "Is this Georgie DiNamico's new enterprise, or one of the cousins'?"

He retrieved a printout of the placement offer, reading the details to them. "According to this, the intern will be working directly for Georgie DiNamico on a small research team. She has specifically asked for an engineer with strong applied mathematics and an interest in marine architecture and hall geometry. I thought of you the moment I read it," he told Aydan with an encouraging smile.

She couldn't bring herself to comment in any way, and watched as the two professors shared a glance.

Dean Winowski asked him to give them some time alone. Once the office door closed the dean looked at her with concern. "Aydan, I'm not a counselor but what I'm about to tell you is important. What I need you to know is this is my personal opinion, not the opinion of the university or anyone else. What I'm about to share is personal and difficult but I can see you're in trouble and for what it's worth I want to help. Do you understand my warning? This talk is just between you and me. Two adults talking about life, understood?"

"Yes, Dean."

"Okay, let's start there. Please call me Sandy. Technically you're not an undergrad anymore and we already decided we were just having a friendly chat, so…"

"Okay, Sandy," Aydan offered with an amused grin. She had always liked the dean and loved her class.

"I understand you need to complete your co-op time before you can graduate, and I also know your mother has set some boundaries which you have respected since the day you started here. Tell me Aydan, how old are you now?"

Startled by the question, she stumbled to answer, "I'll be thirty-seven—first of March."

Clearly the dean wasn't surprised. "You've been at this a long time. I admire that. Frankly, I think you're one of the few students who has completed a degree in the maths and sciences one course at a time. That takes dedication and tells me you want this." At her nod, the dean pushed on. "Okay, good. That's good to know but here's the hard part. Engineering is usually a full-time endeavor. Oh, there are lots of people, especially women, who do well working at it part time, but almost always after putting in several years full time first. Now, I know you have obligations at home…"

"It's not that…"

Dean Winowski sighed, sat back and crossed her arms. After a long moment, she seemed to become aware of her body language, dropping her arms and her judgment. "I can't imagine growing up in this day and age in such a sheltered manner. Don't get me wrong. I respect the effort and the love any family must have to protect their children. It's just that sometimes they can mistakenly protect them from the very thing that could make their lives better. Take this placement with Georgie DiNamico. First, the woman is a big out-and-proud lesbian and that's a problem, because…?" she prompted much as she would in class.

"My mother believes her morals are corrupting."

"What do you believe?"

"I…It is a sin for a woman to live as a man."

Dean Winowski nodded. "I'm with you there, sister. I also happen to think women and men should be free to live as their conscience dictates so long as they don't impinge on the rights and freedoms of others. By the way, Georgie DiNamico is a friend. I haven't known her long. I was introduced on New Year's Eve by her partner Professor Tyler Marsh. The one thing I can guarantee you is that Georgie DiNamico does not live as a man."

Aydan colored at the comment but wanted to fight back, to defend her mother's point of view but before she could think of a suitable comeback, the dean added another fact.

"You can't really be this sheltered. Come on, it's 2017! And regardless of the disgusting rhetoric fueled by last year's election, sexual orientation is still protected by law in this state. Gays and lesbians have been able to marry anywhere in the country for almost two years now. Hell, I think it was made legal over the border more than fifteen years ago! You don't really expect me to believe you're scared to work in the same office as two women who happen to love each other?"

As Aydan's face colored at being called out. She watched as Sandy's brows raised practically to her hairline. "Oh good God!" She stood as if to pace but there was literally no place to go except out of the tiny office. Instead she sat back down, her face now devoid of any emotion. "I'm going to be frank with you, Ms. Ferdowsi. Georgie DiNamico is a UB alumnus and a great supporter of the engineering program, both financially and with jobs, scholarships and internships. For example, the internship we are discussing here did not exist two weeks ago. When we met on New Year's Eve it was to discuss a donation to the Applied Mathematics program. She didn't just listen politely and write a check. She listened, asked questions but more than that, she asked how else they could help. We came up with this new internship, an internship that pays a completion bonus and offers a chance at a real full-time engineering job at a company with more women engineers, not to mention management, than any in Buffalo. When she made the offer, I immediately thought of you. It's a small team, working on a variety of challenges, in a supportive and safe environment. I thought it was the perfect place for a shy, socially naïve young woman. That you're concerned that Ms. DiNamico won't respect your boundaries because you're a woman is completely delusional.

"First let me tell you a few things about her. One, she is a veteran, a vet who suffered some serious injuries over in Afghanistan. Every day she has to deal with serious deficits. Deficits that would have left anyone else to rot in a VA hospital, but her family loves her and brought her home and did all they could to help her get better and adapt to her new reality. They hired my friend Tyler Marsh to help with work and communications for her. My friend Tyler fell head over heels in love with that woman. Do you want to know something interesting? Tyler had to give her written permission before they could begin dating. Yes! And you know why?" she asked, not waiting for Aydan's reply, "because she created very strict rules to protect her employees from being taken advantage of by more senior staff. My friend Tyler, who you should know was already out as a lesbian to her friends and family before going to work there, admitted it was the most eloquent policy she had ever read, and she writes that stuff for a living!

"Now, let me tell you something else. Georgie DiNamico does not willingly suffer fools. You, young lady, may have the best marks, and are perfectly matched to this opportunity but that doesn't mean you deserve it. If you were seventeen and sitting here and telling me you were scared about working with a big old dyke, I would be happy to spend some time counseling you, providing the kind of basic information and knowledge needed to come to your own conclusions. But you're not a child, you're a grown woman. I can't and won't speak to your home life but neither will I accept your excuses. There doesn't seem to be a limit on how many students want this job. So, if you don't want the placement at DynaTech Research, no problem, you can keep hiding behind your mother's wishes. You will not get a placement and you will not graduate. Or, if it's really your morals you fear for, then I suggest you take the job at the meat packing plant. You can punch in at eight a.m. and spend your days writing reports on how to improve the slaughter, storage and packaging of local pork. All the engineers there are men so you won't have to worry about lesbians. You will have to fetch coffee and put up with being treated like a secretary, but the job is what you make of it. I can't say it will lead to employment. They have never hired any of our interns. Of course, I can't say anyone was interested."

When she stood again, Aydan knew it was her last chance. If she didn't say something, do something, it would be Cornell all over again. "Please Dean...Sandy...My mother..."

"No. Start with what you want, not your mother. Understood?"

She nodded, pushing past her fear and doubt to try and explain. "I have no income. I...I'm supposed to marry. It's all arranged. I tried to convince my mother I should finish school, but when I told them about the internship she was...She doesn't understand why I would want to work for free and then when I told them who they were, she had my brother look it up on the Internet. He showed them the picture of those...your friends and told them how they were..."

Still standing, the dean moved behind David's desk and leaning over the computer, input the URL for DME. She clicked on the tab for Media Releases and scrolled down to click on a recent link. When it opened she smiled, then turned the monitor for Aydan to see. "Is this what your mother saw?" she asked.

On the screen was the press release announcing the engagement of Major Georgina DiNamico Jr., USAF Res (ret.) of Buffalo, to Dr. Tyler Marsh, PhD of Williamsville, New York. Looking at the professional engagement photo had lightened the dean's mood. The picture, taken outside in winter, had the two women in jeans and ski sweaters, leaning against the end of a picnic table. On the table between them and proudly embraced by both was a huge chocolate Labrador retriever. "Tell me, do you find this photograph offensive?"

"My mother..."

"Not your mother, Aydan, you! Do you find this photograph...to hell with that. Are you really offended to work for someone who would pose for her engagement photo with her dog at center stage?"

Shamed, she was silent, desperate for a thread of response. She never got the chance to explain that her mother would kick her out, and had threatened to do much worse. The dean turned for the door, wishing her luck in her academic endeavors, walking out.

Aydan had chased after her and down the hall. "I want the placement," she begged, "Please Dean…Sandy."

Turning back, the Dean studied her hard before asking, "Why?"

While a million warning bells went off in her head, she pushed away all the nonsense and biases she heard every day to utter the only thing that truly mattered, "I want to learn."

Clearly Dean Sandy Winowski was considering her words carefully. At last she nodded. "I'll tell David to go ahead and set it up. I am quite sure your education and modesty will be as well respected by the lesbians at DME as they were during our unchaperoned meeting." With that said, she turned and marched away down the hall.

It was easy now to remember how shocked she was. Had Dean Winowski just come out to her? She had waited for David, her academic adviser to return. After everything that had just transpired it seemed almost stupid watching him go to the lengths he did to make sure she was comfortable in his presence. She had never noticed that before. How he never shut his office door or how he always made sure to schedule her appointments when his admin assistant was in. She had just spent ten minutes alone in an eight by eight cube of an office with a lesbian. How she wished she had the courage to throw that in her mother's face.

She had never imagined it would be her mother who would turn on her. The names she had called her, the threats she had made. One would imagine she had become a prostitute or slept with one hundred men all in one night. Marriage, her mother had advised, was much more important. Only women of low status would take a job and only those of the lowest character would work for such vile and sick women. She had ached from all the crying, and fighting, and all because she wanted to work as an engineer. Nothing she said made a difference. Her mother would not approve. In the end it had come down to taking the placement and lying to her or giving up.

She knew she wouldn't get away with lying to them for long but naïvely believed she could convince them of the merits if they could see she hadn't been corrupted. Unfortunately, her story of spending her days at the university library flew for all of two weeks. During the third, just days before Ms. DiNamico and Ms. Marsh returned to work from the Miami Boat Show, her baby brother took it upon himself to follow her. That night when she returned home her mother was waiting with sewing shears in hand.

"If you insist on shaming us then you give me no choice." Her brothers held her in a headlock while her mother snipped savagely at the colorful scarf that covered her head, then her long dark hair.

Aydan had spent the night alone in her room, curled in a ball and crying. All evening she kept imagining her mother coming to her. She would say she was sorry for overreacting, but she never came.

It was after one a.m. when she finally ventured out. As she made her way downstairs, she couldn't help but note all the lights were off. The kitchen too was spotless. There was no dinner plate in the microwave or fridge. Nothing had been left for her, as if she had already disappeared from their lives. That thought didn't actually coalesce until she went into the family room. She remembered closing the door so as not to disturb anyone and sitting down at the corner desk to use the family computer. She wasn't sure what she was looking for but she had to have some answers in place by morning or she would have to give up on the internship. There had to be a way.

She opened up the browser only to have a password dialogue box pop open. That didn't make sense. She closed Google, then reopened it to have the box pop up again. She tried bypassing it, even switching to another browser, but without luck. How long had she sat there staring at the stupid password prompt? She would be thirty-seven in a few months and her mother didn't even trust her to surf the Internet without supervision?

The tears had come with the comprehension of the betrayal. She had done everything they had asked. She was modest and humble. She had never spent a single night anywhere but under their roof. She had never been with a man yet she had been accused of that—and why? So she would marry some stranger. Someone she didn't know, didn't love, and might never love. And for what? To please her mother? Maintain their standing in the community? Appease God?

It felt like sleepwalking, at least it did now, standing in the women's locker room, staring at her reflected face, remembering. That night she quietly made her way back to her room and waited patiently to be sure no one would take it upon themselves to come check on her. When she was sure everyone was asleep, she silently packed, careful to take only her books and work clothes. All she wanted from this life that she was leaving. From deep in the closet, she retrieved a small box. It contained the only gift her grandmother had ever given her, a delicate gold ring, and her personal savings of eight hundred dollars. It wouldn't go far but she owned her little car and could always sell it too. Whatever it takes, she had promised herself then.

Now, heaving her knapsack up, she shouldered her way out of the locker room. "Whatever it takes," she promised herself again. She wanted to learn and after three months at DynaTech Research she could honestly say Dean Winowski was right, this was the place where she would learn and where she was fast coming to understand she would be accepted and respected. She wasn't becoming a whore like her mother warned and she wasn't being treated like one either.

CHAPTER FOUR

It was just after ten when Tyler tapped at the lower level door to Marnie's office. She had spent a significant amount of time here when it had been Georgie's office. During the first months of the reorganization, they had continued to work with the team imbedded with the DME Engineers on the seventh floor, and with Georgie still in the big two-story executive office. Then the problematic Lou had fucked up, again, jacking up the rent for the long-term tenant occupying two, three, and four, plus half the lobby level. The tenant had gone to Marnie to intervene but she had hit that old familiar wall of Lou's pride and ego. Instead of giving in, even just a bit, he had insisted on the full increase of rent and fees. The tenant had countered with notice and now they were gone. Marnie, mad as all get-out, couldn't overrule him then. But what she could do was control which company resources were made available to the other divisions.

The new R&D company, DynaTech Research, was immediately relocated to the second floor and they had successfully moved Georgie into a quiet corner there too. They had lots of room with the entire space available for their use.

They had chosen that floor because the space needed the least amount of work and was basically all open concept. Something Georgie wanted. She wanted to create the same working atmosphere she'd had in a smaller scale in the machine shop and Tyler had agreed as long as they also had a quiet space for Georgie to fall back on. The two corner offices on the east side were perfect. Tyler had taken the smaller one and put a meeting table, couch, and Georgie's private desk in the other. Her work desk Georgie insisted be out on the floor with her engineers. Everyone had worried about that decision but Tyler backed her up knowing she could make changes, if need be.

At Marnie's bellowed greeting, she strolled into the familiar showcase office. With Marnie now in residence the decor had changed significantly. Gone were the volumes and volumes of books, replaced with industry awards, Best-in-Show yachting trophies, plaques and other items that recognized the company's years of corporate charity and community involvement. There was even a long shadow box that displayed over forty Pee Wee hockey jerseys in an overlapping arrangement and with a printed time line highlighting the forty years DME and the DiNamico family had been supporting Buffalo kids in sports.

Tyler wasn't surprised by the changes, only by how long they had taken. "Have I walked in on a family meeting?" she asked, a bit confused to see Lori and Leslie both present.

"Come on in." Marnie waved without any further explanation.

"Hey, Tiger!" Lori called jovially.

She wasn't sure which surprised her more, Lori attending a meeting in person, or that Leslie, her younger sister, was there. After all, Leslie Phipps not only avoided family politics, she was a chef and operated the upscale Fleet Street Grill on the street level, which was where she should be at this hour. Before she could comment, she heard someone following in behind her.

"Sorry guys, just had to pump."

It was Kira, Tyler's sister. She had been named counsel to the DME board back during the original shake-up. At the time she was also nine months pregnant. Once her maternity leave had ended, she had taken up her new post to find that Tyler and

Marnie had created a day care program right in the building. It was perfect. With the now thirteen-month-old Ella just a floor away, Kira, and pretty much everyone else, would drop in during the day for playtime. It was an unheard of luxury and was especially welcome for the single and first-time mom.

"Okay…now I'm worried," Tyler said. "Marnie, what's going on?"

"Relax, kiddo," she offered in her usual wholehearted way. "This is more of a family discussion," she added, drawing a circle in the air to indicate the family she was encompassing included them all, DiNamico, Phipps, and now Marsh. She waited until everyone had settled into the meeting area. It was still set up much like it was when this was Georgie's office, with a long couch across from the fireplace and the big-screen wall monitor.

Tyler joined Lori on the adjacent love seat. The one opposite them had been replaced with an upholstered chair more to Marnie's liking and let her sit closer to the fireplace. Tyler noted the heavy Pendleton blanket tossed over the back of Marnie's chair, her proximity to the blazing gas hearth, and was struck by a frightening thought. *Holy shit, Marnie's going through menopause! Oh, no…she's four years younger than Georgie.*

She turned her mind to a more pleasant topic. They had just started planning their wedding. It had never occurred to her that she should be thinking of kids so soon but she wanted kids and seeing how great Georgie was with little Ella and even her own teenage nephews, she was sure Georgie felt the same. *Didn't she?*

"Tyler, I don't want to put you on the spot but what's the plan for housing your division?" Before she could answer, Marnie added, "Here's the thing. Leslie and I have been talking about business needs and we both agree that the current vacancies can be better put to use than for rental income. Leslie has come forth with a business proposal to expand her restaurant to one or two floors of banquet facilities. The return on investment surpasses our current rental income with just twenty percent occupancy, which I believe Leslie can meet. Your two votes," she pointed her ballpoint pen at Lori and Tyler, "are all we need to proceed."

Lori nodded. "I'm in. Good work, sis. I know it'll be great!"

When the expectant faces turned to Tyler, she nodded. "Without actually reviewing the proposal…Wait, can I ask, are we intruding on Lou's territory? I don't mind, but I would like to be prepared."

Surprising her, it was Kira who answered. "Actually, Lou screwed the pooch when he tried to strong-arm the tenants into a huge rent increase. The terms of Uncle Henry's assignment of responsibilities specifically forbade anyone from the type of thing he was trying to pull off. Henry was firm that each of the Phipps kids play fair or lose control of that aspect of their job. As expected, control of the DiNamico building has reverted to the board, so, basically, you three."

"Well, then." Tyler acknowledged the point knowing they'd have to deal with Lou's crap at some stage. "Normally, I would want to discuss a board vote with Georgie. Technically, I am representing her in these things but we both know she will see this as a win/win. Congratulations Leslie, and please tell me which floor will you start with and will it be ready in time for me?"

Grinning, Leslie nodded at the possibility that she could be open in time to host Tyler and Georgie's wedding reception.

Marnie cleared her throat. "Here's the thing, kiddo. I know you just got my sis settled on the second floor but we think it's the best choice for Leslie."

"Really? I would have thought you'd want to take over the ballroom on eight. Engineering on seven has a nicer view too."

"True," Leslie admitted. "But either choice would require a second kitchen and more staff. We'll still have to get someone in to rip the walls open and access the old dumbwaiter, gas lines and water pipes anyway…"

"And refurbishing a mini elevator and installing a few bar sinks is cheaper and easier than setting up what would basically be an entire second restaurant?" When Leslie nodded, she confirmed, "I get it and I'm not too worried about Georgie. She's adapting really well. I think having a small team and a buffer are all making a difference."

"Come on, Tiger," Lori injected, giving her a love tap on the arm. "Admit it. As long as you're at her side, she does better. You're doing great!"

Tyler colored slightly at the compliment. "What I can't tell you is how long it will be before I can move our division out to the boatyard."

"Yeah," Lori said, tacitly admitting to stalling on her part. "I plan on dragging Georgie around the peninsula as soon as it warms up a bit, which brings me to the reason I'm actually sitting here today and not calling in as usual."

Marnie cut her off. "Tyler, I need you to move your team upstairs."

"Back to seven?" she asked, her brows arching. "I can't put Georgie—"

"No, eight. I know it's not ideal but it's more than enough space and has the advantage of being right across the hall from Georgie's—"

"The ballroom? Is that what you're talking about?"

"Well, we have been using it as a ballroom for the last ten or so years, but before that it was office space and we have money in the facilities budget to make capital improvements."

"What's this all about?" Tyler wanted to know.

"It's simply long-term planning. If your division is still destined for Cattaraugus Creek, then putting you on eight gives us the freedom to update the vacant floors to the same standard as the rest of the building, plus take the time to control the expansion to Leslie's business. Now all we need to know is when you can have your people ready to move again."

Tentatively Tyler nodded her agreement. "Understood. What I would like to do is take Georgie up there and propose it to her for suggestions. Once I know how she envisions the setup, then I can sit down and hammer out the dates. I take it the contractor is ready to go?"

"They're set to start Monday."

"Don't let Georgie see them until I get her upstairs and she's decided this was all her idea!"

Marnie actually laughed at that. "Good God, you do know my sister. Can you make that happen soon?"

Tyler nodded. "Today. As a matter of fact, I'll drag her up there after her team meeting. I'll bring her new intern as an excuse to look the space over."

"Okay," Marnie said, now absently clicking on her pen. "That brings us to another situation, one your sister brought to our attention." When Tyler looked to Kira, Marnie corrected her assumption. "Your other sister."

"Megan?"

Kira nodded. "She's proving to be quite a diligent peace officer. But I'm afraid we're a little confused about what to do with her latest investigative findings. Maybe I should let Amazon Woman explain it to our ethics officer."

Lori grinned; she liked it when Kira called her that; as much as she liked playing the big sister to her and aunty to little Ella. "So here's the thing. A young woman seems to be living in our parking lot, in her car. We both let it slide at first, not wanting to cause her any problems. She's gone all day, so we figured she probably had a job and would be okay, but then Megan came to me yesterday, really worried. Megan tells me she's been through every inch of surveillance tape, and she was sure, and I agree, the girl looks like she's scared to death. She parks under the most brightly lit spot closest to the stuffing shed between three surveillance cameras. And it's still winter in western New York. Now I'm totally freaked—between who or whatever has that kid so scared and her possibly freezing to death, we have to do something but I didn't know what to do."

"And you do now?" Tyler asked.

Instead of answering, she tipped her head to Kira.

"It seems our little sis is an insistent thing. This morning she followed the young woman from the boatyard to her place of work."

"Oh, God no! Please tell me she didn't get in trouble?"

"Oh, it's worse than that," Kira confirmed as she opened a file on her tablet. "She followed her to her place of employ, and by accessing the security records on site, identified the young woman as an employee of DynaTech Research."

With four expectant faces staring at her, Tyler considered it best to work out the implications aloud. "Before we even touch on the fact that a young woman in our employ needs help, do we need to discuss the privacy infringement and unauthorized access to personnel records?"

"Tyler," Marnie intervened, "Kira believes we're covered. While Megan may not be justified in following someone from Irvine to here, she has a right to challenge the access credentials of all employees. Accounting for our employees on property, all properties, is also in her job description. What I think we need to resolve is how to help this unfortunate young woman and if we can address her safety concerns without prying into her situation, embarrassing her or making her any more vulnerable."

While appreciative of their adherence to the rules she had set for discussing privacy-related issues, she understood the situation required the involvement of everyone in the room. "You know, I only have two women engineers—well, three if you count…oh no, Aydan? I knew there was something wrong!"

"Explain," Marnie ordered.

"She started in January, just before we left for the shakedown cruise. On her interview she struck me as very timid and shied away from the guys, so I gave her a cataloging job and had her report to one of the women engineers. She did a great job; she even built a database for Georgie to search all of her aunt's papers and designs. I had high hopes but the last few weeks have been rough. She's become more and more difficult and even less willing to work with the guys. And she's complained about assignments, constantly comparing herself to the salaried professional engineers. She's been impatient with Georgie and yesterday snapped at her in a team meeting. Frankly, I almost dismissed her then and there. Georgie stopped me and quietly asked for a few more days to work with her and I agreed."

"Hey there, Tiger, no worries," Lori assured her. "We all roll with Georgie's requests."

Marnie's incessant pen clicking brought them back to the point at hand. "Tyler, I'm not saying she's your problem but she is on your staff. Do you have any idea how we should handle this, other than just giving her the number for the nearest shelter?"

"Honestly, no…yes, well maybe, maybe we can kill two birds…Let me explain. Georgie wants some time to talk to her and try to sort out her attitude. Why don't I take them upstairs for lunch, then I'll introduce the idea of creating the high-tech lab she wants right up there in the ballroom. There would be no waiting for the right lot to open up, or architects, or building permits and construction schedules. I can tell Aydan she's there to take notes and measurements for Georgie, then leave them alone to talk." At their expectant faces she explained, "Best-case scenario, she opens up to Georgie and tells her what's going on. Georgie will then solve it or bring it back for us to solve in the open, without impinging on anyone's privacy. Worst-case scenario, Georgie fires her ass, in which case security will escort her off the premises. If that happens, we can provide her with information on shelters and community programs both here and close to Cattaraugus Creek."

Marnie retrieved the blanket on the back of her chair, draping it around her shoulders, "Goddammit Doctor Marsh! Why does reasonable sound so cold?"

"Because we're women," she answered with brutal honesty. "Reasonable doesn't keep you warm, or protect your kids, or put food in their bellies. Reasonable laws and ethical behaviors can't dictate the depth of human kindness, or define those deep connections that make us who we are."

"Uh-oh, Pumpkin's in deep," Kira noted of her sister. "What's made you so reflective?"

Caught out, Tyler colored deeply. "That is a discussion I'd best have with my intended first."

"I knew it!" Leslie said before giving the equally happy Kira a fist bump.

Lori asked, "What?" She was notoriously ignorant of straight girl jabber.

Marnie stood, indicating the meeting was over. "Tyler, this is our number one priority, both the eighth floor and the young woman. I want a full report before…" she checked her watch as she settled behind her desk, "four p.m."

With that said, the meeting was indeed over and Tyler found herself being dragged through the corridor to her old office, now occupied by her sister. She sat on the couch, surprised to see Lori and Leslie join them.

"Holy cow, Tiger...You and Georgie popping out babies? Cool!"

Tyler had to laugh at the look on Lori's face. Clearly Leslie and her sister had discussed the idea and if their bright faces were any indication, they were supportive. "Lori, we haven't talked about it yet."

"Yeah yeah, that's cool. Whatcha girls think about it—I see you two making eyes—you two've been chewing on this for a while, right?"

Under Tyler and Lori's scrutiny, Kira finally confessed. "We couldn't help but notice how cute Georgie is with Ella and I know you have always wanted kids, so we kind of talked about the idea."

Tyler wanted to scold them, but their enthusiasm was encouraging. She knew Lori would back any adventure Georgie considered, including having kids, but the fact that the more conservative Leslie, not to mention her own twin Kira, were both in support did feel wonderful. "You really think Georgie..."

"Are you kidding me?" Lori plopped down on the couch beside her, dropping her arm around Tyler's shoulders. "Georgie practically raised all of us and we turned out pretty good."

"Except for Lou," Leslie noted with some disappointment.

"Oh, Lou's okay," Tyler said, but amended her opinion. "Just out of his depth."

"Yeah well, so are we on this homeless kid," Lori added.

"It might surprise you to know she isn't exactly a kid. She's in our age bracket." She made a circling hand signal much as Marnie had to include everyone in the room.

"Huh!" Lori was stumped. "She looks so young on the surveillance footage. Maybe it's being scared and alone that does that?"

"Actually, she may be our age chronologically, but she's led a very sheltered life."

Sitting down at her desk, Kira opened the portion of the young woman's personnel file she was authorized to see. "Her recommendation came from Sandy Winowski at UB. You two are friends, right? Did she have any concerns?"

"None at all," Tyler said. "She did warn that this would be her first full-time position. She explained, as did Aydan, that her family limited her academic efforts to part-time study. Still, you have to give her credit; she stuck with it doing just one course per semester. All she needs is her cooperative work time to qualify for her Professional Engineering accreditation."

"Any idea what the issue is with the family?" Kira asked.

"She mentioned having a strictly traditional Muslim family," Tyler answered. "She never said any more and I didn't think it appropriate to ask. I still don't, except for the fact that she's in some sort of trouble and we all want to help."

Leslie, who unlike her sister, had received their father's dark coloring, looked sympathetic. Lori, the eldest of the Phipps children, was long and lanky like her dad but had inherited her white mother's wild crinkly carrot top hair. She seemed a complete opposite to her petite sister and Lou, their baby brother. Until you spotted the three side by side. There was no denying the shared features of their proud African American father. In all the only hint to their mother's race were the piercing blue eyes common to each of them.   Leslie asked the one thing they had each been wondering: "What's your plan?"

Tyler took a deep breath, and getting to her feet, offered, "This is actually something Georgie is better at. She may not realize it but her engineers trust her and for some reason feel safe to open up to her when given half a chance. What I'm going to do now is tell her everything, then see what she comes up with."

Returning to the second floor and wending their way through the organized chaos of the engineering space, Tyler and Lori headed directly to the closed-door corner office. It was just after eleven when Tyler knocked, and she was relieved to see Georgie wasn't upset by the interruption. As a rule, Tyler made sure she was able to work without disruption until eleven thirty every day. It was a policy that had helped Georgie focus her concentration while sparking a level of creativity the company had never seen, not even before her blooding in Afghanistan. "Look who's here," Tyler announced.

Georgie stood, walked around her desk to give Lori an affectionate fist bump, then waved both her and Tyler to the seating area.

The grouping was furnished with odd pieces Tyler had found in the lower basement storeroom. When they had first set up on the second floor, Georgie had asked only that she bring up all the equipment from the machine shop. They had the space and it made more sense than having the group running up and down the stairs all day. Even with all the desks for her engineers and the extra workbenches, the place still looked sparse and lacked meeting furnishings of any kind. Instead of delving into their very new budget for overhead expenses, Georgie had directed her to the lower basement where they had been storing excess office furnishings for years. The place turned out to be a treasure trove of historical pieces and everyday furniture. Everything from old Luigi's first desk to the original art deco couches that once graced the lobby were stored and available. Georgie had told her to use whatever she wanted and she had taken it to heart. Now several couches framed the work groups on the open floor, and Georgie's meeting area was finished much as it had been upstairs.

Plopping herself on the closest couch, Lori announced, "You, me, and the missus have us a situation."

Tyler grinned at her. It didn't matter what was going on, there was always an air of casualness about Lori. At six feet, and with the build of an athlete, she was a good-looking woman but it was those blue, blue eyes that always did women in. Like her father, Henry Phipps, her skin was the color of rich hot cocoa. Her hair and eyes, though, they had come from her mom Gloria, a sweet Newfoundland lass with deep Celtic roots, which accounted for Lori's unruly red hair, and she did curse her mom now and then for giving her such disorderly curls. She had, on occasion, loudly envied her sister and her tight, perfect afro. Brother Lou, however, had inherited a combination of both parents and wore his hair combed the way her cousins in Newfoundland did. The look always sparked a vision of the sea under strict control, as if you could somehow harness row upon row of ridged curls. Of course, Lori being Lori, she had laughed her ass off when someone accused him of wearing a weave.

"You okay?" Georgie asked her cousin, taking a seat across from her.

"You know I am. I was just thinking about Mom."

That made Georgie smile. Since Henry had fully retired, he rarely made it into the office and Georgie didn't much like visiting the big house. Tyler had pressed her on it and she had complied, understanding the need to push past her demons of loss if she wanted any quality time with her uncle and best friend.

"Ah...Gloree-bee!" Georgie exclaimed. It was Henry's pet name for his long departed mate.

That made Lori smile. "Thanks, buddy. Listen, why don't I grab us a cup of tea while Tyler fills you in?"

"Actually," Tyler interrupted, "I'd like to run a little experiment. Do you mind?"

Lori sat back. "Experiment away."

Tyler moved to the office door. "I'm about to do something I swore I would never do." She opened the door and called to Georgie's intern, "Aydan, will you please bring in Georgie's tea set with four mugs?" With that, she closed the door without looking back.

Georgie, just as surprised as Lori, grabbed her tablet and sat down beside her cousin. She opened the security app, scrolling to the security cameras and expanding the one covering the break area where the coffeemaker was housed and a kettle, teapot, and a tray of mugs. They watched scrunched together as the woman went about making tea and gathering the milk container, a spare sugar jar, and the bottle of lemon juice they kept on hand for Georgie. As they watched her go about the menial task, they could see she was not pleased with the duty. It wasn't the kind of thing either Georgie or Tyler ever did to female subordinates. They both knew the sting of being expected to do that sort of thing simply because of being born a woman, but they also believed in starting at the bottom. That meant the most junior person sometimes got stuck with the crappy jobs. By the time the kettle had boiled and the tea had steeped, Lori and Tyler had filled Georgie in on the situation involving both Aydan and the impending office move.

Lori watched Georgie close her security app as the young intern made her way to the office. She warned herself that Aydan was neither young nor helpless. Who knew what her story was. The important thing now was to set the stage for her to open up. Lori stood with her cousin, as Tyler opened the office door.

"Thank you, Aydan, please join us." Tyler waited while the intern set the tray on the table before making introductions. "Aydan Ferdowsi, I would like you to meet Lori Phipps, president of DynaCraft Custom Yachts." Aydan reached out to accept Lori's open hand just as Tyler dropped her first bomb. "It's a rare day when we can drag her up from the boatyard."

The woman's arm froze in midair, but she seemed to push through her shock, delivering a trembling handshake.

"Nice to meet you," Lori offered with a sincere smile, waving her to the couch. "Have a seat," she said, watching carefully for any reaction. Like the reluctant handshake, she gingerly sat on the love seat adjacent to the two parallel sofas, without comment or question. Lori couldn't imagine a more miserable looking soul. But Tyler was right. She wasn't a kid. Up close, even with the drab old headscarf thingy, she was clearly in the same age bracket as them. That didn't account for her eyes though. Deep brown and innocently large, her gaze was a mix of fear and childish hope. The mix was incongruent yet somehow familiar. Something about her, about scared angry Aydan, pulled at her in a way she had never experienced. For the spark of a moment she worried for her own feelings before pushing them aside. *Why worry?* She was Lori Phipps and she had been born with a Teflon heart.

Tyler began the conversation as planned. "We have a new project to consider. We are going to be taking a look at the division of space and future use considerations. Georgie will take the lead on this but I would like you to drive it. You understand, create the layout diagrams and usage tables."

Clearly Aydan hadn't been expecting that. She nodded, asking, "Will we be looking at a particular space?"

Jumping in, Lori surprised herself as much as Tyler and Georgie, announcing, "Actually, we need you to take a look at everything, the whole building here and everything out at the boatyard. We'll need to bang a schedule together too." She checked her smartphone for the time. "I've got to meet with Lou in ten minutes. You know what a turd he is if I'm late. How about lunch? Would that be a good time to meet and hammer out a plan?"

Tyler nodded. "That's perfect. We had planned on having lunch upstairs. Why don't you join us after Georgie's team meeting?" At Lori's agreement, she turned to Aydan, "What about you? Do you mind joining us for lunch?"

She agreed before asking with timidity, "Upstairs?"

"Yes. In our condo." Tyler made a hand signal that encompassed her and Georgie. "It's on the ninth floor. You don't mind joining us there?"

"No," she answered, but her downward gaze and her body language was anything but accepting.

Lori wasn't sure what that meant and would rely on Tyler to spell out the mushy stuff. Standing, she gave her cousin another friendly fist bump before offering her hand to Aydan. "It was nice meeting you. I can't wait to get started and I promise I'll try and make it fun." For her effort, she was rewarded with a weak smile. While their eyes did connect, if only for a nanosecond, Lori was shaken to realize it was something she wanted to see again.

CHAPTER FIVE

Aydan walked from Georgie's office to the studio space they had set up near the elevators. It wasn't really a studio so much as open space they were using to digitally capture old blueprints and design documents that were far too big for even the large-scale flatbed scanner. Instead of sending them out, they had gone old school, pinning each blueprint to the wall and taking a photograph with the digital camera. Aydan's company laptop was connected to the tripod-mounted camera and sat next to it on one of the portable standing desks. She noted the drawing she had completed, and saved her database entry before disconnecting the camera. There was still some time before the pre-lunch team meeting.

As scared as she was of being caught out by this Lori woman, she wanted to prove she was a professional. It was hard for her to understand why it meant so much. Up until this moment she had been considering calling her academic adviser and asking for another placement. All that stopped her was the threat that it could be worse than this. Certainly being forced to play serving girl had irked her. Still, when she thought of it, it wasn't as if she was always treated like that. She didn't like it when one of the guys stopped to chat with her but it was clear they thought her assignment was something special. Even Skip Phipps, who she didn't mind so much, was in awe, offering to switch his coding assignment for a glimpse of his great-aunt's legacy. Maybe this wasn't such a bad place to work. Once she was officially an engineer, she would expect assignments with a little more bite but she did have to admit the stuff she was digitizing was interesting. Certainly, getting an inside look at the rest of the company would be interesting too but having lunch with her boss and her boss's boss was slightly overwhelming.

The thought of being in their...home was frightening. She had to wonder if they would act differently without the team around. Frankly, they were a little too open about their... their situation for her liking. Still, they didn't kiss or anything disgusting around the staff. And they didn't seem like anything her brothers had ever said about those women. Both were attractive in different ways but neither looked like she couldn't get a man. And neither looked as if she wished to be a man, although she would have guessed Ms. Marsh was the man because she was taller and the boss, but her boss Georgie was definitely the take command type. Did that mean she wanted to be the man? Didn't Tyler say that Georgie and Lori were co-captains of the sailboat they took to Miami? Did that make her the wannabe-man? Maybe her brothers were wrong. It wasn't as if they knew everything. They did have a life and friends outside the Ferdowsi home but that didn't mean much. She had seen videos online from the Ellen show. Ellen didn't look like she was trying to be a man, and her woman was certainly beautiful. Still, Aydan couldn't bring herself to describe Portia de Rossi as another woman's wife. Was it right to judge others if their happiness had no influence on her own? She wasn't sure and as nervous as she was at having to join her boss, Ms. Marsh, and the other women for lunch she was determined to keep her prejudices to herself.

Feeling extremely self-conscious, Aydan stood at the foot of the staircase, trying desperately to look like she wasn't feeling out of place. She had followed the company president upstairs to *their* condo, bristling inside at the idea while chiding herself for her own trepidation. It wasn't as if she hadn't met any lesbians before. It seemed like half the women in her engineering classes were gay. She had kept her distance from them just as she had from her male counterparts, but she had been curious. Her brothers always had such terrible things to say about those women, things her mother would pounce on as proof of Aydan's own misdeeds. How her mother would weep to know she had willingly entered the home of two of those women. For all she knew this Lori woman was one too. Forcing her attention back on the conversation between the Lori woman and Ms. Marsh, she took her time surreptitiously surveying the extravagant apartment.

The space was nothing like she had ever seen. Two stories high with an ornate brass circular staircase leading down from the level on which they had entered, it reminded her of a spread from a magazine. The dining table, set for four, was situated right in the bullnose of the building's west end. The room itself was open concept with a large designer kitchen and the living area across from it was tastefully furnished. She blushed to realize how her married sisters would gush over the décor. Beautiful built-in cabinets adorned each wall and the space was large enough to accommodate an intimate seating area in front of a fireplace, and a large more formal grouping.

Everything is so...elegant and...normal. What was I expecting? She very much doubted the company president trolled the discount shops on Transit Road for furniture or clothing but this...

"Wow, Tiger! Look at this place," Lori exclaimed. "Georgie said you had it squared away but this..." She whistled, spreading her arms to encompass the entire apartment. Turning to Aydan, she filled in the blanks for the first-time visitor. "Georgie has lived up here for about, what, five-six years and never thought to buy furniture."

Slightly stunned by the comment, she wasn't sure what to say.

"Oh, it wasn't that bad," Ms. Marsh said, explaining, "It's okay, Aydan. She wasn't sleeping on the floor or anything like that. She had a couch, a TV, and every game console they make."

Making herself at home in the kitchen, Lori got out glassware before raiding the fridge. "We've got juice, pop, iced tea and... something green," she said, holding up the glass canister for all to see.

"That's iced green tea. I'm trying to wean Georgie off the caffeinated stuff in the evenings."

Lori put it away without comment. Clearly she understood what that was about and again Aydan didn't want to ask, although lots of interesting facts were surfacing from Lori's rambling dialogue. She imagined it would wear on people but it was working to keep her calm. It was almost as if the woman knew she needed someone to fill in the silence. She was far too intimidated by Tyler Marsh and dreaded the idea of being alone with the woman. There was no way for her to tell if this Lori was purposefully acting as a buffer or if she was always this way. It gave her comfort in the moment and for that she was thankful.

"Oh, there's milk too, unless you would like wine or a beer, Aydan?"

Suddenly caught out not paying attention, she cleared her throat, asking with rising color, "I'm so sorry, Ms. Phipps. What were my choices?"

Grinning, Lori repeated her list before adding some additional choices. "And please call me Lori. Look, if you want something else, just say the word and I'll have them bring it up with our lunch."

For a moment she wondered if this was a test. What was the best answer?

When she didn't say anything, Lori simply poured her a glass of ice water before waving her over to the redecorated formal living area where Tyler was already seated. "Nice going, tiger," she complimented her again, lifting her cold drink in a salute.

"Thank you, but it's not all me. Georgie is just as much a part of the changes up here as she is with the rest of the company... companies," she corrected.

"I hear you, sister. Is she still burning the candle at both ends?"

"Oh, it's not that, Lor. She just worries over how much pressure she's put on everyone. You know what she's like."

"Yeah I do, but you of all people should know it's nothing compared to how much she's handled for all of us over the years. In a way, things are much more balanced now, and I think all of us and all the companies will do better. Besides, we're all still leaning pretty hard on her. God knows she really made the design changes for the boat line so much more doable. Christ, I've got half the boat builders in Europe begging to use the transient bulkhead system she created for me. We're selling a shitload—"

"Lori," Tyler warned.

"Oops. Sorry for the potty mouth, Aydan. I guess you can take the girl out of the boatyard but you can't take the boatyard out of the girl."

Aydan was watching Ms. Marsh and imagined she had somehow missed the fact that this Lori woman had only apologized to her. When she noted the crooked smile Marsh gave her, it gave away her fondness for Lori Phipps. *Was there something to that? Were gay girls like that? Did they practice monogamy? Did they even understand it?*

Before she could speculate further on any hidden meaning, Ms. Marsh asked, "Aydan, Lori and I need to talk to you about Georgie and some other more delicate issues. Are you comfortable with that?"

Am I comfortable? Since when does my comfort factor into anyone's perspective? No, she wasn't comfortable with anything and hadn't been since learning that her new boss was a gay girl, woman... *lesbian.* She didn't like that word. The way her brothers would say it with a sneer of contempt always popped into her head whenever she thought of it.

"The first thing I need you to know is that you are not in trouble. Understand?"

She didn't but nodded.

"First things first, how do you like working for Georgie?" Tyler asked.

Of all the things she had feared being asked this wasn't one. "It's fine."

"F-I-N-E!" Lori spelled out, "Fucked-up, Insecure, Neurotic…"

"Lori, really?" Ms. Marsh snarled.

"Sorry Ty, but Georgie will be back soon and I'm hungry, so stop beating around the bush."

Aydan almost laughed at the battle of wills going on between the two divisional presidents, and all over the language being used in front of her. "My brothers have said worse," she offered.

"Still, we have a code of conduct in this company, the family of companies, and Ms. Phipps knows better."

"Aw, come on, Tiger. Sorry, I was just lettin' my hair down but you're right, I do know better. Let's get back to business, shall we?" At a nod from Ms. Marsh the Lori woman turned directly to her. "Aydan—can I call you Aydan?"

She nodded, surprised to be asked. Her personal feelings on a subject, even if that subject happened to be her, had never been taken into consideration at home. This was strange and disturbing in a way. Maybe this was what her dean had meant when she implied working for a company led by women meant the atmosphere and underlying environment would be different. At the time she assumed those differences would be subtle or unworthy of attention, perhaps even distasteful or anti-male. Only here she was, and no one was anti-anything and everyone, including the males, were considerate and respectful.

"Georgie is my cousin and best buddy but she's pretty complicated. I'm talking about her health issues, complications…"

"Limited oral communications skills," Ms. Marsh explained.

"Yeah, what she said. Listen Aydan, do you know about her head getting scrambled and all that?" At Aydan's nod, Lori continued, explaining, "See, the thing is Georgie needs an assistant. Now I know you have your hands full with your internship stuff but well, Georgie likes you. In case you didn't know it, that's not a given. As a matter of fact, she can be a real hard…" Lori Phipps gave Ms. Marsh a guilty look before correcting, "Hard boss. She can be tough on her people, but it's only because she's so hard on herself. Tyler, help me out here."

Ms. Marsh took over. "There are several things you need to know. One, your internship will not be affected by accepting a part-time role within the company. I already checked with Dean Winowski and she confirmed that point. Actually, she was really supportive and believes it will give you a much better glimpse into the day-to-day efforts involved in leading a new tech company, with the bonus of working as a project leader, side by side with the VP of engineering. Is that something you think you would want to do one day?"

"Be a project leader or secretary?" She hadn't meant to sound so harsh in her reaction but she didn't like that they had gone behind her back to the dean. *Just who did they think they were?* She recognized her mother's condescending voice a second before she saw the ice in Ms. Marsh's eyes.

"Whoa there, kiddo," Lori Phipps cut in. "That's not what we're offering you. Yes, being an assistant sucks sometimes but you also get to work closely at Georgie's side. Two, you get paid and I don't know anyone who couldn't use a few more bucks, right? Besides, we all started at the bottom in this family. That tea-making duty we had you pull wasn't because you're a woman or anything. You're the junior guy up there so you get the duty. That's how it worked for all of us and as much as I hated it back then I get it now. Georgie believes, and we agree, that you have to learn to do before you can lead. There are no managers in this company and it's the same out at the boatyard. You're either a leader or a worker bee and even worker bees who earn their chops reap a share of the rewards. You'll see that too, if you stick around."

That stunned her. Not the starting from the bottom, which she didn't believe in, but the quip about sticking around. "So I have to take the job or…" She couldn't believe it much less say what she was thinking.

"Aydan," Ms. Marsh intervened. "Nothing you say here today will affect your internship. Only your performance and attitude have any weight where that's concerned."

She didn't answer. Shaking, she didn't trust her voice not to crack. *What was it with these women?* She wasn't sure if they were inappropriately alluding to something she didn't understand or just trying to be helpful. *Why would they? Unless...*

"There are actually two part-time positions open but before I explain the different duties, I want you to know how dependent Georgie is on her assistant. And there is a reason why we're looking internally. You see, Georgie is a very private person. She is also very sensitive to change. It's my goal to make the transition to her new assistant seamless, so as to not upset her work. That would be much easier to do if her new assistant was someone she already knows and respects."

That caught her attention. *The boss respects me?* "You said you were looking internally. What did the other interns say?"

"The other interns," Tyler explained without rancor, "are working with the legacy group. Georgie doesn't really know them. I haven't spoken to them and for that reason I won't. At the moment there are three candidates in house, of which you are the top choice. Now, would you like to learn about the job duties, or are you set against it?"

"Who?" she asked without thinking, "are the other candidates?" She was shocked by her own boldness.

Ms. Marsh shook her head. "I'm sorry. That would be a breach of privacy, just as it would be for me to repeat any portion of this conversation with them."

"Aw, come on, Tyler. I'm a little curious myself to know which of our employees would voluntarily sign up for babysitting duty."

"Lori, really, I don't remember you thinking it was such a bad job back when you and Marnie were begging me to take it." Turning to Aydan, she added almost as a challenge, "Yes, I started here as Georgie's assistant."

"What?" Now Aydan was more confused than ever. "But you're the president. She works for you."

"Oh boy," Lori groaned, before teasing, "Yeah, you're the president. How does that work?"

As if having some sort of sixth sense, Tyler Marsh stood as Georgie's service dog bounded in, heading right for her while

Georgie herself followed with a waiter and serving cart on her heels. Aydan watched in fascination as her boss's boss scolded her boss. "Georgina DiNamico, you're covered in snow, again! Upstairs this minute and take Maggie with you." If she hadn't seen the smile on Ms. Marsh's face, much less heard Lori's hearty laugh, she would have imagined them fighting.

Still laughing, the Lori woman challenged her boss, "Oh, you are so busted, buddy. What were you two doing, rolling in the snow or something?"

Georgie, all smiles too, shook her head, "Slipped... crossing..." She pointed out the window toward Erie Street and the lake.

"And you just had to roll around in it while you were down, eh?" Lori continued to tease.

Ms. Marsh was now at her boss's side. She watched the two, frozen with interest at the unfolding scene. She had braced herself, presupposing anything nearing intimate interaction would make her sick. It's what people always said, what her mother always said. Was it disgusting? Would it make her sick to see? While the Lori woman began preparing tea, the waiter from the restaurant finished setting out their lunch. As he departed, each woman thanked him by name. It all seemed so normal then...then Ms. Marsh stepped up to her boss, brushing snow from her hair and collar. Aydan was so caught by the familiarity she stared shamelessly at the pair.

"You okay, baby? Where did you fall?" she asked with more than gentleness.

Aydan had never heard two women speak in such intimate tones. Had she ever heard any two people talk like that? *Maybe*, she admitted, when she was young and her father was still alive.

"Crossing Perry...snowbank...icy."

She watched Tyler Marsh reassure the woman, the whole time caressing her face. Then she did the one thing Aydan had dreaded seeing. They embraced and were actually kissing, right there for the whole world to see! A sudden pressure against her leg pulled Aydan from her trance. The dog, Maggie, was at her side and leaning heavily on her leg. That was the other weird thing about these people. They let this dog wander around the office as she pleased. "She's leaning on me. What does it mean?"

"She likes you," Ms. Marsh said as she led her boss up the circular stairs.

"Come give me a hand here, Aydan?" the Lori woman asked.

There wasn't much she could do but comply. The sooner she got through this the better. "Do they always do…that?"

"What, take off just when lunch shows up? Naw, those two are well behaved. Trust me; Tyler will have our girl cleaned up and back down here in minutes."

Not really comfortable being alone with the other big boss, she did realize this might be her only chance to ask things she wouldn't dream of voicing to anyone else. As she began, something sparked in the back of her brain. *I trust this Lori woman.* "I understand she's a veteran and disabled, but why does everyone cater to her?"

"Georgie?" The woman was clearly surprised. Aydan's intrinsic trust in this stranger was immediately confirmed. Smiling, Lori noted with clear joy, "I see you haven't spent too much time with our niece and resident gossip Zoe, or you'd be up on the 411. So here's the short version. Georgina DiNamico is the eldest of all the cousins and was the heir to the family company. You do know her grandfather started this company, DiNamico Marine and DynaCraft?" At Aydan's nod, she continued. "Okay well, old Luigi started the company and did real well for himself. He had three kids, Georgie's dad, my dad Henry, and our great-aunt Georgina for whom she is obviously named. Old Georgina was closest to our Georgie. Anyway, Georgie was raised to lead the company until some ass…sorry! Until a surface to air missile took out her whole crew and left her flat on her back for a year. The Georgie you know today is a vast improvement over what the air force shipped home to us."

"Is that why you keep her on? For her service, I mean?"

Lori Phipps stood up, looking down at her from her whole six feet. "I don't think you're getting the picture here. Georgie *is* the company. She is single-handedly responsible for seventy, maybe eighty percent of the new patents and innovations we're building on and all of the new revenue outside the yacht manufacturing stream."

Aydan wasn't sure which was more shocking, the fact that her boss had actually been groomed to lead, or how much Lori's tone and demeanor had changed. "I didn't mean any offense. I…don't you worry about how it must look, with her…disability I mean?"

Sighing, the woman remained standing rigid, but her eyes were kind. *Kind eyes—kind blue eyes.* "Considering the current politics surrounding Muslim Americans, people could say the same thing to us about you. I bet Georgie never even batted an eye when you walked in with your head scarf thingy and all your winter layers. She doesn't see people like that. She's got some special thing where she just sees the best in everyone. And you need to know, there is nothing she can't do. Yes, she has some challenges speaking off the cuff and it's one of the things we'll go over if you take the job."

"She, Ms. Marsh…"

"You do know it's Doctor Marsh, don't you? The woman has a PhD and she's brilliant!"

Stunned by this news as well, Aydan colored, realizing that in the weeks Georgie DiNamico and Ms…*Doctor* Marsh had been back from Miami, she hadn't given any thought to their achievements or credentials. "Does she, Georgie I mean, does it bother her not to be in charge? I mean it would bother me if I had prepared for it all my life."

"Are you kidding me? Well, you'll get to know this on your own but try to understand that she doesn't care about things like that. For her it's always about what's best for the family and the business and always in that order. As for—"

The kettle picked that exact moment to blare its message. The dog, still glued to Aydan's side, howled along with it. She watched as the Lori woman grabbed it, hitting the off switch as she pulled it from its base. She filled a teapot identical to the one used downstairs and set it to steep. "Do you like it strong? Georgie has a sensitive gut, so we always pour hers first."

"I must admit it is a pleasure to have the option of tea at work. At school it was just coffee or pop. I used to take a thermos of tea to class with me. Mostly chai but sometimes black tea like this. I don't know this brand though." For a moment she considered how easily she seemed to open up to this woman, before pushing those thoughts aside.

"My aunt in Newfoundland sends us a supply every few months. They can't live without their Red Rose down home!"

"Down home?"

"Are you two ready to eat?" Doctor Marsh called from behind Aydan's shoulder. She was making her way down the stairs with Georgie, in a fresh suit, following behind.

Was she really the woman who had been groomed to take over? A woman! She had not quite absorbed that part. Lori said they had groomed her from the start. She knew there were more family members in the company than just these two and there were men. Had this family, this company, really chosen a woman over a man, a man from their own family?

She followed Lori to the table and helped her remove the plate covers. Within minutes they were absorbed in the comforting aromas of the meal and Lori's jovial retelling of some adventure. It was interesting to listen to her but Aydan was learning so much more by watching. She could admit the woman was stunning with those deep blue eyes and her lean, sporty-type frame. She herself was considered a tall woman, especially in her family where she stood head to head with her brothers. She had gotten used to her height and often used it to distance herself from others. She met very few women who were taller than her and she liked that, liked being able to distance herself both emotionally and physically. When she interviewed with Georgie, she actually believed she would be able to physically intimidate the woman because she was shorter. That hadn't been true and of course Doctor Marsh was taller than Aydan too. Not by much, but still it had unsettled her. Now here she was lunching with three women she couldn't pull any of her old tricks on. For the first time ever, she felt no necessity, no compulsion to pull away. She sipped from her water glass, casually taking in the view of Lake Erie. At that moment the simplicity of the situation was as clear as the late winter sun. *I don't have to bully my way with these women to earn their respect.*

* * *

Aydan watched as Georgie used an infrared device to make measurements of the vacant space. Entering the dimensions on a tablet as Georgie read them, she now knew the company had referred to this office space as the ballroom and had used it exclusively for years. She had to admit it was remarkable. Tall ceilings, brick walls, exposed iron I beams, and the highly polished wood floors all added to the warm retro environment. It was nicer than the second floor although only about two-thirds the floor space. That probably wasn't an issue, since they were using less than half the space on two anyway.

Over lunch Aydan had listened with interest as Dr. Marsh and her counterpart, Lori Phipps, discussed the estimated usage needs their businesses would face over the next ten years. It was interesting to watch them deferring to Georgie as if she was their boss, not the other way around. Of course, learning that Georgie was supposed to be in charge did make her think about the situation. Why would someone willingly hand over control of her company, a family company, to strangers? Lori had said she and Georgie were cousins. She didn't know how that was possible, one being Italian American and the other African American. They certainly didn't look like relatives, and what about having your lover take over as president? *How could she trust someone like that?*

"Total square feet?" Georgie asked her.

"Just shy of thirty-three hundred." When Georgie didn't comment, she rattled off the exact footage of the empty space.

"Okay…enough for…"

"I don't know what it's enough for!" she snapped. She wasn't sure what was worse, trying to communicate with this woman or how she always assumed you had an answer for her stupid questions. Surprising her, Georgie walked across the room, retrieving two folding chairs from a heavy rolling cart and carrying them back to set them near the south facing windows. She sat down without comment, waving her hand to the empty seat.

Not sure what to expect, Aydan dragged herself over, slumping down without comment. Why bother? It wasn't as if this woman could carry on a conversation. What she didn't expect was being completely ignored by her. The woman took out her phone and was tabbing away furiously. Aydan was seconds from giving up and just walking out when a message popped up on the tablet she was holding.

"Read it," Georgie ordered.

Confused but curious too, she opened the IM to find Georgie had written her a long note. Shocking her more, the woman began reading from her own copy; reading without the hesitation or omissions that drove Aydan mad. *What the…*

"Do you remember giving Dean Winowski permission to discuss your academic profile when your name was submitted for this post? And do you remember that we supplied a written release which you also signed allowing her to share personal information with your supervisor?"

Aydan opened her mouth, but nothing came out. What the hell just happened? Thirty seconds ago, this idiot couldn't string more than three words together and now she was what, all back to normal? *This is bullshit!*

"Answer the question!" Georgie demanded.

Somewhere between running or fighting, she choked out a yes. She watched as her boss began tabbing through her phone again.

"From my Tyler's…notes: New Year's Eve Open Pitch, 2016. Guest: Doctor Sandy Winowski, Dean of Engineering, attending with her…

"Note 1: The dean was sincerely thankful for the company's long-term support of the engineering program. The two interns currently placed with DME have successfully transitioned to their new training spots. One is now working on legacy patents…The other has joined the Standards and ECN team at the boatyard. This student reports, in his mid-placement critique, that he has learned more in a few months than his first three years in university.

"Note 2: With the reorganization of DynaTech announced, the dean was enthusiastic about adding more interns to the work/learn program. While she was hoping to place two students with DynaTech, GD," Georgie looked to her, pointing to herself in case Aydan missed the GD reference, "was not confident that her young team could provide the leadership necessary to offer work of value to the intern. When pressed, GD offered to personally supervise one intern next semester. Dean Winowski considered but urged GD to accept her select student immediately. Winowski was eager to discuss this student's personal needs. I advised her that we would require a signed Non-Disclosure Agreement before discussing personal information. She agreed.

"Note 3: NDA emailed. Once signed, the dean will schedule a Skype meeting to discuss the student selected for this special internship.

"Note 4: I advised the dean that this internship would be very special. If UB wanted to place a student with the majority owner of the corporation and originator of three-quarters of all company patents, they had better be more than good. This is a once in a lifetime opportunity and I will not have it wasted. Dean Winowski agreed, promising she was sending her absolute best."

Shocked, Aydan's voice croaked out her confusion. "You can talk? What the hell…"

Georgie held up her hand, turning the screen of her phone toward her as if she could read the document from that distance. "Are you the best?"

Her objections and confusion petered out all at once, like someone letting the air out of a balloon. *Am I the best? Is that really how the dean sees me?*

"Aydan…in three months, you show…intelligence and… skill, but…working with," again she pointed to herself, "challenging. I know. I live it…this!" This time she pointed to the strip of pure white hair above her temple.

When there was no response, she started reading from another file she opened on her phone. "In 2011 I was flying a Blackhawk helicopter in Afghanistan. I love flying and I love my country. When the opportunity to serve a second tour was presented I did not hesitate. My primary purpose was not to fight or kill but to save lives and I reveled in that purpose."

Georgie set her phone on the windowsill, turning her complete attention to Aydan. "I see your eyes. Have seen...so many times, this...disappointment. Now, here," she pointed to her lock of white hair again, and then to her mouth, "don't... not direct..."

Suddenly she stood and Aydan could see the frustration on her face, and something else. *Was it hurt?* Could she have hurt this woman, this woman who was clearly struggling to communicate? It had never occurred to her that her boss's problem was not a mental deficiency. "Wait, you own this company. Then why aren't you the CEO or at least the president?"

Georgie slumped back down but her expression remained open. "A smart leader...best person for each...job. I...think, design, and...I love that, good too. Why do...Marnie Pulaski, my sister...much better CEO. All paper, people...yikes! Tyler, true president...leader, planner...she is perfect. Lori too, builders respect...she loves...it. It shows. Now you...What do you...want, no...love?"

Dumbfounded by the question, she sat in silence, unsure how to answer. How could she explain her family's displeasure with her life choices? How could she explain wanting to please her mother to someone like Georgie, someone who probably never had to please a mother and probably rejected all things family? Except she said her sister was CEO and that the Lori woman had mentioned her father's retirement from the company. Skippy had said that his dad was president of another division and even his sister worked here. "Why does, I mean, does your family accept your..."

"Head injury?"

Aydan blushed. "It's none of my business. Sorry," she added, head down and feeling miserable.

"Look at me," Georgie said but it didn't sound as harsh as the order she had delivered moments ago. "Ask...please ask."

It took a long time to consider not only what she wanted to ask but how and more importantly if she wanted to ask at all. "You and Dr. Marsh…they say you're getting married and your family…" She trailed off, afraid to voice her confusion. Was it confusion? It wasn't as if she didn't know what lesbians were. The truth was, she had kept her distance from everyone, not just the guys, or the gay girls. Sitting here, now, with this woman, she realized she didn't care about orientation. Actually, if she was truthful, it was nice—no, refreshing to meet people living their lives honestly. And that thought hit her like a bolt from the sun. These women are the honest ones, not her family, not her brothers and their narrow views. "How long were you a soldier?"

"Airwoman or Guardswoman," Georgie corrected, but the smile was back. "Yes…I lied to join. Had too but…times change. You ever think that you…"

Recognizing where she was going with the question, she jumped in, offering, "The military? No, not me, I think my family…" And without warning the tears began to fall.

Georgie inched her folding chair closer but never touched her. She just sat nearby and patiently waited. Embarrassed, Aydan was desperate to get herself under control. As the tears dried up, her nose went into overdrive. What a time to not have her purse nearby! Surprising her, she felt Georgie moving closer. Panicking and humiliated, she looked up, ready to lock horns, only to see her intention for what it was, a gesture of comfort. She hadn't touched her or anything weird. Her boss, the majority owner of this respected and successful company, was sitting here in her expensive suit with her boyish haircut and what was she doing? *She's handing me a hanky of all things.* She accepted the soft cotton handkerchief, wiping her eyes before politely dabbing at her nose.

"Blow it," Georgie ordered with a maternal grin. "Good cry…good blow. Feel better?"

It was hard not to smile or ignore the charm of this woman. Maybe that's what she had missed, that aspect of her the rest of the team so readily recognized. She blew her nose with the gusto of a toddler who had just mastered the trick. After patting her face dry she sat up straighter, desperate for a modicum of composure. "Why are you being so kind to me? I haven't exactly been—"

"Why not?"

"What…you, it's not exactly business as usual."

"Why not?" Georgie repeated with the look she had seen before, whenever one of the engineers would tell her something couldn't be done. Aydan had learned she would accept a no-can-do but it had to come with a precise explanation. And she was usually right to push. The answers were there. Even as the team intern, she knew some of the things they fought against were doable. She had to give her boss credit for that. She never forced them to back down. She would send them away to research their arguments. That usually ended up being all the catalyst they needed to give it another go or look at things from a different perspective. She liked that.

"I like working here, a lot. It doesn't feel like a conveyer belt. You really let everyone dig into the new ideas and new technologies. It can't be the most cost effective way to run a company."

Georgie shook her head, admitting it without rancor. "My Tyler worries. We," she indicated the two of them, "duty to innovate…help. We can help."

"Why is that important? I mean, I think it's the way to go, but I was told by my professors it was naïve. One even accused me of being a communist!"

That made Georgie laugh, "Professor Mironelli?"

"What, how did…you really know those guys over there. Oh, he was always pounding us on cost of innovation."

"Rebel Rifle?" she asked with a wicked grin.

"Oh God! I thought his head would explode when one of the students brought it up as argument against his costing algorithms. Wait, how did you know?"

Georgie tapped her chest with pride. "I wrote it…back when…"

"You wrote the Seven Cents Per Life paper?" Now she was laughing too. "He was so steamed he just stormed out of the lecture hall. He must have gone straight to the dean. We could hear him screaming one floor down. What an ass. He actually tried to argue that Rebel had made the right call by investing an extra three cents in product insurance instead of spending the seven cents to fix the safety fault. I was so mad! Listening to him go on and on about cost over everything else and all I could think about was all those people who died because spending seven cents didn't compute." She bristled at the memory. "Why do they let people like that teach?"

"Tenure."

Nodding her understanding she added, "I heard a rumor. They say that happens every semester, him getting clobbered with your paper." It seemed crazy that her boss could somehow influence students at UB, but the grin on the woman's face said otherwise.

"Plenty like him…"

"But if you can get a few students to question what they are being taught?"

Georgie just nodded. Clearly she agreed, but more than that she was doing something about it, both with her business and with old bean counter Mironelli. "May I ask…personal, questions?"

Would she? Suddenly fearful again, she pushed past her discomfort. How bad could it be if the woman was asking permission? That was something to consider too. Had anyone ever asked her permission or even her opinion within her own family? Not since her father died. Realizing that, the tears threatened again.

"You are in…trouble?"

How could she explain, how could she let her see how out of control her life was, how much she hurt? This woman was a stranger. How could she possibly understand the demands her family made? How could she understand the threat of losing your family, the people who cared and loved you? *The people who threw me out for not being what they want!*

"Aydan…please."

And that was all it took. As the renewed tears cascaded down her cheeks, the entire story poured out without restraint.

She talked about her father being an engineer and her love for him. The night after night he would spend at the kitchen table helping her with math and physics homework. She spoke of his praise and support, and then his untimely death. It had rocked the Ferdowsi household and upset the balance of power. Since her freshman year at UB, her mother had been calling the shots with counsel from her elderly and extremely traditional parents and had fallen prey to what she believed was an ultra-conservative mindset.

Aydan had begun her undergraduate career as a full-time student. By her second semester that had been whittled down to one course while she helped in caring for her elderly grandparents and her younger brothers. She had younger sisters too, but unlike her they had serious boyfriends which somehow earned them a pass in her mother's eyes. The worst part was how quickly her younger brothers had gone from being the fair-minded and inquisitive boys her father raised to the close-minded little bastards their grandfather so easily influenced. That she could even continue at school with one course probably only happened because her father had set aside money in his will for her education. Aydan was sure he knew how easily her mother would be influenced by her own father once he was gone. What he could not have anticipated was how easily her brothers had gravitated to a place of prominence and influence in their mother's world. And they had reveled at being given authority over her.

"They have control of my life, my brothers I mean." Realizing more explanation was probably needed, even for her empathic employer. She began again, "I was born in 1980, in Paris. We had just escaped from Iran, my family I mean. My father was American. He was a military adviser and assigned to my grandfather's command. He was a general and a cruel man, but still he allowed my mother to marry my father. Sometimes," she admitted, "I wondered if he did it to save themselves. My mother was very beautiful. I imagine the only daughter of a high-ranking general could have any man she wanted. Choosing my father may have saved her life and those of her parents. I have three uncles; one was just a boy and came with them. He lives in New Jersey. The other two both died in the revolution. When we came here, I think my grandparents had trouble adjusting. They often speak of their grand homes and servants as if they have been robbed of something they earned. It always irked me, but my father would be so kind. He always reminded me to sympathize with their situation. He was a good man."

"Ferdowsi HVAC."

"You know it?" she asked, shocked to know her boss was familiar with the company her father built and her brothers inherited. "How?"

"We used to...approved vendor."

"But not anymore?" she asked. When Georgie nodded, she was not really surprised. "Let me guess, they said or did things that were sexist and you wouldn't put up with it?"

"My father...asked...I was at UB...like you. Your father agreed...internship," she pointed at herself. "Your grandfather rescinded...no women."

She wasn't sure which she found more shocking, that Georgie knew her father, that their fathers had known each other, or that her firsthand experience with the Ferdowsi family had not colored her opinion or the opportunity she provided. "You knew?"

"Knew they were...not you, not your granddad." She didn't press the issue. Instead she pointed to Aydan's head cover. "Why the...hijab?"

"What? How dare you question my rights. You can't..." Georgie's look of pained amusement halted her protest, a protest she had long practiced, but had never used until now, now, when it was most inappropriate. Her boss wasn't challenging her religious freedom. Even if she didn't understand the subtle difference between the simple scarf she preferred to the more formal hijab.

"Before we left...you wore...silk, jacquard? Now, gray, heavy...different. Why?"

No, her objections were not about modesty but the change in conveyance of such. Of course she noticed the difference. The woman was the most innovative engineer she had ever met.

As much as she hated to admit that, she knew it was true just as she knew all Georgie wanted was to help. How had she missed that?

Instead of trying to explain, she untucked her headscarf and unwound it, revealing her humiliation for all the world to see but it wasn't all the world. It was just Georgie DiNamico, her internship supervisor, and she was starting to believe she could be a friend. Certainly the next few moments would tell. Georgie let out a slow breath, standing and moving closer but never touching. At length she sat back down. Her face said so much, but having spent all her time trying to ignore the woman, she couldn't exactly describe what she saw: anger; confusion; pity? *Please, anything but pity.*

"Your brother?"

"Brothers," she corrected. "They wanted me to quit here. They said it was an embarrassment to the family. The only reason I was allowed to continue with university was my father set money away for me, for school, but they said an internship didn't count." Unable to hold her head up, she spoke as much to the floor as she did to Georgie. "They showed my mother your engagement announcement and used it as proof that working here would be…inappropriate. They said terrible things. I am so sorry. I should have defended you, but I didn't know what to say. I lied to them to take this internship. I said I was going to the library every day, but they caught me. I was lucky though, my mother remembered your family name. I didn't know why but now it makes sense. When we first moved here, my mother actually worked, mostly as my father's bookkeeper. She would have remembered the larger customers. She didn't tell me why but agreed I could try it for a few weeks. At the end of the first week, my brothers agreed I could continue only because they knew you and Dr. Marsh had left to test that new boat, and I was working on my own. I didn't say anything when you returned but they found out. It was horrible. They were yelling at me, calling me…I'm sure you know all the things men call women to belittle them, but now they had all this extra ammunition, with you and Dr. Marsh being…"

"Lesbians? Aydan...it is just...a word. Words don't..." She pointed to Aydan's ragged hair and the angry red wounds from shears that had bitten the scalp, in what had obviously been a violent struggle to cut off all her hair.

"The silk scarf I used to wear, it was a gift from my father. You have a good eye. It was a Jacquard; he bought it in Paris the day I was born. He often told me of that day, calling me the ray of sunshine in a world gone mad." Not able to finish, she stalled, taking a moment to restore her hijab. Finally, she admitted, "I'm not really religious. I've been wearing this to hide what they did. I never wore anything on my head when my father was alive. Not that he wouldn't have it. He was so tolerant with my mother, and her parents. Maybe it's why their intolerance of me is so...confusing."

"They are scared...scared people...scared men do bad...did they..."

Aydan looked up, meeting her eyes. "No. They cut off my hair and slapped me around a bit, but mostly they just threatened and berated me. They...I don't know where it comes from, but they have this sense of entitlement that they expect the world to fill." Head down again, she admitted, "They forbade me from returning to work here and sent me to my room like a misbehaving child. I waited until they were asleep, packed my clothes, and walked out."

"And sleeping in...car."

It wasn't a question. Clearly, Georgie knew she had been living in the Ford her father had given her as a gift for starting university. Thank goodness he'd had the foresight to put it in her name. The funds he'd set aside for school included a vehicle allowance. She had been living off her gas station credit card which had yet to be canceled. She wasn't sure why that was. Maybe she had her mother to thank for that but she wouldn't bank on it. She smiled wryly at her pun. It was a better bet that her internship counted as part of her academic credits and as long as she was in school, her father's Last Will and Testament was supposed to provide enough money for tuition, books, fees and a full vehicle allowance. Clearly her father never imagined she would be homeless or she was sure he would have addressed that contingency too.

"Come," Georgie said.

She led the way from the ballroom and back up the stairs to the ninth floor. She swiped her hand over the door sensor to the private suite she shared with Dr. Marsh. Pushing the heavy oak door open, she stopped on the threshold and pointed to where she had swiped her hand. "See sensor?"

"No, actually."

Georgie nodded. "Good…feel," she added, pointing to a place along the door molding.

Doing as ordered, Aydan immediately realized that she was touching a pressure panel. Pushing it in, she let it pop open to reveal a numeric pad. She looked up, amazed. Pushing it closed, she examined it again. "I can see it now but only because I know it's there."

"Remember that," was all the response Georgie gave. Leading her back into the foyer of the condo's upper floor, instead of heading back downstairs, she turned for another closed door. This one was unlocked, and she waved her in.

Aydan almost stopped dead in her tracks. Why was her boss, this lesbian woman, taking her into her bedroom? She gulped back her panic, unwilling to look anything but in control.

"Guest room…bathroom," she said, pointing to a door across the room. "We will respect…" She pointed to her, explaining, "Your privacy. Stay…as long…" She didn't finish, just rolled her hand as an indication Aydan now recognized as her signal to continue the sentiment for her. Did this mean she wanted her to stay, uninterrupted, here, with them? She shuddered to think of what her brothers would say and what her mother would think.

"Your choice…other options too." Georgie seemed to be examining her, not looking at her, but looking inside her.

It felt invasive and she balked at the offer. "You're…you're… My family will never allow it."

At that declaration, Georgie laughed. She actually laughed at her. She then removed her smartphone and started tabbing away. Expecting that she was about to be clobbered with some file or paper as explanation for her humor, she stood by with the company tablet at the ready. Two could play at this game. When the notification pinged, she opened Georgie's note to find a list of family members who would offer her sanctuary. Seconds later a security notice pinged and she opened it to find she now had access to the penthouse, plus the guest room security locks had been set for her and her alone. The third item she opened was not a lengthy plea or some paper she was offering as explanation. It was just a simple text: "Aydan, don't be afraid of things you don't understand. This is your life, make your own choices, and we will respect the choices you make."

What choices had she made?

Have I ever made a choice? Staying in school even after all the fights, that was my choice, and leaving home? I made that choice too.

She read the text again: "Aydan, don't be afraid of things you don't understand. This is your life, make your own choices, and we will respect the choices you make."

What am I scared of? They can't hurt me any more than my family has. Respect? She speaks of respect as if it's the easiest thing, an automatic thing and I know that's not true. Yet, she has been respectful. They all have been respectful.

"I have no money to pay you."

"Friends help…okay?"

Friend? Was she? "I can help out. Dr. Marsh said you need help. I'll work for my room."

"Room and board…and pay."

"But I want to earn my way. I don't want anyone to think I'm taking advantage. It wouldn't be right and—"

Georgie held up her hand, halting her protestations. "My Tyler, you two…work it out. Now, we…" she pointed to the tablet, "have a project." Just then the dog padded in, circling around Aydan before giving her a brush-by doggy hug. "Maggie approves."

In that moment, all the months of tension Aydan had been carrying melted from her shoulders. She was still a bit apprehensive about staying with these lesbians, but the issues in the forefront were more about not making a fool of herself in front of her boss and the company president. These women held the power to influence her entire career, yet here they were, opening their home to her. Opening their home when her own flesh and blood had turned their backs on her and with such cruelty. In a way, she might as well stay here and let her family think what they wished. They could call her a whore and a dyke all they wanted, but she was going to finish university, pin the PEng designation to her name and do the kind of work she and her father had discussed a million times. Decisively, she said, "Thank you."

Georgie just nodded. Checking her watch, she showed the time to Aydan before adding, "Look around...then office... fifteen..."

Smiling, she understood she was being given time to settle in. She was also learning to translate Georgie's militarisms. "Understood. I'll be in your office a three o'clock."

Georgie again nodded then retreated from the guest room without another word, the dog Maggie at her side.

Alone, and starting to relax, Aydan took her time examining her new living space. It was neither a small nor a large room. It seemed to have been designed around the furniture, giving every piece the appropriate space and setting. Built-in sconces were in just the right place to provide lighting over each bedside table and framing the queen-size bed. The bed was covered with what she suspected was a family heirloom quilt, judging by the shiny gloss of the well-worn cotton and the number of variegated patches and repairs. It was easy to imagine it had been kept, used, and cared for, for quite some time. She wondered which family it came from, Georgie's or did it belong to Dr. Marsh, and now she had to wonder about the protocol for addressing someone she was living with.

Is that what I'm doing, living with them? Contemplating the strangeness of life, she turned to the small sitting area. It had a love seat set opposite a large screen television. On the low-slung cabinet underneath the TV sat more game consoles than she even knew existed. But it was the wireless keyboard that caught her eye. She made a note to ask if she could access the Internet. Uplifted by the thought of open access to the world of information, she was propelled toward the TV. A sticker on the keyboard identified it as Wi-Fi enabled. Some of the game systems, she knew, would connect with the Internet for all of those multiplayer games her brothers played. Curious, she cracked open one of the two top drawers of the cabinet. She wasn't surprised to find it crammed with a variety of game controllers. The drawer below was tightly packed with games of every sort. Moving on, she opened the opposite top drawer to find it packed with DVDs, a jumble of animated favorites and action hero adventures preferred by every kid and teen on the planet. Surely these couldn't be the type of movies her bosses watched. Did other people watch TV here, younger people, kids? The thought upset her until she realized she was judging again, seeing things through her family's eyes.

She opened the last drawer to find another assortment of DVDs. These titles, though, she didn't know. She did recognize the actress on the cover of one. There was no mistaking someone as distinguished as Olympia Dukakis. She flipped the case over, scanning the write-up for *Cloudburst…lesbians on the run from a nursing home!* As if shocked by electricity, she dropped the DVD case. Feeling caught out, she stuffed it back in its spot. About to shove the drawer closed, she stalled, curiosity overriding her more cautious self. Pulling another DVD from the collection, she read the description. This one was about lesbians too. *I Can't Think Straight.* She studied the cover with the eyes of an investigator. The copy on the back named it a popular lesbian drama. Were lesbian movies so common they could be divided into genres? Before she could finish browsing, a notification sounded on her tablet, bringing her investigation to a halt. She carefully reordered the DVDs, closing the cabinet drawer.

It was a text from Georgie. She was to report to Dr. Marsh immediately. The time display on the device showed only 2:40. That could only mean trouble. Was Dr. Marsh upset to learn Georgie had offered her a room? Dreading what was about to come, she took the elevator back to the second floor.

When the doors opened, she hesitated. If Georgie and those two big bosses knew she was in trouble, did that mean everyone else did too?

The two spacious offices at the east end were partitioned in old-fashioned glass and oak panels. Like the well-worn maple plank flooring, they were all original. She spotted Skip. During her first week, Skip had taken it upon himself to give her the whole history of the building, or at least the whole history of Dynamic Marine Engineering. She had imagined him trying to impress or intimidate her with his knowledge and family connections. She had shied away then but was starting to see him just as a friendly and helpful guy.

He caught up with her as she made her way to her doom. "Hey dude!" he said, and offered his standard fist bump. She usually pretended not to see the gesture, but his enthusiasm buoyed her for the moment. "I just heard. That's so cool! Listen, if there's anything I can do, just say the word."

Confused, she stopped, and turning to face him, asked as plainly as she could, "You know?"

He grinned. "Oh, I know it's all hush-hush, but Aunt Lori kinda let the cat out of the bag. Boy, I can't wait to see what you and Georgie do? This is so cool!"

She felt blood draining from her face. How could he be so callous—and what on earth did he think she would consent to do with her boss? What had she gotten herself into? Her desk wasn't far away, maybe thirty feet. *Just walk over, grab your coat and purse, and go.*

"Skippy!"

Too late! She was frozen in place. Dr. Marsh was standing right behind her.

"All right, Mr. Social Butterfly, back to work. And don't even think of pestering Aydan for a sneak peek at the new office layout!" She turned to the open office, addressing their dozen engineers. "As Skip here has already spilled the beans, I might as well make it official. We will be moving our division to the eighth floor and before anyone starts to complain, yes it is less space than we have now, and yes it's twice as much space as each of the guys on seven get. Good enough?"

There were a few grumbles but she continued, "Georgie and Aydan will be designing the upgrades to the old ballroom. This is happening, folks, so figure out what changes, if any, would improve on what we've got now. No idea is too crazy. But you have to get them to Aydan ASAP. Understood?"

While Dr. Marsh fielded a few questions, Aydan slowly recovered her composure. Skip hadn't been talking about her. He was excited for her. How very interesting.

She followed Dr. Marsh into the corner office and stood by the guest chair waiting to be offered a seat. Instead she was waved into the small corner seating area made up by a love seat and two upholstered chairs. She chose the closest chair before noticing several items set on the table in front of it.

"Go ahead, Aydan; those are for you to read."

"I…have I done something wrong?"

Dr. Marsh looked genuinely surprised by the question. "Why would you think that?" When Aydan didn't answer, she reached for the stack, setting them on her lap and sorting them carefully.

It would be difficult not to notice Tyler Marsh. She was poised, carrying herself at her full height. The women in Aydan's family were all tall too but not elegant like her, not strong. They hid their height, cowering to their men and the world. And there was something more; Marsh and her peers were unapologetic about their appearance. They stood tall with such pride.

"Let's start with this," she offered, handing Aydan an envelope and a receipt. "That is an emergency education bursary. We usually hand out a few every year. Please sign the receipt. Usually we just issue a check but I took it from petty cash just in case you couldn't get to your bank…"

"I don't have a bank," she admitted without taking her eyes from the receipt clipped to the envelope. It was made out to her, with a frightening amount listed: "Twelve hundred dollars? I—"

"Aydan, listen to me. We will help you with everything, okay? Please look at me."

Forcing her head up, she was reassured by the kindness she saw. "Why are you being so nice to me? I haven't exactly been—"

"You've been a little bitch, especially with Georgie. Having said that, I expect your personal situation has played a big part. That and the challenge of working with our sweet but complicated Georgie. Now, tell me, have you thought about taking the assistant job? And before you pooh-pooh it, let me tell you about my situation when I started here."

It took her about twenty minutes to tell the story and go over the basic requirements for anyone assigned to babysit her partner. By the time she wrapped up, Aydan had gained a new respect for the company president. It was easy to understand why she was in charge.

"Sign the receipt for the bursary and read through the job descriptions. There are two openings. Neither will interfere with your internship. Unfortunately, you have to choose one or the other. Your internship won't allow for the hours required to fill both slots. Still, you should be able to get by on your part-time wages. Now the other thing I want you to know is that you are welcome to stay with us for as long as you want, but we are working on an alternative for you. There are two other units up on the penthouse. One belongs to Lori Phipps's sister, Leslie. She operates the Fleet Street Grill on the main floor. The other is their father's, but now that Henry's living out at the big house—sorry, the family estate, it's sitting empty. We may not be able to secure it as a full-time residence for you but you could probably have it for yourself on weekends if you're interested."

"Please, Dr. Marsh, why are you being so kind?" she asked again. Again she saw only compassion, no judgment or superiority, just simple humanity. These women her brothers had berated so cruelly were nothing like they had alleged.

"First off, it's Tyler. I won't have you calling me Dr. Marsh and tiptoeing around our home. Now, coming from an academic background like you, I too found all this first-name nonsense disconcerting at first but they make it work. Just remember, for the time being you're low man on the totem pole. They like all the camaraderie that comes with being on a first-name basis, but in the end they still expect everyone to remember the hierarchy, understood?"

"Yes ma'am, sorry...I mean Tyler."

She smiled. "You're learning. Now, why are we helping you? It's simple, you're a person who needs help, and believe it or not, this is one of those places where they do strive to help people up. I'm sure you've noticed it's almost all family here, but it's not just DiNamico and Phipps anymore. Even my two sisters work here. As a matter of fact, you will meet my sisters tonight at dinner. You will be home for dinner?"

Home. It sounded so normal coming from her. "Home for dinner," she had said. Was that it, now she had a home and suddenly life called for normal things like being home for dinner? She nodded before forcing a squeaky, "Yes, I'll be home for dinner. Yes, very...thank you."

Tyler nodded her approval then picked up her always present smartphone and started tabbing away. The one big difference between Tyler and Georgie was her ability to carry on a conversation while she typed. "What's your cell number?" When Aydan didn't immediately answer, she looked up, sensing the problem. "Okay then, let's get you a phone while we're at it."

Aydan's company tablet chimed and she read through the instructions that Tyler had sent. "Georgie wanted to see me at three."

It was already five past and clearly Tyler wasn't concerned. As explanation, she held her phone up. "I still control her schedule. Lori Phipps will be joining us for supper too, so you three can go over all your ideas then. In the meanwhile, get over to the bank. They know you're coming. Once you're done there, hit the cell phone place. It's just around the corner. We have an account there and they know what our requirements are but just in case...there, they will be expecting you too. How does that sound?"

"I..."

"That's what I thought. Go run your errands and we will see you upstairs. And don't worry; Georgie's already programmed your access credentials. Just use your employee badge to get in."

"Can I bring anything...for dinner, I mean?"

"That's a nice offer, but I'm sure Lori will bring some wine. She always does and God knows Megan never shows up without a bucket of double chocolate ice cream for her and Georgie."

"Megan, is that your sister?"

Tyler stood, gathering the signed documents and ordering them for filing. "Yes. You should know Megan was the one who figured out you were in trouble and she can be a bit on the pragmatic side. Will you be okay if she starts asking questions?"

"You have a right to know—"

"Whoa there Nelly; no one has a right to your personal business. As far as anyone here is concerned, I have asked you to stay with us while you learn the duties associated with being Georgie's assistant. Personally, no one will think twice about it. Before I started caring for her they had half the family on duty, several caregivers and still she needed help. Don't get me wrong. Georgie is brilliant and kind and good God I do love her, but she has to fight every day with so many things we take for granted. Trust me, the only thing anyone will ask about you working and staying with us is how you got saddled with such a heavy workload."

Finally, Aydan stood on shaky legs, holding the tablet close. "I'll go do these things then. What time should I come upstairs?"

"It's your home now. Head up there when you're done with your errands and you might as well drag that duffel bag up from its hiding place in the women's locker room."

Aydan colored but asked, "Did Megan..."

"She's a very inquisitive girl," she said absently as she returned to her desk.

CHAPTER SIX

Lori Phipps stood up from her chair to stretch her aching back. "Frig it, Marnie! If I have to read one more financial report—"

"It comes with the territory," Marnie said without easing up on the pounding she was giving her keyboard.

Working her way through several stretching exercises, Lori asked, "What the hell are you working on? The way you're punishing that keyboard, you'd think the twins are in trouble again. Oh shit! They're not in trouble are they?"

"Not this week. Don't jinx it for me." Marnie finished her typing and, closing the file, she watched her cousin's restless pacing. "You just can't sit still, can you?"

"Hey, you were always the same. What's changed?"

"I have too much goddamn work to have time to get all ADD. Now sit down and tell me what you think."

Lori groaned. "You really want to know? I think its bullshit. The numbers don't make sense and I'm not even sure we have the right to risk the employee pension fund on these bright ideas of Lou's. What did Georgie say?"

"Same as you only in fewer words, but she did say she would back his plan if you, me and Leslie agreed with this."

"So that leaves you and Leslie. What did she say?"

Marnie gave her the most ironic look. "If you have to ask… Look, we're all on the same page here. I'll tell him it was a tough call and the board was interested but not ready to move ahead."

Lori shrugged. "Why do you coddle him?"

She pushed back from her desk, clicking the ever-present ballpoint as she did so. "You know, Lori, you could go easier on him. Yes, Lou fucked up and tried to run an endgame around us, but it failed. It didn't just fail, it was an epic fail and he's going to pay for that for the remainder of his career. I actually feel bad for him," she admitted. "Like me, he knew nothing about Cattaraugus Creek. We didn't know Aunt Georgina's company share had been left completely to Georgie. Frankly, if I had been standing where he was, I might have taken a run at the top job too."

"What?" Lori was stomping mad. "You do have the top job and we couldn't tell you about Cattaraugus Creek. We signed a gag order. Blame Aunt Georgina, not me!"

"What the fuck, Lor! When did you start keeping secrets from me? We have shared everything since the crib. Why didn't you tell me about all of this?"

"Marn, what the hell? Why are you bringing this up now?"

Standing behind her desk, Marnie dumped the ballpoint onto her blotter and assumed her infamous superhero pose. Then she started laughing. "Oh God, I can't get mad at you, but I was a little pissed to think you kept something so…so cool from me." Walking to her office door, she leaned out into the hallway and called to her new assistant, "Tony, will you bring in coffee please." To Lori she said, "Let's sit down and chat about a few things and yes, the twins are on that list."

"I knew it! What did those two little peckerheads do this time? Oh, I know this will be good." Lori noted that even with the fireplace on Marnie looked chilled. "What's with you lately? You're like an old lady, always too cold. I thought menopause was supposed to be all hot flashes and stuff." She stepped up to

Marnie's chair and wrapped the Pendleton blanket around her shoulders before crashing onto the couch.

"I think it's this damn office," she said, waving her hand around the two-story executive suite. "What I would give to put Georgie back in here. I even tried to unload these two floors to Leslie."

"Only you. You finally score the best office in the place, the only one, I will remind you, with a fireplace and you want out. What's up with that?"

Marnie groaned, pulling the blanket tighter. "Don't laugh, I think it's all the ghosts in here."

Lori did grin, but she quickly twisted her expression into a look of concern. "Ghosts, hmm. What about voices, hearing anything in your head?"

Marnie picked up and threw her pen at her. "Smartass! You're worse than the twins. Are you ready for this? They came to me with their latest scheme. They want to sign affidavits that they self-recognize as LGBT so they can inherit some of Aunt Georgina's land. Don't worry," she cautioned as Lori's jaw dropped. "They only plan to change teams until they claim their inheritance, then they will 'come out' as straight. They even used the fact that so many gay people come out later in life, even after having been married and having kids, so they figured it could work the other way too."

"Holy crap...so what's got you more steamed, the fact that they don't get the whole straight privilege thing, or that they have no idea how hard it is for normal people to come out? Or that it didn't occur to them to simply ask for what they want, and that Georgie and I would happily give it to them?"

"Yeah, that one's my top thing. Then the faking being gay so they could rip off their aunts. I didn't raise them to act like Lou. I did manage to knock some sense into them and their father is on their asses big time. I'm not sure which part upset him more, the idea that they would lie about being gay just to get something, or that they were willing to tell the world they were gay. Although, I don't think they actually thought that part out. When I told them we would send out announcements and have a huge coming out party, they started to sweat."

"I'm not sure who you're mad at, the kids for acting like the little conniving prick my baby brother can be, or your husband for being homophobic?"

"Yeah, Jack's attitude did surprise me. We had a long talk later that night. I don't think it's really homophobia as much as a not-my-sons thing. Although he did assure me that if one or both turned out to be gay he would still love and support them, he just wanted them to know how people would react and the reality around coming out."

"And you?"

"Jeez, Lor, I thought I raised them better than this. At this point I don't even want Georgie to consider giving them anything, even if she could."

Lori sat up straighter, her attention piqued. "If she could—what's that about?"

Marnie's shoulders sagged. "You were here. You saw Tyler's face. She wants babies. You've seen Georgie's will. Tyler will inherit her money but the kids, my boys and Zoe and Skip, would have inherited all her real estate holdings. I'm not saying they deserve it or anything but...I don't know. I guess I never thought she would have a family."

"Slow down there. It's not as if it can just happen. Making a baby for a lesbian couple is a complicated business. Besides, who's to say she wants babies?"

Marnie just gave her that look again. "Let me put it this way. If Tyler wants a baby, Georgie will make sure Tyler gets—"

"—a baby. Yeah, I know. She'll move heaven and hell to make it happen but that doesn't really address your problem. Why are you really upset about this?"

Marnie took her time answering. "At first I thought maybe I was being reactionary, like Jack. Then I had to ask myself if I considered Tyler family and I do. At the same time I don't accept Bonnie, Lou's little white trophy wife. It's not like she ever involves herself in the family." She sighed, not having a ready answer. "Maybe I'm just worried. You don't think she's a bit old to be thinking about having babies?"

"I'm no expert but thirty-seven is not too old to be popping out kids."

"Thirty-seven, no, I'm talking about Georgie."

"Oh." Lori nodded, trying to think that through before she started laughing. "Oh Marns, Georgie will not be popping out any babies. That I can guarantee!"

"How do you know? Maybe she wants to be a mother?"

Lori retrieved the discarded ballpoint from the couch cushion and threw it back at her bundled-up cousin. "Trust me on this, and don't ask me to explain it, it's a lesbian thing. If Georgie and Tyler decide to have children, they will probably adopt. We can do that now, you know, but if Tyler wants babies, Georgie will find a way to get her in the family way. She won't go all girly and want to carry the baby herself, unless they get some two for one deal. I saw a movie like that once. Patty Duke and this really cute Canadian actress were lovers and both got pregnant at the same time."

"Oh jeez! What the hell would we do if they were both out on maternity leave?"

"Oh, now we get to the real issue. You're worried about who will run the new company if Tyler's out playing new mommy?"

"I know, it's stupid to worry about it now, but I sit in this office, surrounded by everything our dads built, and worry if I'm doing it right."

"Oh Marns!" Lori sat forward. "You're doing a great job. Revenues are up, orders are up, and employee morale is up. You can't ask for more."

"That's all down to you, Georgie and Tyler. I don't know what I would do without you three but the real issue is me. You and I know this office was built for Georgie and I just don't know if I can fill her shoes."

"This office was built by Luigi to impress, nothing more. There are no ghosts here and no big shoes to fill. This is you. You made this job what it is and if I, and Georgie, and Tyler too are contributing in a big way it's because of your leadership. You cut the strings that were holding each of us back, especially so with Georgie and Tyler, and good call on that kid. She is turning out to be the best business planner I have ever known, and better than that, she speaks Georgie!

"Do you remember all the heartache you suffered over putting Georgie in this office in the first place? It sucked and everyone fought you, but you were right. Her productivity soared. She was protected, supervised, and had the room to work. Getting Georgie out of this office was about establishing your authority while giving her the creative space she needs. I'm actually stoked about Tyler taking her team up to the ballroom. It's the perfect size and on those days when Georgie can't cope, she can just walk across the hall. As for Tyler, I don't think we have to worry about maternity leave. Even if she takes it, she's right here and will always be on call to handle Georgie. Plus, I don't know if you've noticed but Georgie's...well, she's almost Georgie these days. Yes, she still can't string more than three or four words together at a time, but that doesn't stop her anymore. Her team too, shit, I think Tyler's taught them all how to speak Georgie! You should hear Skippy these days. I swear he hears everything she says, fills in the missing words, and regurgitates it up at dinner every night."

"Oh God, Lou must hate that."

"Yeah but it makes Henry smile. That and his Sundays when Georgie and Tyler come for dinner."

"I'm glad they started doing that. I'm proud of Georgie for facing down her issues about the big house. Maybe I have Tyler to thank for that too."

"She's special, Marns, like your Jack is too. They're part of this family and deserve our respect."

Marnie retrieved her pen from where it had landed on her blanket. "Understood. Just don't ask me to tack her name onto the holding division. DiNamico Phipps Pulaski is long enough."

"Could you see Lou's face? Besides, DiNamico Phipps Pulaski and Marsh sounds pretty good to me."

"Speaking of Lou," she said, "Zoe has asked to be moved back to HR."

"Uh-oh. I guess being Daddy's personal assistant isn't as glamorous as she thought. You're not going to take her back, are you?"

"What, and move little Tony? Not on your life. That kid makes the best coffee in the universe and he knows enough to ignore his cell phone when he's in my office. That makes him an all-star assistant in my books."

"Mine too, so let me guess, you want me to take her?"

Marnie walked to her desk, retrieved a personnel file and handed it over. "It's really up to you. She is a good assistant."

"A good assistant who failed the loyalty test in a massive way."

"Lori please. Just consider it. The acceptance/rejection sheet is on top. If you don't want her out at the boatyard I understand, I do, but go easy on the loyalty thing. It wasn't as if she backed an outsider. It was her dad, for freaking sakes. Tell me, which side would you have chosen if a power struggle had broken out between your dad and mine?"

"I get it. Here, give me the file." She took it and the pen, signing the placement acceptance form. "Okay, we'll do this your way since I just spent an hour telling you how freaking smart you are. I want you to know I'm feeling tricked. And you better read that kid the riot act. She can report in Monday, bright and early," she said with less and less enthusiasm. "Wait, does dipshit know our niece wants to bail on him?"

Marnie grinned; this was turning out to be a pretty good day after all. "Not yet. You want to be the one to tell him or can I?"

"Ooh…" She rubbed her hands together like a super villain. "Let's do it together. I love it when you make him report to you. I swear his junk shrivels up every time he walks in here."

Marnie just shook her head, retrieving her smartphone and sending a text. Tony, her new assistant, walked in with the coffee tray. "I'm so sorry for the delay. Accounting keeps borrowing the carafe from our coffeemaker. With your permission, I'd like to order another so this doesn't happen again."

"Order two," Marnie instructed. "One for accounting and a spare for us, but before you do that, please ask your mother and Kira Marsh to join us as soon as Lou arrives. You will have to bring coffee for him but ask Susan and Kira to bring their own."

"Anything else, can I get something sent up from the restaurant? You haven't eaten today," he reminded her. "Or anything for you, Aunt Lori?"

Lori shook her head and waited until he was out of the office before asking, "What the hell, Marns! You're not eating and you're cold all the time. You're not sick are you?"

"I'm just tired."

"So, take some time off. Come on, you've been at this twenty-four seven since Lou started this up. No, since Georgie came back from Afghanistan! Isn't it time you took a break?"

She nodded, as Susan Chan, the Director of HR and Tony Junior's mom, along with Kira Marsh carried in their tablets and coffee mugs. "Maybe all I need is a mini-break. Kira, do you mind if Lori and I visit the day care after this? I could use a little Ella time."

"Knock yourself out. We're joining you for dinner with Tyler and Georgie, so the more you chase her around now, the less energy she'll have to wreck their place later."

"Oh jeez, I forgot all about the wedding planning thing."

"Well, you guys should definitely get your Ella time in now. Once she sees those two, that's it."

Lori waved them over to the meeting area. "This is going to be some planning dinner. Between all of us, Leslie, Megan, and now Aydan, our girls have a full house."

"How is the thing with Aydan?" Susan asked, clarifying her question after noticing their strained looks. "Has she made a choice on which of the assistant jobs she wants to take?"

"Not yet, but you can bring it up tonight."

If that fact surprised Susan, she hid it well. Lori marveled at how well the women, both those born to the family and those who married in, just fit. It would have been interesting if Marnie's ghosts were real. It would be something to see how those men reacted to the girls now running the show and what a spectacular job they were doing. She couldn't help but think Uncle Danny would be pleased. God knows, her own father, Henry, certainly was.

* * *

In the kitchen Aydan turned from where she was helping Lori throw together the salad to see Leslie push open the sliding steel door that separated the main floor living area from the eighth-floor foyer. She had wondered how the waiter had entered the condo to serve their lunch earlier without coming down the stairs. She scooted over to offer assistance. She wasn't really sure what else to do with herself. She had dragged her few possessions up from her car to deposit in the guest room. This was the night she usually spent at the Laundromat. She had neglected that duty with an eye toward being a good guest and taking part in this, whatever it was. She would have to ask Dr. Marsh, Tyler, about local laundries, but not tonight. She didn't want to be a problem and wouldn't risk upsetting anyone.

Instead she helped Leslie wheel the catering cart into the kitchen. Leslie waving at everyone and calling, "Anybody order a rack of lamb?"

Lori teased her little sister, "Very funny, squirt. Maybe you should do one of those Doctor in the House jokes too."

"Let me help. You probably have to get back to the restaurant," Aydan offered.

"Not tonight, Miguel's on it."

"The way I hear it, Miguel's on a lot of things these days, including you?" Lori challenged her with a wide mouth grin. Before Leslie could answer, or flee, the other women offered up their oohs and aahs.

"What, he's nice! Besides, do you have any idea how hard it is to meet a decent guy these days?"

"You're speaking to the choir, sister," Kira offered. She had tossed off her suit jacket and her heels and was comfortably ensconced in the old nail-head chesterfield sofa.

"Huh! You think it's hard to meet guys, you should try—"

"Lori!" Marnie interrupted her, subtly tipping her head toward Aydan Ferdowsi who stood stiffly between Lori and Leslie.

"Wait!" Kira interrupted. "If Leslie has a new man in her life, I want to hear about it."

Aydan watched with interest as these powerful women gossiped and carried on. At first she was disappointed, somehow expecting the evening to resemble an intellectual salon, but these women were smart. They were running a successful enterprise. She didn't really know just how successful they were until she had had unfettered access to the Internet through her work-issued laptop. She'd spent her previous evenings at the Buffalo Library or coffee shops with free Wi-Fi, researching companies in the region, looking for successful businesses that demonstrated a willingness to employ women and minorities. She had actually been hoping to isolate two or three prospective employers she could approach for a starting level position that might consider assuming her internship. It had been a fruitless search with one exception; DiNamico Marine Engineering continually popped up as the best employer in the region and had awards and commendations to prove the claim. They also showed up as the best company for new engineers, the best company for women, and the best company for minorities. According to everything she found she was already in the best place she could be in.

Now, standing here, judging these women, she scolded herself. From the start they had done nothing but be supportive and provide her with opportunities she was just starting to understand didn't happen every day. This was her mother and her brother's influence. Having seen and heard so much from their perspective hadn't just skewed her opinion, it had crippled her ability to see people for who they were, not how they fit within the right-wing Ferdowsi viewpoint. Maybe it was the real reason her sisters had cut and run, each marrying the first man that would take them out of the family home.

Lori touched her shoulder. "You okay there, friend?" At Aydan's startled look, she quietly added, "Don't worry. Once Megan gets here and we eat, if you want you can slip upstairs and escape this craziness..."

Blurting out, "It's my laundry night." Aydan hurriedly added, "What I mean is, do you know if there's a Laundromat around here? I don't really know this part of town," she added as an excuse for a question she wished were still in her mouth. For all her concern, this Lori seemed more amused than anything else.

"Follow me, princess, and I will show you the way." She added a wink and headed for the circular stairs.

Feeling somehow caught out, she fell in behind her, her head down, embarrassed. She didn't venture a look at the other women until she was halfway up the stairs. Georgie, with her dog, was sitting on the floor in front of the fireplace, busy teaching baby Ella colored shapes on an app she had created just for the toddler. Mrs. Pulaski and Kira Marsh sat in front of them on the couch, drinking wine and chatting. Dr. Marsh, Tyler, had changed into jeans and a sweater. She looked different, so casual, and was joking with Leslie the chef as they finished setting the large round dining table. As it hadn't been there at lunch, she could only assume it was borrowed from the catering tables and chairs stored on carts next door. These women were certainly resourceful.

"Okay, I'll take you for the nickel tour, but we'll have to work out the details with Tyler. Don't worry," Lori offered as reassurance as she led her into another bedroom. "Now there are only two ways into the laundry room. You'll probably want to use the other one but you might as well know where everything is if you're going to be Georgie's right-hand man, er, woman. Shit, you know what I mean," she said before realizing she had sworn again. "Oh God, sorry Aydan, my mouth gets away from me most of the time and—"

"I don't mind."

"You don't?" she asked but Aydan didn't say anything else. "So, this is Georgie and Tyler's bedroom…"

"What? I can't be here!"

"Will you relax? This is the way to the laundry room."

Trying desperately not to look around, she shuffled her feet, asking, "You said there was another entrance."

Turning to face her square on, Lori challenged, "Okay princess, spit it out. Have you got a problem with my Georgie and the Tiger? I want to know right now!"

Suddenly scared of losing the job offer, her internship, and maybe even her living space, albeit temporary, she stood frozen, head down and lost for words.

Gently, using just the tip of her index finger, Lori tipped her chin up, forcing her to meet her eyes. "I won't tell. I promise. If you have a problem I want to help and that includes helping you to get comfortable with my cousin and her lifestyle. Those women downstairs, they're my friends, my family, and my business associates."

"It's...I don't..."

Lori dropped her hand and moved over to the polished sleigh bed to take a seat. "Okay princess, I see the fear and the shame and I know life hasn't been easy for you, but that's all I know. It's all any of us know. We want to help you, Aydan, but I'll warn you, a lot of that comes from Georgie and what she sees in you. The truth is we all see something good, some potential, real potential, but I also see you need to leave a lot of crap behind. I can't tell you what that is, but I can help you with what you're facing now. Here, sit down," she said, patting the bed beside her. "Let's have a good old-fashioned girl talk."

It took a moment for Aydan to propel herself from her holding spot. She sat on the edge of the bed and as far from Lori as the frame would allow.

"Jeez girl, I'm not going to bite, wait...oh God, why did I not see this? You're scared of us, us lesbians! Let me guess, your family raised you to believe some hypocritical religious garbage about all gays being deviants and baby eaters and we're all going to hell, or something like that?"

"I—"

"Keep your peace, sister! I've heard it a million times and I don't care what your religion is, any institution that uses hate and lies to hurt others sounds like more patriarchal bullshit to me." She was on her feet pacing, then turned sharply on Aydan. "Just tell me, do you think we're hurting anyone? Have we done anything to earn your judgment? Honestly, we—"

"No! I...I can explain, please," she pleaded, realizing she needed to state her case, but where exactly did she stand? "I... you're right. My family is very conservative..."

"Really?" she challenged. "I want to hear what you think."

She sighed, but kept her head up. The last thing she wanted to do in front of this strong woman was show just how pathetic she had become. "It was different before my father died. He taught us to accept our differences, even celebrate them. He encouraged me to pursue an education and career, but after he died I guess I let my grief get the best of me. By the time I was ready to take responsibility for my own life, my mother had deferred all family decisions to her father."

"And let me guess, the old coot decided you would do better barefoot and pregnant. Do you have sisters?"

"Yes, two—both younger, and yes they are married and none bothered with university although they each seem to believe their idiot male offspring are entitled to inherit the universe."

That comment seemed to break the building tension and made Lori smile. She sat down again, asking, "So, how sheltered was this life of yours? Sorry about your dad—when did he die?"

On friendlier ground, Aydan was able to talk about her dad for the first time in years. Discussing her father had been a taboo subject at home because her mother would wail of her permanent grief at the mention of his name, while her younger brothers were unwilling to consider much less kowtow to the contrary beliefs of a man long removed from their lives. It was a relief to tell Lori the whole story, even the part about the beatings she had received at the hands of her brothers, all intended to put her in line. Then she told her about their hateful words about Georgie and Tyler, and how, when she was still undeterred, they had held her in a headlock while her mother had brutally sheared off her hair.

Lori looked appalled, but her words seemed an attempt to lighten the mood: "Is that why you ditched the pretty blue scarf for that ugly penguin wrap?"

"Penguin? I don't understand."

"Yeah, I'm starting to get the idea you don't know a whole lot about a whole lot." Lori pointed to the gray hijab. "When we were really little we would go to church every week as a big family. My dad's Episcopalian and Georgie's was Catholic. So, each Sunday we would switch churches and all go to one or the other. The Catholic service was very showy. I was always fascinated to watch the priest walking around swinging that smoke bomb thing and followed by his boy-band entourage all in their frilly flowing whites. It always bugged me that they got all the floor time while the penguins sat in the back with us."

From Aydan's look of confusion, it was clear she still had no idea what she meant. "Oops. Oh, you really are a newbie. Okay, here's the deal. I will be your personal and secret translator of all things starting with penguin which is slang for a Catholic nun. You do know they wear the same headscarf type thing and they probably think it's for the same reason but it's a lie. Covering your head does not make you modest. Being modest makes you modest."

"That could be considered a circular argument," Aydan said, her confidence returning at the pledge of support. "It would be helpful to have an interpreter for this new world."

"Ah, a sense of humor! Who knew?" Lori teased. Hearing Megan calling them down to dinner, she said, "Okay, princess. The kid's here. Are you ready to face your savior? And don't worry, Megan won't say anything about the boatyard to embarrass you."

"I…"

"Here's where you say thanks Lori, and follow me down to dinner. And, we can finish the tour after supper while the girls argue over the seating plan, or bridesmaid dresses, or some such wedding blissfulness." Lori stood, offering her hand.

Accepting the unrequired assistance, Aydan smiled to see this woman and her confidence. "Thank you, Lori." Setting aside the millions of questions floating around in her head, it was all she could say. The smile it garnered was warming. Was it possible to really have a place here? If this Lori was to be believed, it sounded like she already did.

* * *

Maggie padded out of the master bath with Georgie on her heels; Georgie was toweling her short bushy hair after a bedtime shower. Tyler had long adjusted to Georgie's military ingrained need to be prepared by showering at night and organizing for the day ahead. Tyler had already set out her clothing for the next day. It was only a suggestion but on most days, Georgie was more than pleased with the assistance and donned what had been chosen for her. Still, no one could say she wasn't her own woman. Now and then she would carefully put everything back and select what she really wanted to wear. She still needed to rely on the codes created in her closet to help her know what was suitable and for which occasion. She could still be counted on to pull strange combinations together, but now she would turn to Tyler for advice before wearing just anything. Tyler was slowly adding color to her conservative outfits, and adding more casual clothing. As their relationship had progressed, so had Georgie's social calendar and Tyler had been able to add items like jeans and sweaters and even a cocktail dress in which Georgie looked smoking hot. It was a nice change from the uniform-inspired business suits. She seemed younger too, especially when she threw on jeans and got down on the floor to play with her dog or now little Ella.

"Hey, welcome back," Tyler called. She was sitting up in bed, legs bent, and reading from her tablet. "What did you think of Leslie's idea for a buffet dinner?"

"Newfie supper."

Tyler watched as she carefully folded the towel before hanging it back in the bathroom. Asking, "Why do they call it that?"

"Grandma would say…" Georgie tossed her robe across the foot of the bed, crawling in buck naked.

Tyler waited patiently, knowing Georgie needed to stop moving before she could engage her mouth and continue her explanation. She didn't mind the delay and certainly couldn't complain about the view. She did ask herself, as she did pretty much every night, if she would ever feel differently than she did at moments like this. Georgie was a sensuous woman. She slept in the nude, not as a statement or provocation—she liked a cold room at night—but she had, without a second thought, turned up the temperature in the bedroom to suit Tyler's desire for a little blessed heat. With Georgie fully veiled between the cool cotton sheets and under their duvet, Tyler told her, "I will never tire of watching you come to bed."

Georgie smiled, moving in close to offer a kiss. "My Tyler... you, I love."

Setting her tablet aside, she pulled her wife-to-be closer. It was easy to get lost in her lips, her mouth, and those kisses. Pulling away to see her eyes, Tyler teased, "Oh no, no changing the subject. I want to hear a Grandma Collins story from the Rock...first." She winked, noting Georgie's trademark grin. The one reserved just for her.

"She said...everyone brings food...you make food...so much. All the tables..."

She used a hand signal Tyler recognized, "Covered? Every table is covered with food so no one can sit down to eat?"

She nodded, smiling, and added, "All night...to celebrate."

"They serve the buffet all night? Oh my God, I can't even begin to estimate how much food that would be."

Georgie was laughing, and shaking her head she explained, "We won't, not like that...Too much waste. Just regular..."

"You're still grinning! You have something planned, don't you?"

Georgie shook her head, moving in to cuddle and finally offering, "No...just want it, perfect...for my Tyler."

That earned her extra attention. Switching off the light, she shimmied down under the covers molding herself into Georgie's arms and body. It was like sleeping with your own personal heater. The woman was always hot from head to toe. It was overwhelming and comforting at the same time and Tyler was beginning to find it almost impossible to sleep on the nights they didn't spend together. That was rare these days; still, it did happen now and then.

"Baby, I was thinking about building the house out at the beach." The beach was how she referred to the property at Cattaraugus Creek. "Maybe we should wait and build the house once we decide on a building for the division office. I would hate to get the house all done and not be able to use it or worse, spend two hours each day commuting back and forth. We're comfortable here, more than comfortable. I love this apartment and it works for us, at least for now."

Georgie's nod signaled her full agreement, before she noted the condition. "For now?"

Tyler groaned, then pulled away just enough to meet her eyes, "I...What would you say about a baby? I know we haven't talked about it but I see you with Ella and I can't help but think you would be a great parent and I guess my clock is ticking—"

"Yes."

"Although we could adopt, I don't really care how, and I know it would be a change and a challenge and—"

"Yes."

"Yes? Just like that?"

"Yes!"

A squeal of delight escaped her as she wrapped her arms around Georgie's neck. "Baby, I don't know why I even worried about it. You really want kids?"

Georgie nodded, wide-eyed and grinning, brushing her hand across Tyler's cheek then through her hair. "Little baby Tyler's...perfect. Oh...how many?"

"Okay, don't laugh but I think I would like two, you know, so they'll always have each other?"

"Like my Tyler...and Kira...Marnie and Lori, good but... what comes first?"

"Like the chicken or the egg?" Tyler joked.

That made her laugh again. "Baby or house?"

Tyler sat up, tossing off the duvet before straddling Georgie. Taking in her open joy and enthusiasm always worked to wash any doubts away. She pulled the old Aim High T-shirt she'd worn to bed over her head and tossed it on the floor, leaning down and bracing her arms on each side of Georgie's shoulders. "You make me so happy. I can't believe we're getting married in just four months. And you..." Before she could finish the sentiment, Georgie leaned up to steal a quick kiss. "How is it you always say and do just the right thing?"

"You get me," she said simply. "That is everything... everything, my Tyler...my love."

Tyler settled her full weight down on her. It was hardly an imposition. While she barely tipped the scales at one-thirty, Georgie was the strongest woman she knew. She settled her head down, tucking it so close to Georgie's that her lips brushed her ear. "I was thinking we could start a family before we build the house. Babies don't need a lot of room to start with and we have our work here so it wouldn't be a big imposition."

"Nursery?"

That got her attention. "Would you mind if we put a crib in here? At least for the first few months. Once we're comfortable, we could move her into the guest room. I know it will be a bit of an imposition not to have guests but I was thinking about that too. Maybe we should buy Henry's condo. We don't need the whole space but maybe we could just add one room from it to this apartment and then we could still use his place for guests or lease it out?" She could feel Georgie nodding her agreement. It was always that simple.

"I will ask Henry...remind me?"

"Oh course, baby. So you like the idea?"

"Yes...Her?"

"Her?"

"The baby...you said her."

"Oh God, you're right. Would you want a girl or a boy or does it matter?"

She shook her head, "Just...your baby...babies...my little Tylers." She closed her sentiment with a steaming kiss as her hands, which she had held in check until now, were free and roaming the soft curve of Tyler's shoulders and back.

"Ooh baby, wait! You only want kids if they're mine?"

Georgie's hand stilled. "Do you want?" She moved her hand on Tyler's abdomen.

Leaning away, just enough to add her own hand, Tyler entwined Georgie's fingers with her own. "I want to have children. I don't think I realized how much until today. We were sitting in Marnie's office and somehow the subject came up. Well, I think it came up between Leslie and Kira, and they were baiting me to see if I was interested." Recalling the entire conversation, she sat up slightly, showing her concern. "I'm not sure how Marnie feels about it."

Georgie raised the intertwined fingers to her lips, taking her time to kiss Tyler's hand. "Tell me?"

"It was during our meeting. Kira and Leslie baited me on the baby thing and when I admitted I might want children, Lori was all high fives but Marnie was...well she just changed the subject. And there's something else. I...is there any chance she might be going through menopause? I mean I know she's four years younger but..."

"Yes...I think so. Maybe...having kids changes...stress too."

"Stress can be a catalyst for menopause? Oh my God, if that's true we better get started now!"

Georgie pulled her back on top before taking her face in her hands, "No worries...my love. Start now?" she asked with a grin.

"Hmm, I'm not sure it works like that but we can certainly try," she said, struggling with a bombardment of sensations as Georgie's lips began to trace a path her hands were blazing. Being touched by her, touching her, the way it made her feel, she had never imagined it could be like this. Love and desire had been instantaneous for her lover, but for her, for reserved and cautious Tyler, it had been a slow burn. She never denied her feelings, but her expectations and hopes, all her hopes, had been slow to coalesce. Maybe it was trust that took time.

During those first few months she had examined Georgie's intentions from all angles, determined not to fall prey to anyone or thing. Navigating the halls of academia had been more treacherous than she had ever imagined, and she had learned firsthand that Ethicists were all the rage in business schools just as long as they didn't examine the ethics of that school's policies. And then there were the failed relationships with faculty members and the management of student expectations, especially those with more than academic intentions. She had found it exhausting and demoralizing. It had been a step up from the lousy and fruitless job search that had left her unemployed for over a year, and living at home with Mom and Dad. Still, it hadn't been a complete bust. Twin sister Kira had moved home too.

Kira's situation was completely different though. Her law career was proceeding well but her love life…not so much. Deciding she couldn't wait for Mr. Right to make his presence known, she had chosen artificial insemination. When her parents learned she wanted to start a family alone, they had begged her to return home. Tyler marveled to think of how supportive her parents were. They had welcomed them both with open arms, offering unlimited support for her and her twin. They even offered to build an addition to the family home with two separate apartments, one just for Kira and the future baby, and the other for her. Kira hadn't wanted that, and Tyler had enjoyed having her twin for company again with the old adjoining bathroom between their childhood bedrooms, their one-time late night secret meeting place. And her parents had been super supportive with her too, insisting she take her time to find the right job instead of accepting just anything she could get.

It was Tyler who, after more than a year of unemployment, decided to aim lower. She had grown desperate to get back to work when she answered an ad for an executive assistant. At the time she believed she had reached the lowest point in her career, but she'd swallowed her pride and applied for the job. The online job description had provided all the details required and she simply regurgitated them back into her cover letter and improvised résumé. The first interview was pretty much as she suspected with one exception. During that time, Susan Chan who she now knew to be a real straight shooter, had been cagey over certain details like whom she would be executive assistant to and what the job would entail. It wasn't until the second interview, when she walked in to meet shy and complicated Georgie DiNamico, that she learned her ruse had failed. Georgie had researched her applicants, choosing Tyler because of her academic credentials and knowing she had lied to get her foot in the door. She had called Tyler on it, asking her not to do it again while conveying her understanding for the ploy.

Entwined in their bed, Georgie's lips found their way to her small sensitive breasts. Moaning, getting lost in the moment, she still had so much on her mind. "Wait, baby, ooh…"

Rolling Tyler onto her side, Georgie doubled the pillow under her head then waited, smiling as her fingers began tracing each rib along her side.

"You…why are you so patient with me? No, don't answer that. Baby, I want to have our babies…"

"Good."

While her fingers traced a hardened nipple, her lips found Georgie's mouth, and quickly devoured any lingering discussion. She had long learned she would receive no protest from Georgie. She'd had older lovers before but none as eager or yet as complicated as her soon-to-be wife. They were perfectly matched that way and even learning that fact had been a revelation. Everything about them, at least from the outside, looked to be so different, even incompatible. Nothing could be further from the truth. In some strange and unfathomable way, they needed each other. Accepting that had been the last of a long line of barriers Georgie struck down and Tyler couldn't imagine being happier.

CHAPTER SEVEN

Lori stood in the security cottage, coffee cup in hand, staring out the office window. Since she had been running the production line, she'd made a habit of arriving before seven each day. First order of business was a perimeter check which she did with the day shift security guard. Then she and Megan would unlock the production shed and any outbuildings the crew might need to access that day. Most mornings that took a little over forty minutes. Afterward she would return to the security cottage to hear Megan go over the list of scheduled visitors, deliveries and any actions that required either her approval or her attention. She also used this time to track just who did and did not arrive on time. Working for family had led some individuals to believe they could get away with behavior that wouldn't be tolerated elsewhere. They were wrong, more so than ever, especially since this was the Monday her niece Zoe was supposed to report in as her personal assistant.

She really didn't want to admit she needed an assistant but the days of business as usual were truly over. The updates and changes she and Georgie had put in place over the last year had done more than ramp up boat orders. Suddenly, DynaCraft was the go-to place for industry consultation or just plain spying. It wasn't as if they weren't willing to share, she just wanted to make sure the company received fair compensation for their hard-earned innovations. Having an open yard with full public access made that a challenge for her sole security guard. Zoe's arrival would take a number of items off Megan's list, giving her more time to do her job. Tracking material shipments and Lori's appointment schedule would now fall to Zoe but she also wanted her to understand how important Megan's job was. She was the eyes and ears of the boatyard and formed their first line of defense. She needed to understand, right from the beginning, that Megan was part of her core team.

"How's our lady friend doin'?" Megan asked as she printed out the day's visitor badges and sign-in sheets.

"Lady friend?"

"Yeah, Ms. Aydan," she offered casually, her eyes focused on the spreadsheet she was working on. "You know, the one stayin' with Tyler and Georgie."

"Ms. Ferdowsi?"

"However you say it…"

"Hey. Don't do that. A good cop learns about the people she is sworn to serve and protect."

"I didn't mean anything."

"No, you didn't even try. You pulled your white privilege card and decided you didn't need to learn her name because it wasn't like yours."

"Whoa boss, that's not—"

"Isn't it?" She swung around to look her in the face. What she saw was Kira and Tyler's big-eyed and clearly confused baby sister. "Shit! Listen kiddo, I'm not going to apologize. Maybe I should but—oh hell, I know you're better than that and I also know you're going to make a great cop. I guess I'm feeling a little protective of Ms. Ferdowsi. She's really been through hell."

Megan stood, and retrieving Lori's empty cup explained, "Me too. I kinda feel like we did good but we screwed up in the first place. I wish I had figured out sooner that she was in some sort of trouble."

"Yeah, me too," she lamented, watching the kid as she made her way to the tiny kitchenette. Megan returned with two steaming cups, handing one to her boss. "Are you still mad at me or is this more about Zoe coming here?"

Lori took the mug in both hands, cradling it in defense from the cold damp weather. "I'm not mad at you, but I am a little strung out thinking about the Aydan situation and the Zoe thing. Actually, you're going to be working with Zoe more than I will. Maybe I should let you worry about Zoe."

"I can handle her."

Lori smiled, taking a cautious sip of her second cup. She was not the type of woman that did well when idle. She liked to work, liked to keep her hands busy, and since giving up smoking and being promoted, that was oftentimes hard to do.

"Can I ask about her, Ms. Ferdowsi I mean? It's bad isn't it, what happened to her."

"First off, let's remember to respect her privacy. I trust you completely and as her savior you're entitled to a little information. I just haven't decided what information that is yet. If you can be patient, I promise to keep you up-to-date. One thing though, let's not talk about it with Zoe around. Aydan's having enough trouble adjusting without the company gossip having a field day, or worse…"

"Worse? Oh…"

She turned to look at Megan. "Oh, what?"

"It's okay, boss. I've got a gay sister for frig sakes. Half the girls who work here are lesbians. I'm totally there."

Lori checked her watch; it was now five to eight. "You're totally there? First off, Aydan isn't gay although she was accused of it because her family looked Georgie and your sister up on the website and found their wedding announcement."

"Ugh, my mom has those pictures all over the house, those and new ones of baby Ella every week."

She laughed at the picture of Debbie Marsh, superhero mom. Why couldn't they all be like that?

"Is that her?" Megan asked. They watched a vintage red Chevy pull into the lot. "Holy crap, is that a Corvair?"

"Yeah, my idiot brother bought it for her when she graduated from high school."

"Oh man!" she whined as she grabbed her coat and headed out with a parking sticker for Zoe's car. "Boss, you want her to come in here or meet you in the loft?"

"Here," she called after Megan, before mumbling to herself, "might as well get it over with."

* * *

Aydan stood listening as Leslie and Tyler argued with the contractor. Tyler had issues with their contract she believed were not being adhered to while Leslie was frustrated by the list of things he believed couldn't be done. Aydan had spent all weekend with Georgie inspecting every floor in the building, taking measurements of every space and compiling a list of improvements from what was immediately required to what would be nice to add. All in all the DiNamico building was in excellent condition and had been well cared for with the exception of the leased floors. They had taken a beating but now that the tenants were gone it was a golden opportunity to bring those lower floors up to grade. At the moment they were standing in the unoccupied section of the second floor listening to excuse after excuse. She did wonder why Tyler didn't shut him down, then she remembered the one detail Georgie had drilled into her head. "This is your project."

She closed her eyes, acknowledging her discomfort and anxiety. Taking a deep breath she propelled herself into the scrum. "Mr. Fener. I'm Aydan Ferdowsi. I'm the project manager. I have been listening to your concerns—"

"Ferdowsi? You Ben Ferdowsi's kid?"

The question, while straightforward, hit her like a gut shot. No one had spoken to her of her dad in fifteen years and the recent battle with her family had renewed the rawness the mention evoked. The best she could do was nod and pray he wouldn't wax on while she battled the pain of her loss.

He seemed to settle down with that minimal information or at least it made him think. He opened his contractor's clipboard and pulled out several printed sheets, clipping them to the top. "He was a good guy. Sorry. If you're running the show then how come I got this thing saying I couldn't pick my own subs?"

Tyler stepped in giving Aydan a chance to regroup. "Mr. Fener, our contract specifically forbids you from hiring subcontractors who do not meet the Corporate Standard of Ethics. You agreed to that when you were hired and—"

"I'm even more confused now," he said, turning his back on Tyler and all his attention on Aydan. "You want me to fire your company?"

"I want you to honor your contract."

"But it's your family?"

"That's where you are wrong, sir. Besides, Ferdowsi HVAC was on the blacklist here long before I joined the company and frankly, I'm very proud to work in a place that stands behind its people and policies."

Fener looked like he wanted to argue but dropped the subject, moving instead to those issues delaying his workers. "How the hell do you expect me to maintain a schedule if I can't even get full access to the space?"

"Before you worry about access why don't you tell me why safety pads haven't been installed in the elevators, or why the temporary partition curtain hasn't been hung on this floor, or why the rigging hasn't been installed for the demolition chute and why the construction bin hasn't been ordered, or why you haven't chosen a spot to—"

"All right, already. Geez…you really are Ben's kid. Okay, I'll get my guys working on the scaffolding and bins and stuff, but I want to know what's next. I need to have some idea who and when to bring them in."

"We understand that," she assured him. "That's why we're all here right now, to get this thing going and going in the right direction. I'm working on the detailed plan for the eighth floor and will have it for you next week. For now we need you to concentrate on prepping this floor, and three and four. Once the construction bin is in and the scaffolding secure, have your men work on stripping all the walls down to the brick on three and four. Once that's done you may bring in your HVAC sub, one preapproved by Dr. Marsh, and the elevator people to find and repair the dumbwaiter. If you're still twiddling your thumbs, feel free to start in on the restoration of the maple floors."

Fener stared at her before making a note on his clipboard. "Okay, boss. That works for me." Tucking his clipboard under his arm and heading out, he stopped at the fire exit door, offering casually, "Just for the record, your dad was a good guy. It's too bad your brothers are such shits."

Aydan didn't know what shocked her more, the sight of Tyler standing with her hand clamped over her mouth, or Leslie Phipps's backslap of her and her hearty howl. She was just as stunned by her assertiveness, but worried she had overstepped the line with her boss. "I'm sorry Dr. Marsh. I…"

"I have never seen Fener back down, even with Dad or when Uncle Danny was alive." Leslie cried, "Aydan rocks!"

Tyler was laughing too. "Oh my God, you were great and please you can call me Tyler anytime. I will be so happy to tell Georgie you speak Fener!"

"Can I ask a question?"

"Aydan, of course you can. This is your project to run. Only you know what information you need to do your job."

"Did you blacklist my brothers' company because of me?"

Leslie stepped forward to explain a story that predated Tyler. "Actually, it was Georgie and she did it about seven, maybe eight years ago when I was opening the restaurant. I'm sorry but it was an older man she was dealing with."

"No need to apologize. My father died sixteen years ago. My grandfather ran the company. Now my brothers have taken over. He was not a kind man and neither are they."

Was that the nicest thing she could say about the men in her family? It wasn't that she couldn't or wouldn't admit to these strong women that her brothers, in the absence of her dad, had become conservative fear-mongering control freaks who thought nothing of taking out their disappointments in life on her. Their treatment over the years and especially in these last few months, made their beliefs and behaviors even more intolerable. For her there was no forgiving them; but she had never imagined the outside world might judge them as harshly. Maybe a part of their ignorance had been pounded into her. They might never have to answer for their actions personally, but there was a whole new justice in them being blacklisted from a job she was managing.

"Do you know what they did to be blacklisted?"

"Oh I know…I was there," Leslie said. "So that was your grandfather?"

Aydan nodded.

"Well, good old granddad kept arguing with me over the layout of the kitchen. I've worked in a lot of bad kitchens and I knew the changes he was suggesting were for his benefit not mine. When I wouldn't amend the plans he started demanding to talk to the real chef. He was sure *the guy* in charge would understand the technical issues. I could have called Dad or Uncle Danny to deal with him but this was my project, my restaurant, so I called Georgie down. She was COO back then and had final say on anything in the building."

"Aydan," Tyler added, "this would be before Georgie's head injury."

Leslie nodded. "So she came down and listened to his complaints, then spent an hour discussing everything from building codes to work flow. He kept trying to shut her down, coming up with one excuse after another. When that didn't sway her, he tried bullying her, saying only he understood how to do the job. You should know, Georgie really tried with him, but when he got belligerent, she busted his balls for a dozen things from code violations to thingamajigs. He did not take it well. He stormed out, then sent a scathing email. She sent one back informing him that his services were no longer required on this project."

"Wait…" Aydan closed her eyes, remembering her eldest brother's venomous attack on one Georgina DiNamico. "It all makes so much sense now. My brother BJ went to work for my grandfather right after dad died. The way my brother reacted, especially after my youngest brother Alan went online and told him the women of your family were now running the companies, tells me he remembered something. Probably just the awful things my grandfather said. Still…" She smiled at the irony. "No wonder he was so upset to hear the company was doing so well. This economy has been particularly difficult for their industry."

"Oh, Aydan…" Tyler's concern for Georgie's intern and assistant had already been riding at DEFCON 2. Knowing Aydan's family's protest had been partially fueled by Georgie herself, not to mention the announcement of their engagement, was heartbreaking. "I am so, so sorry."

"Not at all. Please," Aydan assured them. "I should have stood up to them a long time ago. Actually, this is nothing new for them. So this is why Ferdowsi HVAC is blacklisted, the restaurant fiasco?"

"Actually, that was just the start. The old bastard tried to sue us for breach of contract. When that didn't work, he tried to name the company in a suit claiming racial discrimination," Leslie added with a grin. She still enjoyed the irony of old man Ferdowsi accusing a family that was half African American as racially discriminating against him. "That one got as far as the preliminary hearing. Were you there for that, Aydan?"

Now she was smiling too. "Sorry no, but how I wish I had been."

Leslie nodded, turning to Tyler to say, "You should have seen it. The clerk read out the docket thing and the judge asked who was representing Dynamic Marine. You should have seen his face when my very black father and our white but olive-skinned Uncle Dan stood up. Then the judge asks exactly who the complaint is against and Georgie and I stand up. I think it was one of the first times in my life I remember being truly proud I was African American and part of this crazy family. And you know how dark my dad is and Uncle Danny, well he was so swarthy he could pass for Middle Eastern. You should have seen it. Marnie and Lori, Lou, even Susan were there, and all stood up. It was like our own little United Nations. The judge scolded your grandfather's lawyers for bringing a nuisance lawsuit into his court, and that was it."

Incredible, it was absolutely incredible. She wouldn't call it a coincidence—she didn't believe in them—but she would now consider the connection between her family and this one. How incredibly different their upbringings must have been. "Thank you, Leslie, for telling me this story. I can't tell you how proud I am to work here. I just hope my family's behavior both now and then won't—"

"Nonsense," Tyler interjected, while Leslie gave her another more cautious slap on the back. "There's something you should know about working here. It's an assurance I was given pretty much every day for my first six months. This company is family. I thought it meant a lot of people working here were related. I was wrong. When someone says we are family around here, they really mean we are all part of this extended amazing clan."

"Tyler's right," Leslie added, "and don't think you're the only stray to be welcomed by our happy mash-up. I'm so sorry your family isn't in a place where they should be, but you've got us now. We're not perfect, but we take care of our own."

"Besides," Tyler joked, "now that we know you speak fluent Fener, you definitely have a place in the pack."

Aydan wasn't sure which lifted her more, their enthusiasm for including her or the simple relief at knowing they too knew what her family was all about and had stood up to them, never backing down.

CHAPTER EIGHT

When Aydan sat down at her desk the next day she still had a few good hours to work before Georgie's morning seclusion ended. She wanted to get a jump on her drawing for the new space on the eighth floor. She was confident that contractor Fener had plenty to keep him busy for a week or two. She was determined to make sure she had a finalized plan by Monday. Georgie had wanted to spend a day out at the boatyard, but lucky for Aydan, Tyler had asked her to finalize the building updates here before addressing the needed changes out there. She had just finished adding the last of the change requirements into her project plan when she sensed more than felt a presence nearby. Looking up, she smiled to see Skip waiting patiently for her attention. He was such a strange young man and so different from her brothers.

"Hey, dude," he said, "I heard you're working on the floor drawings. Want me to show you how to put them up on the worktable? It's cool if you don't. I just thought it would be easier than trying to look them over on your laptop. Hey, is that a new phone? Look it's the same model as mine!"

For the first time since starting at the company, she smiled at him. He was young and kind and trying so hard to make her feel included. It had taken awhile for her to understand him and understanding was turning slowly into trust. "Thanks, Skip. I know how to open a file on there, but I'm not sure how to make amendments. Will you show me that?"

You'd think she'd just named him Prince of all the World, the way he beamed at her response. "Okay, save your file to the Cloud, then we can open it over there. Oh, you can use a stylus if you like or the keyboard graphic. I just like to scribble on everything, but Georgie, she can really type, so she uses the keyboard GUI a lot."

He spent the next hour helping her check the figures on each layout before leaving her alone to work on her ideas. Someone in the group had started calling it the R&D Lab and Skip had repeated it with glee. His enthusiasm really was a boon. That, and feeling like she was actually doing something, something that mattered and would have a long-term effect on the company and her coworkers. Getting this right wasn't just about proving herself as an engineer or a project manager but returning the trust they had placed in her. Complete strangers were trusting her, housing and feeding her, and never once had they judged her.

The first few days staying with Georgie and Tyler had been nerve-wracking. She had managed the first evening with ease mostly because they had guests—well, a house full of women planning a wedding, a lesbian wedding no less! She had been mostly forgotten by everyone except Lori and Megan. They'd both lost interest in the planning session about two minutes in. Aydan was pretty sure Georgie's eyes had glossed over early too, but it was her wedding and she was starting to understand that if it was important to Tyler, it was important to Georgie too. She admired that, admired her devotion to her woman and Tyler too, who oversaw every aspect of Georgie's life. She didn't understand it at first, even sneered to think Tyler would kowtow to someone like Georgie but she wasn't a "someone like." She was a real person with a disability. Maybe disability wasn't the right word. She was certainly one of the most talented engineers she had met. And Georgie had given her a chance, a real chance to prove herself, not to mention given the kind of support her own family denied.

While the rest of the women were hammering out the guest list, Lori took her and Megan on a private tour of the entire ninth floor. Megan had been in Georgie and Tyler's place many times but Henry's only once, when she was invited for her first DiNamico New Year's party, just weeks before Aydan started her internship. Making their way through Georgie and Tyler's private space was less overwhelming for Aydan with both Lori and Megan along. Megan fawned over their antique bedroom furniture and they both listened intently as Lori told the story of Aunt Georgina and how she adored little Georgie. She glossed over the family tragedy of the older Georgina, focusing on the tale of little Georgie deciding at eight years old that it was her responsibility to take over her aunt's job in the family company. For a moment, she recognized the common loss Lori had suffered and marveled at how she deflected her own pain. They all did it, Lori, Leslie, even Mrs. Pulaski. Telling stories about Georgie had become a way of coping for all of them. She could only imagine the trauma for the whole family of almost losing the woman. That sentiment hit her hard as Lori took them through the walk-in closet. She had never seen anything like it, not even in movies.

"I don't know if you'll be managing any of this. I know Tyler does it all now, but it is part of the assistant's job."

"What part, like laundry?" Megan asked. She had stopped in front of the section housing Georgie's Air Force uniforms.

"No, no, cleaners are in here twice a week and they do that. It's just making sure things get replaced when needed and her wardrobe gets a once-over every year. That's always fun. This year Tyler and I went out to old Uncle John's, he's got a tailor shop in Williamsville. Anyway, between them, I think they have this covered."

Megan was still drooling over the assorted uniforms when Lori opened a small drawer for her to take a peek.

"Oh man! Are these hers?"

"Of course," Lori said, taking out the set of mounted ribbons and medals and handing them reverently to her.

She pulled out a few other items, and although she wasn't sure what Aydan thought, she didn't have to guess with Megan.

"Oh man! Are those her wings? Boss, those are master aviator wings! That star is for combat, isn't it? What else does she have?"

Megan's eyes almost bugged out when Lori showed her the second pair of silver wings.

"Holy cow, she has jump wings too! Oh man!"

"Who is this man you keep referring to?" Aydan asked unable to keep a straight face at Megan's confused look.

"She got you there, kiddo." Lori chimed in, enjoying this jesting Aydan. "Come on, Aydan, we'll let Megs here do a little more drooling while I show you the laundry room. Meet you in Henry's, okay? And make sure you put everything back just like the chart in the drawer. Understood?"

"Yes ma'am!" Megan offered with a grin. She had her phone out and was comparing Georgie's fruit salad of medals to the USAF website's description of awards. "I want to see what all of these are for."

Lori led Aydan into what was once Georgie's safe room. It still was, but here too Tyler's touch was undeniable. She had added a treadmill and some free weights, making the hospital bed in the corner look less clinical. "When my cousin first came home she had bad PTSD plus every time she fell or even moved too quickly it affected her head injury. My dad and Uncle Danny both lived up here—I'll show you their apartments in a minute—but basically they brought her home and added this funny little room. It used to be part of the foyer. Anyway, they took turns every night sitting watching over her. When we learned it was helping, we all took turns. After Uncle Dan died, we got the dog. That really helped too."

Shocked by the commitment it must have taken from the entire family to care for this one woman, while they also had their own families and work, she asked, "Does she still…"

"I don't think so, at least not when Tyler's here. I know you only know her like she is now but, well, we all just assumed she would take over one day. I don't think any of us really took our work too seriously until they shipped her home from Afghanistan. The first year was hell on everyone, but we were all trying to pretend nothing had changed. Then my dad and Uncle Dan sat us all down for a family meeting. And when I say family I mean everyone, all the cousins, DiNamico and Phipps, even the second cousins, any and all family working for the company. We sat down in the boardroom and the old boys laid it all on the line. We could all step up or walk away, no questions asked. No more cruising and letting Georgie shoulder our future expectations. I think everyone was a little stunned at first, mostly because we were all being called out, but they were right. Back when she was chief operating officer, we had each made her life a living hell. She's almost five years older than Marnie and me and we were spoiled brats, Lou and Leslie too. And we were all like, why me? I have to hand it to our dads, they stayed cool with us, but they made it clear we needed to shape up or ship out. 'No hard feelings' they said. Anyone who didn't want to work for the company anymore didn't have to. Then they started telling us these stories of all the times Georgie had bailed our asses out, literally and figuratively. Holy cow, those old guys knew every secret we had!

"They knew she had bailed me out for drinking under age, went to court with me and paid my fine. They knew about me getting in fights and her taking time to talk with me and get me to a counselor. They knew about Georgie pulling Marnie out of cars with bad boys, and they knew a million other things she had done to save our skins. By the time they were done, I don't think there was a dry face in the place. They left us to talk without them. I remember us all hitting the wine a little hard, but that didn't take away the sting. The truth was Georgie had been groomed for the top spot right from the start. Not because she was oldest or anything like that, it's just that she had earned it. She had been working toward it from the time she was eight and decided she needed to get to work because old Aunt Georgina was gone. She worked harder than all of us put together and she took care of us in a million ways we didn't even think about."

Lori stopped when she heard Megan behind her. "Sorry, I got on a rant there. So here," she said, pulling the closest door open, "is the laundry room. And that door over there goes to my dad's apartment." She led them into a darkened hall flanked by bedrooms. "That's the master and this, this is the guest room, which is mostly used by Zoe and Skip these days, but lucky for us not that often."

"Where is your father?"

"Oh, he lives out at the Big House. Most of the family lives there."

"You should see it, Aydan," Megan enthused. "It's out at Eighteen Mile Creek just across the river from the Frank Lloyd Wright house and it's way better! Wait till you see it and you'll love Henry. He is so cool! He knows everything about everything, but he doesn't talk to you like you're stupid or anything. He's totally a blast!"

Lori shook her head, grinning at the running gush of admiration for her father. She wrapped her arm around Megan's shoulders for a sisterly side-hug. "Hey dude, he thinks you rock too."

Beaming from the compliment, Megan suggested, "Let's show her the piano. Come on, Aydan, you have to see this. It's a real baby grand!"

Watching as Megan sped down the hall, Aydan in tow, Lori realized she was grateful for the kid. Her enthusiasm was contagious, so much so, she was sure she had glimpsed a bit of a smile from the reserved Ms. Ferdowsi. It was easy to want to see Aydan doing better, but Lori felt a pull she didn't quite understand. Maybe it was simple responsibility, whether misplaced or well-earned. The woman had been hiding from trouble in her very own yard.

She often thought of herself as the unofficial Mayor of Cattaraugus Creek. Since building her house out at the beach, her neighbors and tenants had come to depend on her and her resources, like the yard security officer, to solve problems when the police or fire/rescue were too far away. She had used the boatyard tractor to pull cars out of snowbanks, the yard crane to move storage containers on and off the beach each season for the local sports association, and the yard plow to clear driveways for area seniors after each snowstorm. It only made sense that they would turn to her to arbitrate their disputes. It was why she paid attention in the tightknit community. It paid to be vigilant. *If I was so vigilant how did I miss Aydan hiding in her car in the boatyard lot every night?* Before she could take the thought any further, she heard music coming from the living room.

She made her way quietly down the hall to find Megan standing at the piano and Aydan playing a piece she didn't recognize. It was beautiful and haunting, and drew a warmth from the woman she had not yet seen. Long slender fingers stroked keys in combinations evoking heartache and hope. Was it melancholy in sunshine or clear skies in winter? Stepping a little closer, she was curious to see what music she was playing. Since her mother's death the only people who played the baby grand were professional musicians Marnie hired for special events. None of the children ever took an interest in piano lessons. For years the extravagant instrument had sat in the big house collecting dust. It was Georgie who insisted on moving it here for Henry. While everyone objected, assuming it would bother him, or because they didn't want to be bothered, Lori had taken Georgie's side, hoping having it around would provide some solace for her long-widowed dad. It had been the right move. The piano became an item of pride, and he was pleased to show it off to visitors. For him it was a solid connection to his lost wife and the mother of his kids.

Stepping up behind Aydan, she realized she was playing without music. Had she memorized this piece? Maybe she had a memory like Georgie, photographic. Aydan stopped, immediately starting to apologize. "Hell no, you don't. You sit back down and finish whatever you were playing. It's…I don't think I know the right words to describe it."

"Me neither, boss," Megan said. "How do you remember all the notes without the music?"

"I wrote it," she said quietly.

Megan let out some indecipherable encouragement, and Lori asked, smiling, "Please play it for us?" While Aydan obliged without comment, Lori carried over two nearby stools for her and the kid.

They sat transfixed by the melody. Aydan too was transformed as if the trauma of the last dozen years were washed away. One could almost imagine the ghost of her dad standing at her side. It was ethereal and enchanting and in this moment, for Lori, the woman was beyond beautiful too.

Uh-oh, I think I'm in trouble!

CHAPTER NINE

Aydan looked up from her breakfast preparations to watch Tyler make her way down the circular stairs. She was dressed as she always was at this time of day, in a fluffy white bathrobe and fresh from the shower, her hair wrapped in a towel. Her eyes were fixed on her tablet.

"Morning," she offered absently with a smile.

There was no denying the woman's charm. She could certainly understand her boss's attraction to her. Besides that, Tyler did just about everything for Georgie. She wasn't sure what that meant or why a woman with her education and experience would want to play nursemaid. She watched as she brewed her coffee from the single cup dispenser, adding cream before taking a tentative sip. Obviously pleased, she smiled over the rim of her mug. "I can't tell you what a lifesaver this machine is. Before we got this, I was drinking instant coffee every morning. Now we can enjoy a decent cuppa joe."

"I guess it didn't make sense to brew a whole pot just for one."

"Actually, I would have happily brewed a big pot every morning but the smell upsets Georgie's stomach."

She had been accumulating a long list of things prohibited in Georgie's world. The coffee in their office was brewed in the restaurant and delivered in carafes. "Is that why our coffee is made downstairs?"

Tyler nodded absently as she started setting out ingredients. She had her partner on a strict menu. Georgie started her day with scrambled eggs and chopped spinach which Tyler always made for her. It wasn't that Georgie wouldn't cook, but she was Tyler's first priority.

Dropping bread into the toaster, and taking out fresh tomatoes, she began slicing one. "I have no idea where Leslie found these, but they look amazing. Would you like some?"

Aydan requested two slices, before asking, "Does Leslie buy the groceries?"

Tyler nodded, checking the time on her tablet before wandering over to the nearest window. "This has been the weirdest spring. Last year we barely got shoveled out from one snowstorm before the next hit. This year it's below freezing one week and in the sixties the next. And this rain…" She shook her head at the sight of cold drizzle and the sound of bracing winds.

"You worry about her. You all do."

Tyler turned to Aydan, arms tightly wrapped across her chest.

"I mean, that's good."

"But?" There was no rancor in her voice, just a look of interest.

She respected that. "There's no but, it just…"

"You wonder what we get in return? Or are you asking what I get from my relationship with her?" When Aydan colored, Tyler smiled, returning to the kitchen island to butter her toast. She sat on a barstool with her toast and tomatoes, still smiling at Aydan. "Few people see just how much she does for others. For her family, it's about supporting her now out of respect for all the support she provided them over the years. For me, well…let me ask you this. Have you ever been in love?

No, don't answer that. Think about it this way: how would you feel to know someone loved you so unconditionally, you could count on them for everything and anything, and just so you know, Georgie puts my wishes first in, well, everything. Can you imagine how that would feel if that person was someone to whom you were deeply attracted?"

"I…no."

Tyler's head tilted as if she were seeing Aydan from a different perspective. "I know things have been excruciatingly difficult for you since your father's death, but what about before that? Any boyfriends in high school? What about your first semester at UB?"

"I…there was someone but…it wasn't, it didn't work out." She blushed to remember the heartache of betrayal, something she had barred from her mind for so long she had erased that singular painful brush with longing. How had she forgotten that long night crying in her father's arms, his patience with her and his complete understanding and support? She had been ashamed then. She was ashamed she hadn't been completely honest, ashamed she hadn't told him everything. More than that, she was ashamed that her personal prejudices had tainted her last cherished time with him. It had haunted her, compounding her ever-present heartache at his death.

Seeming to understand, Tyler offered a sympathetic "Ouch," before noting in a consoling tone, "You're free now, Aydan. You can do and see anyone you like." She held up her hand, adding, "I'm not saying you have to run right out and fill up your dance card. Just know the decision is now yours and yours alone."

Aydan nodded, appreciating the effort everyone was making. In the weeks she had been in residence, they, and all the women of their families, had made an effort to include her in their plans and camaraderie. At first she imagined it was all just part and parcel of her added duties as Georgie's executive assistant, but by the end of her first weekend, she had to accept it was much more. She was welcome here, even wanted. The experience bordered on the fantastic. "I can't imagine someone caring for me the way you do her. I don't mean that in a bad way…"

Tyler took her breakfast plate to the dishwasher, then loaded another K-cup to brew her second coffee. "It's hard to explain," she said, adding cream. "I like taking care of the little things for her. She is much more self-sufficient than people realize. What she can't do herself she can certainly afford to have done for her. For me," she added, leaning against the counter, "taking care of the little things lets her know how much I love her."

"And what exactly does she do to show you…I'm sorry. It's none of my business."

"Aydan, Georgie and I want you to feel free to ask anything. I know our life, so much of what we are is new territory for you, but don't think we're not willing to answer questions. So let me try to explain…For me, the reward comes in just seeing how much I mean to her. Surely you remember that feeling?" When Aydan didn't answer, Tyler frowned. "Boy, he really did a number on you. Well, don't you worry, once you get your footing, I'm sure there will be no end in sight when it comes to men asking you out."

Before Aydan could even contemplate what that meant or decide if she should explain, Tyler turned at the sound of the upstairs door and the clicking of Maggie's paws as she ran down the stairs and straight to Tyler's side. Aydan missed whatever that signaled, watching as Tyler leaped to her feet and raced from the kitchen and up the stairs at breakneck speed. Not knowing what she should do, Aydan followed, curious and concerned, to watch as Tyler ripped the towel off her hair to drape it around Georgie's shoulders. "You're soaked to the skin baby, what happened?"

"Erie…truck…did not see…us."

"Oh my God!"

Aydan watched as she began examining her partner with the thoughtfulness of a trauma surgeon. "Baby, your ear is bleeding. Are you hurt anywhere else?"

"Cold," she said as violent shivers wracked her body. Her clothing, soaking wet, was hampering Tyler's investigation.

"I need to get you in a hot shower then we can take you to the hospital."

"I...no," Georgie began to argue until the moment Tyler took her arm to lead her to their bedroom. Without making a sound, the pain from just that tentative touch sent her to her knees.

Tyler was right there. "You didn't just fall, did you? That asshole hit you! Oh baby, I think your arm's broken. Aydan, help me get her into the bathroom. I have to get her warmed up, and then we need to get to the hospital."

Immediately, Aydan took the uninjured side, helping get her back on her feet. With Tyler's arm around her waist, and guarding the injured arm, they managed to get her to the bathroom. Not sure what to do next, she turned her back as Tyler began stripping her silent employer of her wet sweats. Embarrassed to overhear Tyler's tender coaxing and gentle reassurances, she turned for the door intending to return to the kitchen until called.

"Aydan, I need you to grab my phone from the other room. Quickly please."

When she returned, Tyler was standing in the large open shower, still in the bathrobe, and stripping the last of Georgie's running clothing. Even from where she was standing, Aydan could make out fresh bruising all down her left side. Her right hand hung from above the wrist at an unnatural angle.

As Tyler began pulling her wet tights down, she let out an involuntary cry, "Oh baby, that bastard! Why didn't you call us? Did he even stop? I can't believe you made it home without help."

Aydan was so transfixed it didn't occur to her that she was standing there watching her naked boss until she felt a pressure against her leg. Looking down, she wondered why the dog had taken an interest in her then remembered how she had communicated the urgency of the situation so easily with Tyler. "What can I do?"

"Send Sanjit a text," Tyler ordered. "Have him pull the truck up in front of the side door and keep it running. Then send Marnie a text. Tell her I'll call from the hospital."

Aydan sent the building security guard the urgent note then reconsidered the order to text the CEO. As much as Marnie

Pulaski intimidated the hell out of her, it would be better if she called. She checked the time on Tyler's phone first, realizing the woman would be in her car and halfway there. Perhaps it was better to send the text, at least until she was out of her vehicle and could carry on a conversation safely.

Maybe I should call Lori. She said I could call for anything. This is probably one of those things she would want to know and she probably won't be in her car at seven twenty in the morning. Didn't she tell me she walks to work?

She grabbed her new smartphone from her room, fumbling through the GUI, hunting for her new contact list, then listening to the ringing on the other end as she kicked off her office shoes and began pulling on her boots.

"Hey there princess! To what do I owe the—"

"She's hurt!" Aydan blurted. "Georgie!"

"What's happened?"

"She was out walking her dog. A truck hit her. She's badly bruised all up and down her left side and her arm looks broken, and maybe her wrist."

"Where is she now?"

"Tyler's taken her into a hot shower and I've got Sanjit pulling her truck out so she can take her to the hospital."

"Okay…Well, if it's just a broken arm we may have gotten off easy. Who else have you called, other than the Sandman?"

"Nobody. Tyler told me to text Mrs. P…Marnie, but she's probably in her car right now so I called you first."

"Good. You did good, princess. Don't call or text Marnie. Let me handle that for you. Now here's what you're gonna do."

Off the phone she tucked it in a pocket before retrieving her winter coat. She went down to the library as ordered and began collecting the documents Lori believed the doctors would need to see. Relieved to see everything in order, she recognized Tyler's hand in the organization, including a cover sheet detailing the steps to follow in an emergency just like this. She made her way back up to the master suite, sending Sanjit another text and was relieved by his instantaneous 'Affirmative, Ready' reply.

At the bedroom door she stopped dead in her tracks. Georgie was sitting on the edge of the bed in her underwear, her body racked with violent waves of vomiting, her head braced against Tyler, who was holding a wastepaper basket for her.

Aydan saw what she had missed before, what they had both missed. Something was wrong with her left shoulder. That arm looked unharmed yet it hung as uselessly as the other did, but different somehow. Tyler handed her the basket. "Sorry…can you bring some fresh towels?" she asked, before mouthing, "Call 911!"

Scurrying into the bathroom, she closed the door, dialing 911. The emergency operator was well trained, quickly asking all the pertinent questions. She sent Lori and Sanjit a short text, grabbed towels and more towels.

In the bedroom, Tyler had lifted and was examining Georgie's face. Her complexion was like chalk. Sweat poured down her brow and temples.

"Help me get her dressed. In the walk-in…she has a blue zip up sweatshirt. It's with her Air Force PT gear. It's sleeveless."

They were able to slip it over each arm then zip it up. Getting her track pants on was relatively simple after that. The 911 operator had told Aydan the ambulance was six minutes away. That meant they would be there any minute now. "Tyler, please get dressed. Everything's ready except you. I can hold her. Just show me were to put my hands."

"Here," Tyler said, carefully stepping back and holding Georgie's head steady.

Aydan cautiously placed one hand on each side of her brow, holding her head like an unexploded bomb. She kept her focus as she sensed more than saw Tyler flitting about. In what seemed like seconds she had donned jeans, a sweater, her boots and finger combed and braided her wet hair. She was back at Georgie's side and about to resume her care when they heard Sanjit calling from the foyer.

"We're in here!" she yelled.

Two paramedics, pushing a stretcher laden with medical kits and bags, pushed ahead of Sanjit and immediately got to work. Aydan relinquished her hold, moving back to give them room, and listening while Tyler answered questions and provided the details Georgie could not.

Tapping her shoulder, Aydan turned to see Sanjit's worried face. "Lori called me."

She stepped out into the hall, beckoning him to follow, she asked, "What does she want us to do?"

"Did you find all the hospital stuff?" When she nodded, he rushed ahead. "Good. All right, first thing is we make sure they take Tyler in the ambulance with her, and make sure she has all the papers. Then we are to wait downstairs for Mrs. P and Kira Marsh. We must get them to the hospital. She doesn't want either of them to drive. She's sending Megan to take Kira but if she doesn't get here first, you're to take her, right away. I'm to drive Mrs. P and you're to take the Land Rover to the hospital in case Tyler needs you to do anything or take her anywhere. What else?" he asked himself. Pulling out his phone, he checked the time. "I can't imagine she will be here for at least another twenty minutes, her, or Mrs. Pulaski. We must not inform anyone of what's happening. Ms. Phipps was insistent she would take care of that."

"Of course," Aydan reassured him as the paramedics began rolling the tethered, ashen Georgie from the bedroom. Tyler was on her heels and looked like she had no intention of being left behind.

Aydan scrambled to grab the accordion file with Georgie's medical information, her coat and one for Tyler. With Sanjit in tow they all squeezed into the elevator. While the paramedics tossed out numbers and spoke in acronyms, Tyler was clamped onto Georgie's hand, speaking in hushed and comforting tones to her immobilized and barely conscious partner.

When the doors opened, Marnie was standing there. If the woman looked harried before, her stress was now elevated to a level none of them had ever seen. Gray-faced, she followed them out to the ambulance, fully intending to climb aboard. At first they refused citing some dim-witted regulation, but under pressure they finally conceded to one passenger. Marnie, completely out of character, acquiesced to remaining behind, insisting Tyler stay with Georgie.

As the ambulance pulled away Sanjit stepped up. "Lori is on the way. Aydan is going to wait here for Megan and Kira. I'm to take you over to the hospital," he asserted respectfully. At her incredulous look, he leaned away, clearly intimidated. "Please Mrs. P, Lori said I must drive you."

She blew out an angry breath. "Who the hell decided Lori was in charge around here?"

Shocked by the anger in her words and the fire behind her eyes, they both stood mute in the cold gray rain.

"Fuck!" she screamed, pounding her fist on the hood of her Navigator. "Fucking—fucking—fuck! This is not supposed to be happening again...FUCK!"

"Mrs. P," Sanjit, braver than Aydan, tried again. "Shall we go? Do you need anything from the office first? Please, tell us what we can do?"

Seeming to cave in front of them, Marnie handed her keys to him. "Did anyone talk to Leslie?"

"Lori told me to let her take care of all that," Aydan said, "but I can go up to her apartment right now, then I'll get Kira and Megan to the hospital."

Marnie nodded, opening the passenger door to her truck. "Go see Les, then tell Megan to get her sister over to the hospital. You wait here for Lori." With that said she climbed into the SUV. Sanjit handed Aydan the keys to Tyler and Georgie's Land Rover, still parked in front of the building's side door.

Watching them go, Aydan stood in the rain, transfixed as employees with parking privileges began pulling into the lot. A few waved, most took her in with a curious glance, but none stopped to talk or ask questions. Word had gone out last week that she had been named as Georgie's executive assistant. Many had offered some level of congratulations, also warning of the "craziness" that came with working in Georgie's inner circle. Clearly, whatever they assumed she was doing was related to some universal belief that Georgie was always up to some stunt, so anyone working with her was either crazy or just plain up to no good.

She had just turned for the building when she saw Kira's minivan pull onto Pearl Street. Kira stopped sharp, opening her window to Aydan. "I know! Amazon Woman called me. I've got to get Ella up to day care first."

"I'll help," Aydan offered, following in behind the van as Kira parked in her reserved spot.

Kira was out of the vehicle in a second, tossing Ella's diaper bag to her and retrieving her baby daughter from her car seat. They were heading for the entrance when two police cars screeched to a halt in front of the building.

"Here we go," Kira commented, tipping her head to the cops. "That's the deputy chief. Get them inside the boardroom before anyone sees them. I'll join you as soon as I get Ella settled in."

Aydan surrendered the diaper bag and ran through the rain to meet the police. She led them to the main floor boardroom, introducing herself by name and title. She knew the family or at least the company was well respected, but this show of brass was a surprise. The deputy chief explained that he had assigned two of the officers present to investigate the hit-and-run. He had just started asking her for details when Megan blew through the door.

"I'm here, Aydan! Where's Kira, I gotta get her…Chief?" She jumped to attention, all but saluting the police brass.

Before they or Aydan could explain, Kira pushed in with Leslie on her heels.

"Will someone tell us what's happened?" Leslie demanded.

Sucking in a deep breath, Aydan forced herself to speak up. "Georgie was hit by a truck this morning crossing Erie at about ten after seven. She was walking Maggie…her dog. She was having some difficulty talking, so I have no details on the truck."

"She'll remember," Megan asserted. "She's got a friggin' computer for a brain."

"That's right," Leslie added. "Do we know how bad it is? Did you see her, Aydan?"

"Yes." Aydan had seen a lot more of Georgie than she ever imagined. "She has bruising all down her left side. Her right arm appears to be broken and the left shoulder may be dislocated."

"What about…" Clearly Leslie couldn't say it and Aydan wasn't sure she should. Out of nowhere a hand touched her shoulder.

"It's okay, Aydan, I'm here now," Lori assured her. "Go ahead and tell us everything." Seeming to understand her anxiety, she took her hand, giving it an encouraging squeeze.

Buoyed by Lori's endearing support, she began tentatively. "I think we just thought it was bruises and the broken arm but then she almost passed out when Tyler tried to get her in the shower." At their confusion, she explained, "She was soaked from head to toe and shaking like a leaf. We were trying to get her in the shower to warm her."

One of the officers was scribbling notes in her memo pad while the other stepped into the lobby, his mouth pressed to his shoulder mic. "You're doing great, princess," Lori told her. "What happened next?"

"Tyler asked me to call Sanjit to have her truck ready to go, you know, so we could take her to the hospital."

"And that's when you called me?"

Nodding, she explained, "I got those papers you told me about, but when I got back to their bedroom…Dr. Marsh, Tyler, was holding her head and she was vomiting. Tyler told me to call 911."

"What about her head?" Leslie asked. "Was she hit there again?"

"I don't…" Almost whispering she admitted, "There was blood coming from her ear and it looked like her nose had been bleeding. And there's one other thing." This she definitely didn't want to share but somebody had to help her. "The dog, I think she's hurt too."

Leslie, who was already crying, wailed at the news. Kira, who had wrapped a consoling arm around her, pulled her in closer. Even Lori groaned. "Shit. Where is she?"

"In her bed, the one in the safe room. She was soaked too. When I tried to towel her off she cried then growled at me. It's not like her."

The second officer came back in with Skip on his heels. The officer reported, "They found the accident site, right behind here on Erie. Looks like he hit her in the curb lane, right in the pedestrian crossing. The storm drain is clogged. They say there's more than a foot of slush. I don't know if we'll find any—"

"Get public works on the line," the chief ordered. "I want the drain opened now and have them strain every goddam thing once the water starts moving and get patrol to pull all the traffic footage coming off Route Five and along Erie for at least a mile. Canvass for witnesses."

"Chief?" the second officer started to protest.

"Just do it!" he barked. "If you can't find the truck that struck down one little woman, I've picked the wrong officers to investigate a simple hit-and-run."

The cop frowned at being called out in front of civilians but promised, "We'll get him."

While he stepped away to ask Aydan a few more questions, Lori filled the newly arrived Skip in on the situation. "I know you want to go to the hospital but I need you. You, and Aydan. Someone has to get Maggie over to the veterinary emergency. If something happens to that dog, well, you know how bad it could be. Can you handle that for me?" He nodded, and she added, "I've sent your sister to wait with your granddad. The rest of us will head over to the hospital, all except your dad. I've asked Lou to hold down the fort here and prepare a press release. When I know something I'll let you, Zoe, and your dad know, and I need you to do the same for me. Take Georgie's Land Rover. And Skip, use a furniture cart if Maggie can't walk. That dog weighs over a hundred pounds. Even I couldn't carry her all the way to the car. Got it?"

"Yes, Aunt Lori. We're on it," he said, stepping over to wait at Aydan's side.

Lori turned back to the deputy chief. "Thank you for coming here to personally see to this. I'm going to take the girls over to the hospital. Will you keep us informed?"

"If I can't, one of these two will. They're on it until we find this asshole and we will. Erie is one of the few roads with unbroken video surveillance. We've got coverage on every block." With that, he exchanged a few more words with his officers before heading out. The fourth officer in the room, the DC's driver and aide, gave Lori a respectful nod as she followed.

Lori hooked her arm just long enough to give her thanks. When she called that morning, it was as a friend needing advice, not looking for top-level intervention. She had forgotten two essential points when dealing with Buffalo First Responders. They respected Dynamic Marine's community contributions, and more specifically, the generosity and longtime support of the DiNamico and Phipps families. The other was straightforward: the local cops considered Georgie, a wounded veteran, an equal. Not quite one of their own, but a peer nonetheless.

Sensing Aydan waiting for her, she turned to see a veiled look she didn't understand. "Princess, come on now. I thought you were going to trust me?"

She nodded, but didn't explain.

Lori took her hand again, holding it in both of hers. Waiting patiently, hoping her comfort would instill some trust, she said emphatically, "You did everything right."

Across the room Skip and Kira were consoling Leslie. She needed to get them all to the hospital and she had to talk to Marnie too.

Trying desperately to explain everything she had seen, Aydan was struggling, "She…" Aware of Lori's closeness and with their hands now intertwined, the moment seemed to stand still for her. Something about Lori's deep blue eyes and her dark smooth skin was incongruent and pleasing all at once. "I think she…the vomiting, it was like milk, watery milk. I've seen that before…"

Lori remained silent, holding both her hands, she seemed to be encouraging her from some place Aydan didn't quite understand.

"She…I think she was having a heart attack. My father…it was just like that."

Lori wrapped her arm around her shoulders, offering gently, "I'm so sorry you had to relive that. That is not what you signed up for."

"I'm okay. What you and your family are going through and Tyler…"

"I know," Lori reassured her. "We're going to take care of her too, but right now I need to know if you're up to helping Skip with the dog."

"I...I'm embarrassed to admit it, but she scares me."

"That's okay. Skippy knows her well." She added with a wry smile, "And he hasn't got enough sense to be scared of anything except his sister. Will you help me?"

"Yes, yes of course," Aydan said, giving her an impulsive hug.

She headed quickly over to join her workmate and partner in dog rescuing. Without looking back she followed Skip from the boardroom, but could hear Lori soothing her sister and Kira as they walked to her Jeep. At the elevators she looked back, wishing she could have gone with them or that Lori could have come with her. Lori was strong, so strong; Aydan imagined the situation might have turned out differently if she had been there from the start. That was crazy though. Tyler Marsh was a smart woman and had done everything right. The only thing she couldn't do was turn back the clock. She could do what she had been asked and she could pray. What else was there?

* * *

Lori set takeout cups in front of her sister, but held onto the one for Marnie. Beside her, Tyler's father, Carl Marsh, carried the coffees intended for his wife and daughters. "Any news?" he asked.

Debbie Marsh shook her head, pointing toward Tyler and Kira. They were huddled with Marnie in a corner of the hospital waiting room in what looked like a very serious conversation. Something in their posture and expressions would have scared a saner man away, but Carl Marsh inserted himself in the scrum anyway, even when Marnie visibly seethed from his interruption. "Looks like you ladies might need some muscle. If so, I'm your man. Well, me and Lori." He pointed with his thumb over his shoulder. That comment was enough to defuse Marnie's rage.

"If we don't get some answers, or they don't let Tyler in to see her soon, I may just call on you two to break some heads!"

He nodded. "You got it, coach."

She offered up a half smile. Ever since Lori's call had interrupted her leisurely drive up Route Five to work, she had been like an angry machine, grinding out orders to everyone around her. She liked Carl Marsh. He was a lot like her husband Jack, somehow irreverent and respectful all at once.

Just then two doctors stepped into the waiting room. "Are you Georgina's family?" one asked. She looked older than her male counterpart by at least twenty years, and Lori was immediately relieved that they didn't have some kid working on her cousin.

Tyler was so shaken by their arrival, Lori found herself supporting her on one side while Carl held the other. "Please, she isn't…"

"No," the younger doctor reassured them. "She's stable. We just have some questions."

Lori moved forward to introduce everyone. "This is Tyler Marsh; she's Georgie's, Georgina's fiancée. These are her parents and her sisters. This is Marina Pulaski, Georgina's sister."

"And I take it you are Georgina's nurse?" the younger doctor asked.

That pushed Marnie to DEFCON 1. "Listen ASSHOLE, You're Talking to My Cousin. I Will Not—"

At that precise moment, Margaret O'Shea, Georgie's former partner and a general surgeon at the hospital, rushed into the waiting room. "I just heard, oh my God, Marnie—"

"Oh Jesus Christ!" Marnie cried, slapping a hand to her forehead. "And the hits just keep on coming!"

Lori grabbed Marnie. Not so much to settle her down as to keep her from killing someone. It was Tyler who once again proved to be the calming voice. She took Marnie's arm, pulling her close. "Doctors, we need to know what's going on. Is—"

The woman doctor stepped toward them. "I'm Doctor Poulan. She's taken a hell of a hit but saying that, I want you to know her head CT is good. Not perfect but compared to the baseline records you brought, I have no concerns in that area. Your initial speculation was right Ms. Marsh—"

"It's Doctor Marsh!" Marnie corrected with a snarl.

Doctor Poulan took the correction in stride. "Of course. You were correct, Doctor Marsh. Her left shoulder was dislocated; we have reset it and expect it to heal completely, as we do with the fracture in her right arm. The hematomas are widespread along her entire left flank. They of course will heal as will the other fractures."

"Other fractures?" Tyler choked out.

"Yes, I'm afraid she sustained fractures to her left hip and left tibia. All of which are expected in a high-speed impact. Now, I'm afraid we have…May we speak privately?" she asked Tyler.

As tears began to fall on Tyler's dazed face, Marnie surged forward only to be pulled back by Lori and Carl. Their joint physical restraint did nothing to curb her mouth. "I DEMAND TO KNOW WHAT'S GOING ON RIGHT NOW! That's my sister in there and if you people ever expect to get another cent from this family, a family you have already deeply insulted, answer our questions! NOW!"

"Whoa Marn, let the doc talk, okay?"

"Yes," Tyler said through tears. She visibly pulled herself together. Squaring her shoulders, she drew herself up with a fierceness to match Marnie's. "Whatever you want to say to me you can say in front of our families."

The doctor nodded but did not seem pleased. "She's been asking for someone…else. And her injuries, the distal radius and ulna fractures to the right arm don't fit. It's not the type of injury I would expect from a hit-and-run. I most often see this in cases of abuse where someone has super flexed the wrist, twisting it to straining or in this case the breaking point."

"More like tried to break it right off," Margaret O'Shea said. She had a tablet in her hands, and appeared to be reviewing the x-rays. She leveled her accusation directly at Tyler. "To cause a radial fracture of this severity—"

"Whoa now, Mags!" Lori said, stepping in between the pair.

"I'm sorry to ask this," the senior doctor continued, "but she fought the sedation. Some patients do and I see from her records it's happened in the past. While she was lucid, she asked for you and another woman. If there is abuse involved I need to report it and speak with this Maggie person immediately."

"*Maggie?*" Venom spilled from Tyler's mouth as the assembled group turned to Margaret O'Shea. "Margaret, if you did this—"

Lori cut her off, pulling her away from Margaret O'Shea. "Hang on everyone! Doc, show me how this wrist twisting/breaking thing could happen." Lori stepped forward, offering her own arm.

Demonstrating the type of movement used by most abusers when grabbing a victim, Dr. Poulan pointed out telltale signs to look for, depending on the angle and direction of the attacker's pull.

Taking a deep breath, Lori exhaled much of her pent-up frustration, explaining to them all, "Maggie is the name of her service dog. They were out together when she was hit. Is there any way this was caused by Maggie trying to pull her to safety?"

The doctor's eyes widened. "Well...it would have to be a very large dog. Does she walk with the leash wrapped around her wrist?"

They all nodded. "She has to," Tyler added, explaining, "she sometimes...wanders. It's the dog's job to bring her home."

"Among other things," Marnie growled. "And she weighs almost as much as my seventeen-year-old sons and she's stronger than the two of them combined!"

"Not to mention smarter," Lori quipped, regretting the untimely joke the moment she made it.

Looking abashed, the doctor apologized. "I'm so sorry. You must understand how—"

"Can I see her, please," Tyler begged.

"Don't worry, Tyler," Margaret O'Shea offered consolingly. "We'll get everyone in there the moment she's back from the cath lab."

At this mention of the cardiac unit, the ensuing uproar was difficult to temper, but between Lori and Carl they calmed the group enough for the doctor to continue. Lori had to marvel: *Looks like Georgie was hit by a truck and Maggie broke her mommy's wrist trying to save her life even though she was hurt herself. Good girl! And Aydan's right. Georgie was having a heart attack. Huh?*

They listened as the doctor explained. The heart attack was relatively mild as these things go. Still, it was hard for Lori to understand how anyone as fit and careful about her diet as Georgie could have a blocked valve. They were assured that the hospital's best was with her and the procedure relatively simple. All they could do now was wait.

While Carl and Debbie Marsh worked to bring Marnie down and hold Tyler up, Lori slipped out into the ambulance bay. What a day to be a new non-smoker! She stood under the portico, selecting Aydan's number. She took a deep breath, clearing any trace of anguish or concern from her voice, unwilling to upset her with the news. She would have to tell her and Skippy about the heart attack and the broken bones but she'd do it without a hint of concern.

"Lori! Is she—is everything—"

"She's fine, princess. Everything's fine." She listened to the crystal clear sound of relief emanate from her phone. "Is Skippy nearby?"

"He's in signing the papers for the surgery on Maggie. Oh Lori, her shoulder is broken; something called an ACL or something like that. Sorry, I tried to remember the details but she looked so sad..."

The sound of choking back tears rang as clear as Christmas bells. "Hey now, take a breath, I'm right here...There you go. You might find this interesting. You were right about Georgie breaking her wrist but we have Maggie to thank for that. It looks like she may have tried to pull her to safety. I have a feeling she was hurt trying to save Georgie, either before she was hit or immediately after. Either way, that dog's a hero in my book for getting her home. What do you think of that?" she asked, waiting for Aydan to settle. "Take your time. I'm in no hurry, princess."

"Why are you so nice to me?"

Lori's lighthearted laugh echoed around the portico. "You, princess, need to get used to it because nice is what I do. Well, it's what I do when I'm not kicking butts or taking names." When she didn't respond, Lori asked, "Hey, you okay?"

"Yeah, yes, sorry I...oh, here he is."

"Good, can you put me on speaker?"

Skippy's voice was clear, but sounded troubled. She held a calming tone for him too, coaxing them to provide an update on the dog. The vet was sure she would be fine with surgery, recovery and probably some physical therapy. She shared with Skip her belief and Georgie's doctor's agreement of how the injuries were sustained. It made sense that Maggie had gotten hurt at the same time as Georgie. Once she assured them they had done everything they could for her, at least for the day, it was time to give them her news.

"First things first, the docs think Georgie's going to be fine. She got broken up bad, but nothing compared to what's she's seen before. Just simple fractures which they said will heal in four to six weeks. The most important thing to know is her head is okay. They did a CT and it's no worse than her last one. The only thing—and Aydan I'm so glad you were there and so sorry you had to see it—but you were right. She was having a heart attack. It was very mild and she's going to be fine." She could hear both her nephew and Aydan sharing expletives. "Hey guys, listen to me. She is fine! She really is. Now I need to know what you two are planning to do next. I can't have you report back to the office until Marnie, Lou and I agree on a statement."

"Aunt Lori, can we come there?"

"I was going to ask you two to head home and sit with your granddad but Zoe's with him so, yeah come on over. Oh and Skip, stop and grab us some decent coffee."

"You got it, Aunt Lor. Anything else?"

"Just take your time and be safe. We can't afford any more upsets today. Got it?" They chimed in their affirmatives together then ended the call. "One down," Lori said to herself. Next it was time to get her brother up to speed. She knew some messed up part of Lou's brain would see this as an opportunity, but the rest would know enough to do the right thing. She was just finishing her update to Henry and Zoe when she spotted Georgie's Land Rover with Skip and Aydan in it. "Listen Dad, I've got to go, but I promise I will call as soon as we have more information and the minute they say we can see her, you're the first in."

Skip looked as broken as Aydan. And Aydan, God she was an attractive woman. It was hard to understand just how sheltered her life had been. Or had it? There had to be more to the story. Even with that ugly gray thing she wore to cover her head, there was no denying the woman was a beauty. Tall and fit, she was curved in all the right places. Lori shook herself. *Just what you need, a messed up straight girl. Good God, get your head in the game!*

* * *

"Marnie, why didn't you come to me sooner?"

She stared across the examination room. Doctor Margaret O'Shea, Georgie's ex and all around pain in the ass was reviewing the list of symptoms she had described. "Margaret, I swear to you..."

"Hey...it's just you and me, patient and doctor. I can leave the family part out if you can?"

Giving in, Marnie explained, "My family physician sounded so convincing when he said it was early onset menopause. I actually thought that was a real thing until Lori confronted me."

"Well I don't normally comment on other doctors' opinions, but that's all it is without a complete workup. Let me run some blood work to start with then we can drill down on what the underlying concerns are. Yes, this could be serious but I don't want you all stressed out. You probably get enough of that at the office."

Marnie sighed heavily. "It's something every day. The minute you get one fire out another dozen pop up. Now this Georgie thing. I swear..."

"How is she?" Margaret asked with real concern. "I was so hoping she was getting better but I see she still needs her full-time helper at her side."

"Helper...oh Tyler. It's not like that, at least not anymore." Marnie watched as Margaret schooled her expression. It seemed she wanted to know more, but this was Margaret O'Shea. She might be a talented surgeon, but she was also Georgie's ex.

"It's okay Marnie. I just want to see her happy. Just like I'm sure this is something simple, something we can fix. Let's get you down to the lab for blood work and as soon as I have some results so will you."

CHAPTER TEN

Stomping into her parents' kitchen, Tyler dropped her duffel bag then kicked it for good measure.

From the family room, her parents, who had been watching a movie, stared at her in silence. "You okay, honey?" Debbie asked cautiously.

Her back to her parents, she grunted, "Fine," before kicking her duffel bag again. Without warning she kicked it again, then again and again.

Carl grabbed her arm. She whirled around in anger, collapsing in his arms, sobbing incoherently.

Debbie shared a look with her husband. After thirty-six years of marriage, they had long developed a silent language. Debbie would go upstairs and check on Kira who was putting the baby down, while Carl dealt with their sullen child.

He waited until his wife was out of earshot. "Your mom made decaf, but I can put the real stuff on if you're up for it." When she didn't answer, and wouldn't or couldn't look at him, he did what good dads do, pulling her in tighter for a papa bear hug. "It's okay, pumpkin, Daddy's here." Used to Tyler being the more stoic of his children, he was barely prepared when her sobs turned to a full-on crying jag and she cleaved herself more tightly to him. She cried inconsolably and he held her without speaking. There was lots of time for discussion. He was a patient man, more patient than his wife, and he knew his daughter. She would tell him everything when she was ready and not a moment before.

It was a good twenty minutes before Kira and Debbie made their presence known. By then Tyler was sitting next to her dad at the kitchen table. Fresh coffee was hissing and spitting its way into the pot. She had stopped crying, but only just. Her face displayed all the torment of her emotional flood, along with a nose so red a reindeer would blush. She was busy fighting to control hiccups, a result of a long hard cry.

"Ty," Kira probed tentatively, "what's happened?"

Looking to her sister and mom, she broke into tears again, dropping her head back onto her dad's shoulder. The arm and shoulder of his sweatshirt were already soaked and misshapen from her crying and tugging to hang on. He didn't mind, understanding his part was to provide comfort and solace. His wife was in charge of sorting out the rest.

She cleared the already substantial collection of spent tissues from the table before setting out to pour their drinks. At the counter, she spotted the coffee carafe knowing he had made it to please their notorious caffeine hound of an offspring. Reaching into a side cupboard and pulling out a bottle of Baileys, she doctored their four coffees.

Tyler lifted her head, using the last of the Kleenex to blow her runny nose. They sat patiently, letting her collect her thoughts. When she finally looked at them, tears rolled down her cheeks again, "It's over," she said with finality, her heartbreak palpable.

Everyone sat in silence, watching her battle her emotions. While tears continually cascaded, she struggled to clear her nose, and the hiccups were back with a vengeance.

"Honey, please breathe," Debbie encouraged, while Carl added more Baileys to her still untouched coffee. "Come on, take some big breaths, honey, and then try a couple of big gulps of your drink. It should clear your hiccups."

It took a few more minutes and a few more big gulps before she could trust her voice. "It's…she…"

"Honey, just tell us what's happened," Debbie begged.

"She…Georgie," she sniffled, blowing her nose before continuing. "She…we're over."

Carl pulled her protectively back into his arms while Kira swore in shock but it was Debbie who would have to dig for the heart of the matter. "Oh, pumpkin, what's happened? I thought you were taking her home today. Did something happen at the hospital?"

"This doesn't make any sense," Kira cut in. "You're getting married in less than three months for God's sake. What the hell happened?"

"Easy, Turtle," Carl warned his other twin daughter in a soft low growl.

She held up her hands in surrender. "Sorry, I just…you were supposed to take her home today. Something must have happened at the hospital. This doesn't make sense. Georgie is head over heels in love with you!"

"Head over heels over me," she said through sniffles.

"Don't say that," Debbie consoled. "Your sister is right. Something must have happened. Please, honey, can you tell us more?"

"Where is Megan?"

"She's in class tonight," Carl answered. "Should I call her and get her home?"

Shaking her head, she said, "No, just wondered if she was hiding or something."

They let her take her time organizing her thoughts. It took a few more minutes and a few more sips of her coffee before she could begin in earnest. "She's gone to Eighteen Mile Creek, to stay at the big house."

"Oh, honey." Debbie felt a moment of hopefulness. "It makes sense. She's probably just worried about how much pressure would be placed on you having to run a new company and care for her…" She trailed off at her daughter's look. "Why?"

"She thinks she's a bad bet. She doesn't want to leave me alone with a kid or kids, if she…"

"Oh, my God, this is about the heart attack?" Kira asked.

Tyler nodded. "That idiot doctor scared her. The blockage... they analyzed it, identified it as a foreign object, it's what caused the heart attack. It was left over from Afghanistan...what do they call it?"

"Shrapnel?" Carl offered.

She nodded.

"But...how come, wait, why didn't the military get all that crap out?" Kira continued her examination. "The hospital should have seen shrapnel in her x-rays or scans or something, shouldn't they?"

"He said it was Kevlar, probably from the shattered rotor blade. She would have been fine but that idiot had to go and tell her there may be more!"

"So." Debbie was struggling. "Now that they know what to look for, can't they go get the rest out?"

"That's the point, Mom. There really isn't any but maybe this one little piece and it wasn't going anywhere until that stupid asshole ran her down."

Debbie didn't call her on the language. She was right. The guy who hit her was a complete waste of space. The cops reported that he had partied most of the night and put himself behind the wheel of his work truck jacked up on caffeine pills and Jack Daniels. The worst part was his complete indifference to what he had done. It was at times like these she questioned why the country was so consumed with concerns of terrorism when hate and apathy were more truly the national threat. "She's worried she'll let you down."

"No Mom, she's sure she will leave me barefoot and pregnant with nothing and no one to care for me. She absolutely believes I would do better elsewhere!" Her head was down again and she leaned it heavily on Carl's shoulder. "She won't even look at me."

Debbie watched as Carl, an arm around her shoulders, pulled her closer. Tyler held her mug cradled in both hands, something she had done for years. It reminded Debbie of those days when the twins were in their early teens and began to display all their authentic adult mannerisms. Tonight, she just looked older. They had all known disappointments, all her girls, but this was one none of them had envisioned.

She had worried, back at the beginning, when Tyler and Georgie first became involved. Most of her common mom concerns centered on how much care her future daughter-in-law would require. She had listened to the stories of her battle to survive and then recover from her catastrophic wounding in Afghanistan. Wounds she should have succumbed to on the battlefield. The type of which had killed everyone else, including the bigger and stronger among her crew. But Georgie wasn't the wounded warrior Debbie had been expecting. She was intelligent and kind, and while her verbal communications challenges upset the woman deeply, it never prevented her from doing her best. Debbie respected that, respected Georgie. This, whatever this was about, went much deeper than a mild heart attack. "Honey, is there any way she's just scared?"

Tyler sucked in a harsh breath. "She is!" she asserted. "I know that. I just can't get her to see it. She's just…"

"Easy now," Carl advised kindly.

"I…it's like something broke in her. Even Lori and Marnie are confused. We all just stood there listening to that moron talk about the Kevlar being almost impossible to detect and I could see it, see her shutting down. We all did."

Debbie nodded. "Honey, you may not want to hear this but I don't believe this has anything to do with you. Yes, she's taken it out on you, on the two of you, but what I'm hearing is she's scared."

"I know that! I just…" She was sniffling again.

"Ty," Kira said, "I think Mom's on to something but this isn't just a fear thing. Georgie's the bravest person we know. Well, other than you, Dad." He smiled at the inclusion. "I knew I should have gone with you and Amazon Woman. I just had a feeling."

"What are you thinking?" Debbie asked.

"Let's look at it logically. I bet that's how she's figuring things, right?" At Tyler's nod, Kira went on, "This is her second major health thing. Even the surgeon said she was the toughest patient she'd ever met. What was the phrase she used?"

"Incredible will to live," Carl furnished.

"Come on, think about it. She gets shot down. Her whole crew is blown to bits all around her and she still manages, with all those broken bones, and her head smashed in, to crawl away and hide. This time she gets hit by a truck, she's knocked unconscious and her dog drags her out of a swollen gutter before she can drown, and she manages to walk home as if it's nothing! A woman like that doesn't just give up on someone she loves."

"I know!" Tyler cried.

"No, wait. That's not what I'm getting at. It's got to be something more…something scarier than being shot down or run over."

Debbie almost choked, "Oh my God. That's it. Why didn't I think of it?"

Kira made a restless motion. "Come on Mom, spit it out."

"I think you're right. Actually, I'm certain you're right. Honey, I have a feeling I know exactly what's going on here and Kira's right about it being too frightening for her."

"What could be that frightening? She's never afraid."

"Not as an adult but think about her childhood. She's lost every woman she has ever loved. Her mother, her aunts, her grandmother…"

"That bitch Margaret."

"That unpleasant, social climbing woman, yes her too. And she left when Georgie was at her most vulnerable…"

"I would never—"

"Easy," Carl soothed again. "She knows you're not her, pumpkin. In case you never noticed, the women in our family are particularly smart. You should listen to them. I do."

For the first time since storming out of the hospital, a ray of hope began making its way into her shattered heart. Yes Georgie was scared, but she was stubborn too. Maybe it was why she was so damned hard to kill. *Well, I can be like that too.* "I think you're right but how…I don't know what to do?"

"Maybe I do," Kira suggested. "Let me call my favorite Amazon. I'm sure all we need is more information. If she thinks breaking up is the best thing she can do for you then maybe all you need to do is find a more logical argument for staying together."

"Happen to know any good lawyers who might argue my case?" Tyler, blotchy faced, asked wryly.

Kira smiled along with their parents. "As a matter of fact I do. But you don't need me. You just need the facts. Once we figure out what ghosts are really fueling this, I'm sure you'll be ready to drive this one home."

Tyler managed a half smile.

Debbie and Carl looked at their daughter. At last there were signs of life where her eyes had seemed so hollow just minutes before.

"Well what are you waiting for?" Tyler exclaimed. "Go get on the phone!"

* * *

Aydan sat in the darkened living room of Georgie and Tyler's apartment. After a month the place was starting to feel like her home too, but as tired as she was, she just couldn't bring herself to climb the stairs and go to bed. The last two weeks had been exhausting. Between her regular intern duties, learning her job as Georgie's executive assistant, and trying to be supportive for Tyler, she was tired but more than that she felt thoroughly muddled.

She had started out with serious prejudices around her boss and her relationship, believing their public openness had offended her family's good opinion—not just theirs but hers too. Now she could confront herself.

Just who am I kidding? The last family member to hold any type of positive opinion of me was Dad. I've spent the last fifteen years trying to be less and less of me and more of whatever it is they want but it was never ever going to be enough. I thought it would be horrid to work here, with women like them every day. Yet here I am. Complete strangers have been kinder and more respectful of me, and to me, than my own flesh and blood. And I worried they would offend me? Instead I lied to protect my humiliation, my weaknesses, and myself. Yes, I lied.

That's the true offense here. I didn't just lie to them, I've been lying to myself and for so, so long.

She hadn't recognized the sentiment eating at her in the dark until she remembered just how angry she was at the hospital. She had grown to respect Georgie, even appreciating her process, but more than that she had fallen for the intimidating and accomplished Tyler. Not that she was in love with her, but she could appreciate the woman's charm and beauty. That had been a two-fisted blow and the thing she had been stewing over for hours. Realization had crashed in on her the night before Georgie was physically struck down crossing Erie.

She had been in her room reading and was up much later than usual. Seeing the time and wide awake, she was anxious to sleep. Deciding a glass of warm milk was worth a try, she headed for the kitchen. In slippers and making her silent way in the dark, it wasn't until she was almost on the top stair when she realized someone was on the couch. Stopping dead in her tracks she was about to retrace her steps when her eyes adjusted just enough to recognize what she was witnessing.

Georgie and Tyler were on the couch and while the blanket that usually hung across the back was pulled over their bodies, it was more than obvious they were without a stitch of clothing. They were making love in the dark with nothing but the light from the fireplace and each other as witness. She had wanted to back away, even run away, yet she didn't, couldn't. Standing in the dark, she had been a voyeur to something she had long classified as nothing more than some bodily need for release, a need easily overcome with diversion or discipline. *What a lie!* There was nothing mechanical or even unfitting if that could be applied. A passion she had suspected between the two telegraphed into something more than she could comprehend. Tenderness, desire, pleasure in and of one another and something more: they were a world of one, and in that moment she knew nothing could challenge that.

With that revelation, came the crushing memory she had long since blocked. The one who had hurt her all those years ago, that one first tentative and scary foray into love, the one

Tyler had characterized as "the guy who had done a number on her." Only the guy wasn't a guy and she was ashamed at not admitting it, if not to Tyler, then at least to herself.

"Sarah, you broke my heart and I let it shape me. Shape my relationship with my family, and shape my future. I did that. I let that happen, let it color everything in my life. Let my grieving mother and conservative and ignorant grandparents use it as fuel to control my life and shame me into obedience."

She had tried to shake it off, but the image of Georgie and Tyler making love was seared indelibly into her brain, awakening something she long believed dead.

I want that, want what they have, had…no, have. I don't know them well and yet I feel I know them as well as I do myself.

If she could lose fifteen years over a teenage heartbreak, no wonder Tyler was behaving like a wounded animal. How many nights did her father sit up with her even after she came clean and told him everything?

If I were Georgie and loved a woman like Tyler, would I walk away to spare her and her heart? "Oh Georgie, you hardheaded thing!"

Standing with purpose, she climbed the stairs and strode to her room. Picking up her phone, she noted the time but didn't care. The world had been turned upside down and if she valued her place here, with these women who had welcomed her, it was her responsibility as much as any of the rest to help make this right.

Selecting her most frequent contact, she pressed connect.

"Hey princess, you okay?" Lori answered.

"I want to help. What can I do?"

CHAPTER ELEVEN

When Tyler walked into the office at eight a.m., she could feel the tension on the floor. Clearly the word was out and a rill of anger seeped through her. Affording a perfunctory smile, she made her way to the corner office. She wasn't surprised to find Lori waiting in Georgie's office, or even Aydan, but Henry was unexpected.

"It's awfully early, Henry. Shouldn't you still be in bed, enjoying retirement?"

He grimaced before explaining, "I figured you could use a lead engineer."

Plainly he was not so confidant the situation was something she and Georgie could resolve. "Don't tell me she's quit the job too?"

He winced at the rebuke and she almost cried out at his nod. Instead, collapsing into the chair next to his, she asked, "She's quitting?" At his saddened look, she qualified, "Everything?"

When he nodded again, she sat in silence, her emotions perfectly schooled. "Excuse me, I need a coffee."

Before she could move, Aydan was on her feet. "I'll get it, anyone else?" Henry accepted and Lori followed her out of the office, leaving them to talk.

Once the door was shut, Henry, reaching out and taking her hand in his own, explained, "I love that girl with all my heart, but she is as stubborn as all get-out! Now just tell me, straight out, is she worth fighting for, or is your heart too cross to forgive?"

"I..." Her lip quivered. She'd expected him to be forthcoming. That was just who he was. But the added tenderness always stripped away her façade of control. There was such kindness and wisdom in the man, and a respect she appreciated most. His respect of Georgie she adored and understood. His respect for her, she had earned, and that in itself was a gift. "You don't need to worry," she said quietly. "I'm still committed to doing the best job I can. I just...Henry, what are we going to do without her? I might be in charge, but she is the company!"

He nodded. His weathered face conveyed his concern and something more...maybe remorse.

"What is it? Please, it can't be any worse, can it?"

"Just tell me little girl, have you given up on her?"

"What?" Dropping his hand, she stood up and distanced herself from his knowing presence. But she couldn't deny the pain propelling her these last sixty or so hours. "I'm mad. I'm hurt. I'm a million other things. But I am not giving up. I...I just don't know how to fix this."

"Georgie's been the family fixer ever since...since we lost..." He stood, taking cautious steps to her side. "Baby girl," he fretted gently. "She's in trouble. I don't know what that so-called doctor said, but something's broke in her. We all know you're the one bearing the brunt of all this, we do. It's new territory for all of us."

She bristled at the "we all know" comment. "So, I take it the whole family knows? What'd she do, give a press conference or something?"

Henry chuckled briefly. "Now, none of that. It was just the gruesome twosome and me. We got to talking...after they brought her home."

She gave him a pathetic smile. "You call Lori and Marnie the gruesome twosome? I'll have to remember that. Please, sit," she said, waving her hand to the upholstered chair she knew he preferred. "How are your knees today?"

"Oh, no complaints," he answered, settling in. "All this rain has been hard. I feel it in my bones and I think old Maggie does now too."

"How is she? I haven't seen her since Lori and I picked her up from the vet."

"Better now that she's back at her mistress's side, but she's as blue as a second moon, maybe even as blue as our girl."

Tyler waved Lori and Aydan back in, accepting a fresh cup of coffee before taking a seat beside Henry. "I assume you three have something to tell me. Something that you think will help us, meaning Georgie and me?"

"Not quite," Lori answered. She set her cup on the large coffee table Tyler had chosen for Georgie.

They had been waiting in Georgie's office, not hers, when she arrived and Tyler was grateful for the show of deference, especially under the circumstances. With a real possibility that she might have to lead this company without her lover, she knew setting an example was how it was done. She wanted to be the leader they needed to make this enterprise a success, but without Georgie she was hard-pressed to even care much for the prospect. Pushing out a ragged breath, she said plainly, "I'm listening."

"Well," Lori said, "Friday, after we got her up to the house, I went for a little drive. I guess something's been eating at me since the whole thing about old Aunt Georgina's will blew up and everyone learned she left Cattaraugus Creek to Georgie and me, the big ol' lesbians in the family. So—"

Sounding more like Marnie than herself, Tyler cut her off. "Please tell me you didn't go harass the woman. Jee…Jupiter, Lori!" She would not curse in front of Henry no matter how upset she was. "Breaking someone's heart is not a capital offense. Even if it was, I think the statute of limitations is long over for a forty-five-year-old breakup between old Aunt Georgina and her Helen."

"Come on, Tiger, cut me some slack. I just went over and introduced myself all nice like. Helen was the one who invited me in. She said she knew exactly who I was and even remembered me from when Marnie and I were tots. She was cool and nice. A lot nicer than I imagined and I learned a lot, some not so nice, but it explains some stuff."

"I'm not going to like this am I?"

"Aydan," Henry interrupted. "Why don't you and I go put your design for the new office on the big table and have a look-see?"

She nodded without comment and got to her feet. Once they were out and the office door closed, Lori moved to sit across from Tyler. "You okay?"

Tyler just stared. She was sad and mad and a million things in between, but okay? Not so much. "I know you're going to tell me some crap about every woman in her life walking out, but I didn't leave. She dumped me!"

"Hey Tiger, I know, I know, no one's blaming you here. We all think she's lost it, but we know some stuff, stuff we never knew before and I think it'll help you." When Tyler didn't object or comment, she pushed on. "Anyway, things between Helen and Aunt Georgina did not go down as we thought."

"We?"

Lori groaned. "Okay, me. I thought she'd bailed on Aunt Georgina and married some guy. I couldn't be more wrong."

"Let me guess, old Georgina bailed on her just like my Georgie..."

"Your Georgie didn't bail! Well, she did, but she thinks she's doing you a biggie! That dumbass thinks this is honorable, letting you out now as opposed to dropping dead on you sometime down the road when you need her most." Seeing Tyler's expression, she pleaded hastily, "Come on, Tiger, you know she's scared. Do you want to know what we think the problem is?"

It was all Tyler could do not to go straight over the coffee table and pound the living daylights out of her. "Good God, you're infuriating, Phipps!" But Lori was right, she did want to know what the hell had sparked this disaster. Georgie was a loyal woman, as loyal as they get, so why had she done this thing, this one thing Tyler was sure she would never do? Yes, she wanted to hear, to know, so she sucked back her rage. As usual, it took time for Lori to wend her way through the story. It was hard listening patiently. She liked Lori, liked her storytelling, but she missed the simplicity of communicating with Georgie.

At the end of Lori's recounting of the separation of Helen and Aunt Georgina, Tyler shrugged and said simply, "If this is true and Georgie's dad is complicit, it's, well it's tragic, but what has that got to do with us, and me. Unlike her dad, there's not an abusive bone in Georgie's body."

"No, you're right, but it explains why Georgie clung to Aunt Georgina and why Aunt Georgina stayed in the big house. She built that beach house for her and Helen, but instead of moving in she had Helen's brother take up residence to keep her safe from Georgie's dad. I think she was scared for Helen, just like she was scared for Aunt Winnie and Georgie too."

"You think he hurt her?"

"No, and neither does Helen, but then again, they kept Georgie with them day and night. They tried to get Aunt Winnie to leave, even offering her and the kids their own place down at the beach."

"And where was Henry during all this and what about your grandparents? Old Luigi and Sophia must have known something was going on."

"What the hell? What's with the attitude?" Lori demanded.

"Look." Tyler stood needing to move or scream. "It's horrible to learn that Danny DiNamico—that Georgie's father was the kind of man who enjoyed pounding on women, but I don't see how that helps or explains anything…Wait, you don't think I'm…" She couldn't finish, but the horror on her face conveyed everything she was thinking.

"What? No!" Lori asserted, astonished by the assumption. "Crap. I so suck at this. Geez Ty, no one thinks that. We all know you're the one shining light in Georgie's life. We don't want her to lose you and vice versa. Hell, if there's anything to this, it's her worry she's going to turn out like her father, let you down, or leave you alone with no love or support. Come on!"

She stood, but didn't crowd Tyler's space. "I think the real thing was Aunt Georgina's loss. We all lost something that day, but she was really the only one who knew what was truly going on. I mean it must have been hard on Dad, but he still had us, and we had Sophia but…Look, maybe a lot of Georgie's drive to work for the company, and keep all of us in sight, was about protecting us from Uncle Dan."

"That's a stretch don't you think? You already said he never touched her."

"Yeah, but that doesn't mean she didn't need to protect us."

Tyler slumped back down on the couch. Lori was right, whether they needed protection or not, Georgie would have seen it as her lifelong duty to take over where her aunt had left off. No wonder she had isolated herself, both as a child and an adult. Between her military service requiring her to lie about her sexual orientation, and her protection of her family siblings among which she included Henry's kids, she must have endured constant pressure. "You once said you thought Georgie grew up isolated…lonely. Maybe she likes it better."

"Ty!" Lori begged, planting her ass on the coffee table in front of her. "You know that's not true. Two months ago, when we were on the shakedown cruise, she sat me down for a big talk. Wanna know something she told me? I think you do," she insisted when Tyler held up a hand to stop her. "She said my girlfriend Peachy wasn't the one or I would know. She was sure Peachy would live with all the tears and holes and black spots on my soul, but if I waited for the right one, it would be different. She said you fill all those dark places in her, shining light where even she has always feared to go. She begged me to have fun, but not to settle for tolerance and acquiescence. They always fall short, she warned. Better to risk it all for someone like you, someone who fits so perfectly." Intertwining her own fingers in front of Tyler to demonstrate her point, she added, "She told me you were everything to her and that you more than fit her, you were her complement, and her…damn it, what's that musical term…um, counterpoint? Yes, complement and counterpoint. Who the hell even talks like that? I had to Google it for chrissake!"

"And still she left me."

Lori grabbed her own head in a fit of frustration. "She's broken, Tiger! Broken like none of us have seen before and believe me, we thought we'd seen it all! You didn't see her this weekend. You were home with the family. Kira and I were texting, Megan too. If it helps, your baby sis threatened to beat the shit out of her."

Shaking her head at Megan's newly formed protectiveness she finally broke into a weak smile, but couldn't bring herself to speak.

"I can't begin to know how you're feeling but Kira seems to think you still care. Do you? Would you take her back?"

At that, the tears began to fall and she sat frozen, feeling numb and broken.

"She spent Friday in her old room, Aunt Georgina's old room," Lori explained. "You might remember the fact that you two have all the furniture from that room in your condo. The kids have been using it as an exercise room. She wouldn't even consider anywhere else or let us move any crap out. We ended up dragging a couch in from the TV room. That's how she's sleeping, on a fucking couch after breaking her fucking hip! Then on Saturday, after we managed to get her meds in and her bandages changed, she wanted to walk the dog on her goddamn crutches! We helped her out to the patio but she and that dog, who's just as banged up, crutched it to the fire pit, and wouldn't come back. They stayed out there all day sitting on that old bench. I had to take them both blankets. She's not eating, and she's spending every minute she can just…just staring at the lake and yesterday…"

"Nice try, Lori, but it rained all day yesterday, and there's no way she—"

"WE COULDN'T GET HER IN! She sat there in the fucking freezing rain all the goddamned day! Lou had to order the boys put up the old gazebo room around her. All we could do was keep her supplied with dry blankets. Even then her only concern was for the dog." She trailed off, looking away, distressed.

"What…" Tyler cleared her throat. "What do you think she's doing?" Upset as she was, the last thing she wanted was for Georgie to hurt herself. She had seen her retreat before, but in the past it was always about her feelings being hurt and it never lasted longer than a few minutes. Usually that was all the time she needed to push her ego aside and ask the kinds of questions that went beyond herself in an effort to understand the situation. She would always tell her team to remove themselves from the equation first. Using that practice on herself, she knew succeeding in the process required a change in perspective.

It was more than her work policy, Tyler had learned, it was her saving grace. Georgie worried that any empathy she held had been permanently injured when the main rotor blade made contact with her flight helmet. To compensate, she had made a practice of examining the point of view of all parties in any situation, especially when she was upset. As a couple it had made learning all of those personal push-button issues much less volatile. She could still be a brat sometimes, but usually it was the other way around. How many times had Georgie caught her pacing, head down and arms crossed, wallowing in her own self-pity? She never pushed, but she wouldn't let Tyler push her away either. Reassuring and patient, she had promised to always be there. "She promised…Why? What is she doing?" she asked, drying her eyes and wiping her reddened nose.

Lori took Tyler's hand and waited to be sure she had every inch of her attention. "I think she's trying to die."

Tyler tried to pull away, but Lori wouldn't let her.

"She knows she can heal from broken bones. God knows she's broken more than the rest of us kids combined but that heart attack. I…it's just too much like Uncle Dan. Then that asshole doctor goes and tells her she might have more of that shrapnel crap and another bump could dislodge one and kill her in seconds. What the fuck! Why not just hand her a gun and tell her to pull the trigger?"

"That's not—"

"No?" Lori dropped her hand, stood and paced to the window. When she finally turned back Tyler could see the tears in her eyes. "We have to do something. If we don't…Tyler please. You're the only one with a hope in hell of breaking through to her."

"What about Henry?" Even with her own pain clawing through every inch of her, there was no way not to feel Lori's anguish too. "He's always gotten through to her," she said, wiping at nose.

Lori shook her head, and said quietly, "He cried last night. I haven't seen that since…since my mom died." She sat down again but this time in the chair across from Tyler. "I didn't even know I remembered the funeral but seeing him like that…" She was up from her seat again, pacing to clumsily cover the fact she was crying too.

Tyler stood, and carrying her ever-present Kleenex packet, joined her by the window. Standing side by side, looking out onto Pearl Street and the morning downtown traffic, she finally admitted, "I haven't given up. No way. I'm just shocked, and hurt. And I'm…do you really think this is about Danny DiNamico— her own father—being a bastard, or is she that scared she might drop dead the next time she takes a slip?"

"Both, but it's the dropping dead on you that's freaking her out. Look," Lori said, "none of us really understand what goes on in her head, but Helen said Georgie had an amazing memory, even as a child. She watched Uncle Dan hurt the people she loved. Then Aunt Georgina leaves Helen and rides in on her white horse to save the day. It's not just what she did that's been ingrained in her but how she did it. She gave up on having a normal relationship with Helen so she could be there to protect Winnie and all us kids. It's what she knows, and the one example she has been trying to live up to all her life. She must believe this is best for you, for everyone. It's like wham, if she's not in your life, you won't have any more worries."

Tyler stood silently contemplating everything she had heard.

Then Lori added one more concern. This one so disturbing, she whispered, "Just so you know, Marnie's out of patience. She's meeting right now with the family lawyers. If we can't get Georgie back on track, she has every intention of shipping her off to the funny farm. She won't stand for her just sitting there, withering away."

"Don't even joke about something…" At the look on Lori's face, a horrid dread began making its way through her gut and pushing hot bile up her throat.

"Sorry Tiger, but she only needs two signatures and you know Lou would bend over backward to sign on the dotted line."

Returning to Georgie's computer and opening her appointment app, Tyler pulled up the daily production schedule and milestone list. Tapping in a few changes, she asked, "How much work can I reasonably give Henry? I mean, is he really here to work?"

Lori nodded. "He's not a young man, but he wants to help. I was thinking maybe Aydan could run point on whatever you need him to do. That way she can handle emails and stuff and let him catch a nap when he needs it, if that's okay?"

She agreed, even if she didn't. It wasn't as if she could ask an eighty-year-old to put in eight hours a day. "There's nothing I can't push back, nothing except the one project that was most important, the design of the new office."

"When does Fener need the new drawings?"

"Two weeks ago. Leslie's got him busy on the third floor and Marnie's given him a list of improvements to keep him busy but…"

Pulling out the chair across from her, Lori sat down, suggesting, "I think you might have something sooner than later. Dad and Aydan spent all weekend working on it. I think they were just trying to get her interested, but when they didn't, well, Aydan didn't want to let you down, and I think Dad's kind of in the same boat."

"Henry's worried about letting me down?" Of all the ridiculous things she had heard…

"We all are," Lori said, quiet again. "But Dad…I kind of freaked out on him, you know, after talking with Helen. I guess I sort of lost it. I was…kind of loud. I wanted to know why he didn't stop it and how he could be sure Uncle Dan never pounded on Georgie."

"Weren't you worried for Marnie or your own siblings?"

She shook her head. "Me and Marn shared a room, and Sophia, she slept in the nursery with Leslie and Lou…"

"Did Henry know?"

She was silent for a long time. Finally, she explained. "Remember that letter from Aunt Georgina the lawyers gave us each to read and how it said it was a different time? I guess that was his excuse too. If it's any consolation, he's really ashamed that he thought he had to respect Uncle Dan's privacy." At Tyler's hostile expression she added, "Please. I know its bullshit, but I kind of see where he was coming from, considering everything."

"Really?" she demanded, back on her feet. "What excuse is there for letting a man beat his wife, or worse, letting a seven-year-old child witness the whole thing?"

Lori was on her feet too, arms out, hands open as if to prevent a spooked horse from bolting, "Hey now, Tiger, we don't know that. We just know she understood that Aunt Georgina had to leave Helen and move back out to the big house to protect her family. And yes, my dad screwed up, but come on. Old Luigi welcomed my African American dad into his Italian family, treating him like a son and true equal to Uncle Dan, his flesh and blood. Even you must wonder what it was like to be a black man living with this white family. Everything good in his life, his wife, his kids, his job, were all connected to his friendship with Uncle Dan."

Caught by that revelation, she had to think about Lori's words. She couldn't remember when, or even if, she had thought of Lori or her dad as African American. The DiNamico/Phipps clan were so familial it just seemed impossible to think of them as black or white. They were unapologetically family. Race wasn't invisible so much as respected for the varied paths that had brought them all together. Still, she had a point. Times were still hard in this country for people of color. Hell, life sucked if you were anything but a straight white middle-class male. She might not know what it was like to be a black man in the seventies, but she was familiar with the perils of being a woman and a lesbian in this day and age and while things had improved vastly, there was even now such a lack of parity in every imaginable field. She sighed at the revelation. "I think I get it. I don't like it," she warned.

At the desk computer she updated her schedule, then closed her apps. "Here's what I'm willing to do," she stated. She wanted to make sure Lori understood exactly what she was saying, as she laid out her demands. When she got no argument or bullshit, she nodded. Marnie was right, Lori might play the joker most days, but when it came to crunch time you could count on her to rein it in. "We are going to go out there and make sure Henry and Aydan are on the right path. Once I'm comfortable with what they're doing, you and I are taking a drive."

"Great, I'll drive us out to the big house then—"

"No. First we are going to visit this Helen. Once I'm satisfied there, we will drive out to the big house and we will take my truck."

"Sure, okay but wouldn't it be better if—"

"If I'm going to do this it's with one goal in mind. I'm going to get to the bottom of all this family crap then I will sit down with my fiancée and talk some sense into her!"

"Okay, that sounds good."

"And if that fails," she warned, "we will bring her home anyway and by any means!"

That got Lori's attention. She held Tyler's gaze, gulping in air and then offering her agreement, however awkward. "You're the boss, Ty. I'll do whatever it takes to make this right, even if that means I have to drag her broken ass out the door. I promise!"

* * *

Aydan sat down at her desk to organize her task list for the rest of the day. She wanted to have the drawing changes completed by the time Henry was back from his nap. She almost snorted at the irony. Part of her new job was to babysit the VP of engineering. It had never occurred to her that all the engineering veeps, past and present, needed babysitting. Henry had been at her side since arriving early that morning. She had taken him and Lori to Georgie's office thinking it would be wrong to let them into Tyler's, or worse, make them sit on the bench outside. Both Henry and Lori had assured her it was the right thing to do, and while Lori paced, she and Henry discussed some of the old DME drawings she had been cataloging.

They had spent the weekend hammering out details for the new office. It wasn't anything they had been asked to do, but Georgie's accident and subsequent withdrawal had pushed them, and cleaning up her boss's work priorities seemed to be their one common ground.

She liked Henry. He was soft-spoken and unpretentious, much like she remembered her father being. And he was a gentleman. How rare was that in this day and age, a gentleman who immediately treated her as a fellow professional. Skippy too was good that way. Obviously his grandfather had taught him well.

Then there was Lori. Lori Phipps was like no woman she had ever met. Yes, she was obviously a lesbian but not in some unreasonable way. She carried herself tall and proud for the whole world to see and she didn't care what they thought of her personally, just as long as they didn't insult her boats! She considered herself a craftsman and so did the people who worked for her. She was hands-on in every facet of the boat building business. So was Georgie, but this was different.

Spending the weekend at the DiNamico/Phipps estate had not been part of the plan, but after arriving Saturday morning with a backseat full of stuff deemed necessary for the family to care for her employer, Lori had asked her to stay. At first she agreed, worrying over Georgie's health and confused about what had happened between the time Tyler had left to drive her home from the hospital and when a panicky call had come in asking her to pack Georgie's clothing and meds. She didn't immediately worry when Tyler didn't come home Friday night, but when she got to the big house on Saturday she knew better.

How could something like this happen? It had been more than a month since her move into their guest room. It had taken much of that time for her to relax. They hadn't pushed her to join them yet always included her whenever she was interested or confident enough to accept their invitations. From watching movies, to quiet dinners, or joining them for a walk by the lake, she was always welcome. After the hit-and-run, she had fallen into the same pace and schedule as Tyler and the family, focusing on Georgie, while keeping the company humming. And Georgie too had been upbeat and so forgiving. Not like Lori or even Skip, for that matter.

She'd expected Skip to act out, doing the male protective thing, but it was Lori who had gone ballistic. Aydan was sure she called in every favor she had to bring the deputy chief himself in to immediately launch an investigation. They hadn't wasted any time, identifying the vehicle with its damaged right fender from traffic cam footage collected all along the route where Georgie was hit. With extensive high definition video, it was easy to trace the truck to the trucking yard where the vehicle was registered. Lori's cop friend, the sergeant on the deputy chief's staff, had described rolling with five other units on the yard. They found the driver sleeping it off in the office. The truck too had been easy to spot. So was the bucket of soap and water the company owner was using to wash away Georgie's blood from the front grill and fender. They had arrested both of them, shutting down the entire trucking yard until they had gathered all their evidence and investigated the legality of the operation.

The really odd part was the aftermath, the reactions, Georgie's and Lori's. With blood vengeance in her eyes, Lori wanted the guy handed over so that she and her men could handle it themselves while Georgie worried for the other trucking company employees, the law-abiding men and women whose livelihoods were now in peril. Aydan could appreciate both positions, but something about Lori's protectiveness, while misguided, had struck a chord with her. That's what families were supposed to do, stand up for one another, protect one another.

Holding herself back from these people, from everyone really, was how she had been living her life since her father's untimely death. Yet, just months after being tossed out of her family home, her life had been completely turned around, and all it had taken was for one concerned member of their extended clan to notice her situation. Their immediate response was to talk to her, protect her, and offer her the tools she needed to take care of herself.

It was at that moment she understood time meant nothing. For more than a decade after her father's death she'd had to survive by her wits, living with complete strangers who considered her inferior and unworthy of even the smallest morsel of esteem. *A decade and a half lost, a whole fifteen years! And just months with these people, these complete strangers, and I feel more at home than I ever have been.*

She respected Lori's strength and her boldness, even when it sometimes seemed wrongheaded. Lori was good. Like the rest of the family, she treated her as an equal, and more than that, she was a friend, a protective and caring friend. How had that happened? She could only imagine that Lori's protective nature had recognized in her a woman in peril. How strange to have a complete stranger care—except she didn't feel like a stranger.

Not like she did around Georgie. It was harder to get to know her or even feel completely free in her company. Not that the woman did anything to alienate her or make her feel unwelcome. She just lacked any mechanism to comprehend someone else's discomfort. It was fascinating to watch Tyler educate her. It was also a bit annoying, but Georgie wouldn't hesitate to pause a movie to ask for Tyler's explanation of some emotional plot twist. It was always amusing to hear Tyler and Lori debate the situation with Georgie. That was another sweet thing she had been doing. Whenever Tyler invited her to join them she always asked if she would like either Lori or one of her sisters to tag along. It was a relief to go out and not feel like a third wheel. Better was just going. Having fun. Even if it was just a burger at Milo's, it was still so much more. Georgie had been the opportunity she desperately needed while Tyler provided support and guidance—but Lori was her friend. Even with everything going on, she smiled every time she called or stopped by. It was sweet to think about, sweet to know she had someone to count on, someone who would stand up for her, maybe even protect her too.

Stalling her thought process, she fought to push another idea from her head. *How can I think of her like that? I'm not imagining her sticking up for her buddy over a minor misunderstanding.* The picture she had seen was as clear as day. Lori, with a protective arm around her, Lori with her arms around her, Lori...*How can I think like this? She would never think this way. No one thinks I'm like that and I don't even know if I'm like that! Am I like that? So I liked a girl once, does that make me a lesbian? It was just one girl in school...and now another at work. My brothers are ignorant brutes but even they think I am...why did they have to put a label on it? Why did they have to make it all so sordid and vile? Can't I be attracted to someone regardless of who it is?*

When Zoe touched her shoulder she almost jumped out of her skin. "Oops there, Aydan. Sorry, I didn't mean to startle you." Pulling a spare task chair up beside Aydan's desk, she smiled, noting, "You're as bad as Georgie when you're concentrating on your work. I swear I could have let a bomb off in here."

She shook herself out of her funk, offering Zoe a polite greeting. She didn't know the young woman well and felt self-conscious around her. Something about her constant joviality, mod clothing and stunning beauty unhinged Aydan. She was beyond intimidating. Lori had even made a joke that Zoe had that effect on men and women.

They'd been enjoying a casual dinner out with Tyler and Georgie and Lori had tagged along. Somehow the subject of Zoe and her new position came up and Lori began laughing. "You should see my guys, and when I say my guys I mean all the women and men out there. I swear, every time she takes a walk through the production bay, coffees are spilled, tools are dropped, people fall off ladders, and she has no idea she leaves them all busting at the seams! Even the old-girls in the sail loft fawn whenever I send her up."

Tyler was laughing too but Georgie was slightly behind the eight ball and as usual Tyler had to provide a metaphor she could understand. "Remember when we docked in Barbados and you took us to the airport to see the British Airways Concord?" When she nodded, Tyler coached her, "Now, think about how that aircraft makes you feel and compare it to the average airplane. You know them all. Can you see the difference, baby?"

Georgie smiled at them all. "You are saying...niece is smoking hot...perfection?"

Lori had smacked her arm with affection. "Sweet baby Jeez...jellybean, with those looks, she could open any door she tried. As our dearly departed Carrie Fisher would say, 'She won the DNA lottery!' Now if she would just decide what she wants to do with it."

"Lori," Georgie counseled, "she is young."

"We weren't like that."

"Could not be," she advised, "different generation."

Before Lori could argue or solicit Aydan's opinion, something she did more and more often, Tyler asked plainly, "How is it going with Zoe?"

Serious for the first time that night, Lori reminded them that the conversation was privileged, before answering with some hesitancy, "Better than I imagined. She's organized, she pays attention to detail, and she's asking questions. I didn't expect that. I hate to say it but I think she actually likes working out there. Although," she added with a wry grin, "she still wears her heels in the office."

Tyler explained for Aydan, "Everyone has to wear safety boots out there, which is why we haven't taken you out for a tour yet."

"Aw, you should have said something," Lori teased. "I just happen to know the boss out there, I'm sure I can wrangle an after-hours tour. That's an open invitation Aydana-danna. Just say the word and I'll be happy to show you around the place. As a matter of fact, it's about time you guys came out to my place for supper…"

They had sat in Milo's for another hour that night, drinking beer and trading stories from their childhood.

"I'm sorry, Zoe," Aydan said now. "I guess I'm a bit worried about everything going on."

"Understandable," she offered with sympathy, squeezing Aydan's arm encouragingly, "but there's not really much of anything we can do, not at the moment."

Aydan didn't ask what she meant and worried silently, waiting for her to explain her presence.

Handing Aydan her phone, Zoe clarified, "Henry asked me to take pictures of all of those old office panels and the big oak doors stored in the millwork loft. He said you might want to use them somewhere. Can you put them up on the table thingy? I'd do it myself but I'm embarrassed to admit I don't know how. You won't tell Skip, will you?"

She nodded, starting to relax. "I can show you, if you want." She expected Zoe to wave her off but instead she pulled her chair around beside her. "Thanks Aydan, it's bloody time I learned this stuff."

CHAPTER TWELVE

Stumbling on the cold sand, Tyler managed to catch herself from falling. She hadn't realized how far she had walked until now. She had meant to just step outside for some air. Now she was standing dead center on the very spot where Georgie wanted to build their home. After listening to Helen Jensen for the last few hours, she needed to think, needed time alone to decide. It was hard to believe she could be more upset.

Unbelievably, Lori's stupid idea was more valid than she had imagined. Trying to sort her way through everything she'd heard she had marched out to the beach, only intending to walk a few yards. Looking around, she shivered painfully. It had been a strange spring. Last week's warm weather had melted all the snow. It looked like spring until you actually stepped outside. This week's deep freeze made the sand feel like hardened cement. The wind, vicious in its determination, blew in hard off the lake. Tyler's arms, wrapped defensively around her chest, were as numb as her feet and heart.

Could it have been as bad as she's saying? She didn't know and the weight of it was exhausting. She kicked a loose rock, wanting nothing more than to lie down right there. Lie down, close her eyes, and pretend none of this had happened. *How could one random event so completely derail our lives?*

Before storming out, needing to think, she had wanted to know why no one said a negative word about Danny DiNamico, or even his mother Sophia for that matter. She couldn't blame Lori or Marnie, they really were too young to remember much less understand, but what about Georgie? Did she not remember? Or had she long forgiven him? This man the DiNamico/Phipps clan so respected was a bully, a wife-beater, and during the darkest time in the family's history, he had done the one thing all lesbian and gay lovers fear. He had barred Helen from the hospital where Georgina lay dying, barred her from his sister's side. He had kept apart two women who loved each other and for appearance's sake? Helen had told them of going to Sophia in tears and begging to see Georgina. The woman, even in her own grief, had remained a tyrant, ordering her to never approach her daughter again.

Tyler had wanted to scream right then, but there was so much more to learn. Henry, who she had so hoped would prove to be the voice of reason, had reached out to Helen, even working behind the family's back so she could sneak in to the ICU after hours, but a nurse had blown the whistle. During the three weeks Georgie Senior fought for her life, Helen had seen her twice and for only a few minutes. Her one consolation was in knowing she had been able to tell her she loved her. Needing to be with her, she and Henry were working on another plan when they learned a restraining order had been filed and she would be arrested if she stepped inside the hospital again. Tyler couldn't really blame Henry for giving up then; after all, he had just lost his own wife and had a house full of kids to raise and a company to run. With the loss of Georgina, their president and CEO, DME was suffering a leadership vacuum. Even in retirement old Luigi was still a force within the company and without them both, Henry found himself cornered. He had chosen the children and company first and she knew that rationally she couldn't blame him.

She understood why he buried his memory of that time but Georgie, her Georgie, had never said a word against her father. According to Helen, she had witnessed everything. She had been the one to open up to her aunt and confess to what was going on behind closed doors and she was the reason Aunt Georgina had moved home. At least she'd had the wherewithal to ask Helen's brother to move into the beach house to protect her.

Danny, she explained, was an angry drunk. Sober, he was his father's son. But loaded, he turned into his wrathful mother, with muscles. He had shown up at her door late the night of Georgina's funeral. Helen had been warned not to show for the service and she had respected that wish, however painful. It didn't stop her from sending flowers, or visiting the graveside after the family was gone. Once again, someone thinking they were doing the right thing had tipped him off to her presence. He had raced out to the beach, intent on putting her in her place. Luckily her brother was there and prepared for trouble.

Tyler had sat motionless, listening to Helen tell the story of Danny showing up and demanding she leave, warning that he now owned the place and wouldn't have her infesting his property. If the energy he used to kick down the door wasn't warning enough, his rage at spotting a stack of unopened Christmas gifts, addressed to both big Georgie and little Georgie, his sister and daughter, pushed him over the edge. Helen had been sure he had every intention of killing her. Her brother had defended her while she called the police. By the time they arrived, he had managed to push Danny out the door, but Danny DiNamico was a big strong man. There was no abatement to his rage. Even when the cops showed up, he had been livid, demanding they forcibly remove Helen and her brother on the spot. The worst part was hearing how the cops almost did. Fortunately for them, Georgina had kept all her personal papers at the beach house. Whether she had seen this coming or simply considered this her real home, it had saved Helen that night.

The officers responding to her emergency call recognized Danny or at least his family's influence and assumed he was in the right. But with a copy of the deed to the house and

Georgina's will, Helen had convinced them she had a right to be there. They'd had her brother in cuffs sitting in the back of a cruiser when a supervisory officer ordered him released and drove Danny home.

Thinking about the police turning a blind eye to an attempted attack had forced Tyler to question the influence of the family—when just weeks before she had been so thankful for it. A hit-and-run accident, especially when it didn't involve a child and where no one had died, would rarely receive the type of attention and resources that were put to work to find the man who had struck Georgie down. One call from Lori and the deputy chief had thrown everything at finding the asshole. One call! She had been so thankful for the DiNamico influence then. She couldn't think about it now. The ethics of influence had always been a subject that fascinated her. And Georgie, for all her worry of fairness, had never said a word against her father. Maybe it was why her stories regarding him never seemed to stretch back beyond her wounding in Afghanistan.

The sound of a car horn startled her and she turned to see Lori making her careful way along the beach in the Land Rover. Thankful, she pulled open the passenger door only to see someone in the back seat. "Helen?"

"I'm coming with you. If my little Georgie's in trouble, then I'm going to help. I couldn't be with her then, but I'll be damned before anyone keeps me away now."

Tyler just nodded, pulling on her seat belt. She wasn't sure how old Helen was, but she had mentioned retiring last year after almost forty years of teaching high school science and math. She was an interesting woman and kind too, considering all the DiNamico/Phipps clan had done to ruin her life. It wasn't enough that she had lost her life partner, Danny had wanted her out of the beach house and when that failed, he had gone after her job and he had done it. It had taken her three years to work her way back into the system. She had been let go in the early days of Buffalo's court-mandated integration program. By 1985, the program had seen the end of the education oligarchs, with the Board of Education now operating twenty-two advanced learning centers, new high schools in need of teachers with advanced skills. In the time between being fired and hired back, Helen had gone back to school, finishing a Masters and a PhD in applied mathematics. With those accomplishments she could have gone anywhere, but she loved teaching kids and returned for the chance to step back in the classroom. Tyler admired that, admired her. Henry, Helen told them, had offered to pay for it all. His secret effort to keep her informed.

She'd pulled a carefully wrapped and stored box from her room, setting it out for them to see. It contained letters and mementoes from then and since. There were love letters from Georgina, wrapped lovingly with a mauve ribbon. Christmas cards from Henry with photos of all the kids and mimeographed copies of Georgie's school report cards. The most heart wrenching had been a series of drawings, notes and creations her Georgie had made for Aunt Helen. She called them little Georgie's inventions.

At that moment, the enormity of Georgie's loss and her years of playing solitary protector to her siblings all made sense. How many nights had she herself lain awake watching Georgie struggle in her sleep? Everyone said she was much better now, but Tyler knew she fought a war every night. She had imagined, like everyone else, that it was Afghanistan and the crash that haunted her. Now she wasn't so sure.

Oh baby, you've been fighting this battle all your life, no wonder you've given up.

* * *

Lori's brother Lou Phipps, standing alone in the family room, was staring out past the patio to the beach. Lori had already explained that they were taking turns keeping an eye on Georgie. It never occurred to Tyler, after everything that had gone down over the last year that Lou would be concerned much less willing to help out. Welcoming them, it was easy to see the pain on his face. Tyler was impressed when he didn't waste time interrogating Helen, the newcomer. Instead his only question, "Are you here to help?"

Helen assured him before she wrapped a motherly arm around Tyler and suggested patiently, "Let me try first. Is that okay?"

Choking on the kindness in her tone and the woman's reverence for her status as Georgie's fiancée, she nodded her consent. Watching Helen make her way toward Georgie, Tyler would not consider failure. "Please," she begged under her breath, "please listen, Georgie. I can't lose you to your fear and this wrongheadedness."

* * *

Sitting at the shore's edge it was easy for Georgie to believe Erie was the fiercest of the Great Lakes even if she was the runt. The very last of the winter ice was disappearing right before her eyes. There had been a moment when she wanted to measure the melt back, record the yards of reduction each day or map the disappearing flow, and then she remembered: there was no point. Why bother starting anything she wouldn't be around to finish. She was leaving so many things incomplete, there was no way she would burden anyone with any more.

"Little Gee…it's Aunt Helen."

Georgie froze at the sound of the voice and distant memories. The sights, sounds and scent of the big house sparked nothing but remembrance. She had almost forgotten how hard it was to come here, forgotten how much easier it had been since Tyler.

"Georgie, I'm here now. It's Aunt Helen. May I sit down?"

Frustrated by the constant bombardment of emotion, she turned away from the annoying ghost only to watch Maggie raise her head. Turning, she looked up at the visitor but couldn't make out a face with the winter sun high in the sky. The voice, though, struck something in her. Raising the broken arm, she tried shielding her eyes. It took a minute, not to recognize her, but to comprehend what was happening.

"You're dead!" she said, and turned her attention back to the wind and the lake.

"I assure you I'm not."

When Georgie didn't respond, Helen moved closer, offering her hand to Maggie. The dog sniffed it with little interest before laying her big dog head back in Georgie's lap. "She's gorgeous, Little Gee. I understand she had a hand in saving your life."

Georgie eyed her with suspicion, watching as she pulled over a chair and sat down.

When Georgie made it clear she would be spending her days out on the back lawn just feet from the water's edge, the twins had dragged out the expensive patio furniture, not caring if it was ruined in the rain. Even if they couldn't keep her in the house, they were trying to make her comfortable. They built a bonfire right there on the beach and they had kept it going all weekend, even stacking enough wood for her to use. She wasn't interested but they'd kept it burning all day. Now she had company. It was hard to believe they still didn't get it. She wanted to be left alone.

"I said—"

"He told you I was dead, didn't he?"

With the cast on her arm, it was hard to maneuver her hand to block the sun. Seeing Helen clearly and more confused than ever, she nodded, choking on her distress.

"It's all right Georgie…"

Reaching for her crutches, she looked like she was trying to get up.

Helen grabbed her before she tumbled. "Careful…"

Suddenly Georgie's arms were around her neck, awkward cast and all. "He said you…died too…you did not…get me? I thought…I believed…I…" Her verbal jumble was tempered with tears and soon she couldn't talk at all. Maggie too seemed to understand something significant was happening and had squirmed out from under her blanket to stand leaning against the pair.

Helen let her cry, holding and soothing her, much as she had when she was a child. "I tried, Little Gee, I tried," she said over and over. When Georgie's sobs began to subside, Helen helped her back onto the wicker sofa, wrapping the blankets carefully around her and the dog.

It took time for Georgie to pull herself together. None of this made sense to her, the reality trampling on her well-ordered memories. "He *lied* to me...I fought him...I wanted... you, I wanted...like me and Big Gee...He said...*dead*." Shaking her head she confessed, "I knew...lied. I knew but...you never came..."

Helen nodded, reaching out to gentle the fingers fisted at the base of Georgie's fiberglass enclosed arm. "He filed a restraining order. I'm so sorry, sweetie. I missed you so much, but I couldn't fight him."

Her crushing anger was a potent desiccant for her tears. "I hate him!"

"No you don't, sweetie. I know you. Maybe you don't love him the same way you did your aunt, but you shared a bond. Your aunt used to tell me you were just like him but without the baggage. Why else would you pursue an air force career at a time when women were barely tolerated and lesbians prohibited?"

"I...you know?"

"Which one, sweetie, that you have a beautiful fiancée or that you served in the Air National Guard?"

Georgie tried to sit up straighter. At times like this she always did better on her feet, but that was impractical with a broken leg and fractured hip. Thank God the hip was just a hairline fracture or she'd probably still be in hospital. Of course, sitting vigil at the lake's edge all day, every day, probably wasn't such a good idea. Stiff, sore and confused, she looked to Helen, watching as she moved her chair closer again.

"Should I start from the beginning?"

At her nod, Helen took her hand again, giving it soft strokes. "After the accident, I wanted to be with you, at least for the funeral, but your grandmother was very distraught and wouldn't hear of it. Your Aunt Georgina was in the ICU and the hospital wouldn't let me visit. Back then it was policy to only let in family, and no matter how we felt about each other, I wasn't family to them. Georgina had prepared a medical power of attorney, which did get me in once. When Sophia saw me there, she had a meltdown and your father asked me to leave.

Georgie, I need you to hear this," she continued in a rush of words. "He was good at first. He promised to keep me informed and work out a time to visit when Sophia wasn't there. We thought Georgina would...the doctors were hopeful she would make a full recovery. I knew the future would be challenging for everyone and I convinced myself that your aunt could better manage Sophia if I played along for the time being. I realized too late what was happening. Your dad called me every day but his attitude, usually friendly, was becoming combative. Then he stopped calling and wouldn't return my phone calls. I was desperate and needed to see Georgina. I loved that woman so much, Little Gee. We had planned to spend our lives together and here she was, all alone and fighting for her life. Henry managed to sneak me in when Sophia was taking a rest break, but one of the nurses mentioned it to her and that was it. I can't really blame your dad, I think his grief and his guilt made him desperate to please her."

"No!" she argued, "not good enough."

"Oh Georgie...think about it. He had just lost his father, and Luigi was the most influential man in his life. His best friend and business partner had just lost his wife. His sister was in the hospital in serious condition and the loss of your mom, along with his guilt over the way he had hurt her..."

"I get that...I..."

"Sophia was an intolerant woman who worried more about how your family was perceived than anything else. She accepted Henry despite him being black, grudgingly, and it took time. Your grandfather's high opinion of him made all the difference. I didn't have that advantage. Sophia rejected me, and our relationship, before I even had a chance to earn Luigi's respect. Without it, there was no way into the family. I think your father fell into a trap of trying to make your grandmother happy. Maybe he thought it was better for you kids—who knows. All I know is that your Aunt Georgina did all she could to protect me, but it wasn't enough. In desperation I tried to sue for access to her, but it took longer than she had time to live. I didn't give up. I kept thinking if I could keep from provoking your grandmother, she might one day consent to me seeing you. I even agreed to stay away from Georgina's funeral, but when she learned I had been at the graveside later that day, well, it was decided that action was needed. I put it down to ignorance, intolerance, all the 'ances, really."

"Did you...remember me?" Georgie asked, fighting the tears again.

"Oh, Little Gee, I have never forgotten you for a single minute. I even tried to petition the court for access to you, but back then there wasn't a hope in hell. It was over before it started. God bless Henry. He has kept me up-to-date all these years. I've seen all your report cards and your science fair ribbons. I have every one of your school pictures, plus one of you in your air force uniform and another with your helicopter and crew in Afghanistan."

"You know?" And now there was no holding back the tide.

Helen was out of her chair, and leaning in awkwardly, hugged her as tightly as she dared. "I know what you're trying to do and I can't let you. I've waited a long time to have you back in my life and I'm not giving up on that now. Do you understand me?" Georgie was trembling, from her emotions and the cold. "Little Gee, I know you're in pain. I recognize so much of her in you. I'm here and I promise I'm going to help you fix this. Do you trust me?" She leaned back to look her in the face.

Georgie choked words out between sobs. "I...I messed up... Aunt Helen...How..."

Helen pulled her close again. "That's all right. We can figure it out together, I know we can."

* * *

It had taken all of them to load up the landscape cart and get Georgie back up to the house. Lori was stressed, worried she might have to manage Tyler if Georgie kept up her bullshit. Now she was even more concerned. It had taken only minutes for Helen to drag her into the house. They hadn't sorted anything out yet, but it was obvious Tyler was pissed. Grabbing

Tyler's arm, Lori pulled her back, slowing her pace. "Easy there, Tiger. Let's give them some time to talk."

Tyler spun around to her. "She's had all goddamn weekend! It's my turn now!"

Lori grabbed her again, restraining her. "Hang on!" she ordered. "For fuck sakes, Ty, will you listen to me?"

"Fine," she snapped. "Fine, just let me go!"

Lori eased off slowly, half expecting Tyler to bolt. She took a deep breath searching for the right thing to say. "Oh geez, Tiger, I know you're mad and hurt and every other fucking thing but…" She groaned in frustration. "*Ragazza stupida!* Do you have any idea how intimidating it is to talk to you? I swear, sometimes I feel like a simpleton."

"What are you talking about?" she hissed.

"You, Doctor Tyler Marsh PhD, that's who!"

Tyler crossed her arms. "Don't be ridiculous. You have an MBA. It's not as if you're uneducated or ignorant. What the hell is your problem?"

"You. You leap in here and sweep her off her feet, turn her world around, and give us back the Georgie we thought was dead."

"Lori, I don't know what you're saying."

"Please hear me out. I'm not good at this stuff. Not like you. I don't know what you're feeling. Frankly if it was me, I might have killed her by now, but you're not me you're the one she loves. I think you might be questioning that now, but you of all people should know this isn't about you. Hell, I don't even think it's about the heart attack. At least not the way we think."

Tyler, head down, kicked at a clump of dead sod. "I'm listening."

"Okay, here's what I'm thinking. We know her head injury fucks up how she works through problems. God knows she can work her logic through the toughest technical challenges in the book. But emotions, well, not so much. And then you come along. You found a way to make that part work again. I think we all started to forget how hard that is for her, you know, her trying to get both sides of her brain working together. She's so much better with you that we've all been acting like she's all fixed, but she's not any different at all. Yes, loving you has changed so much for her but that's your doing, your way of getting through to her, not some miraculous healing. Tiger, I can't believe she did this to you, but I think I understand. This is the first and only decision she's made without you to temper her ruthless logic."

"She makes decisions every day."

"Think about that. The decisions she makes every day are about things like a line of code, or technical standards, or millimeters of change to a design. When was the last time she handled anything outside of all her tech stuff without you helping?"

"My engagement ring," Tyler insisted. "That wasn't technical and she did it all by herself."

"Really?" Lori asked but she was glad to see Tyler was still wearing her cousin's ring. "Do you really want to hear all that went into getting that sorted?"

Closing her eyes for just a moment, and groaning at the truth of it, Tyler finally asked, "You helped her? Let me guess, Marnie must have been in on it too."

"Oh Tiger, let me just assure you. When you're not at her side it takes all the DiNamico-Phipps women to make it happen. And when it's for you, it usually means your sisters too."

"You were all there? You all helped pick out the ring?"

Smiling, Lori wrapped an arm around her shoulders. "Even your mom was in on it. Georgie would not choose a ring without their blessing."

"If Marnie was there she would have taken over," she lamented, studying the ring carefully.

"Not at all. She is bossy, but not when it comes to what Georgie wants for you. She mostly wanted to make sure the jewelers were being patient with Georgie and listening to what she had in mind. Only your mom and Kira got a yay or nay but that wasn't until she got down to the last three."

"The last three? How many rings did she look at?"

Lori hooked her arm, liking this strolling talk. "Let's see, we went to four jewelers, and looked at a few hundred rings at each. I tell you, it was quite an education. I thought choosing the setting was hard but then she wanted to hand select the diamond and know about the gold. Even that had to be perfect. We got her through that but it took a whole friggin' team. Starting to see where I'm going? And don't be stubborn. I know you want to freak out on her like she's a normal person, but you know she's not."

Tyler turned them back toward the big house. "I'm not saying I agree, not completely but…"

Lori stopped her on the spot. "I would give anything to have what you two have. Please Ty, please think about this before you do anything. This whole thing is nothing but her stupid fucked-up robotic brain making brutally logical decisions. It's all zeroes and ones to her. It's like those crazy algorithms she makes up. You know, something like, 'Tyler's love times the number of days together, plus X if married, and multiplied by the number of children you guys have.' I bet if you run the numbers too, it would make perfect sense for her to leave now instead of sticking around, letting your relationship grow to love her more. As fucked up as it is to hear, I really think she believes she's doing the right thing by you."

Tyler was walking with her head down, but she gave Lori's arm a bump. "My family said the same thing all weekend, along with 'don't give up.' I don't want to. I just…hurt."

"I wish I could make that better, but it's really up to you. She may never be one hundred percent but she's still pretty good, don't you think?"

That comment generated a wolfish smile. "Do you really think I'd be this upset if she was just pretty good?"

Lori hadn't been expecting that and laughed, her mood picking up immediately. "Who knew our Georgie Porgie could be so smooth!" They had reached the patio and Lori stopped her one last time. "What's the plan?"

"All right, here's what we're going to do. Let's get her home and comfortable and let her and Helen talk for as long as they want. Did you drive Henry in today?" She nodded and Tyler said, "Good. Call Leslie and tell her we will all be home for dinner, Helen, Henry and Aydan too. Let's give Georgie the homecoming we were planning."

"Okay, and then?"

"And then...don't worry. I know how she's hurting, physically hurting, on top of everything else. All I want is to get her home and make sure she's safe and comfortable. Sometimes it's hard waiting for her to talk, but she does. I'll be patient, I promise."

Lori nodded. "Well then, let's get this show on the road."

CHAPTER THIRTEEN

Aydan had spent most of the evening trying to be helpful or at least stay out of the way. She had raced with Zoe to help them get Georgie in the building and upstairs. She and Zoe dragged her personal items in, and chatted amiably with the newcomer. For Aydan, everyone was new, but she was surprised to learn this new aunt was a complete stranger to Zoe, Skip, and even Leslie and Lou.

Their first priority was to get Georgie comfortable. Aydan assumed they would put her to bed, but when she insisted, they set her up on the couch in the formal living area farthest from the kitchen. Tyler wanted to give her some privacy. Aydan wasn't sure what she meant until Henry arrived and he and this Helen person pulled the upholstered chairs close to Georgie.

Even just watching clandestinely it was obvious the conversation was a roller coaster of emotion for each of them. She watched too as Lori, Leslie, Skip with his dad, Lou, and late arrivals Kira, Megan, and Marnie all worked to comfort Tyler while they jointly prepared supper in the open kitchen. With her Fleet Street Grill closed on Mondays, Leslie had loaded up everything she needed and carried it upstairs. The constant chatter among the group as they chopped and stirred was pleasant. Even Zoe, who had tagged along to help and never quite left, was playing nice.

After everyone had eaten and cleaned up from dinner, Georgie was exhausted. Lori and Tyler helped her upstairs to the bedroom, Aydan following at Tyler's request. She had pulled out sleepwear for Georgie, helping them get her changed and in bed. While Tyler stayed with her, she and Lori headed back downstairs to see every one out. Zoe and Skip, with their father, Lou, offered to drive Helen home. She would be back in the morning, planning to spend her days helping her niece get back on her feet. Leslie went across the hall and Henry over to his apartment too. He would be staying there while Georgie was out of commission. Aydan was seated in the living room, reading quietly and trying not to worry over the circumstances of the last few days.

"Good book?"

She jumped at Tyler's interruption. "I'm sorry," she said. "I found this in the library. I should have asked."

Tyler smiled at her. "You don't have to ask," she said as she passed by heading for the kitchen. "Although I can't believe you found anything worth reading in there. There's nothing but old company manuals and…" She stopped to look at Aydan, a curious expression on her face, asking, "Feel like a little treat? I'm going to make coffee and Baileys. I'll make it with decaf if you're interested."

Feeling caught out, but not wanting to look ashamed, Aydan straightened her shoulders, holding up the book she was reading and showing off the cover.

"Good choice," Tyler offered casually, waving for her to follow. At the kitchen counter she found mugs and selected two K-cups. "This is the one you like, right?"

Nodding, she stepped up to the island, taking a seat at one of the comfortable stools.

"You know, you can talk to me or ask questions." When she didn't answer, Tyler pushed her gently. "With all that's been happening over the last two, three weeks, we haven't had a chance to talk about how you're getting on."

"I'm enjoying the work."

"That's not exactly what I meant. How are you doing, you know, with all the changes happening in your life? I can imagine this whole DiNamico/Phipps family can be a little overwhelming. I don't know which is the greater anomaly, the number of twins in this family, or lesbians."

Aydan smiled weakly but the rising color in her face betrayed her discomfort.

Tyler let it go, taking both their doctored coffees over to where she had been reading, setting Aydan's cup down beside the overturned book and taking her favorite place on the hearth with her back to the fire. "The first time I read that book I was in high school. I remember being so mad when the husband hires a slimy detective and threatens to take her daughter away. I wanted to scream, but more than that I wanted to talk to someone about it. I wanted to understand why people could be so mean."

"Did you talk to someone?"

"Eventually. At first I tried to talk to Kira, she was my best friend growing up, but she is so much like my mom. I do love them to bits, but shades of gray they do not see." She sipped at her coffee. "I read a few more books, pretty much every book I could find. They're all in there along with a few hundred Georgie read when she was trying to come to grips with coming out too."

"Is that what you think I'm doing?"

"What I think is irrelevant. What I know is you have lived a sheltered life, at least since you lost your dad. We do a lot of growing in our twenties and early thirties, a lot of lessons learned that you've missed out on." When she didn't answer, Tyler pushed her gently. "Aydan, there's no rush, you have lots of time to learn who you are, the real authentic you. And you will always have good friends here willing to help. Please don't ever think you're alone, no matter what you're going through."

Silent but wanting to talk she finally blurted, "It wasn't a guy."

"Who wasn't?"

"We were talking, when I first arrived, and you said you thought some guy must have really hurt me."

"I'm so sorry. May I ask?"

She nodded, her head down. "I...it was my fault. She wanted me to tell my parents, but I was scared. I was worried about them hating me or not letting me go to college. Of course," she lamented, "that's exactly what happened after my dad died. I would have been better off risking it, but I just wasn't sure about myself."

"Are you now?" Again she didn't answer so Tyler got to her feet, moving over to sit on the couch. "You know, there is no hard-and-fast rule. Deciding what you are, deciding what you feel and who you feel it for, can't be qualified or measured or put on a schedule or in a project plan. Hell, many young people today refuse to even accept a label, using instead terms like queer, fluid sexuality, or what was the one I heard the other day...pansexual human. All I'm saying is being you, whoever that may be, should be about you learning what makes you a better person."

"You really believe that?"

"I swear to you, some days, our true selves are all we have to keep us going. That doesn't mean you don't prepare or stand up for what you believe in—it just means anything can happen and often does. If nothing else, these last weeks have been a sobering reminder of that."

Finally agreeing, she chanced to ask, "Are you, I mean, are you two okay? Sorry, it's none of my business."

"I don't think that's true. You're our friend, you live here, and part of your job gives you some responsibility in our lives. This is where you should remember the part about me saying you can talk to me about anything."

It was said with such simplicity and affection that Aydan smiled. "I do want to talk, but I guess I'm more worried about you and Georgie right now. I...I just don't understand what happened. Sorry..."

"Aydan, will you please stop apologizing. You have a right to ask, and honestly I could use someone to talk to, if you're okay with that?"

"Yes of course," she said, sitting up straighter and cupping her coffee mug in both hands in imitation of Tyler. She listened quietly while Tyler filled in the specifics surrounding Helen and the late Georgina's relationship, providing details that had been avoided or glossed over at dinner. "It's so horrible! Part of me can't believe any family would act that way. But they can and do, my own included, and I still don't understand."

"You and me both," Tyler agreed. "All we can really do is be patient with them and be ready to help them understand if and when they want to try."

"Why do you think he did it, I mean, Mr. DiNamico, keeping Helen away from her all these years, especially after his mother died. I don't understand who he thought he was protecting."

"Fear, self-preservation even, it's usually a combination of things. I'm sure it was exactly as Henry explained, at least until Sophia died. At that point they had both lost so much and he had lied to little Georgina to keep her from continuously demanding to see Helen. He told her she had died too. Imagine if you had just turned eight years old when all this was going down. You're big enough to see everything, but not old enough to truly understand the family dynamics, social issues, or even the legal system. I think her father was in pain and wanted Georgie for himself. Certainly her grandmother figured into the mix. After that, it may have been his need to keep the girls close, or maybe he was too embarrassed to admit to her that he had been lying. It would have been hard to do when she was ten but imagine the blowout that would have occurred if he did so later in life, like when she came home from Afghanistan."

"Henry did say he thought about it a lot. I can't help wondering if my mother will ever think about what she's done."

"According to my mom, and now Kira, that's all moms do, think about every decision, every word they said to their children, second-guessing everything."

"I'm not surprised by the second-guessing, but when does reality seep in?"

That spurred an ironic grin from Tyler. "That, my friend, is the million-dollar question. For me, the hardest part of coming out was working up the courage to talk to my parents. Usually, Dad and I talked. Kira and I worked part-time in the body shop. She helped my mom in the office and ran the customer counter, but I wanted to be in the back with Dad and the guys. I loved the smell of the place and watching a wrecker get turned into something special. Most of his work is fender-bender repairs, but every once in a while someone would come in with a restoration job. Those were the cars I loved working on." At her raised brows, Tyler explained, "Don't get too excited, engineer girl. My job usually involved hand sanding and prep for the paint booth, you know, taping over lights and windows and such. What?"

Aydan was grinning at the description. "I just can't see it. You all dirty, sanding cars? You're always so...put together."

Tyler stood. "Come on, let's have another coffee, and as my mom would say, we'll add a little Irish."

While she made two more cups of decaf, Aydan found and examined the bottle. "This actually comes from Ireland, huh?" she said, reading the label. "So it's made from whiskey? I never would have guessed." Noticing a similar bottle, Aydan pulled it down to examine it too. "What's this one?"

"That's my secret weapon, Baileys Chocolate Cherry. I suggest caution on that one. Talk about the ultimate panty remover!" The minute it was out of Tyler's mouth she colored, slapping her hand over the offending orifice. "Oh Aydan, I'm so sorry..."

She was laughing. It was really the first time in ages. She had recognized a look, a look Tyler only had when she was thinking of Georgie and now she had a good idea what those quiet thoughts were considering. "You are so busted, boss!" She was still grinning when she picked up her mug. "Thanks for that. It's been so long since someone just talked to me like a friend, uncensored comments and all."

When they sat down again, Tyler picked up the novel Aydan was reading and flipped to the front matter. "This must be

Georgie's copy. It's an even earlier edition than mine. You know we have the movie upstairs?"

"They made a movie? How long ago was this?"

"Just last year. They changed the title for the movie to *Carol*."

Excited, she sat up on the sofa. "The one with Cate Blanchett?"

Tyler nodded amiably. "Yes, have you seen it?"

Aydan groaned, rolling her eyes. "I've seen nothing, absolutely nothing. I feel like I've been living in a time warp for the last decade."

"Well then, we can all watch it tomorrow night."

The first thought that popped into her head was that she would like to invite someone, but she wasn't ready to admit that to Tyler; she wasn't sure she could admit it to herself. Instead, she asked something just as difficult, just not as difficult to her own self. "Is everything going to be okay with you two? I mean, I think you both love each other very much but…"

"But this was a test and we have so much talking to do and I need to do some healing. If you're asking if I'm going to try and fix this the answer is absolutely yes. I love her too much to give up, especially if Lori is right."

"Lori." She felt a slight tingle race through her at the mention of Lori Phipps, almost as if the woman had been standing behind her running a teasing finger down her spine.

Tyler's head tilted slightly. Sipping from her mug, she explained Lori's theory of Georgie's decision-making process, a process she had described as brutally logical.

"If she's right, will it change anything?"

Setting her cup aside, Tyler let her head fall against the back of the couch. "Yes and no. I know I can't react when she pulls something stupid like this, at least not until I've had time to talk to her and help her reason her way through things without resorting to creating some computer app to decide for her. I knew better on Friday, but I was so upset I just reacted. Part of me feels like a shit for not recalling how hard it is for her to understand any unquantifiable nonlinear thing. And I'm mad at her for not remembering the rule that she talk things through with me. Mostly I'm mad at that asshole who ran her over and left her facedown in a foot of water. I'm mad at the idiot doctor for scaring her when we specifically told him to bring all clinical information to me. Most of all I'm angry at her dad for being a wife-beating bastard who was too much of a coward to tell his daughter her Aunt Helen was still alive and kept that information from her all these years."

Silenced by her intensity, she did understand the frustration. She watched as Tyler retrieved a wad of tissue from her back pocket, wiping indignantly at her tears, and mused, "Sometimes I wonder what lies my father told me."

For some reason the gentle statement soothed Tyler enough for her to ask, "Tell me about him. How did your parents meet? I mean Iran isn't exactly on the Best Getaway list."

"My dad was in the army," she said, "this was back when the Shah was still in power. Dad was assigned to my grandfather's command as a military adviser."

That got her attention. "Your grandfather's command, what was he?"

Pushing out a hot breath, Aydan almost whispered, "Deputy Commanding General of the Army."

Tyler whistled. "Wow, your dad must have been high up in the army too, to get so close to his family."

She shook her head. "Actually, that's one of the things I've been thinking might be a lie." Tyler's brows raised but she held her tongue. "My dad wasn't that kind of adviser, at least not the kind you see hobnobbing with generals. He was a US Army staff sergeant teaching sergeants in the Iranian guards how to be better firearms instructors. My mother tells this story of them meeting at a grand ball and seeing him in his dress blues and falling in love."

"You don't think that happened?"

"Oh, I think they met and fell in love, but I know a thing or two about the army, both ours and theirs. Enlisted men, even American advisers, do not get invited to social functions where officers will be, especially general officers. I think there's a better chance they met in a bar or nightclub, they had them you know, especially back then when things were so pro-American."

"So, she created a fantasy. Do you think she was ashamed to admit she was a normal young woman going out with friends and meeting boys?"

"I'm sure shame is involved. My mom has always been cagey about their anniversary date. She would say she left that all behind in Iran and would only think about her new life here. I bought that right up until Dad died. I was helping get all his papers in order and found their marriage certificate. It was issued in France just a week before I was born. When I showed her, she just flipped it off, saying they remarried in France because the church insisted on it. I know France is mostly a Catholic nation but still, it sounded like BS to me."

"Interesting," Tyler noted. "So, what's your theory?"

"My theory, they met in Tehran and were sneaking around behind my grandfather's back. I'm guessing he found out and cut it off, even when they realized she was pregnant. I'm sure my grandfather's pride would not let him consider such a low-ranking soldier as a husband for his only child. Then the Shah fell. My dad was extracted with his unit, but my grandparents must have thought they could ride it out. They were very wealthy and may have imagined their money and station would keep them safe. Then the Ayatollah ordered his boss be hung for crimes against Islam and I'm sure my grandfather believed he was next. The CIA exfiltration team brought them out that night with nothing but the clothes on their backs. They were very bitter over the situation and the loss of their family holdings, and remained so until their deaths. I had the impression that they went to Paris thinking everything was temporary and the French banks could recover their money. When they realized they were penniless, living in the most expensive city in the world like they were still aristocrats, they must have panicked."

"I bet. I know I would have. Was your dad there?"

"In his army record file I found a list of all his postings. According to that he was stationed at Fort Benning Georgia, teaching Green Berets."

"Wow! That's a long way from the Paris Opera House."

"See, I'm not crazy to think this, am I?"

Tyler shrugged. "I guess the real question is why it was so important for your mother to lie about it. If it was just a point of respecting her parents' pride I can almost accept it. If it's shame, well, it could be another factor in the puzzle of your treatment compared to your siblings. I'm sorry I don't know much about the Muslim faith. What's the party line when it comes to unwed pregnancies?"

Now it was her turn to shrug. Silently, she removed her hijab. It was the first time she had done it anywhere except her bedroom and that one time with Georgie. "I never wore one of these until my dad was gone. He never said anything, but I have a feeling he laid down the law with my grandparents. It's not as if we were raised as Christians either. When we were little and friends were going to Sunday school, he would always say we had lots of time to make our own decisions about faith and advised us to wait until we were adults to make that choice."

"Smart," Tyler agreed. "I take it that decision was overruled when your dad died."

"The very next day. I really thought my mom would get everything back to normal once she had some time to grieve but, well, it just never happened."

"I'm so sorry, Aydan. It sounds like he was a really great guy." Maggie stretched up from her dog bed and making her way to Tyler leaned against her legs. "Is it time, girl?"

"Let me," Aydan said. "I'll take her out for a walk, then bring her to your room, if that's okay."

"You don't mind?"

Aydan was up, grabbing the empty mugs. "Let me just straighten up first, then I'll take her for a walk. How far should we go? I mean, her shoulder must still hurt."

"I'm sure it does. I think a loop around the building should do." Walking to the stairs, Tyler stopped and said, "Aydan, thanks for everything." With that she headed up, disappearing into the master suite.

"Well, Miss Maggie, do you think you can teach me this dog walking thing?" The dog, limping slightly walked to her and leaned against her leg. She had seen her do it before, but almost always with Georgie or Tyler. "I guess that means we're friends again."

* * *

Maggie had sauntered throughout her walk, taking her time to sniff every corner of the building before relieving her bladder at the one location Aydan knew Georgie didn't like her to go. The postage-sized strip of still-hard grass on the building's northwest corner had once connected Erie with Cathedral Park and had necessitated the original bullnose feature to fit the lot. Now the tiny greenspace formed a triangular-shaped parkette with a few trees, a small Victorian iron fountain, and a single city bench. There was no point in scolding the dog; she was probably too sore to make it much farther. With their business done and cleaned up, they headed back inside and upstairs. All the way up in the elevator, the dog sat at her side, leaning heavily on her leg until the doors finally opened.

Then everything changed. Aydan recognized the dog's sudden urgency, familiar from the morning Georgie was hit. Fumbling through her pockets for her employee pass, she begged under her breath, "Please dog, just this once be wrong."

The moment the door lock disconnected, Maggie pushed through, racing around to the master bedroom and pushing her way in. Aydan was trying to decide if she should just go to her room or check on her bosses when she heard Tyler.

"Aydan, can you come here, please."

Sticking her head in cautiously, she said in alarm, "Oh no, not again."

"I don't think so," Tyler said kindly, never taking her eyes off Georgie. She was sitting up in bed. Tyler, still in her street clothes, had squeezed her way in behind her back, giving Georgie something to lean against while she was sick. Tyler had a towel in her hand, wiping at the sweat beading on her shoulders and neck. "It's just the pain meds. I'm going to have to call her doctor tomorrow and get her to prescribe something else."

That made sense and was much better than the alternative. "Here Georgie, I can take that. You're done, right?" she asked carefully, reaching out and taking the loaded kidney bowl from her shaking hands. She didn't look so hot, but she did look a lot better than before.

With two younger sisters, two baby brothers and a sickly grandmother, Aydan had seen her share of barf. Nothing could shake her on that level and what people, even big tough bastards like her brothers, would balk at often shocked her. *Bastards!* She prepared a washcloth then grabbed a fresh towel, carrying everything back into the bedroom.

Tyler had moved to sit on the side of the bed. She sat leaning over Georgie, propping pillows behind her head, reassuring her as she wiped away the slow stream of tears trailing down her cheeks. "It's okay, baby. We're big girls; we can handle a little barf. You never got upset when Ella threw up on you Christmas Day, so we won't get upset now either, right Aydan?"

It was easy to admire the woman's devotion. Her eyes were always on Georgie, even when she was trading points with someone else. "Tyler's right, boss. I have seen ten times worse come out of my brothers and believe me they never had an excuse for it."

Georgie was smiling now as color slowly seeped back up her face. "Thank you," she said, making eye contact before repeating it for Tyler. Suddenly her tears were back but from a completely different cause. "My Tyler...sorry, so sorry...I thought..."

"I know, baby. You thought you were doing the right thing. Please don't worry. I'm not mad, but we will have to talk about it."

She watched as Georgie nodded solemnly to her future bride. Handing over the damp cloth, Aydan set the kidney bowl on the nightstand along with the clean towel. Quietly she told Tyler, "I'll put that call to the doctor on the top of your priority list for tomorrow. I take it you're pretty sure it's the meds?"

She nodded. "Although the cheesecake Leslie made is definitely on her no-no list. Remind me to let her know. I think she made it as a treat, but it's not something she does well with anymore."

"Complicated," Aydan said quietly, noting it without criticism. "Let me grab a clean T-shirt for her. Any preference?"

"Yes, but first will you help me get her over on the other side of the bed?" Tyler explained to Georgie, "Baby, I think it would be safer if you sleep on the other side. I don't want to risk hurting your leg or your hip."

Georgie held up her right arm, showing off the fiberglass cast. "Might hurt," she said, concern in her eyes.

"Don't worry, Maggie will warn me if you're having a nightmare. I'll have plenty of time to wake you up or run for cover." This last bit she added with a grin.

It was nice to see them like this again, joking and playing together. "Which will be easier, walking her around the bed or do we just help her scoot over?"

"No scooting," Tyler warned them both. "The doctor specifically said no playing Twister! So, how about we get your air cast back on and walk you around nice and slow?" It didn't take long to get her up, moved, and settled back in.

"Thank you, Aydan," Tyler said as Aydan went to the bedroom door. "I can't tell you what a relief it is to have you here."

Back in her room, Aydan picked up her phone to plug in the charger, only then realizing she had missed two calls. She wasn't used to having a phone much less carrying it around everywhere like the rest of the world. Two text messages, one from Zoe and another from Lori, had been sent within minutes of each other. She didn't think it was too late to call, but didn't want to be reporting on her boss without Tyler's permission. She was sure it would be okay with Lori. It seemed she and Tyler, along with Mrs. Pulaski, oops Marnie, all shared information freely but not so much with their niece. It was hard to figure out what that was about, but families were complicated. She of all people could attest to that. She sent a quick response text to both, and headed off to prepare for bed. She stopped suddenly, facing the mirror. She had completely forgotten she had removed her hijab earlier. She ran her fingers through the uneven short hair. It was growing back in nicely and thick. She could feel all the places where the shears had brutally cut through hair and scalp as she struggled to fight off the bastards. "I like that. The Bastards!" she said, smiling at her reflection. The wounds had healed well and were impossible to see in the mass of dark thick locks.

In that instant she decided she would get her hair cut this week. *Something perky!* Maybe she would spend some of her first precious paycheck on a cheap scarf too, something with some color. Something she could wrap over her head casually, and remove without anyone thinking it was some sort of unveiling or political statement. *Tyler's right, this is my time to get to know me.*

CHAPTER FOURTEEN

Tyler woke from a fitful sleep. She wasn't used to sleeping on the other side of the bed. The truth was, other than these last few weeks, she couldn't remember sleeping with Georgie and not being in her arms. She wanted to cuddle up but her fear of hurting her held her back, that and a teeny tiny sliver of residual anger. She needed to talk and she needed to connect, but that would have to wait. She had been patient before...hadn't she? Certainly that first night, when she had waited and waited in her room for Georgie only to realize that she needed to go to her.

Yeah right, just who am I kidding? I barely lasted thirty minutes back then and I was ready to break things!

Carefully, she rolled on her side, wanting to watch her sleep.

"Hi," Georgie said quietly, with a welcoming smile.

"Baby, you're supposed to be sleeping. Is something wrong?"

Georgie nodded, tapping the fingers of her casted forearm against her chest. "I thought...forgive me, my Tyler?"

Taking her hand in her own, fiberglass cast and all, she soothed, "I forgive you, I do. I don't quite understand you, this, but I know you'll tell me everything when you're ready."

"Ready," Georgie said as an errant tear escaped.

Rolling as close as she dared, Tyler stroked the fingers poking from the cast, carefully kissing each one. "God, I wish we could cuddle. We have the best talks like that and I miss you so much."

"Can," she reassured, lifting her right arm to wrap it around Tyler's shoulders.

She had long grown used to sleeping like that every night, with Georgie's arms around her, engulfing her, protecting her. Nothing else in the world could compare to being held, loved, and adored by this woman. The adored part was especially pleasing. "You're sure? I don't want to hurt you, baby."

"First rule," Georgie said, prompting her to remember the first time she shared that sentiment.

"Always mean what you say." She snuggled in, grinning with pleasure, taking care to be sure Georgie's shoulder had plenty of support. At least with sleeping on this side, there was less chance of accidentally rolling onto her hip or leg, or the still stiff shoulder. It only took a moment to find that warm soft place that brought her so much peace. She was so tempted to just fall asleep and wake up tomorrow pretending none of this had ever happened.

"Okay, here goes," she said, kissing away another silent tear. "I'm hurt, not because you did this, but because you didn't talk to me first. I thought we agreed it was my job to translate the world, at least the non-tech world for you?"

"Yes," she answered, nodding.

"Yet you made a unilateral decision for us, both of us."

"Yes…wrong."

"Baby, I'm not asking you to admit fault. We all know you take the fault around here far too freely. I just want to understand what you were thinking."

Tyler felt light fingers trace along her back. She almost laughed to realize the path they followed was predicated by the limited arc of Georgie's cast. Still, it would be hard to guess her forearm was wrapped in fiberglass. That was the thing about Georgie; she was a life in contrasts. She was gentle curves under straight-line suits. She made the best use of her brilliant analytical skills, often to the point of overwhelming her diminished verbal abilities. Her personal interactions bordered on deceptive simplicity, but she wasn't without emotion. On the contrary, her passions ran deep and often unsuspected. She was rigged for silent running and that comprehension offered Tyler the key to learning and understanding more. Tilting her head to see Georgie's face, she explained, "Everyone thinks you did this out of some misguided belief you were saving me—wait!" she ordered. "I see it in your eyes. I also need you to listen, really listen to me, baby…We are in this together, no matter what. Anything can happen and no, I never for a minute thought we would be looking at health complications this early in our lives but so what, life happens, and the reality is anything can happen to either of us any day. You, of all people, know that."

When she looked again, Georgie was smiling. Tyler sighed. "You make me crazy, you know?"

She nodded slightly before apologizing, "Sorry."

"No more apologies, it's time for a science lesson. I want to hear what you were thinking. It's important, baby, I need to understand how you process this stuff, so I'll know how to help."

"Who helps Tyler?"

She rolled a little higher on her side, gingerly resting her arm on Georgie's chest, wanting to look in her eyes. "You do, every day. You make me feel loved, you make me feel adored, and you make me feel smart and capable and a million other things. You gave me your trust and you gave me your respect. To tell you the truth, back when the university cut the funding to my program—well, to the whole department—and shut us down, I really thought I would have to leave Buffalo. She may not be the greatest city in the world, but I love it here. It's my home, but staying looked like a long shot. It's ironic how it all turned out. I'm exactly where I feel I belong with you and with our work. They are irrevocably intertwined."

"Comingled?"

Tyler laughed at her version of the situation. "Yes baby, our work, our lives, our future are comingled to the extent that the very act of disentanglement could have catastrophic effects elsewhere."

"I did not...wrong assumptions."

"I'm listening, baby," she offered, snuggling her forehead against Georgie's cheek. "Why don't we start from when Doctor Stupidity walked in."

It took a moment before Georgie began to explain. They often spent long hours talking like this and always with great success. Here in this quiet room, with just the two of them, Georgie's deficits were at their lowest. Getting her to talk was as simple as turning out the lights and letting her close her eyes. She wouldn't speak publicly with her eyes closed, at least not for more than a few seconds at a time. But here, with Tyler, all remaining misgivings vanished.

"The Kevlar...talking about how I got it...trying to explain, he was not patient enough...it made me mad. The Kevlar... hard to imagine but...think aluminum honeycomb core then... Kevlar. Also wires, sensors, heat element...then aluminum outer skin to sandwich. I...no one listened!"

"Okay baby, let's make sure I understand this. The helicopter rotor is made of a core material, some kind of aluminum honeycomb?" When she felt Georgie's nod, she pushed on. "The rotor blade you showed me was very thin and only flexed in one direction, so I'm going to assume the core is what gives it strength. I'm guessing the Kevlar is used to encapsulate the core or any features needing to be protected. Would that add to the strength too?" Hearing a positive grunt, she had a better idea where this was going. "So, you believe because of the way the blade is constructed, it would be rare to have wounds from just Kevlar? That means some amount of aluminum, either from the skins or the encapsulated core should be present too?"

"Yes!" Georgie let out a frustrated breath before kissing Tyler's nose.

"That makes more sense than his theory that the Kevlar had been broken down into threads running wild in your bloodstream. What an idiot!"

"So mad, could not think...Then he showed one removed. I looked...looking...easy to see aero-primer green but no aluminum...Panic, what if...what *if* there is more? It broke me...the thought..." She was silent but Tyler waited patiently, knowing she was struggling. "I remember every detail...Mom's funeral...Papa's and Aunt Glory too. One, two, three," she said, turning her head to kiss Tyler's brow. "All in a row...So strange to see...one, two, three...then we go again...Aunt Georgina. I can count...where is Aunt Helen? They promised...she promised, everyone promises, but everyone leaves.

"No, not for my Tyler...no more loss, no more!" she asserted painfully, sucking in a breath. "One tiny piece of Kevlar? Mild MI...what if more? Not right for you...Not right, I thought. I lean so much, need so much...you give, and give...what for... why, my Tyler? I am so broken...now more!"

"Do you really think it changes anything? Oh baby, I wish you could understand all you do for me. Jeez, you read my thesis before you even met me. That was a first. Then you put me to work, real work. It wasn't just you believing in me; the point was, you just believed. You believe in the same standards I do. We both ascribe to the same work principles and ethics, both in human interaction and technical development. The difference is you gave me a platform, you trusted me to take the lead, and you insisted I take credit for my work. I have never worked with anyone so...egoless. If I wasn't already in love with you I know I would be now."

"This work...you were born to...all you. I am lucky."

She was quiet for so long, Tyler raised her head to see if she had fallen asleep. She was met with those ever-changing green eyes and a wistful look she knew belonged to her and only her. "Right there," Tyler said, explaining, "the way you look at me says so much and makes me feel beautiful and adored. Only you have ever done that to me. And then there's the other thing. I know you say it's what I do to you, but I feel the same thing too."

"I love you deeply...my Tyler...I made...wrong math. I know now but...are you sure? What if..."

"We already covered this so now I will tell you with kisses. Maybe this way it will sink in to that thick skull of yours. Let me see," she said, propping herself on her elbow and looking her over carefully. "I haven't kissed this shoulder in a while. I'll start here," she said, nibbling her way across Georgie's shoulder, collarbone and to the hollow of her neck. "Hmm, another place missing my attention," she added, before beginning a more languorous exploration. "Starting to get how this works, baby?"

"Working...oh, yes."

"Oh no you don't. There is no nooky for you. The doctor said nothing strenuous remember?"

Georgie opened her eyes, smiling. "Promise," she said, offering a pathetic rendition of the Boy Scout salute with her hand and forearm in a cast. That had Tyler laughing, really laughing, and Georgie's pleasure was more than clear. She stroked her fingers through Tyler's dark hair, finally risking moving her painful left shoulder so she could lift both hands to hold Tyler's face. She took her time, and without a word, traced the contours of her cheeks, the line of her jaw, then up along her brows, finally cupping her cheeks gently. "I understand now... This..." She closed her eyes to frame a reply. "Losing what could be is...more painful than any loss we may face. Are you sure...the risk, you want that?" she asked.

Tyler, half on her side and half-on top of Georgie, had tears in her eyes but she wasn't upset anymore.

Georgie promised her, "I can't...won't live without...my Tyler, my love." Wiping the tears from her cheeks she offered her solemn vow: "I want to live...I want to marry you...I want to sail with you...our babies, everywhere...together...now, my love...no time to waste." She pleaded, "Enough lost...time for my Tyler."

"I don't know if I should kiss you, try to hug you ever so carefully, or just go scream off the roof! Oh baby, you make me so happy. I knew you would understand if you just waited for the entire dataset before considering a solution. Now kiss me and tell me how brilliant I am."

Georgie did so without hesitation, wrapping both arms, cast and all, around her. "Aunt Helen...may be godmother?"

"To whom?"

"My Tyler's babies."

"My Ty...just how many babies are you planning on and why am I doing all the heavy lifting?" She liked this, no, loved this, lying in bed with Georgie and talking about the most silly and important things, all with the same joy and reverence. "Come on, spit it out. How many babies did your algorithms say we should have?"

She held up two fingers, and then showed her four.

"Let me see, either you want two, or you want four, or I've got it all wrong and you want twenty-four kids?"

Georgie snorted at that thought. "Finally, enough to play!"

"Play what, all-out no rules lacrosse, no way! Have you seen these hips? No way is this woman pushing out twenty-four anythings, but if you'll settle for two I think I can get on board for that."

"Twins?"

"Is there no end with you? What is this, some new bravado gained from surviving death once again?"

Now Georgie was grinning. "Marry me?"

"I am marrying you, in just three months. Or has your recent adventure robbed your memory of that little detail?"

"Tomorrow."

"What about tomorrow? I haven't looked at your sched…"

"Marry me," Georgie insisted, "tomorrow."

Tyler, her face just inches away had forgotten to breathe. "You want that?" she finally asked.

"Life is short…I want, hope for many…as your wife, my wife…Never again…not without you."

Laying her head down and burrowing deep into her neck, Tyler sighed. "This is what I missed, what I was so terrified to lose. Baby, I love you so much. I want every day with you from now on, no matter what."

"Done," Georgie said quietly, pulling her closer and holding her tight. "Always, done…my Tyler, my love."

* * *

Lori looked over the expansion drawings one more time. "Geez kiddo, you did a great job on this. I'm really pleased."

Zoe practically swooned at the compliment. "What a relief."

"Was Megan any help?"

"Actually," Zoe admitted, taking a seat behind her desk, "she was great. She helped me check all the dimensions and clearance requirements. Plus, she is so sweet; she's always reining in the guys when I need to visit the assembly bay." Her smile telegraphed her pleasure at the efforts their lone security officer made for all of them.

Lori groaned, gathering the drawings and signing the approval block on each page. "You do have a way of attracting attention wherever you go. But still, if those jerks ever say or do anything other than drool let me know. I will not put up with any of that boys-being-boys bullshit!"

"I can't say I blame them. I must look a sight whenever I pull on those ugly safety boots and stroll down there in a skirt."

Finishing up the approval signatures, Lori smiled, but wanted her to understand the point. For her, it was always unsettling when women bought into the notion that they were somehow responsible for the actions of men or even other women. "Don't even go there, kiddo. I've been very impressed with you. The clothing you wear to work screams professionalism. I know what you're thinking," she said, halting any response. "Marnie told me you were top-notch when it came to this whole assistant gig. I'll admit I had my doubts, but that wasn't fair. As far as work goes you're the best thing that's happened out here. As a matter of fact, I've asked Marnie if we can move you over to the management side." She held up her hand, adding, "She said we need to send you on some courses first, but..."

Zoe squealed with delight. Zipping around the desk with the grace and speed of a rambunctious child, throwing her arms around her aunt, she shrieked, "Thank you, thank you, thank you! I promise I will not let you down!"

Lori returned her enthusiastic hug with care. "Before I forget, I want you to remember something about working here." Wanting to make sure her niece understood, she explained with care, "I know society, schools and the university, hell everybody, tells young women how to act and how to dress. Worse, they blame women whenever they're victimized by men. I won't have that here. The standards Marnie and I set for you are about business and the fact that you're a Phipps, nothing more. I know people tell you you're beautiful all the time but it really is an understatement, and I will not have the guys or anyone else acting like it's okay to ogle you, or whistle at you, or worse. Please remember this: You are only responsible for you."

"And this office," she said with a grin.

Lori just shook her head. Twenty-one and astoundingly gorgeous, her niece often suffered bouts of insecurity and Lori was more than aware of it. She believed it to be the driving force behind her aggressive behavior with women. "Peachy says you haven't been out to the club in months, lost your dancing shoes? Or did you just find something better to do with your time?" She watched as Zoe colored. She hadn't seen that happen since she was a teen and Lori had asked straight out if she was a lesbian. "Okay, no pressure but hey, even I've had bouts of monogamy. They don't take your player's card away for giving it a try."

Just then both their phones beeped notifications. Before Lori could even open her text messages, Zoe read hers aloud. "Marnie wants to see the finalized plans."

"Let her know you have them finished and I've signed the approvals." Looking at her own phone, she noted the time. "Ask her if she can fit me in at lunch. That will give me a chance to pop in and check on Georgie before we sit down."

"Can I come?"

There was so much hope in her eyes, Lori grinned. "Oh, so I take it your interest can be found lurking in the DiNamico building? So, spill kiddo, who is she?"

Zoe blushed, waving off her insinuation. "It's not like that, we're just friends. She helped me with these and I—"

"Aydan!" Lori reared to her feet, her body language and tone revealing her distress. "No way, Zoe!" She paced the tiny office, needing room to move. It was one of the reasons Zoe had added more office room to the expansion plans. It was a good call, but this wasn't. "Look kiddo, I don't want to be a bitch but leave Aydan alone. She's a bucket full of broken and doesn't need any of your..." Suddenly aware of her language and threatening posture, she backed off.

Looking like she'd just been slapped, Zoe fired back, "None of what? My bullshit?"

"Look, I didn't mean it that way. It's just that she's been through a lot. Besides, she's not even a lesbian."

Zoe snorted at that. "You really are a big dumb butch sometimes! You think she's straight just because she wears that scarf thingy or because she's pretty? Really Lori, this isn't about you unless…Oh my God!" She clamped her hands over her mouth. "You like her!"

"Do not!" Talk about sounding like a stupid lovestruck teen. *Maybe I do like her that way. Oh shit, now what do I do?*

Triumphantly, looking like she had bested her aunt, Zoe stuck out her hand. "May the best woman win."

Recoiling, Lori forced herself to think. Did she really want to go head-to-head with the hottest lesbian in town? "We can't hurt her that way. I won't—"

"I won't do anything untoward. Let's make this a gentlewomanly wager. We will both continue offering our friendship only. If things progress to a kiss, and only a kiss, the kissee wins." Lori was still panicking when Zoe added, "If I win, you take me to Aunt Joanne's dress shop and buy me anything I want. If you win, I'll do the same." At Lori's raised brow, she amended, "Fine, I'll buy you something butchy from Uncle John. Better?"

Normally, Lori would never consider such a thing but Zoe's mischievous grin and her own desire overrode her common sense. "Two, no three rules!" At Zoe's mounting enthusiasm, she listed her conditions, ticking them off on her fingers. "This is a secret bet. If anyone learns about it, especially Georgie, Marnie, or Aydan, the bet is off and I'll tell everyone it was your idea. Second, no funny business, you have to pledge to treat her with respect. She's been through enough—let's not make her feel used too. Got that?" At Zoe's nod, she added the last point. "If, and I mean if, she kisses one of us and wants to, you know… no! I don't mean sex you pig. If she's interested in one of us and kisses one of us, it has to be her starting things. Then the other one backs off completely. Agreed?"

Zoe stuck her hand out again. "So, will I be accompanying you to the meeting with Marnie?"

Lori groaned for show but couldn't hide her grin. She liked having the kid working at the boatyard, liked her irrepressible spirit, not to mention her mockery for anything she considered in her way. "Well I guess it would be ungentlewomanly of me to say no." Rolling up the large-scale prints of the construction plans, she slipped them into a cardboard tube. Then she sat down again. "Okay kiddo, time to spill. You've been pissed with this whole Georgie thing for weeks."

"I...I just don't see it. Why does everyone run to her? It's not as if she's the prettiest or anything. I mean, she can barely carry on a conversation yet you're all there at her beck and call."

"What else?"

"Nothing, that's it. I'm just...why do women go for her? I mean she's..."

"That's your ego talking, chicklet, and women don't go for her or at least they haven't in years, unless...aah, Tyler. You want to know why Tyler would fall for her and put up with her bullshit?" When Zoe didn't answer, she knew it was the true question. "Let's see, Georgie is a lot older than you so you should have the upper hand in that category. You're hands down better looking; even Tyler will admit you won the DNA jackpot and that's coming from a woman who thinks we're all pretty hot. What else, hmm...you know how to have fun. You can outdance anyone and you are charming. It makes sense you're confused. Anyone would look at the two of you and agree you're the hands-down winner. So then, why did Doctor Hot-Body choose our broken leader when she could have grabbed the diamond in the crown?"

Lori watched as the kid lifted her head. She was embarrassed for raising the subject but looked very much as if she needed to hear the answer.

"Sweetie, I think she fell in love. I know it doesn't make sense, but that's how it works. At least that's what Marnie always says. If you want my theory about those two, I think Tyler fell in love with Georgie's intensity and intelligence." Holding up a hand, she begged Zoe to listen. "Whoa there, kiddo! I'm not saying you're not intense or not intelligent, but no one has those two things in spades like our Georgie Porgie."

Before Zoe could argue, her phone beeped and she checked her message. "Marnie has already ordered lunch for all of us to be served up at Georgie's. I guess she wants Georgie and Granddad to be part of the final signoff, but she wants us in her office at half past eleven."

Checking her phone for the time, Lori nodded. "I'm going to run next door and make sure everything is in order. Meet me at my Jeep in twenty."

"It's a wee bit early, don't you think?" It was just past nine.

Lori couldn't hold back the smartass grin, challenging, "I thought we had a little gentlemanly wager going on?"

"Gentlewomanly," Zoe corrected with a grin before returning to her phone and replying to the text.

* * *

Lori hemmed and hawed over the selection of scarves. "These aren't really doing it for me, Uncle John. Do you have anything...I don't know, more special?"

"Everything I carry is special, especially as a sweet *memento*." Watching her roll her eyes, he pantomimed slapping her upside the head. "Tell me about this customer—or is it a supplier who is so important you are giving your favorite uncle such a difficult time? Hmm, help me out here."

"I..." she stalled. In the category of old-school gossip, old John was the family winner, as fast on the phone as Zoe was with instant messaging. Still, if she wanted him to cough up the good stuff, she'd have to give him something. "It's for an employee. Georgie's new assistant. She used to have this really gorgeous silk scarf she liked to wear. I think it was one of those antique ones. Unfortunately, it got wrecked so I would like to get her something nice to replace it."

"Antique?" He shook his head.

"Okay, I know there's a proper name for it which I don't care to learn. Just tell me if you have something...better?"

He examined her carefully, arms crossed over his barrel chest. "And I should ask if our little Georgie knows of your, *uh hum*, interest in this one?"

Trying desperately not to look like a caught-out adolescent, she forced her head up high. Before she could figure out what to say, he began laughing lightheartedly, turning for the back storage room without further comment. She listened as he whistled and sang amiably to himself until finally he carried out two small boxes, setting them on the counter. From them he unfolded several silk scarves in a variety of designs and colors. Compared to the synthetic versions she had already seen these were magnificent. She picked up one that looked like watercolor splotches on snow. Surprised by the difference in weight and the delicate texture, she held it up for closer examination. "This is real isn't it?"

"Of course! Now these are from Vincelli Silk, quite lovely. That one you are holding is a Fattorseta."

"A fat whata?"

"Oh, my girl. Thank goodness Uncle John is here to help you. Now this is House of Fattorini, these two are the exquisite design of *bella* Carolina Fattorini. Are they not beautiful?"

Lori stood in awe, thinking of what it would be like to see Aydan swap out the horrid gray head wrap thingy she had been forced to wear. "Good. Perfect, fine," she choked out. "Wrap them up, I'll take them all."

"All?" He almost choked too. He showed her the retail tags, just to be sure she understood.

The whistle that followed could have cleared traffic for a mile up Niagara Street. "Are you kidding me? What the hell are they made of, gold?"

He grinned, smiling at his god-niece and her lack of fashionomics. "Very few places can still produce silk of this quality. It is expensive, but a piece like this will last generations to come if treated kindly."

"Won't we all," she said. "Okay, I guess I'm getting one. I like this one and this other, the Carolina something or other."

"Fattorini," he corrected. "I cannot help with the price on this one, but if you would also like the Vincelli, that one I have some room to discount. Should I go look at my books and see what the cost was?"

She needed a minute to think about it and told him so. He didn't seem bothered at all, collecting the other silks from the counter and taking them with him back into storage. Lori took a hard look at the remaining two. Each screamed Aydan to her and she so wanted to buy them both. It wasn't as if she couldn't afford them or needed to hesitate, but this was Aydan, practical, sensitive, Aydan. The last thing she wanted was the woman thinking she was trying to impress her, but hell yes, that's what she was doing. Besides, Aydan needed something for herself. Something to help her reclaim her personal identity, whether or not she wore a head cover, that was a personal choice only Aydan could make and Lori didn't care one way or another. The Aydan she cared for was shy and modest and somehow the scarf suited her. Plus she made it look damned sexy. If she ever got her hands on Aydan's brothers, she'd teach them a thing or two about what women can do.

John shuffled back in, handing her a piece of scrap paper with several numbers scribbled on one side. With a heavy discount on the second scarf, he had pared the price down to just below a thousand dollars. *What the hell.* She pulled out her credit card. "So…can we keep this just between us, man to man?"

With a kind, open smile, and snatching her credit card, he promised, "Man to man, my sweet girl, yes I think we can."

* * *

Lori tapped on the open door to Tyler's office. Waved in, she took a seat across the desk and tried to ignore the heated phone call in progress.

"Then let me make myself crystal clear. I am her partner and I will make the final decision, not you."

She couldn't guess who Ty was arguing with, but she knew from experience not to go head-to-head with Tyler Marsh. "Poor fool," she whispered.

"Oh, for God's sake. Margaret, get over yourself!"

That answered that question.

"Be my guest, go ahead call Marnie. Call Henry. You can call the fucking governor for all I care!" Tyler slammed the phone down.

"What the hell is old Mags bugging you about?"

"Argh," Tyler grunted, both fists flying up in frustration. "I hate that bitch!"

Lori smiled, trying not to enjoy her discomfort; after all, she had been through enough already.

"Can you believe it? She wants Georgie put into trauma counseling. I explained very patiently that any needs she may have, both she and I would arrange. She actually accused me of not putting Georgie first!"

"Whoa there, Tiger, don't let her get to you. If I had to guess, I think this is all about old Mags coming to terms with the fact that Georgie Porgie is truly and completely off the market. I never told you this but Margaret's been trying hard to get all chummy with me over the last year, you know, ever since she first saw you with our girl. Oh, she's always chipper, pretending to be checking up on Henry, but she never fails to fish for something on you two."

"Why? Why would she care? She's the one who left Georgie and that was six years ago."

Lori nodded. She liked these talks with Tyler. It was like having Georgie back but without the math. "She walked out on our girl the minute it looked like her 'for better or for worse' pledge was going in the worse direction. I'm sure she thought she'd have some new sugar mama on the hook in no time but in her scheming little mind, she thought she would always have Georgie to fall back on. Then you came along. Geez Ty, she was a bitch on wheels to deal with when she thought you were just the hired help, but when she got a load of that rock!" she said, pointedly looking at Tyler's engagement ring, "I think that fantasy fell apart, big-time." She made a sound of something blowing up, her hands pantomiming the explosion of her head. "Kind of boggles the mind what some folks can tell themselves."

Tyler just sat for the longest time. "I want to say that's ridiculous but…I can't. I will never forget the look in her eyes when she accused me of abusing Georgie. It wasn't so much anger as some sort of twisted glee to think me at fault."

It had been a defining moment for Lori too. Not just seeing Margaret's true colors—she already knew what kind of woman she was. It was in the way Tyler had charged in to protect Georgie, her only care for her lover. Lori wondered if anyone would ever fight for her, respect her, or believe in her the way Georgie and Tyler did with each other. "Listen kiddo, before we go upstairs I need to confess a few things to you." She quickly assured her, "No real headaches, I promise, okay?" She watched Tyler sit back in her chair and force herself down a notch. "Okay, so here's the thing you need to know. When Georgie wants to do something special for you she can't go to her human world interpreter. That's you, in case you didn't know…"

Tyler was starting to smile. "I know she turns to you when she wants help but doesn't want Marnie to just take over. So, I take it you're not too sure about her latest appeal?"

Lori was trying to find a way to talk around the request when she realized she was always better off just coming clean with Ty. "Here's the thing. She's really feeling like a piece of shit. She thinks she let you down…"

"She did let me down," Tyler insisted, "but go on."

Groaning, Lori cleared her throat, stalling for time.

Tyler stepped around her desk and took a seat in the chair next to her. "Yes, I'm mad and yes I will get over it, but with time and attention. By the way, did she mention she asked me to marry her now, as in today?"

It was easy to admire Tyler Marsh. She was tough and forthright and a perfect match for Georgie. "She loves you, Ty. She wants to fix this and she's completely lost as to how. She sent me a list of things she thought would be a good starting gesture but she's terrified of getting it wrong and frankly I'm way out of my league on this one." She fished out her cell phone, opened her text messages, and passed the phone to her.

Tyler read the lengthy text through once then again. "This is…" was as much as she could say before choking up.

"See? She just wants to do something big to prove herself. Don't worry, I told her I didn't think she needed to buy you a new car or a bigger ring. Adding your name to the deed to the condo did make sense. What did you think about the idea of buying out Dad's apartment?"

"I…we talked about annexing one of the guest rooms."

Wrapping her arm around Tyler's shoulder, Lori declared, "She just wants things to be perfect for you, but she doesn't know what you need to see from her. If you want my opinion, I think she should add your name to everything. She was planning to, right after the wedding. But I don't see any point in waiting, do you?"

"Marnie would freak!"

She chuckled at the thought. "God I do love yanking her chain. Don't worry on that point though; even Marns is on board with the make-Tyler-happy plan."

"I don't know whether to be happy or scared."

Lori withdrew her arm from Tyler's shoulder, giving it a friendly nudge. "So, did you two decide on the wedding? Are you moving things up?"

"Honestly, when she asked me last night, I wanted to go then and there. It's probably good we don't live in Las Vegas or someplace where you can get married at two a.m."

It was always a pleasure to see Tyler's stabilizing self. She did that for Georgie, kept her on an even keel, and righted her whenever the winds listed heavy against her beam. There was something else she hadn't quite understood until now. Tyler needed her too, needed Georgie's confidence in her. It was more than need. They complemented each other. That's what set them apart and what she was counting on to get them through this. "I have an idea about that. Leslie mentioned you guys are facing some seating constraints for the wedding. I was thinking we could move everything out to the boatyard. Leslie says she can cater it out there just as easy as here and if the weather cruds out we'll still have here for a backup. We'll get the big catering tents and all the fancy tables and chairs, whatever you want."

"It would make Georgie happy. I'm not sure about walking around in heels on the grass though, and what about the noise and the neighbors?"

"First off, I'll have a proper dance floor built and with the extra room you can invite some of the neighbors. Anyway, it's something for you and Georgie Porgie to talk about."

"Thanks Lori," she offered, looking pleased. Walking back around her desk, she checked her online schedule. "I've just one more thing to do before lunch. I hope you and Zoe have your plans squared away. I don't know who's been a bigger pain in my backside, Fener or Marnie. Why don't you go on up and check on how she's doing? Helen's been up there all morning."

"Will do but first…Ty, please sit down, I have something else of a personal nature to discuss."

Looking uncomfortable, she sat down, ramrod straight.

Lori had decided on the way back from John's tailor shop that she would come clean with Georgie and Tyler before she did anything stupid.

Tyler waved a hand. "Tell her I don't need a grand gesture but," she added with a wry smile, "I'll take the diamond earrings. Just make sure the jeweler comes here to see her. No more traipsing all over the Greater Buffalo Area, understood?"

Smiling, Lori had to wonder what the reaction would be when she finally said her piece. Maybe this was a sign to keep her stupid mouth shut. Or maybe not. "This is kind of about… well…see, the thing is…what I want to say is…oh crap, Ty. I feel like a friggin' teenager! You see there's this girl, uh woman, and I want to ask her out…actually I kind of want to, I dunno, court her, but, well…you see, she works here and I…"

"Oh my God, you're interested in Aydan!"

Lori sat with her mouth hanging open. Why she thought she had to go through this whole song and dance with Tyler was a complete mystery. The woman could interpret absolutely anything that tumbled from Georgie's mouth. It only made sense she would be as intuitive with her. "Please, I don't want you to get the wrong idea. I really like her, but I know she works for you guys. I promise, if she tells me to take a hike, I will, and respectfully. And no, she hasn't said or done anything to make me think she's interested. I just…she's really different than most of the girls who go for me. Is it too soon? Maybe I should wait till she's found her footing, you know?"

She watched as Tyler leaned back in the ergonomic executive chair. Somewhere in the back of her mind she knew Georgie would have personally selected it for her. All the other furniture in the room, on the entire floor, had come from the machine shop or the basement storeroom which was usually packed to the rafters.

"You want my advice, Lori?" When she nodded, Tyler said plainly, "Don't waste any time. Be patient, and be kind. Those are two things I know you can do, but do not wait. I have a very strong feeling other parties may not be as patient as you."

That struck Lori like a gut punch. Zoe! Well she wouldn't let her niece and her juvenile games impede her hopes. She intended to be a rock for Aydan, be her friend, and if she wanted more, well she'd figure that out too. "Thanks. I half expected you to rip my head off."

Tyler simply shook her head. "I know you, Lori Ann," she teased. There had been a lot of ribbing when it was discovered they shared the same middle name. "You're like Georgie on the outside, all cocksure and tough as rocks, but she's a marshmallow on the inside and so are you."

She had to admit Tyler had pegged them both right. "I'm not sure how Georgie would take the 'cock' part. You know what a prude she is." Thankfully Tyler seemed to take that well, you never quite knew if you were crossing a line with her. At least she could count on the woman telling it like it is. Suddenly she fully understood how easy it must have been for Georgie to fall for her. "I think you're the best thing to ever happen to Georgie. Thanks, Tiger. Thanks for being who you are. She needed that, and," she waved an encompassing arm to include the office and its occupants, "so did we."

Harrumphing, Tyler got to her feet. "Unless I figure out how to steer some of Georgie's projects and soon, none of us will be welcome here. Come on," she added, grabbing her phone. "Let's head upstairs. Georgie wants to have a quick look at the new plans. I think it's important to keep her involved and I know she's eager to get back to work."

Lori followed her from the corner office, past the engineers, whom Tyler greeted by name, finally waving for Aydan to join them. Spotting Zoe with a chair pulled alongside Aydan, working closely with their heads together, she tried not to openly react as a green streak ripped through her like none she'd ever known. The last time she had bristled like this was the first time she saw Marnie kissing Jack Pulaski. It was at that moment she knew their special bond had changed forever. They had been the center of each other's universe from the first day they shared a crib, until Marnie fell in love. Accepting that Jack could make her happy was easy, stepping aside so he could take that honored place had been heartbreaking, but she'd done it. That's what you did for the people you loved. Would she have to do that for Aydan and Zoe too?

"Let's go, you two," Tyler called to the cozy pair. "Henry's already upstairs and Georgie needs to see everything before Marnie arrives."

It was difficult, watching them. Aydan gathered up a stack of devices and several rolls of architectural drawings, Zoe, of course, was oblivious to her need for assistance, blabbering on, using every excuse in the book to get closer, taking liberties, reaching out to touch her arm or pat her back. It was all Lori could do not to smack her. She grabbed up all the drawings from Aydan.

"Forget something?" she snarled at Zoe.

Turning on her, Zoe looked ready for a fight, only then seeing the rolls of their own plans back on the worktable. Gathering all the materials they had lugged from the boatyard, she was quickly back, boarding the elevator with them.

Lori leaned against the back of the car, chastising herself. *What the hell am I doing? This stupid bet with Zoe is going to backfire. I'll lose my chance to get to know Aydan. Or worse, she might actually choose Zoe. Then what'll I do?*

CHAPTER FIFTEEN

The dog's paws clicked from the elevator all the way to Tyler's side in the kitchen. Scratching Maggie's head, she ordered her up to her dog bed. "Mommy's upstairs—go." Without a glance back, the dog lumbered over to the stairs, climbing up without much effort.

After a month of assuming dog duty, Aydan could easily admit how much she was enjoying taking her out for this last walk of the evening. Pushing the heavy steel door to the foyer closed, she set the lock, very much expecting this was the last day they would leave it open. With the cast off Georgie's arm, and allowed to begin weight bearing with the air cast on her leg, Georgie could finally toss the crutches.

The apartment was made to impress, the dramatic view from the ninth-floor gallery designed to overwhelm the visual senses. With Georgie's limited mobility, Tyler had bypassed the necessity of the stairs, unlocking the big steel door separating the kitchen from the eighth-floor lobby so Georgie could access the elevator to move more easily between the upper floor bedroom and the main floor library and living area.

In the four weeks Georgie had been home she had progressed without complication and with a resilience even the doctors had admired. She always gave Tyler first credit for her stellar recovery but she never forgot the effort everyone was making. She was working too, from the apartment. And the team, especially Aydan and Skip, were up and down with work and ideas all day long. The police had come and gone, briskly taking Georgie's statement about the hit-and-run. After being presented with the high quality traffic cam footage, the driver had pleaded guilty. There was still a case pending against the trucking company owner for accessory to a felony, hinged on testimony from other employees witness to the arrival of the bloodied truck. It was a good bet now that no further stress would be placed upon Georgie.

"So," Aydan began, looking to Tyler who was making her late night coffee. She couldn't believe how much the woman consumed on a daily basis. She finally understood the term "caffeine thin."

Grabbing Aydan's favorite and loading it in the machine, Tyler said, "She's upstairs reading your plans right now. I have no idea what she thinks, but she is impressed with the initiative, both from you and Skip."

Aydan beamed at the compliment. "It's just, well, the Sea Rescue Rover is such an amazing tool, it only makes sense to add functionality."

Handing her a hot chocolate, Tyler motioned for her to follow. In the months she had been living with the couple, she treasured most her late night talks with the big boss. Georgie too. Aydan was thriving under her leadership, a fact that startled her when she realized just how much her life had changed at the hands of that complicated woman.

She'd found the company complicated as well, and challenging. In the reorganization, the engineering and design departments had been divided three ways. Georgie chose fifteen engineers for her core team, offering them the chance to come aboard the fledgling division; twelve had accepted the offer and were immediately labeled Georgie's apostles. Those reluctant to join were either heavily invested in current projects or worried for the longevity of the startup. Most of the engineers stayed with DME except for those working on patents, and they were transferred to the new investment and holding division run by Lou Phipps. There were some complaints and plain old bellyaching. Whenever Aydan had to visit the DME guys on the fifth floor or the DPP engineers on seven, she was always stressed. There was definitely an attitude about them, with remarks about how lucky she was to be placed with Georgie and her apostles. She was working hard but more than that, she knew exactly how lucky she was and didn't need creepy pissy guys cornering her in the lunchroom to tell her as much.

"Oh no, please tell me Mal Devers didn't corner you again?"

"No, well yes. He wanted to know what I was hiding beneath my habit! I had no idea what he was talking about. Until he offered to save me from the nunnery. I just don't understand why Georgie would hire a guy like that."

Tyler visibly bristled. "She didn't. He was a leftover from her father's time as VP. Yes, he's been here that long. But he's Lou's problem now. Still, I won't put up with his crap."

"That's what Zoe said to him, but not as nicely as you just did." Smiling, she recalled Zoe mouthing off to the old bastard. Not that she needed her to step in. In all the months she had been working here, she was learning to stand up for herself. Devers wasn't so much a creep as he was a guy who had never learned to see women in a professional role. He would address his female coworkers with terms like honey or doll, never for a minute understanding the disrespect of his casualness. "Zoe was saying he's always like that. I guess some guys never get it."

She watched as Tyler sipped at her coffee. She knew this was her time to unwind, and watching her take a few minutes for herself, she wondered how late Georgie would read. Her injuries and rehab schedule were proving to be a test, but she never complained and neither did Tyler. If anything she seemed purely relieved to see her partner healing both physically and emotionally. After the details of Georgie's father's betrayal were brought to light, they were healing together. That impressed her most. Even after the heart attack fiasco, which was what Tyler called it, even after all that they were stronger and more devoted to each other.

"It's none of my business," Tyler said, "but how are things going on the dating front?"

She didn't blush anymore when Tyler asked these kinds of questions. Well, not as much as she used to. "Zoe's fun. Did I tell you about the dance club she took me to? It was…interesting." She watched Tyler as she finished her coffee, setting the empty mug next to her on the hearth. "I had fun," she added, feeling her answer was more than lame. She did have fun, but dancing all night wasn't her thing. Zoe had been understanding, even charming, and it set off all kinds of bells. "We had an interesting chat. She said you two used to date?"

"Date?" Clearly not happy with the description, Tyler said dismissively, "Dating, as in one date, is the history of me and Zoe. Does one date count in your book as dating?"

She had to think about that. "I guess not, but I'm not exactly an expert. I'm sorry; I didn't mean to bring it up."

"Aydan, you're our friend, mine, and Georgie's. If you have concerns, talk. You know that."

She nodded, knowing she was right. She had been a friend, they both had been friends to her, but like Georgie's need for an interpreter, Tyler had become a sort of cultural counselor to her. "She's very pretty, but she's very young. I know she's trying hard to acclimate me to the real world, I just…I guess I'm not sure why." When she realized Tyler wasn't going to comment, she pushed herself to answer her own question. "It's not that I don't think she's attracted to me, she's made that point clear. Still… can I ask, when you were dating, sorry, went on your one date, why didn't you go out again?"

"Good question," Tyler said, sitting up a little straighter. "I'm not sure how Zoe's been behaving with you, but she can be a little aggressive. Then, of course, there was Georgie. I had no idea she was interested in me, but the Monday morning after that one date brought proof positive in so many ways. Zoe and I spent most of the night dancing at the club. What we didn't know was Georgie and Lori were there too. I found out on

Monday after we learned Georgie had been up the rest of the weekend working on a new project just to keep her mind off what she thought was going on between Zoe and me. It wasn't until I told her I had no intention of dating Zoe that I realized how much she cared. There was this aura of relief that seemed to pour from her."

"You are the center of her universe," Aydan commented; then felt suddenly shy for saying as much.

"And she's mine," she admitted gently. "She changed my life, not that it was bad or anything. It just missed that special thing that happens when you find someone who fits you." Tyler's smile telegraphed her conviction. "The thing is, I never really noticed Georgie until that moment. I was sitting in the library there..." She pointed casually. "I was a mess. I'm embarrassed to admit I'd been crying. She sat down with me, thinking she needed to explain company policy to me on relationships with coworkers, but I had thought she was giving me a warning or maybe worse, letting me go."

"Oh my God!"

"I know. I laugh now, but it was really upsetting. The thing is she just sat with me, no pressure at all, but it was more than that. It was really a defining moment for me. Right up to then I had felt I was fighting everything, work, the university, the whole world in a way, and here was this amazing woman, sitting quietly, patiently, as if I was the most important thing to her."

She stood, stretching her back. Turning for the kitchen, empty mugs in hand, she stopped, looking over carefully at Aydan. "At the time I had no idea what I had just put her through. She had seen Zoe and me together and was instantly confronted with her feelings, and trust me Georgie can act out with the best of them. She'd worked without rest, day and night, until she sat down with me. I know it's her emotional stress tell, but being there listening to her reassurances I felt like I had someone in my corner. Setting our one little hiccup aside, I know she will always fight for me, in every sense. So here's my suggestion when it comes to women. Ask yourself, will she fight for me? Not just to protect you or stand up for you, but will she put her needs and wants behind yours or will she expect you to do that for her first? Expectations are like karma, if you don't acknowledge they exist, they often come back to kick you in the pants." With that said she loaded the last stray items into the dishwasher and headed upstairs.

Aydan sat with her book, the warmth of the fireplace to keep her company. What a strange chat. How could just a few minutes of personal conversation with either one of her bosses open doors of thought she never considered examining? *Or have I just avoided exploring myself?*

* * *

Tyler walked into the bedroom to find their bed empty. What she did find was a gift box. It was savagely wrapped and she grinned knowing Georgie must have done it herself. She had learned long ago that her wife-to-be had zero talent or patience when it came to things she called frilly details. It would be tempting to just open whatever it was, but this wasn't just a simple gift, this had become a daily activity. Georgie was still desperate to earn her forgiveness and had taken to barraging her with presents.

Telling her—more than once—that it wasn't necessary hadn't slowed her effort, nor was it really helping. What she needed, longed for, was not this anxious creature but Georgie's solidity. She wanted the heroine back, the fearless warrior, however broken. Shaking the box, she felt something inside slide soundlessly. Probably a sweater, she decided, and was about to leave it and go find Georgie when she spotted the card that had been sitting underneath the box. She opened it and read directions to wear whatever the gift was and head to the foyer. "Okay…so you want to play?"

Pulling off the paper, she opened a shoebox to find the most exquisite pair of handmade moccasins. Not a fan of animal furs, she was pleased to see the traditional rabbit pelt used to make the lining and cuff were of a deep pile fleece. The split moose hide exterior was fully beaded and beautifully detailed but it was the vamp design that caught her attention. It took a moment to put it all together and when she did she almost cried. Blue flag irises stood in gorgeous glass beads. They were the first flowers Georgie had ever sent her and she knew she must have had the moccasins made for her. That was just like Georgie. Instead of just dropping by the Seneca Trading post and grabbing a nice pair, she had ordered exactly what she knew Tyler would want. Without a second thought she slipped them on her bare feet, noting the perfect fit. *These were made just for me.* It was an idea she still had trouble wrapping her head around. Of course Georgie had a handsome income, not so much from her salary, most of which she often rolled into her special project budget and department R&D, but from her extensive investment and real estate portfolio. She herself would always say she had been very lucky, and Tyler was always relieved to see her heart was in the right place when it came to her wealth. She donated extravagantly, spent only on what she needed or what she believed Tyler wanted, and never really imagined needing more. Her only departure from this had been these last four weeks since their breakup fiasco. Thank God Marnie and Lori had reined her in on that front. Who knows how far she would have gone, although it did please that little-girl place in the back of her mind where her princess would shower her with gifts and fine horse-drawn carriages in a storybook effort to prove her love.

Slipping from the bedroom, she made her way to the foyer. The apartment door had been left propped open. Leading from the door was a line of burning tea candles. That made her smile. She had spent some time explaining to Georgie that bigger gifts weren't the answer. She wanted bigger acts. "Show me how much you care," she'd told her. "I know you can buy me anything, baby. That's not what I need. I need to know you're here for me, now and forever."

That had been hard for Georgie to understand. Actually, it had been like pulling teeth but that was the good and bad about her, and they had spent many a long evening discussing all the things that really mattered to each other. That had been an eye-opener, not just for Georgie, but for her too. She knew

Georgie appreciated all the efforts she made at her side but she noticed the little things as well. The woman was like a hawk; she saw everything, everything except for the fact that giving up on them would cause Tyler pain.

Pushing the fire door open, she was surprised by the sheer number of lit candles lining the stairs. Stepping carefully, she followed the trail to the roof as a tingling excitement began its way up her spine. She liked this, loved this, Georgie's rooftop romanticisms. When she and Lori had brought her home from recuperating at the big house, Tyler wanted to do something special and immediately decided it was time to create a full-time rooftop patio. Other than putting out heaters and ashtrays for the annual New Year's gathering, the rooftop sat empty all year long. She didn't know if Mr. Fener, the contractor working on all the changes to the building, held Georgie in such high esteem or was just plain scared of her, but he had the roof patio constructed in days with terraced decking and seating and dining areas. There were large box planters everywhere, and she and Georgie had spent all last weekend choosing and planting flowers and colorful shrubs.

At the top landing, the fire door was propped open and she could see even more candles ahead. Stepping out in the late evening, she marveled at the display. A sea of candlelight blazed in soft contrast against a starry night sky. Standing, staring, she was overwhelmed. This is what Georgie did, orchestrating these perfect moments of pure joy. Stuck in place, Tyler felt her presence. And then she was there. Quietly, Georgie stepped up beside her, gently placing a supportive hand on her back.

"Baby…" Until that moment, she was unaware of the tears rolling down her cheeks.

Unassumingly, Georgie offered her hand. "I'm here," she said quietly.

Georgie led her toward the new patio area. In the wide space in front of the long built-in bench she had arranged what looked like all the patio cushions, some blankets and even pillows. Tyler wasn't sure where the pillows had come from but had a sneaking suspicion Georgie had raided Henry's guest room. It all looked so cozy and inviting, she couldn't help turning and wrapping her arms around her neck. She loved that, the way she could just drape herself over Georgie, and how Georgie's arms, so strong, could encompass and protect her. She had missed this, this feeling of need from Georgie, her complete and utter belief in them together. Easing her tight grip, she consented to stretching out on the makeshift bed. At first she had wondered why the patio daybed hadn't been utilized until she sat down among the cushions. By creating this nest, set so low, they were below the roof's parapet and the wind blowing in off the lake. The cool evening temperature, slightly high for this first week of May, was more than comfortable, sheltered as they were from the night wind. As Georgie fussed with a blanket, making sure she was nestled in safe and warm, she noted, "I can't believe you went to all this trouble."

"For my Tyler...anything."

There was so much sincerity and promise in that statement, she was almost tempted to let everything go, but how could she? "Baby, I know you're trying. God, how you do things, and I'm so glad you didn't jump into the deep end with the gifts and all. And the slippers too, they're beautiful. Irises, blue irises, you remembered..."

At the long pause, Georgie begged, "I'm listening...please, my Tyler...explain."

Nestling closer, she stared at the stars, searching for words. That was the great thing about Georgie; she would wait patiently for as long as it took for her to sort her thoughts or decide how she wanted to raise a painful issue. It wasn't necessary to present them cautiously. The woman always listened and never took offense. She honestly believed that anything Tyler was feeling was valid and worth sharing, even the negative things. She had never known anyone who could so successfully set her ego aside to listen, really listen to personal criticism.

"I'm still so mad at you!" blasted out of nowhere. Admitting it to herself was almost as revealing as Georgie's reply.

"I know...me too."

"Who are you mad at?"

"Me," she admitted easily. "I gave up."

That admission stalled Tyler's racing thoughts. It wasn't as if Georgie hadn't taken responsibility for her actions or explained herself before, in detail, however haltingly. Now, in this moment, she appeared to comprehend her actions more clearly than ever. "You realized something. Is it your long talks with Aunt Helen?"

She nodded, closing her eyes, "That too."

Tyler waited, recognizing that whatever she was about to share she had prepared in advance. That was a good sign. She liked to think Georgie was working on this, sorting it out. She didn't want her feeling sick or guilty, but she needed to understand the true catalyst.

"I have…never given up…Even after Afghanistan…"

"But you left Margaret," Tyler challenged her. Adding, "And then you left me."

Georgie's eyebrows raised as a gentle grin brightened her face. "Oh no…you talked to…her?"

"Yes. Yes I did and you can't blame me!" It was all she could do to remain still. Her natural inclination was to stand and pace whenever she was riled up.

"No blaming, promise. My Tyler…tell you a secret?" At her nod, Georgie explained, "When I came back…remembered no one. No one…I just followed…Marnie, Lori were strangers too."

"What, wait…" She sat up to look at her, then settled back in, resting on an elbow to face her. "If you didn't remember anyone, why would you ask to be moved from Margaret's— correction, the home you and Margaret shared—back to the big house?"

She shook her head. "Told the VA doctors…No more strangers. I want to go…back to rehab, not family."

"I don't understand. What about Henry, you knew who he was?"

Again she shook her head. "Very nice man asked…come stay…hear old sounds…see old faces…maybe remember.

The doctors too…said try. Don't give up…I like a challenge. Margaret too…said she would stay…with me."

"I don't understand then, what changed, why did you leave her?" she pushed.

"Oh no, my Tyler." Georgie's eyes were moist, kindness and honesty radiating. "Aunt Georgie's bedroom…my old room, it was…catalyst." She reached to Tyler, brushing an errant strand of hair from her eyes and back behind her ear. "My room, first…Then Henry. Just his voice…nothing more. Margaret… Margaret was restless. And I wasn't…" For the first time, Georgie looked away, unwilling to meet her eyes.

"Oh no you don't! I know you, Georgina. You just spit out whatever's embarrassing you so much."

Georgie smiled at her flare of temper. "You will be…good mom."

"Stop stalling."

Still not meeting her eyes, Georgie took a deep breath, finally rushing out the story like a misfiring engine. "She wanted…I couldn't…not yet, not then…couldn't explain…she…she was hurt. Then ultimatums…fighting, fighting…made it worse. I just couldn't…she…"

Sitting a little higher, Tyler took in the shame on Georgie's face. She cupped her cheek and turned her head to make eye contact. "Are you saying she moved into the big house with you, stayed in your old room too?" At her nod, she pushed on to the part she knew would have humiliated her partner, especially in the one-sided sexual relationship she shared with her ex. "So you're saying she left when you wouldn't fuck her?"

Even in the candlelight, it was easy to see Georgie was embarrassed. It was amusing and curious how shy she was when it came to talking about sex. Funny too, considering the woman had zero problems expressing herself when they made love. "Baby, I have to say, I hate her and love her." That drove Georgie's brows way up. "I hate her for being such a bitch and yes, what you're saying makes sense and it fits with a few weird things she's said, you know, off the cuff when she wasn't paying attention. And I'm just realizing how thankful I am for that woman's crass, social climbing 'Oh look at me, I'm a victim' bullshit. She gave up on you and that was my good fortune. What I don't understand is why you didn't leave her."

"I made a commitment...even if I didn't...remember."

That made Tyler mad and she was sitting up again. She couldn't look at Georgie. "So you were willing to live up to your commitment to a bitch you didn't even remember, but you have no problem walking away from me? What the fuck, Georgie!" She felt a warm hand on her back, slowly rubbing small circles. Angry and confused, all she wanted to do was shake off that hand. Shake it off and walk away.

"I don't do...scared, very well," Georgie admitted quietly. Her hand had stilled on her back but she didn't withdraw physically, she seemed to understand Tyler's inclination to bolt. "All I could see...all I could think...me letting you down... me leaving you alone...you and our babies...I broke inside. My Tyler, I did not...give up on you. I gave up on me...I gave up. Never been so scared..." She added, almost in a whisper, "Never."

"Afghanistan?" Tyler questioned weakly. "You must have been scared when you went down in Afghanistan?"

"Yes," she admitted, "but different...I had training...I had procedures...and I had pain, pain, my companion." She explained, "Pain kills fear."

Georgie had never confessed to the pain or commented on how she had survived that long night broken and alone. "You never told me that."

"Never told anyone," she acknowledged, moving to sit knee to knee and take Tyler's hands in hers. "With you...with this," she said, tapping a hand above her heart, "I have no...ROE."

"Rules of Engagement?" Tyler asked then questioned, "but how does that..."

Georgie squeezed both her hands, holding eye contact as she explained, "No solution...First time ever. I knew I would...fail you. It killed me, and I...I gave up, not on you, not my Tyler...I gave up...on me...on getting better...on life."

"You were scared," she said in a whisper. It felt almost silly, but something about the idea of Georgie being frightened was so wrong. "I've never known you to be scared of anything. Well, not anything important. Things like people and therapy, but not me, not the future?"

That garnered an immediate smile. "Your first week." Now she was grinning, really grinning. "I could barely breathe... when you...seeing you."

"Please," Tyler laughed, releasing some of her building tension. "You were cool as a cucumber."

Smiling, Georgie leaned in giving her a soft, promising kiss. It was the kind of kiss that always confused her, tempting and promising but patient too. Finally she asked the one thing that had been eating at her the most. "Did you even think of me, you know, over the weekend, back in the big house in your old room?"

"I thought always...I didn't deserve you." She looked away for the longest time, finally saying, "First night, trying to rest, in my room...Aunt Georgie's room, empty. I was empty too. So much loss...everything hurt...this most." She tapped above her heart again. "Felt stupid...failure too...I wanted you but... didn't know how. How do I fix me? How do I find...solution? Heart attack...fear...protect you. No way to fix!"

"Please tell me you weren't really trying to create an algorithm to solve the problem?" She asked this as a joke, remembering Lori's insistence and Helen's agreement that it was the only problem solving mechanism she had. The glimmer she saw in those telling eyes said everything. "Oh my God! You did?"

Without explanation and only the slightest hesitancy, Georgie withdrew a folded sheet of paper from the back pocket of her jeans, handing it over.

Tyler had to reach out for one of the nearby candles for enough light. She examined the paper first. The header read 'From the Desk of Georgina DiNamico.' Tyler had no recollection of ordering custom notepads, then realized the paper must have been from her Aunt Georgina's desk, and noting the aged and yellowing edges, she understood her fiancée must have written this that weekend back at the big house. The first section was indeed a ridiculous algorithm, but more telling was all that followed.

After more than a year of reading through Georgie's project notes she recognized her logic. First she would try to capture all the data points influencing a given problem, create a basic algebraic formula that explained her proposed process, and then list all the unknown variables. This list of variables was more telling than anything she could have said. "You wanted to call Friday night?" she asked, but didn't wait for an answer. They were all right there on that single methodically detailed page. "How could you keep telling yourself it was best for me, if you were so hoping I would come for you?"

"More time...fear for you became...shame in me. And... never been so...terrified."

She sat for the longest time, just looking at Georgie, looking into her eyes. She was like no one she had ever known. "You said babies, plural." It was even included in the problem set, proof positive that leaving a family behind was an issue for her. "Did you mean that?"

"Of course," she said, with an open look that confirmed it was true. "Still, scared for you alone...if I should die but...more scared...living without you."

In that moment it wasn't the gifts, or the promises, or even Georgie's patience that had made the difference. How was it a woman with so many challenges conveying her thoughts verbally could say so much? She would always tell Tyler it was her own listening skills and ability to comprehend her broken thoughts that made all the difference. Whether that was true or not, something was shifting in her, something she worried could never be righted.

"Baby, I have a secret too." At Georgie's questioning look, she explained. "I know you get scared and I know you think you have to pull through everything all alone but you don't, never again. I don't care if we only have a few years—but I have a feeling you're too damn tough for even Kevlar to kill. I want us to spend a long life together. I want our kids to grow up learning cool things from you. I'll take care of the scary stuff, I will baby, I promise. Now you promise me, next time you think you might let me down and don't know what to do, you send me a text. Even if I'm sitting beside you, understand?"

Tyler leaned in, wrapping her arms around her neck and kissing her cheek, she whispered, "Next time, just text '*Stay with me*.'"

* * *

Sitting in her screened-in porch, Lori had been contemplating the darkened beach for hours when she heard a car stop and a door slam. Assuming it was a noisy neighbor coming home from a late night on the town, she was startled when Peachy tripped the motion sensor and set off the outside lights. *Fuck, just what I need.*

After presenting a stunned and stammeringly grateful Aydan with the scarves—downplaying if not masking their expense—she had waited a couple of days before asking Aydan out, and she had been wallowing in her rejection ever since. Oh, she had been sweet, explaining she just needed a little more time. Lori tried to take comfort knowing nothing had happened between Zoe and Aydan, at least not yet. Zoe, she knew, would waste zero time in sharing that victory.

"Helloooo!"

"Geez Peachy, what the hell are you doing here?"

"Nice, Phipps! Who pissed in your cornflakes?" she snorted, making her way into the screen porch without invitation. "Aren't you happy to see me?"

"No, as a matter of fact, I'm not. I'm sorry but I need time alone. I told you that, remember?"

"Oh you big goof, I don't mind dropping by and cheering you up. What's got you all in a gruff anyway?" She was outfitted in a tight-fitting dress, and kicking off her heels, she swatted Lori's hand from her lap and planted herself down, taking her time to shamelessly grind her ass into Lori's crotch.

"Knock it off!" she snarled, getting to her feet and dumping the woman from her lap. "Come on Peachy, we talked about this. I don't want that with you."

"Oh, take it down a notch there, stud. I was just having a little fun."

"You sound like some stupid frat boy." Storming into the kitchen and grabbing herself another beer, she tried to figure out what to do, just how rude she was willing to be.

Reaching into the fridge for her own beer, Peachy offered casually, "Listen, I'm sorry. I just had a bad night and thought, selfishly thought, you would cheer me up. Looks like you're the one who needs cheering. So, what's so eating at you that you're not interested in a little fun?"

Lori took her beer to the kitchen table. As much as she needed to talk she instinctively understood this was not the woman who should hear what was on her mind. If anything, Peachy was the exact opposite. Picking at the label on the bottle, she tried to get as far from her thoughts of Aydan as possible. "So I guess the club was a bust tonight?"

Groaning, the woman slid into a chair next to her before taking a long pull on her own beer. "Ugh! What a meat market. And the women, it's as if they get younger and younger every week. I swear it was like a friggin' pre-school in there tonight. How the hell's a girl gonna get some with a crowd like that?"

"So you figured you'd just head over here for a little servicing?" The disgust in her voice was more than enough to make her feelings understood. They had been through this before and each time Peachy had assured her there was nothing between them. "We're just friends," she would say, before offering additional benefits.

Lori had to question her own behavior. The truth was she didn't see a problem with that or hadn't until she tried to examine Aydan's view if it were to ever come up and somewhere in the back of her mind she knew one day it would. Peachy was just like that. Actually, she was a lot like Zoe. Whenever they spotted some shiny bauble they might like, they went for it with gusto. It was the losing interest most people weren't prepared for and women like Peachy and Zoe could lose interest in a heartbeat. That was the worst part for Lori. She had just assumed Peachy would lose interest in her. This constant boomeranging was wearing her down and fraying her nerves.

"Okay, so you want to be pissy all night. I get it, so you struck out too. Want to tell me about it?"

"No!" Lori refused to fall into that trap.

"Fine already." Peachy shot back. "Come on, grouch. Let's go watch a movie," she suggested as she made her way to the living room, beer in hand. "We can watch a friggin' movie, come on, friends do that you know."

Giving in, Lori shuffled after her. It was just a movie. *And that's all it will ever be.*

CHAPTER SIXTEEN

Waving off the offer of assistance, Tyler poured her own coffee before sitting down at Lori's kitchen table. She watched as Peachy fussed, pulling out the ingredients for breakfast.

"I wish Lori had told me you and Georgie were coming," Peachy said. "I would have used the one-cup thingy instead of brewing a whole pot. Now I feel bad. Will Georgie be okay?"

"She'll be fine," Tyler promised. She had watched Georgie's reaction to Peachy welcoming them in and knew that more than the smell of coffee had driven her back out. With Maggie at her side and Lori's golden retriever on her heels, she had waved off Tyler's concern. "Just need air," she had reassured her, turning for the beach and most probably a quick visit with Helen just a dozen doors away. "Actually, we weren't planning on breakfast. Lori was supposed to meet us at the boatyard. When she didn't show and didn't answer her phone, we decided to walk over."

"Oh that nut-bar!" she offered with affection. Clearly she was in her element, reveling in her self-imposed role as hostess to Lori's guests. "I'm afraid we had a few too many last night but you know what it's like."

Actually I don't and neither does my dismayed and disappointed fiancée. "Why don't you let me start the bacon, so you can go get dressed?"

Peachy was literally barefoot in Lori's kitchen and wearing nothing but a skimpy robe. Of course both she and Georgie had seen a lot more of Peachy during the shakedown cruise but this felt weird, as if they had just caught Lori cheating.

"Oh I'm fine, Ty. Can I make you another—"

"Peachy," Lori growled from the doorway, "go get dressed, I've got this." Her fresh-from-the-shower appearance did nothing to hide the ravages of a serious hangover. "What are you doing here?" she demanded the moment Peachy was gone.

"Really?" Tyler asked, shaking her head. She got up from the table, setting her half-finished coffee in the sink and removing the unattended frying pan from the burner. She hissed, "You were supposed to meet us at the boatyard and your phone is off so give me a break if we were concerned."

Lori looked like she would snap back at her, argue. Instead she slumped into a kitchen chair.

Tyler moved to stand at the patio doors. Looking out onto the beach, she watched as Georgie tossed a stick for the dogs to fetch. When she finally heard the sound of the shower running upstairs, she turned to Lori. "What the fuck!"

"I know, I know," she groaned, this time in shame or perhaps some sort of self-loathing.

"What happened? You've been all gaga over a certain woman we know for months now."

Lori stood, pushing herself to the counter. Her hands were shaking when she reached for a coffee mug.

"Stop!" Tyler said, and told her, "Sit down before you fall down. I'll get your coffee."

Lori slid back into her chair.

"Where's the booze?" Tyler asked then stormed past her, returning with a bottle of Crown Royal, adding a finger to Lori's mug.

Wide-eyed, she stared, "I don't think…"

"Drink it!" Tyler ordered. "I'm not in the mood for your bullshit today, Phipps." She poured another coffee before joining her. "I don't get it. You've been going on and on about Aydan and now you're what, shacking up with Peachy?"

"It's not like that." Lori cradled her head in her hands. Finally, she took a tentative sip of her brew. "I thought you were supposed to drink tomato juice for a hangover."

"Trust me. A little hair of the dog never hurt anyone. Well, as long as you don't make it a habit," she added. "Lori, I know the world thinks you're some sort of lesbian Romeo but I know better, so does Georgie."

"Oh shit, Georgie! She'll kill me. Where is she anyway?"

"Relax. She's outside playing with the dogs and she won't kill you. She will, however, wonder what the hell's going on. Even she's figured out you've got it bad for our Aydan, and you know how obtuse she can be when it comes to these things."

Lori just groaned her reply before finally admitting, "I... you know why. You saw them last night. I'm wasting my time and you know it."

Last night, Marnie and Jack had treated all the sales and marketing staff to a dinner and included all the primaries from the other divisions. It wasn't supposed to be a big thing but Leslie offered the newly finished private dining room on the third floor, wanting to give her staff a less stressful first run. Instead of hosting a small dinner for just his sales reps, the discount Leslie offered allowed him to invite all his staff, their spouses, and close DME family members. Tyler had invited Lori up for drinks before dinner unaware that Aydan had a date with Zoe. She had tried to act cool and pretend it didn't bother her, but even Georgie had seen through that ruse, wrapping a consoling arm around her after Zoe and Aydan were out the door. At least they wouldn't be joining the dinner party. That was something she could be thankful for.

"So, what, that's it? She has one date with someone else and you give up? I can't believe it. The great Lori Phipps thinks a woman's out of her reach!"

"Buzz off," Lori warned, then swore when they heard the shower stop. "Shit Ty, now what the fuck do I do?"

Tyler moved to the glass doors to check on Georgie. She and the dogs, thankfully, were still playing. An involuntary smile crept across her face. Georgie was safe, Georgie was having fun, and she was hers, all hers. "I can't tell you what to do, but I can tell you this isn't it. Look, whether you realize it or not, you're using that girl," she said, pointing in the general direction of the upstairs bath.

"It wasn't exactly my idea..."

"What wasn't your idea, honey?" Peachy asked, strolling back in.

The woman must have set a warp speed record getting dressed. Her hair was toweled dry but hadn't been combed. Her baggy T-shirt, obviously one of Lori's, clung to her soaking back. As she passed the table, she stopped to pat Lori in a commiserating fashion before planting a peck on her head. "Oh, my poor honey. Ty, you should have seen our girl last night." She poured the last of the coffee for herself and began making a second pot. "You know, I think I'll make pancakes. That should help with your tummy, honey."

She turned her attention back to Tyler. "Why don't you have a seat, Ty? I know you can't function without at least two of these," she added, holding up her own cup.

"No thank you, Sue Ellen. Georgie and I have a full day planned and we're already behind. Now that we won't be putting the boat in the water today, I'm going to take her shopping. She needs new boots, plus she's been begging me for a visit to her favorite bookstore. Lori, can I count on you to have someone available tomorrow to operate the yard crane? Or should I have the marina staff schedule it in?"

Before Lori could respond, Peachy cut in, "Ty, it's none of my business but why can't Georgie do it herself? It really is a lot to ask of Lori on her day off. You know how hard she works."

Tyler smiled sweetly as she bristled inside. This was Lori's mess to clean up, not hers. She slid the patio door open, stepping out into the screened-in deck before answering, "Of course it is. Unfortunately, running a company isn't always a nine-to-five job." Turning to Lori she added, "Let me know about getting the boat in. Georgie would indeed do it herself but it's not a one-person job. And Lori, please think about that other project. I don't imagine you want to miss out on that one if you can help it." With that she strolled out of the house and across the beach.

Georgie looked so cute, playing some sort of game with the dogs. When she looked up, she smiled. That was Georgie, her Georgie, full of life and love. Tyler couldn't help herself, walking right to her and wrapping herself into her as tightly as she could. There was no hesitation; Georgie's arms were strong and welcoming. She had come to count on that. "Guess what, baby. It's just you and me today. Feel like doing some shopping? We could hit the shops or head to the mall."

"Old Editions?" she asked with a happy grin.

"Yes, we can hit the bookstore too."

Still grinning, Georgie called to the loping dogs. "FALL IN!" It was her back-to-work command for Maggie, and by habit Izzy, Lori's golden, trotted to her side as well. She connected Maggie's lead before signaling for Izzy to follow them up to the house. A dozen steps in that direction and Izzy broke formation running to her wilted mother who was waiting on the deck stairs.

"Morning, sorry I slept in. Any chance you want some breakfast? Peachy's making pancakes."

Georgie shook her head. "Rest...call later. We will reschedule."

Tyler watched as Lori silently pleaded with her cousin. Eventually Georgie offered a lifeline. It was what Tyler had come to think of as the DiNamico/Phipps Get-Out-Of-Jail-Free card. She said loudly enough for Peachy to hear, "Important project to discuss...Tyler will text...time. Can't put off...understand?"

"Yeah," Lori answered, providing the appropriate look of contrition. "Sorry Georgie, I'll get my act together and bring over those reports you wanted to see. I can have everything at the office by the time you're back from the bookstore."

Georgie nodded, turning to leave, then stopped. "My Tyler...should...leave Maggie?"

She nodded. "Actually that's a good idea. She gets so bored with you in the bookstore and Lori has to come into the office anyway. You don't mind, do you Lori?" It was all Tyler could do to keep a straight face. Peachy was standing in the enclosed porch, arms crossed, listening to every word.

Lori accepted Maggie's leash. "I'll see you two later, thanks for understanding."

As they strolled back toward the boatyard, Georgie reached out to take Tyler's hand. "She okay?"

"I think she's having an uncharacteristic bout of timidity."

Georgie groaned her sympathy. "Been there...especially with...competition."

"What competition?"

She smiled, pulling her closer and wrapping her arm around Tyler's waist. "Competition for you," she admitted simply. "Not like Zoe...I suffered...lack confidence too."

Unable to resist, Tyler planted a long slow kiss on her wife-to-be. "Mmm, I can't believe we're getting married in three weeks."

Leaning back against the truck, she took Georgie in her arms and pulled her close to stand between her legs. "I don't trust Zoe with Aydan but it's not our place to get involved. I've been careful to infuse a little reality with her, but it's really up to her and frankly, Zoe can be charming when she wants."

"Aydan," Georgie asked. "Should I try?"

"No baby, not yet, she'll come to us when she's ready for advice. I know she's not a kid, but maybe we should think of her that way. If we try to influence her now, we may just alienate her and she's already come so far."

Georgie nodded, leaning in closer, taking full advantage of Tyler's exposed neck. She worked her way methodically from just below her ear to nip along her collarbone, before moving on to the pulse points in her neck.

Tyler surrendered her lips and all conscious thought to Georgie's clever, clever mouth. It was easy to get lost in her attention. Her hands were under her spring jacket, skillfully making their way to her breasts when a car horn blasted close by. "Hey you two, get a room!"

"Dad!" Tyler cried, releasing Georgie after a reassuring hug. For some reason her father enjoyed embarrassing the two of them whenever he could and catching them in the middle of a hot and heavy make-out session definitely gave him lots of fuel for his arsenal of jokes. Secretly it pleased her. Even Georgie had said it was refreshing in a way, noting how uniquely accepting the man was of his daughters and their multifaceted lives.

He climbed from his classic Corvette. The top was down and his ears and nose looked red. "So, I see my girls are doing fine, but I don't see the boat in the water?"

"Lori's a little under the weather this morning," Tyler explained.

He laughed good-heartedly. "I tell you, I wish I'd had her stamina when I was half her age. Boy oh boy, the trouble I would have gotten myself into."

"You!" Georgie jokingly challenged, "Debbie had you…" She made a winding signal with one hand around her other.

He was laughing too. "Oh, you are so right. She had me wrapped around her finger in seconds and my head's still spinning from the first day we met."

"You are lucky." Georgie told him both looking amused and sincere.

He wrapped his big bear arms around them both. "As it should be. Come on," he urged, "come on over to the car shed." It was what they were now calling the old millwork building she had made available to him and his Car Club buddies as a free workspace. "Wait till you see our new project!"

*　*　*

Aydan was restless, pacing the open space of the new office. Not everything was in place yet. The office movers were sure they could get everything upstairs in one day but had booked the entire weekend to move the new division from the second floor to the newly finished offices on eight. While the movers took their lunch break, she inspected their progress with a critical eye. The details mattered to her, but they mattered even more to Georgie and she wanted to get this right for her.

On Thursday she and Tyler had taken her to the fracture clinic for follow-up X-rays. When everything checked out, they had removed the arm cast. The air cast on her leg would need another few weeks but she could dump the crutches and was already weight bearing. She wasn't sure who was happier about her progress, Georgie or her very excited dog. She had gotten used to walking the dog and secretly hoped she could continue doing so. It was nice to walk at night, feeling secure and unafraid. It wasn't as if Maggie was a trained attack dog, but she was protective of Georgie. When it was just her and Aydan out for a walk, the dog's protectiveness encompassed her too.

What an interesting sensation, knowing something would stand up for her without question. Tyler and Georgie too were protective in their own way. It was almost comical except for her instinctive sense that she needed their help. Perhaps it explained why getting the new office just right was so important to her. They believed in her and were giving her the opportunities no one else had. She wanted to surprise them both and getting them out of the building and away from the eighth floor for the move had been her one request.

Aydan had been invited out to the boatyard with them. The Memorial Day long weekend was usually when Georgie and Lori got the big family sailboat into the water. She had been interested, not in the sailboat but in the mechanics of moving a fifty-foot vessel. When the annual exercise was added to Georgie's schedule, Lori had offered to teach Aydan how to operate the yard crane. She wasn't sure which part of the invitation appealed to her more, a firsthand chance to operate the big machine, or the time with Lori.

It was strange, really. Up until last night, she had spent a lot of time thinking about women and relationships, and the Phipps women in particular. Zoe was a beautiful girl, no doubt there. Aydan had marveled at the joy of having a young woman like that take an interest in her. She was charming and turned heads wherever they went, but as big a boost as her ego got from that kind of attention, it didn't exactly make for solid ground for a bond. She wasn't so naïve to believe other women hadn't built better relationships on less, but was that really fair? Besides, Zoe was so young, not in life experience like herself, but in so many other ways. Everyone agreed she had grown up a lot in the last year after she'd found herself on the wrong side of a family divide, but she had put in her time with the Dark Side, and was now earning her way into Lori's division. She was proud of her for that, but secretly worried she carried some resentment. Still, it was easy to sympathize, wondering if she too would have backed her father in a family struggle, and knowing that in the end she would have made the same choice as her friend.

My friend! And the truth of that hit her with full force. That's how I think of Zoe. She's not the woman I'm dating, and she's not the woman I want.

She saw Zoe as her friend. Sitting on the edge of one of the large casement windows, she felt a moment of overwhelming pain. *No wonder Georgie creates crazy algorithms trying to figure this stuff out.*

"There you are!"

"Lori!" Aydan stood, strolling over to meet her halfway. "How are you? Tyler sent a text telling me you were coming over later today. I'm sorry I didn't know when or I would have been waiting for you next door."

"Whoa there, princess," Lori offered with a charming smile that always worked to ease her concerns. "I'm just trying to make myself useful. I kind of screwed the pooch this morning. Any chance you might be interested in helping me make things up to Georgie and Ty?"

Not understanding what she was talking about and uncomfortable asking, she simply smiled her interest. "What have you got in mind?" That answer brought a smirk to Lori's face and Aydan almost colored at the pleasure invoked by just being nice to this woman. It was such a contrast to her reaction to Zoe and unlike the warning bells the young woman set off, Lori's indomitable spirit just seemed to lift her from all corners.

"Well, let's see. Have they got anything scheduled for this evening? I mean, we could take them to dinner or…"

"We?" Aydan teased.

"Uh, oh, well I…"

It was sweet to see Lori get so tongue-tied. She loved doing that, rocking the boat with this handsome and confident woman, and she never got upset. If anything, she seemed to enjoy the challenge. Aydan said, "Yes, we can take them to dinner, but I think they would be just as happy with a home-cooked meal and us for company. What do you think? Actually," she added before letting Lori answer, "there's a movie I've been wanting to watch. Tyler said they have it in their library and would love to see it together. It's called *Carol.*"

That idea drove a bigger smile up Lori's face. "Good plan, just one hitch. I can't cook."

Aydan took her arm, casually steering her across the foyer to Georgie and Tyler's living room and kitchen. Proud of her boldness in actually taking Lori's arm, she explained as they walked, "Let's take a look at what we can put together without having to ask Leslie to bail us out."

"That's always an option."

"I know, but Georgie and Tyler don't like fancy stuff all the time. Maybe some old-fashioned comfort food is exactly what they would enjoy."

"Hmm." Lori nodded, and watched as Aydan began opening cupboards and mentioning ingredients. "I don't know what to do with all that stuff."

Aydan, turning to her, was enjoying her discomfort way too much. "Your sister is an award-winning chef, one of the best in western New York, and you can't figure out what to do with sweet potatoes?"

Shaking her head, Lori pulled out one of the stools at the large kitchen island. "I'll have you know, I grill a wicked steak."

Taking in her infectious grin, Aydan challenged, "Okay then, how about we put that new barbeque to good use. I remember Georgie mentioning how she's looking forward to the warm weather and getting up to the new roof patio. It certainly looks like it's warm enough," she said, taking in Lori's T-shirt and jeans. It was easy to admire the woman, not just for her strength, but her casualness in everything but her work.

Zoe too liked to have fun but not with the same understanding of purpose and balance. She probably would in time, but Aydan wasn't willing to wait out her maturation, and watching Lori as she tabbed out a grocery list on her phone, she now understood why.

I may just be coming out and finding myself in this new world but I'm not a kid. I don't want to spend the next decade sowing wild oats when I know exactly what I want.

Dating, flirting, dancing, were all great, but it wasn't her and never would be. Sarah might have been the first woman she felt any attraction to, but she understood now that Sarah would not have been her one great love. Watching Tyler and Georgie had taught her that. Love needed more than attraction. Of course, attraction was a good place to start. Lori was attractive to her, maybe even more so than Zoe. Like Tyler she was taller than Aydan, and Lori was solid, a harder quality to describe. Something about her strong form and irrepressible joy always awoke a sense of fun in her, a lightness she hadn't known since her father's untimely death. Maybe that was it. She was a joker like him and with a tender heart too.

"Okay," Lori said, her eyes still on her phone as she read out her shopping list. "Anything else? Should I get wine? I'm pretty good with that."

"No you're not!" she joked, loving Lori's assertiveness. "You do exactly what I do. Either you ask Leslie to choose or you just buy the most expensive bottle in the place."

"Do not!" Lori argued but couldn't keep a straight face. "Oh, I'm so busted. How did you figure it out?"

"Who do you think I learned it from?"

Lori was laughing as she pocketed her phone and stretched. Aydan stood fixed in place watching as the soft cotton of her T-shirt pulled tight across her cut abs and high small breasts. She couldn't deny the attraction was there, but was it enough? She had thought about Tyler's advice to look for a woman who would stand up for her. She knew Zoe was a fiery sort who took no prisoners, and while that was appealing, she did question who exactly Zoe was trying to protect. Lori, on the other hand, left no doubts as to who and what she cared for.

Lori strolled toward the elevator, stopping at the threshold to the foyer. "So dinner and a movie sounds good. Uhm...so, it's a date?"

Aydan smiled at her, how could she not? "Yes Lori, it's a date," she said, following her out and pulling the steel panel door shut. "I might need your help tonight keeping Georgie out of the new office. I want to surprise her on Monday morning."

"Good luck with that," Lori joked, adding in a more supportive tone, "I'll do everything I can to make that happen for you, but even I have only so much influence with my crazy cousin."

Taking her arm, Aydan steered her to the elevators. "Well, between you, me, and Tyler, we may just be able to pull it off. Of course we could call in your dad and Helen. They've been making great headway with her."

Lori pressed the call button, giving Aydan's hand a light squeeze. "Yeah, they're pretty good, but no one's the equal of the great Georgie whisperer." At Aydan's raised brow, she explained, "The great and talented Doctor Tyler Marsh, PhD."

Grinning, she had to admit it was an apt description of the big boss and her friend. When the elevator opened, she pushed Lori into the open car, telling her, "Go on you. Go find us some perfect steaks and don't forget to ask Leslie about the wine."

* * *

"Come here, baby," Tyler said, getting herself comfortable in the corner of the couch. She had pulled over the long ottoman from the living area to extend the legroom for Georgie.

Grinning and bouncing on one foot, Georgie managed to turn around and back in to nestle between Tyler's legs.

"See! I told you this would work."

"Should we take off the air cast?" Lori asked.

"No need," Georgie said, wrapping Tyler's long arms around her, pulling over the blanket from the back of the couch.

"Aw!" Lori complained, "what if I get cold, or Aydan?"

Georgie just shook her head. Tyler pointed to the library. "The extra blankets are in the window seat. I'm sure you can find something to share," she teased, watching as Lori blushed. She loved embarrassing her especially when she reddened. She was always surprised at how much this woman could blush, especially whenever Aydan's name was mentioned.

Aydan called from the upper floor, making her way down the circular stairs, "I found it." She held up the DVD jewel case as proof. "And I brought a blanket, you big baby." This was directed at Lori and Tyler had to fight not to grin. Thank goodness Georgie was mostly oblivious to the flirting and teasing that had been going on all evening.

"Lori," Tyler asked casually, "I keep meaning to ask how your side is doing with the wedding prep."

"Not bad," she answered, loading up the DVD and handing the remote to Aydan. "And before you ask, JoJo says everything on the dress side is handled, so no panicking."

"Thank goodness for Joanne. I thought I would never get you two in dresses."

Georgie cleared her throat, prompting further explanation from her cousin. "Okay, well, I should probably come clean right here..."

"Lori...you better not have some funny idea about my wedding!"

"*Your* wedding?" she quipped.

"Told you," Georgie said casually to her cousin, but she was clearly enjoying the repartee.

Before Lori could say more, Tyler managed to reach over and hook her arm around her neck. "Lori Phipps, you badly behaved lesbian, I promise nothing but pain..."

"Hey...no noogies. Ty, let me explain!"

Tyler released her hold, snuggling back in behind Georgie. "You've got sixty seconds, Phipps. No beating around the bush."

Lori, sitting with Tyler on one side and a very amused Aydan on the other, was momentarily at a loss for words. "Ah, oh well, um, you see..."

"Fifty seconds."

"Jeez Ty, will you listen already?" she pleaded, even more frustrated by Tyler's clear delight. "Really? Oh, you're a brat,

Tyler Ann! Georgie, how the hell do you tell when she's kidding and when she's actually mad?"

"I wrote…manual. Want to read?"

Now Lori was laughing too, so much she actually snorted. That got the best of Aydan, who offered her a consoling shoulder pat.

"So, Marnie already spilled the beans?" Lori asked.

"Yes, yes she did," Tyler confirmed, all the while chuckling amiably. "And I love that both you and Megan will wear the suits Joanne ordered, and yes, Kira, Megan and Susan will stand up with me. That means you two geniuses need to make sure Aunt Helen is willing to act as mother of the bride for Georgie, and yes, Joanne is ordering in suitable dresses for her to choose from so please make sure you get her over there for a fitting this week."

"Wow, that's great, Tiger. I think it's so cool that you're including Helen."

Wrapping her arms around Georgie again, Tyler pulled her in closer. "That's what you want, right baby?"

Georgie simply nodded. Resting her head on Tyler's shoulder, her lips a hair's breadth from her cheek, she said simply, "Thank you, my Tyler," before offering a kiss.

"Oh boy. Quick, Aydan," Lori begged, "better start the movie before these two forget we're here."

Navigating the opening menu, Aydan clicked play. "You know, everyone around here makes up these great pet names, everyone but you, Georgie. I can't figure out if that's just because you don't like them or don't think that way. If you want, I could help you make some up?"

Georgie gave her a thumbs-up. "Used to have…for Lori and Marnie."

As the opening studio credits began, Tyler explained, "Georgie can't remember what she used to call Marnie or Lori when they were kids. I did laugh to hear Henry admitting to referring to them as the Gruesome Twosome."

"Oh, that's good," Aydan agreed, grinning at the prospect of getting to tease Lori even more. She settled back to watch the movie, enjoying her fussing with the blanket, and covering their legs together. Bolder than usual, she reached under it to take Lori's hand. The arch of surprise on Lori's brow was almost imperceptible, but the smile was not and Aydan relaxed when Lori gave her hand a tender squeeze.

CHAPTER SEVENTEEN

Aydan was holding her breath. Leslie and her caterers would arrive to finish setting up for the opening reception within minutes. Everything had been moved to the new eighth-floor office, and Tyler and the staff had spent all morning getting settled in and making sure everything was in order before they welcomed Georgie back. Now she was standing dead center, in the south side open workspace, looking everything over. The old glass and oak office panels that had been in storage for so many years encompassed the north-facing boardroom, electronics lab and two offices, Georgie's and Tyler's. Tyler's large space occupied the northeast corner, with Georgie's right next her hers. Fener, the contractor, had hinged the panels dividing the two offices so that Tyler could keep the space between them open when she wished. It hadn't been in the plans and Aydan was concerned Georgie would balk. She needn't have worried; if it came from Tyler, she would accept it without question. If anything, she appeared delighted by many of the extras they had cooked up together, especially her office.

Foregoing the meeting area, they had made it a dedicated workspace, with a side entrance to the department meeting room next door. Tyler had wanted to put her couch in there, but the space was on the small side with her desk, loaded bookshelves, workstation, and Maggie's big dog bed. Besides, if she needed a nap or just plain quiet time, their apartment was only a few hundred feet away.

Clearing her throat, Georgie turned to her team. "Excellent work...Aydan, Skip, everyone...This," she said waving her arm around the expansive space, "is perfect for...perfect team." She closed her eyes for just a moment, before reaching out to take Tyler's hand. "We have a chance...a real chance to create. Here, now, together...no limits, no sky."

And that was it. The new space was now approved by their technical lead and it was all the team needed to know. Aydan was sure every one of them had been carefully selected and she was secretly convinced they had been chosen based on their ability to understand their broken leader. They cheered at Georgie's approval of the new space and all the work they had been doing and would be done and they cheered to see Georgie take Tyler's hand. Aydan had never seen her do that in the office, but seeing the reaction she understood: it was simply a subtle statement meant for anyone harboring concerns for their relationship or the future of the division.

Once everyone settled down, Georgie stepped aside, signaling by hand for Tyler to take the floor. She spent a few minutes giving a very high-level introduction to some of the new projects being considered and encouraging them to present their own proposals. She would set aside time in the schedule each week for the engineers to pitch ideas to the whole team. She listed her expectations on the process and everyone's responsibilities, promising to cover everything in more detail later in the week. Right now they were minutes away from hosting all the DME, DPP, and even the DynaCraft employees for lunch and an open house.

Tyler had done something else too. Just that morning, she and Aydan had collected and carried all the awards, plaques, and tributes the company received for Georgie's special projects including the Sea Rescue Rover. That too she had on display, right alongside the 3D printout of the new thruster design. With archival copies of Georgie's original work, the whole team had dug into the stalled project, solving it, and streamlining it in weeks. Aydan thought it was a bit brash to throw in the face of the other guys, since it took their team only weeks to accomplish what the DME guys took a year to mess up. Still, it had made the team even prouder and she had to give Tyler kudos there too. She really knew them.

When Leslie and her people rolled off the elevators, everything shifted into high gear. While everyone was free to enjoy the food and the guests, Tyler had made it clear that they were all representing the new division, and she expected them to stay on point. "This is business, not a party." Aydan knew she would be evaluating their performance with an eye on who was capable of working well outside their group and who, like Georgie, would do best staying close.

"There you are!" Zoe called, traipsing into the new office, dressed in a suit that screamed CEO more than administrative assistant to the master boat builder. She understood Zoe took a lot of pride in her appearance, but she secretly wondered if all the effort masked some insecurity. Among the DiNamico/Phipps clan she was the only one without a degree, something she'd made light of on more than one occasion.

"Welcome," Aydan offered, surreptitiously keeping an eye out for Tyler. She had been very specific that no one, absolutely no one, be allowed into the new office until Marnie cut the official opening ribbon. Casually taking Zoe's arm and steering her back toward the foyer, she suggested, "Let's head next door. Tyler wants all the early arrivals to wait over there to be sure Mrs. Pulaski is the first to enter." Mentioning Marnie's name was a last-minute gambit, something she added on seeing the cringe Zoe involuntarily gave at the mention of Tyler's name.

"At least she still knows enough to kowtow to Marnie."

"What?" Aydan asked, confused. Looking around, she was relieved to see Georgie and Tyler's living room empty. "Are you talking about Doctor Marsh?"

"Ugh! Really Aydan dear, she's not a friggin' real doctor. You don't have to call her that, besides—"

"Zoe, what's with you?" she practically hissed, trying not to be overheard.

Shrugging off the gentle hand leading her, Zoe stormed over to the open kitchen, bypassing the cart of cups and the fresh carafes of coffee and tea the caterers had just rolled in. She searched the cupboards for a tall glass, then added ice from the fridge and rooted around for a Diet Coke. Checking to make sure no one was in hearing range, she stated, "I just don't see what the fuss is. Everyone's acting like this is some big deal! I don't get it. It's a dozen guys sucking up more floor space than all of the finance division, and everyone's acting like she's just opened the Mayo Clinic. It's not like she's curing cancer or anything."

Shocked by her venom and confused by her simile, she couldn't help but challenge her. "Okay, we may not be curing diseases but the work being done by this very small team will save lives. Besides, the finance division has a very conservative business plan. I'm sure your father has explained how he wants to build the portfolio carefully. I think he's calling it his CQO Strategy or 'Cautious Quiet Optimism.' This division has a much different—" She broke off, exclaiming, "Really? What's with the face?"

Zoe's shoulders sagged. "I don't want to fight. I was all excited to tell you I got my invitation. I wanted you to see it before I RSVP'd for us."

"What invitation?" Aydan asked. She was standing with her arms crossed, watching Zoe make herself at home. She wasn't sure what bothered her more, the young woman's self-assuredness, or her assumption that she would be accepting of any invitation.

"For the wedding, you silly goose."

Feeling caught out, she momentarily envied Georgie's ability to stare down any uncomfortable situation. Groaning internally, she knew she should've called this off sooner but she did enjoy spending time with Zoe, just not like that. "I'm not sure why you would even want to go, considering how you feel about them."

That stilled Zoe for a moment, and then she did what she always did, calling on her bravado. "Don't be silly. You know I'm just joking when it comes to those two. Besides, I think we have more than earned a little fun on their dime. After all, we've done all their heavy lifting. Without you and me coming to the rescue, I doubt they would still be together much less getting married."

Transfixed by the absurdity of the statement, Aydan was at a loss for words. There was no point in challenging her. Instead of logically arguing her point, it was Zoe's habit to fluff off any challenges to her assertions. The engineer in Aydan always bristled whenever she did so. It reminded her of her mother, sloughing off any fact she found inconvenient. "I'm sorry, Zoe, but I already have my plus-one for the wedding."

It was a bold move, especially since she didn't have a date and had yet to open her own invitation. Thankfully, Georgie and Maggie arrived at that exact moment, ending the conversation. But Aydan wasn't naïve enough to think Zoe wouldn't raise the subject again, especially given the shock on her face.

"You all ready, boss?" she asked Georgie.

Georgie nodded to them both. "Right shirt?"

"Is that the one Tyler set out for you?"

She shook her head. "Button fell…"

"Don't worry. I'll make sure the dry cleaner repairs the loose buttons, and that shirt is a perfect match. You did well."

Smiling at the compliment, Georgie pulled on her suit jacket, but stilled when Zoe began fussing with her lapels and unnecessarily straightening her clothing.

"What would you do without me?" Zoe asked.

Suddenly Aydan understood, recognizing the insecurities Zoe hid behind her efforts to be needed. What a contrast to her own experience. With her family she was needed, but unwanted. Zoe, it seemed, had misunderstood her place in her family, assuming she was unwanted because she wasn't necessarily needed. Aydan made a mental note to talk to her friend. She was in the enviable position of having a family who wanted her and they were constantly creating opportunities she hadn't quite earned. The "friend" moniker filtered into her brain again just as Lori, Marnie and her assistant strolled in. The smile she saw on Lori's face sent home her understanding. Zoe was a friend. Lori was something else.

Marnie eyed her sister critically. "You look good. Are you ready? Did you memorize your speech?"

"Tyler will give...but ready too," she added, showing Marnie her prepared remarks and assuring her she had memorized them along with several answers to the expected questions.

The whole point of making a show of the office move and the reception was to highlight the parent company's commitment to research. Lou had brought a proposal forward suggesting DynaTech be taken public independent of the family holdings. For once his suggestion made sense, but would still depend on Georgie incubating enough of her profitable ideas for Tyler to steer to market. Lou was sure, and everyone agreed, that two or three years of cutting-edge work would firmly place the tiny R&D enterprise in the limelight. DME's engineering successes were already well respected in the marine industry. A few broader spectrum wins were all that was needed to catapult them into a top public offering. It was a plan even Tyler and Georgie agreed on. Creating a successful company was first and foremost for the two, but after the recent health calamity, they were both determined their life together would include much, much more than just business.

"Good," Marnie said as if announcing something truly important. Looking very much like the grand dame of the pack, she took in the assembled family members. "Zoe, you look lovely in that suit. Lori tells me you're doing great work out at DynaCraft. And just so you know, I have approved the class list you submitted. Take it slow; I don't want to hear you're burning the wick at both ends, at least not any more than usual."

Zoe glowed with the praise. "Thank you so much, Marnie. I promise you won't be disappointed."

"I know I won't, kiddo. No worries there," she reassured her, before looking everyone else over with a critical eye. "Aydan, the new scarf is lovely. It suits you much better."

Aydan fingered the fine silk of the gorgeous scarf Lori had given her. Unused to receiving praise, especially of the personal variety, much less from the boss's boss's boss, she blushed, mumbling out her thanks. Catching Lori's eye on her, she colored even more. How was it she could just look at her and feel so much? As if a current flowed between them, a current of energy, and something so much more. Something she couldn't understand and couldn't ignore.

I don't want to ignore it—her—anymore.

Then she saw Zoe looking from her to Lori and back again; clearly she had noted Aydan fingering the scarf and the exchange of looks between Lori and Aydan.

Zoe bounded over to Aydan and fingered the fine fabric. She called loudly to Lori, "Ooh, Italian silk...Quite the gift, Lori. I call this cheating. No fair trying to win our bet by bribing Aydan into kissing you first!"

Aydan gaped at Zoe. Then stared at Lori whose face was turning several shades darker than her already dark complexion. Without thought, she fled from the room.

* * *

Toweling her hair dry, Tyler walked into the bedroom. "What a day, baby. I can't believe how crazy it got and you—you did so well with that journalist."

"Nice guy," she said, putting her book aside to watch Tyler prepare for bed. It was one of her favorite things, watching this astounding woman methodically review her thoughts about the day as she paced through her evening routine. She was wearing the light silk robe Georgie had given her last Christmas and padding around in her new moccasins. She was mostly a barefoot type but even the wood floors in the updated condo could get cold. It was one of the reasons she had ordered the mocs instead of settling for some silly lady slippers. She knew they would be more comfortable, not to mention warmer, and had hoped Tyler would like them. Judging by her comments, not to mention her enthusiastic lovemaking, she was pretty sure she had done well. That was the other amazing thing about her wife-to-be; she knew how important it was to just spell things out. "I'm so lucky."

Tyler turned to look at her. Her face carried the simplest of messages and the reality wasn't missed by Georgie. "We both are, baby. You know that and so do I." Carefully draping her towel over the back of a chair and walking to the bed, she crawled up to her on her knees. "We have a family thing we should talk about."

"Lori or Zoe?" she asked intuitively.

Tyler shook her head. "I don't know why anyone thinks you're obtuse. I swear you never miss a thing."

"Tell me," Georgie asked, patting the spot beside her.

Pulling back the covers, Tyler unfolded her long legs, kicking off her moccasins and slipping between the cool cotton sheets. She cuddled close without prompting, launching into a detailed explanation of the situation.

"Lori agreed? Betting?"

"I know you're upset, baby, and I agree Lori wasn't really thinking and we both know what Zoe can be like."

"Aydan…is she…"

"Hurt?" Tyler filled in the blank, adding her own opinion. "I think she's confused, mad, and maybe a little bit flattered. She's literally just come out and here she has two hot women placing a wager on her affection."

"Affection or sex?" she asked, not at all happy about the situation. This was the kind of stupid and thoughtless shit Zoe gravitated to. Lori too could be a player when it came to women, but she had always been respectful, until now.

"No baby, this wasn't about who could get her in the sack first. The wager was for a kiss, which is why I think Lori fell for it. It all must have seemed so innocent."

"And now?" Georgie asked, questioning what had changed.

"Honestly," she said, sighing at the situation. "I think Lori's falling in love with her and I have a feeling Aydan might be in the same boat."

Groaning, she asked, "Can…forgiveness?"

"Can Aydan forgive Lori? I think so. I know Lori wants to talk to her but, well, her pride is involved, and she's embarrassed. At least Zoe didn't have her little jealous meltdown in front of staff or guests. I know Marnie's going to be on Lori, and us too, but we're their friends. We need to…"

"Fix it?"

Tyler moved back just enough to look in her eyes. "My first rule when it comes to other couples is the same as yours: butt out. It's just that Lori's your sibling as much as Marnie is. What would you do if Marnie and Jack had some sort of blowup?"

"Beat up Jack."

That made her laugh. "What on earth makes you think it would be his fault? It could be Marnie?" she asserted.

Georgie shook her head. "Marnie's rule one…always right."

"And rule number two is, when in doubt refer to rule number one? Oh, you don't have to tell me. I swear, your sister and I have gone head-to-head more than once and I would not wish that on my worst enemy."

Now that concerned her. "You okay…should I…talk…"

"No baby, I actually don't mind the intellectual head banging with your sister. It's a little like my old days at the university, fighting over the day-to-day details. She keeps me on my toes. Besides, if I let you deal with Marnie, you would have zero time left to dream up all those new ideas the team loves so much. I'm so proud of you."

Snuggling into her, Georgie stroked her damp hair away from her face, planting a few soft kisses. "Prouder of you," she added honestly.

Everything Tyler did for her, for the family, for the company was more than helpful. It made success practical and that was a huge step up from possible. The kiss she received in return conveyed Tyler's gratitude at the compliment. It was important to Georgie that everyone know how much their contributions improved her life, but none as much as having Tyler's love and affection.

She was searching for the belt to her robe when Tyler stilled her hand. "Slow down baby, we need to talk about this mess first." Adding a scorching kiss before she slid up on top of her, and propping her head in her hands, Tyler looked her squarely in the face. "I want to help Lori and Aydan but I honestly think all they need is a little time, without any interference to work this out on their own. If they want to work it out," she added as a caveat.

When Georgie nodded her agreement, she pushed on. "I think we need to help Zoe. I didn't understand it until today, but I think her ego is terribly bruised. I see your look and I know this is a thing you don't always understand. I love you for it, so don't worry about not getting it."

"So...issues...causes?"

"Well, this is a little embarrassing, but Lori told me something surprising today. She said Zoe took you and me getting together pretty hard."

Her brows must have climbed a mile high while she was remembering just how messed up she was when she thought Tyler and Zoe were dating. If Zoe was half as upset as she had been, the poor kid must have agonized over their wedding announcement. "How can we help?"

"That's the million-dollar question. I don't think Zoe was ever actually interested in me; I don't think she was after anything other than a quick hookup. I think the real issue was you and me falling in love. Lori says that for Zoe it kicked in some sort of competitive interest in Aydan. I'm sure she would have gotten over Aydan's rejection pretty quickly but seeing her interest in Lori, must have felt as if she was repeating history."

"Ouch." Using both hands, she brushed Tyler's hair back planting a kiss on her chin and running her hands over her shoulders and down her back. She let her nails lightly rake along her spine, before cupping her behind. "Would not want...not like I felt."

"Oh baby, I don't think it's like that. I have a feeling this is just Zoe acting out. She sees herself as beautiful and glamorous and isn't used to women not falling at her feet. Her ego is bruised, not because she had feelings for me or felt something for Aydan. From her point of view, she lost out to a pair of old fogies."

Skipping over the old fogies comment, Georgie forced herself to concentrate on the issue. "So…why do me when…"

"Yes." Tyler heaved a sigh of relief. "Thank God you get it. Lori got the point when we talked about you and me, but the minute I tried to apply it to her situation, she refused to listen. I swear she's more stubborn than you!"

"Less than Marnie," she joked and Tyler laughed too, snuggling down a little closer. Georgie stiffened when her thigh pressed hard between her legs. "Oh, my Tyler."

"Just you be patient now. We still have to do something to make Zoe feel more, I don't know, welcome. Does that make sense?"

"I could ask…be my bridesmaid?" She was sure it was the right answer when Tyler pressed a warm wet kiss on her lips. She couldn't help responding, deepening her attention, adding just a touch of tongue and soliciting a sensuous moan.

"Hold up there, hot lips," Tyler teased. "I have a suggestion. What if I asked Zoe to be one of my bridesmaids? That way you could ask Skippy if you want."

That made sense and she told her as much, only asking, "Zoe would…like?"

"I think she would be honored to be on the bride's side. I had to laugh today when she referred to you as the groom."

That drew a groan. "Wait till she sees…dress."

"Wait till they all see it! Lori and Marnie both swore on pain of death that they wouldn't let our little secret slip. I can't wait to see you on Henry and Helen's arm. It'll be so perfect, baby."

"You…perfect. I can't wait."

"Hmm, yes, perfect, baby. I can't wait either, now how about helping me get this robe off?"

Georgie just smiled, handing her the belt for the robe.

Tyler snuggled in, nudging her hip in just the right spot. She had learned early on it was Georgie's instant on button and her response didn't fail. Flipping Tyler on her back, she quickly demonstrated her recuperative strength but not without tenderness. Then there were those damn eyes. Adapting to Georgie's silent communications might have been challenging if it weren't for those open eyes reflecting every single thought in her head. It was reassuring and so overwhelmingly exciting to know her every thought, feeling, desire. Tyler had always been a bit of a screamer herself and enjoyed lots of verbal feedback. Making love with Georgie had changed everything on that front. Learning she could just open her eyes at any moment to find her, see her intent, and know her heart, was a revelation, and had opened a world of sensuousness she had missed in all those late night, eyes-squeezed-shut screaming sessions. Those experiences were incomparable to what it was like to have Georgie on her, in her, devouring her, worshipping her. And she too had found so much power and release in that connection. "I missed this, baby, missed you like this."

Georgie's hands stilled, but her pleasure radiated from every inch of her. The other night on the roof, they had made love for the first time since the accident. The hiatus had been only partially necessary due to her injuries. The true barrier was Tyler's feelings. It had taken the month of healing, and healing together for her to feel completely accepting again and Georgie never questioned her need to heal or the amount of time it took. Once she was home, her only concern had been in wanting to prove herself.

Tyler knew that in any other relationship, with any other woman, the situation would have permanently torn them apart. Instead, this whole thing felt more like a simple hiccup. Something she just needed to discuss with her in order to fix. And she could count on that too. She had never met a woman so easy to talk with when it came to her emotions and desires. Georgie wanted to hear her thoughts, wanted to hear her longings, demands, needs, and wants, and she loved to hear her scream! The first night of resumed intimacies Georgie had been tender and patient, just what Tyler needed. Tonight though, "Baby, I want to feel your mouth on me."

Tearing her attention from the small breast she was ravishing with her tongue, Georgie stared transfixed before a wolfish grin began fueling her progression. She took her time settling in between Tyler's smooth thighs, never once breaking eye contact.

It was a little unnerving at times, connecting with such honesty. Digging her fingers into the sheets for a handhold she begged, "Don't hold back baby, I want to feel..." From that point on it was harder and harder to offer any coherent feedback but she tried. Georgie had admitted more than once how she loved to listen to her, hear her and the louder and more suggestive the better. She wasn't asking her to talk dirty or scream obscenities, but to be Tyler, her Tyler, whatever that was and however that came out. And to the woman's credit, the more Tyler let her inside the private world she had safeguarded for so long, the more she was understood and accepted. As for love, there was no limit to her love, affection or respect. She lavished each without limit, and without some sort of quid quo pro.

Arching her back, she tried desperately to hold back the pulsating need to drive herself into Georgie's mouth. Immediately recognizing her mounting arousal, Georgie pinned her hips to the bed with a tender kind of physical strength. Her tongue had worked its way all around and over her clit and settled into tormenting just that perfect spot Tyler adored.

Clawing at the bottom sheet, the intensity of her reaction was almost blinding, and before she could comment or even comprehend all the sensations alive in her, she felt Georgie slip fingers inside, pushing in deep and curling them back with just enough pressure. "Yes, baby. Ohh..." There was no slowing what would happen now. With her hips pinned to the bed, Tyler rocked her shoulders forward as her orgasm mounted, reaching for Georgie with one hand, needing to connect in every way possible. Georgie was everywhere, in her, on her, and there were those green eyes, always open, always offering so, so much more. She let her orgasm wash over her and away with everything she had been harboring this last month. This was them, they were them again, but they were more too.

"Baby..." She couldn't quite talk yet. She reached for her, pulling her up to interweave together in each other's arms. Georgie held her desperately tight, tenderly rubbing soothing circles on her back while aftershocks shook them both. It never ceased to astound her how Georgie could get off just making love to her. Tyler, of course, would never settle for that. Her healthy ego had long accepted that her fiancée was certainly self-sufficient but clearly preferred Tyler's attention. There was no denying that pleasing Georgie, bringing her to orgasm was more than a pleasure; it was a point of pride. If she was shocked at how hot and bothered the woman could get just touching her, her responsiveness under her ministrations was exalting. "Oh God, baby...let me breathe."

"Slow...nice and slow, my Tyler."

Lying with her head on Georgie's chest, she could hear and recognize a subtle change in her breathing. "What's wrong baby?" she asked, tilting her head back just enough to see her face.

"No wrong...I..."

She almost looked helpless. Tyler pulled herself up a little higher. "I'm listening."

"Aydan said about...nicknames. Do you...I am not so good...endearments, sorry."

"Endearments?" she asked before understanding. "Baby, I don't need a long list of pet names. You say more with your eyes, not to mention your hands. I would never wish for that to change."

"But before...could joke and...like Marnie and Lori."

That made her smile. "Actually my love, I have it on good authority that you always sucked in that area." At Georgie's truly amused look she explained. "The other day you mentioned not remembering the nicknames you used for the Gruesome Twosome when they were kids." Georgie smiled at her use of Henry's moniker for Lori and Marnie. "Well, the curiosity got the best of me so I asked. I have to admit, learning how little you've changed was satisfying," she teased. "You called them Eveready and Duracell!"

Georgie smacked her hand against her forehead with amusement. "Oh, so lame."

"Given that, I must say I'm more than pleased with 'My Tyler'. Of course, if you're looking for suggestions…"

Snuggling down so they were nose to nose, she pulled the sheet up to cover Tyler. "Let me try…Gorgeous…Brilliant… Perfect…"

Tyler shook her head, giving her a sweet kiss before explaining, "Those things are compliments, very sweet compliments you are free to deliver any time you like, but as pet names they need a little work. Why don't we try a little experiment?" At Georgie's approving grin, she explained, "I am going to ravish you from head to toe and you, baby, are to do nothing but enjoy my attention. Understood?"

Grinning, she nodded her agreement. "Experiment…what?"

"Oh no, you. I'm in charge here and you get to do nothing but think about all the things you feel for me. I promise," she said, brushing her cheek against Georgie's and whispering in her ear. "Surrender everything, baby, your thoughts, your desires, everything. Now close your eyes and just feel. I'm right here, the whole way. I promise all the words will come the minute you stop searching, asking, questioning. Just surrender to me and let me be everything like you do for me. Can you do that?"

"Yes," Georgie promised, her breathing already hitched at the sensation of Tyler's warm cheek against her own, her warm breath, and warmer words caressing her ear.

It didn't take long to find all those places that thrilled her, pushing Georgie higher. "Breathe baby, just breathe. I'm right here," she assured. She was missing those expressive eyes and wanted that connection back, still she waited for her to find her words.

"Hap…My Tyler," she said, opening her eyes to renew their connection.

Her thigh was between Georgie's legs and her hand had gravitated there too. "Baby, you are so wet. God I love touching you."

"Don't stop," she begged.

"No?" Tyler loved teasing her, loved seeing that questioning look. She drew a wet finger from her clit and all the way up to her chest. The pleading look she received was more than enough to make her grin. "You are so easy," she tantalized her, moving closer, wanting to feel everything Georgie telegraphed in her every move. "What does Hap mean?" she asked, teasing with her fingers tracing an indirect path back down between her legs.

Looking even more aroused, Georgie stilled, explaining, "You said feel…I feel happiness…Hap."

Startled by the admission and its simplicity, she leaned in delivering sweet kisses along her jaw before turning her attention to that gorgeously hungry mouth. Georgie was a sensuous kisser but more than that, she mirrored Tyler's own desires so closely, almost telepathically knowing exactly how she wanted to be kissed. If she wasn't careful Georgie would have her on her back again and as much as she was looking forward to that moment, there was something deep in her that hungered for her release. Maybe it was ego or her own mounting desire but taking her to her complete surrender was as perfect and excruciatingly honest as it got.

Georgie's hands were on her face, her eyes beseeching her.

"Breathe, baby," Tyler warned, the pad of her finger stroking slowly, imperceptibly slow, along the side of her clit. She liked to think of it as her baby's sweet spot and it never failed to push her over the edge. She wasn't in a hurry. She had a few more ideas to introduce, but what she wanted, needed right now was to make her come, and she wasn't disappointed. It was always so incongruous, the effort Georgie went through to convey only gentleness in her touch. Yet in her physical release, she had scarred the headboard, clawing with her nails on several occasions. Tonight, one hand had remained gently cupping Tyler's face while the other had gathered the sheets in her fist, pulling hard, threatening to rip the high thread-count cotton to shreds.

Tyler pinned her down hard, riding out wave after wave. That was the gift, the feeling, the knowing she had pleased her, satisfied her and that she could and would again. "Baby, I love you so much. I can't begin to explain how you make me feel."

Georgie, awash in afterglow, stilled and gently eased Tyler down next to her, never for a moment letting her out of her arms. She couldn't talk, still struggling to catch her breath. Finally, she closed her eyes. "Frightening."

"What is, baby?"

"How much I need...you, like air."

And that was the truth of it. She understood Georgie had spent her life being needed but needing, not so much. If her wife-to-be had an Achilles' heel this was it, the worry of needing or needing too much.

"Listen carefully Georgina, my love. I need you and you need me. It's that simple and it's good. And I promise it will never be too much for me."

"Sure?"

"Oh baby, not only am I sure, I will be happy to spend my life proving it."

"No proving!" she objected.

Tyler settled into her favorite position, intertwined but leaning up on one elbow to see Georgie's face. "What would you have me do?" she asked gently. "So, baby, tell me. How can I assure you?"

"Like this," she admitted. "Talking...cuddling...making love."

"And what about just plain fucking?" Tyler teased.

"Oh you...bad!" she admonished with a sexy grin then asking sincerely, "Is it...what I called you...what I..."

"Hap? Oh baby I love it but I do have one request. Will you keep it just for us?" At her amused look, Tyler explained, "Marnie and Lori already have a million pet names for me. I don't want them stealing yours too."

"Okay," Georgie readily agreed, brushing Tyler's dark hair back from her eyes. "Love you, Hap."

CHAPTER EIGHTEEN

Standing in the foyer just inches from Georgie and Tyler's front door, Lori backed away, trying desperately to control her nerves. After Zoe's spilling the beans on their stupid bet, Aydan had refused to speak with her. It had taken a week of emailed explanations before Aydan would even accept a text much less a call. Another week of late night talks until finally she agreed to dinner. Lori wasn't sure this was a date, but she wasn't willing to mess up a chance to make things better. Maybe Aydan wasn't all that interested in her, she didn't know for sure, but if she was, she didn't want to miss the chance to show her what kind of woman she really was.

She paced back and forth, again looking anxiously over the large bouquet of flowers. When she'd asked Marnie for help on that front, she just rolled her eyes and sent her to see Jack. After he stopped laughing, he gave her the number of the florist he used, sharing the fact that it was the same one Georgie now called whenever she was in trouble. It turned out the florist was not only well acquainted with their misdeeds, she admitted to making weekly deliveries to either Marnie or Tyler. Looking over the purple roses critically, Lori did wonder if it was too much, then remembered something Georgie had once shared about not pretending to be something you're not. *And I'm the kind of gal who thinks a woman should have roses, so there!* Quickly, forcing herself to breathe, she knocked on the door before she could change her mind.

Georgie opened it, grinning. "Waiting...downstairs. Both."

Groaning, Lori almost dumped the flowers, but knew there was no running from this. "Let me guess. Tyler's going to make me explain and apologize again?"

Still grinning, she suggested simply, "Just grovel."

"That your advice or experience talking?"

"Both."

Lori didn't catch sight of Aydan until she was almost down the circular staircase. Caught out by her sheer attractiveness, she missed the last step and stumbled, crashing into Georgie's back. By some fluke the two of them managed to stay on their feet, pulling themselves together to stand facing their witnesses. Completely humiliated, Lori did the only thing she could think of, handing Aydan the flowers without comment.

Accepting the bouquet, she seemed as stunned by the entrance as Lori was. Thank goodness for Tyler. "You two," she accused with amusement. "Georgina, take Ms. Klutzy here over and have a seat, while Aydan and I find a vase."

"Wine," Georgie asked, "my Tyler?"

"Yes, baby. The bottle's breathing, go ahead and pour," she instructed, turning her attention to Aydan and the search for a vase.

A bottle of cabernet syrah sat open on a tray with four glasses. While Georgie poured the wine, Lori sat down next to her, and in a voice just above a whisper, asked her, "How much trouble am I in here, buddy?"

"You are okay...just time for...penance."

Lori groaned, watching as Aydan and Tyler made their way to the living area. While Tyler carried some sort of appetizers, Aydan carried the vase of purple roses, setting them on a nearby table.

"Thank you, Lori. They're lovely," she offered, accepting her wine. "Have you tried it? I picked it out."

Picking up the bottle and examining the label with interest, she asked, "Did you buy this on the big adventure?"

"Oh, Lori," Aydan gushed. "It was wonderful. Georgie warned the trip through the Welland Canal would be slow and boring, but I just loved it. There was so much to see and the lift locks! Have you been through those? Of course," she answered for her. "I'm sure you've done it a million times."

"Actually, I've only done it twice and always with Georgie at the helm. I keep telling her it would be much faster to just head right up the Niagara River."

While Georgie laughed at the joke, it was Tyler who teasingly questioned her navigation, while explaining, "And right over Niagara Falls. Now that I want to see you pull off."

"Yeah, yeah Tiger, I know you're much more adventurous than you let on. Why else would you marry the ringleader here?" She watched them all enjoying the conversation. That was a relief; at least they weren't grilling her for her stupid mistake. It was bad enough she had missed out on the impromptu sailing trip across the border. "So, details, details. How long did it take to get through the canal? Did you make it past Glendale?"

"Just," Georgie admitted. "Anchored at three."

"Wow, you made it to Lock Three and with Frick and Frack running the show? Please tell me Marnie's two miscreants were on their best behavior?"

"They were perfect gentlemen," Aydan reassured her.

"Actually," Tyler elaborated, "they want to use the boat to run charters so Georgie told them she would evaluate them on everything, seamanship, navigation, even hospitality. If they failed one part they failed it all and she wouldn't give them another chance until next summer."

"Wow, cool! Georgie Porgie sets down the law. They must have bellyached about that?"

"Not a word," Georgie affirmed.

"We docked at some little marina by Niagara-on-the-Lake, and cycled over to the winery, actually we went to two of them.

They were each only about a mile away—right?" Aydan asked, looking for Tyler or Georgie's confirmation. "Of course you know that, you've done the wine tour thing."

"Actually, I haven't. The two times we sailed over to Lake Ontario, it was to visit Toronto. I thought that's where you guys were headed."

"That was a ruse Georgie and Tyler cooked up to test Marnie's boys."

"That," Tyler added, "and the fact that it took ages to clear the rest of the locks. I guess that's what happens when you're there on a Saturday."

"I'm so glad you guys took the boys out for this. Marnie says they've really been on her ass, oops rear end, to get checked out to go solo. I can't believe they pulled it off."

Georgie nodded, and Tyler filled in a few details. "Aydan was right, we got to Niagara-on-the-Lake just around noon and docked at this tiny marina, and then Georgie tells them we want steaks for dinner and something fresh, that's all, and sends them on their way."

"Oh my God!" Lori was shaking her head, familiar with all the trouble Danny and Luc could find. "I think that could be construed as an act of war. You do remember you were visiting a foreign country?" She laughed, and clinked her glass against her cousin's. She then turned to Aydan saying sincerely, "I am so sorry I missed all the fun. I promise it won't happen again."

Making eye contact, they shared a connection for probably longer than appropriate, but it was vital that she take responsibility for those actions that had resulted in her not being included in the little long weekend adventure.

"Duly noted," Aydan said, a subtle smile twitching at the corner of her lips.

Her lips were naturally dark and alluring much like her eyes and it was all Lori could do not to lean over here and now and take her in her arms.

Tyler stood, reaching for Georgie's hand. "Come on, baby. We don't want to be late."

"Where are you guys off to? Please don't run out on my account," Lori said, not entirely meaning it.

Georgie shook her head, setting her glass and Tyler's on the tray, letting Tyler explain. "We are taking my sisters to the movies."

"Now?" she asked, checking her watch. It was already after eight.

"You know how nervous Kira gets about leaving the baby. She thinks it's better to sneak out to a late show after she's long asleep."

Lori nodded at the logic. "Kira's a good mom and Ella, I wouldn't mind having a few dozen of those running around under foot."

"You and Georgie," Tyler joked, taking Georgie's hand before explaining to Maggie. "Not tonight little girl, you're off duty."

While the dog listened to Tyler, she did look to Georgie for confirmation. "Stand down." With just those two words, she trotted back over to the sofa, sliding down to lay across Aydan's feet.

Lori stood, offering her farewell. Clearly the dog assumed Aydan was staying in so she would too. Lori waited until they had climbed up the circular stairs and were out of sight before pouring more wine for Aydan and topping her own glass. Almost choking, and forcing herself to meet Aydan's dark eyes, she admitted, "I'm a little nervous."

"Isn't that interesting? And here I thought that would be my line."

Lori sat in silence, cursing herself, forcing herself to say something, anything. At long last she apologized, "Aydan, I am so sorry…"

"Enough," she said gently, reaching over to take her hand. "I have listened to all your apologies and frankly I get it. I'm not happy you fell into this whole thing with Zoe, but I'm not mad anymore."

"You're not?"

"Actually, I'm worried about her," Aydan said.

That caught her, not that she was worried about her niece, but that she was confident enough to willingly discuss the underlying situation. "I am too. Ty explained it to me. I'm kind of embarrassed to admit she had to beat some sense into me, but I get it now and I'm worried too."

"Tyler is pretty amazing."

The jealousy she felt was uncharacteristic. Lori was sure she herself was the only one to blame for this dustup with the kid and subsequently losing time with Aydan. Missing out on the three-day sailing trip had hit her hard, not the outing but the chance to be with this incredible woman. In the last three weeks their emails and then phone calls had become more personal and hopeful with each day. It was all new territory for Aydan and Lori too.

"I see your look, Lori Ann Phipps. How dare you be jealous of my friend!" It sounded like a challenge but the grin on her face betrayed her amusement.

"I...am not!"

At the sound of Aydan's sweet laughter, Maggie's head shot up and she let out a happy yip before yawning and heading for her dog bed. "Even the dog's got your number."

"Yeah, I'm a dork. I admit it. Even the Tiger says I'm a big dumb butch sometimes."

"And her twin sister is madly in love with you."

"What? No!" Lori argued, "the Turtle's my buddy. Just like Ty is. Why would you say..."

"Will you relax? I'm just highlighting the fact that I too could be jealous of all the women who adore you. The difference is that I accept the fact that women will fall for you."

"What women?" Lori asked, knowing somewhere in the deep recesses of her mind that this wasn't the right question. "Sorry, you're right of course. Zoe says my gaydar must be off but still, Kira isn't gay, she's just a friend."

"Oh, you are woefully ignorant of your charms, Ms. Phipps. I am sure you could convert Kira and win your toaster oven."

It was said with such seriousness that Lori sat momentarily stunned, "I, um...you know about the toaster oven joke?"

Shaking her head Aydan stood, offering her hand. "Come on, you. I've got steaks ready for you to barbeque and I made some veggie kabobs to try on the grill."

She accepted the outstretched hand. "You trust me?"

They were standing face-to-face and only inches apart. Aydan, looking up, answered quietly, "I trust you with everything."

It was simple and empowering and a gift, her confidence and trust something she had fretted over, worrying she would never earn it back. She wanted to get this right but struggled with self-doubt. "Can I...I mean, may I...oh hell..."

"Yes, Lori. Now would be a good time to kiss me."

Even with permission, covering that final few inches between them felt like the bravest thing she would ever do. Closing her eyes, afraid Aydan might change her mind, she barely touched her lips to hers but the fullness, and sweet taste drew her back again. Taking her time, she explored her lips, enjoying the feel of her in her arms. Even after she broke from the kiss, breathless and lightheaded, Lori held on. Holding her so close, feeling her strength and confidence buoyed her immensely, and she was reluctant to step away, reluctant to look in those dark expressive eyes.

"It's all right, Lori," Aydan said, promising, "I'm nervous too."

* * *

Zoe stood leaning on the long bar nursing her last drink. It was long after last call and most of the place had emptied out.

"Sorry Zoe," Jersey, the bartender told her. "It's time; I have to take your drink. Can I get you a coffee?"

Before she could answer, another regular patron joined her at the bar. "Well, well, well. It looks like you struck out too!"

"I didn't strike out," she hissed at Sue Ellen Peach. "I just needed a break from those bitches."

"I hear yah," Peachy commiserated, accepting one of the coffees Jersey set in front of them and adding cream. "You want?" she asked, pushing the little basket of fake dairy creamers and packets of sweeteners closer to Zoe.

"You're chipper for a woman who's just been dumped."

"Hardly. I'm just used to Lori's shit. She wanders, some women do, but I've gotten used to it. She'll be back, she always is."

Zoe just stared at her. "I hate to tell you this, Peachy, but I think this one's different. She's even taking her to the big dumb dyke wedding!" This she added with air quotes, vowing, "I'm supposed to be a bridesmaid now but I'm not going." Watching Peachy carefully, she was curious to see her reaction to news of Lori's love interest. Disappointment and confusion were threatening Peachy's control. "You didn't know?"

"Which, that she was taking that...Islamist bitch, or that you don't want to go alone?"

"What makes you think I would go alone, why would I?" Zoe asserted, feeling caught out for even having to defend her ability to attract women. "Plenty of women would be proud to be on my arm for the gayest event in western New York. I could ask anyone!"

"Yes, you could," Peachy agreed soothingly. Her dour face visibly brightened. "But you're not going to ask one of those other women, you're going to ask me."

Zoe studied her. She knew she was drunk and would probably regret this decision. Still, she couldn't resist, and sticking out her hand, she grinned offering her pledge, "Done!"

CHAPTER NINETEEN

Lori stormed into the boatyard security cottage, ducking under the counter, demanding, "Have you been able to get that bastard Fener on the phone?"

"No," Megan answered, "but I think I have a solution."

"Did you find out who did it?" she asked, jerking her head toward the security surveillance system.

"Listen boss, why don't we get this sorted first, you know, kind of find a solution before we get into who did what?"

Lori just groaned. If Megan was reluctant to share her findings, she knew it wouldn't be good news. They were supposed to be making the final preparations for the boatyard to host the big wedding and Tyler and Georgie's guest list of eighty friends and family had skyrocketed to well over four hundred with the additions both Lori and Marnie had insisted be added for the sake of both family and business. They had accepted the situation with grace—well, at least Tyler had. Georgie was a little overwhelmed, but had placed herself firmly in their hands with the singular goal of pleasing her wife-to-be.

It was now Monday and they had just five days to get everything squared away. Thinking everything well under control, she had arrived that morning to find some yahoo had driven a 4x4 off-roader all over their property, crisscrossing the boatyard lawns, and gouging great welts in the turfgrass. She had promised Tyler she would make sure anyone in heels would be able to walk around without problems, and now she wasn't sure anyone could safely step out on the grass without becoming a muddy mess. Reluctantly, she slipped into the chair across from Megan's desk, asking without much hope, "So, what's this idea?"

"Okay," she said, holding up a hand and looking much like the cop she soon would be. "Now, just hear me out. First thing I did was call Kira and don't worry, I swore her to secrecy. So I asked about, you know, what kinds of things girls can walk on in heels."

Lori groaned again.

"Don't worry, she promised. Anyway, she remembered going out to the Seneca Powwow with some friends back when she was in university. She said they put all these cedar shavings down for paths to walk on, you know, so you wouldn't wreck the grass but she said it was soft but really solid too. She thinks the girls, well everybody, could walk on something like that real easy. And she said it looked good and smelled good too."

"I don't know, kiddo, it sounds kind of silly. I don't think laying out a few bags of mulch will solve anything, sorry."

"Yeah but see, that's the thing. These are real fresh shavings, not mulch, and they didn't just dump down a few inches. They laid it down like a roadway. She figured it had to be six inches thick and wide like a driveway and," she raised her hand again, "before you ask, I made a call to the TSC over in Collins. They only had a few bags, but when I said I would probably need several tons, they gave me the name of a guy out on the Cattaraugus Reservation. He has lots and said he would come out and have a look at what we need. And yes, I asked him about walking on that stuff. He had a good laugh at that, but did say they use it for the youth dances out there and some of the girls wear heels, so he was pretty sure it must be okay."

Lori thought about it. "You know, if we cut some tarps to lay out first, to keep the moisture from seeping up too fast and then have him roll that stuff out...Wait, will he do that?"

"Yep! He was real cool. I just have to call him back and he'll come over later and have a look so he knows how much we need. And he said he had helpers so we just need to decide if he delivers everything and lays it out on Friday or Saturday morning."

"Which is better?"

"Well, I was thinking Friday, but he said it smells better if he puts it out fresh that morning but it was our choice."

"Smells better, geez, the place is going to smell like a barn."

"Better than the lake, you know, on certain days."

Lori groaned again. "I don't know. I think I'd prefer the odd smelly fish day to barnyard odors. Still, cedar might be nice. Okay," she decided, "call him back and get him out here. I'm still going to keep looking for a landscaper who can get in here right away and start laying patio slabs. At least Fener's guys finished polishing their cement pour. I know he was a little irked we wanted it polished and ready before the new building went up. Are the party tent people all confirmed?"

"Actually, they asked if they could come out on Thursday to get started raising the big tent. I said it was okay since they're not going to charge us extra. That's okay, right?"

"That's perfect, Megs," Lori answered absently as she tabbed through her own to-do list. "What else, what else?" She wasn't really asking, just struggling with all the myriad things needing to be done before Saturday. "Oh shit, sorry, I forgot about the surveillance. What did you find?"

Megan hesitated for the longest time. Reaching for the remote, she pressed the play button without commenting on the footage she had isolated.

Straining to recognize the vehicle pulling donuts all over the boatyard's healthy rich lawns, she choked suddenly, the recognition hitting her like a fist to the gut. "Fuck me!" she uttered, immediately out of her chair and pacing the small office. This was a problem she herself had created and knowing added to the insult. At least Megan knew better than to comment. She had been right to offer solutions before sharing this upset.

"Boss," Megan said carefully. "Listen, me and Sanjit were talking and, well, we were thinking we should double up out here for the week or at least on Thursday and Friday. Especially once the tents are up and all the equipment is out here."

Lori was about to agree, only then remembering Sanjit would be a guest and Megan was in the wedding party. Even though they could probably handle themselves and the sleep deprivation, she didn't want either of them stuck there all night and possibly facing down her mess. "Thanks kiddo, I appreciate that, both of you. I will miss you guys when you leave for the police academy in September."

That much was true, especially with Megan, who had taken to her job like a duck to water. The kid really was made for this stuff. "I want you guys to have fun, and besides it's your sister's wedding. I'm already in enough poop with Tyler. I think we should call in paid duty cops. Can you take care of that for me?"

"Sure," Megan promised, adding notes to her phone. "What time should they be here on Saturday?"

Lori shook her head. "Bring in two officers for the remainder of the week, evenings and nights until the party company comes for their stuff on Monday."

She watched as Megan's brow inched up. To the kid's credit she knew better than to question the decision. If Marnie or anyone else for that matter balked at the cost, she would pick up the tab herself. Having the cops nab Peachy was a hell of a better prospect than risking having her own staff take her on.

She thanked Megan for the update, and marched back out into the midday sun, wandering around the parking lot unfocused. She finally stopped at her Jeep, leaning heavily on the hood and resting her elbows there. Lost in thought and unaware, she steadily tapped two fingers against her lips. Normally she shared this kind of stuff with Marnie. They were best friends and had been since birth, but Marnie would flip if she had any idea this mess was of her own making. No, calling Marnie to talk was off the table. She could call Georgie. She would understand but she would be disappointed too. She was already disappointed over Lori's involvement with Peachy. She had been good with it on the shakedown cruise back in January. Of course that might have been more about having a fourth person on board, ensuring her more time with Tyler alone. Tyler! She should call Tyler. But this was Tyler's wedding and she would give her a lecture and tell her to come clean with Aydan.

Finally, pulling out her phone, she clicked on Aydan's number, sucking in a few harsh breaths waiting for the call to connect. She didn't need to call anyone else for advice. It was Aydan she was concerned for and Aydan she needed. This was new territory, this wanting someone and caring what they might think. Over the last few weeks she had worked hard to repair the damage from her stupid bet with Zoe and Zoe too seemed to have calmed right down, apologizing to them both. At least that hadn't been weird. Marnie was spot-on when she said the kid was a complete pro at work.

"Well, good day, Ms. Phipps. To what do I owe the pleasure?"

Trying not to panic, Lori offered her standard greeting, "Hello, princess. How's your day going so far?"

"All in all I can't complain, but I am starting to worry for my charge. She's very nervous."

"Georgie?" she asked unnecessarily. "Wow, who knew!"

Aydan chuckled at the response. "Every time I try and talk to her, she just keeps repeating 'make it perfect for my Tyler.' Well, not quite in so many words, but you know that."

"Oh, I do indeed," Lori answered, and then paused, unsure how to broach the subject. She admired how Georgie could stutter out a few phrases Tyler would instantly understand. She wasn't worried Aydan wouldn't understand her. Her hesitation was borne of shame and fear, real fear of losing this thing she hadn't even known she wanted so very, very much.

"Oh, Lori," Aydan said softly. "What's happened, can you talk?"

"Yes, no, I mean yes but I think we should meet. It's important," she added, her anxiety clear.

There was a long hesitation before Aydan asked, "Are you okay?"

"Yes, but something's happened out here. Something I'm trying to clean up but..."

"But whatever has happened, you think it's important I know, or important I'm prepared?"

Lori was so relieved to hear the kindness in her tone. "Ah, yes and yes."

"Is this something Georgie and Tyler should not hear?"

"Oh yeah, that's a pretty good bet but I won't ask you to lie for me. If it turns out I can't fix this on my own, I promise I'll come clean ASAP. Until then...well, you have a right to know and I made a promise. Besides, I kind of need someone to talk to about this, this situation. Is that cool?"

"Of course it is. Actually I'm glad you called. It's nice to know someone appreciates my opinion."

"Appreciates?" Lori almost laughed. "Aydana-dana, I more than appreciate it. You just make things make so much sense to me."

She laughed quietly over the digital line. "Would you like to come into town and get a bite? Or, I could drive out there. You keep promising to give me the full tour and a home-heated meal."

While that idea was more than pleasing, the sudden and probable risk of having Peachy show up was too much. Almost panicking, she coughed out a negative, "Uhm, I'll come into town. Actually, I think I'll stay in Dad's apartment for the rest of the week, you know, just in case G&T need me."

"Uh-huh," she said, clearly aware there was more to say. At Lori's silence, Aydan offered, "Okay...I'll wait until you're here to ask for details. Would you send me a text before you leave the yard? That way I can be ready. I take it we'll be going out somewhere?"

"Yes, yes you decide and yes I'll let you know when I'm on my way. Thank you, Aydan." With that said they ended their call. It wasn't as if they were at that point in their relationship where they were expressing endearments. *No not saying, just feeling. Oh God, Aydan please, please, I so hope you can forgive me again!*

* * *

Hours later Aydan sat in the darkened living room, considering all she had heard. It was hard to understand her own feelings. Part of her was so drawn to Lori she wanted to forgive and forget, emphasis on forget but that wasn't who she was. The question haunting her was how Lori could declare such interest in her while still…still having intimate interests elsewhere. It just didn't make sense. She so wished she could talk to Tyler but the details involved a threat to her wedding and even Aydan knew better than to open that can of worms, at least not with the boss's boss, even if she was her closest friend. Her wedding, their wedding, was too big a deal to add the worry over one of Lori's…encounters, into the mix. She would need to keep tabs on the situation. Megan would be a better contact on that front, and as a bonus, she knew just how important this day was for her sister.

Georgie too was approachable. She knew without asking that her boss would listen, work out a plan with her, and keep the situation as far from Tyler as possible, but she would worry. Adding worry for either of them was out of the question. They had been there for her from the start. Lori, Leslie and Kira too but it was Megan who figured out she was in trouble and Georgie who had come to her offering her support and friendship.

But Lori…not really. She was like the middleman in every interaction. She still contributed in an interrelated way and it wasn't that she couldn't get things done on her own but more often than not, she was the messenger, either delegating orders or carrying her concerns upstairs for Marnie to decide on, or across to Tyler to manage. That wasn't fair though. Lori ran her own division like a well-oiled machine and she had been pivotal in managing the entire situation involving Georgie's accident. She had to acknowledge that Lori's efforts with both women might have been the saving grace their relationship needed to right itself. That was worthy of respect. There was no denying she believed in acting on her feelings and doing the right thing.

Still…it was hard to accept she would just allow some person to ingratiate herself into her life. She understood why Lori would have wanted a companion on the shakedown cruise, but even that idea irked her and forced her to question so much.

Was Lori just a grown-up Zoe? Both women seemed so free with their intimacies. She understood and yet was shocked at the same time. Long before she and Lori began dating, she could admit her desire for this bold attractive woman. Certainly when she had delivered the beautiful silk scarves. She had made a big deal of it being nothing. "Just in case you wanted to swap out the gray one. No big deal." At first Aydan had taken her at her word but she had pondered, slowly admitting to the quality of the silk. She knew they must have been extravagantly expensive, remembering just how much her dad had paid for the beautiful Jacquard the day she was born. The scarf her mother and brothers had destroyed.

She was grateful and flattered by the gift but suspicious too. Who did that kind of thing and why? It was part of what drove her to accept Zoe's invitations first. The young woman seemed to understand her plight, being new to the world and all but she too had her own motives. And Tyler was right, Zoe could be aggressive, but seemed to waffle between being patient to pushing her agenda. She now suspected the "rules" Lori had set for the stupid bet were responsible for reining in Zoe's aggression. And what were Lori's intentions? From the start she recognized her stronger attraction to Lori and had steered toward Zoe thinking her a safer alternative but spending time with Zoe only reminded her that Zoe was young and as much as they had fun together, it was her desire for Lori that never waned.

She hadn't acted on that desire, not yet, but it had been there the whole time, the wanting, and the need, but like any good engineer, she had established milestones, intending to get things right. She had spent a long while contemplating the mistakes she made with Sarah all those years ago and jumping in too fast had been one. It wasn't as if Sarah had been anything but patient too but it had all been too fast and too painful for

Aydan to digest. "Small steps," her father had counseled at the time and she had lived by those words as she worked at building a new foundation for her own solitary and singular life.

She could now admit to wanting to share this new life. Living with Tyler and Georgie had been an education in how beautiful and challenging it was to make a lifetime commitment to each other. Tyler dealt with trials others couldn't comprehend. Lori at least could walk, talk and chew gum at the same time, but she too came with a set of problems, foremost obviously being the legacy of her love life.

Climbing out of the window seat she had been warming, she walked to the library, turning on the spotlights for the bookshelves. Lori had suggested a book for her to read. She found it amusing that the woman would recommend a work of fiction as some sort of explanation for her past. She wasn't sure who had so carefully sorted every title by author and shelved them accordingly but she was thankful, pulling Karin Kallmaker's *Wild Things* from the bookshelf. Carrying it dutifully to her room, she accepted she wasn't in the mood to read. She needed to talk, and with the implications to Georgie and Tyler, they were definitely out of the picture.

She wasn't ready to talk to Lori herself, at least until she had time to process everything she had learned and she didn't think it was fair to pull Zoe into this. Besides, she never really knew whose side she would take. She'd seemed genuine when she offered her friendship. Still, it wasn't right to lean on her after having dated, even if it was only for a few times. Who did that leave in her grand pantheon of friends? That thought actually made her smile.

Six months ago I didn't have a friend in the world. Today I have a home, a job, a really good job, and this amazing woman in hot pursuit of me. A pursuit I very much want her to win. Does her past really change that and why does it make me so damn mad?

* * *

Lori watched as Marnie poured herself another glass of wine, asking if she wanted one. "Naw, I'm good," she said, turning to Helen who had just walked back into the room. They had elected to spend the night before the wedding at Marnie's place because there was room and knowing Georgie would prefer anyplace other than the big house. Skip and Megan, part of the wedding party, were staying too. Skippy had taken a lot of heat for being the only guy in the wedding party, but like everything the kid did he took it in stride, gleefully telling the whole world he was honored to be Georgie's bridesman. Now both he and Megan were in the media room playing video games with Marnie's sons, Luc and Danny, and Georgie was tucked in bed.

They had slipped a mild sedative into her nightcap knowing her nerves had already gotten the best of her. She had spent most of the day pacing and alternatively practicing her vows and obsessively checking her gown and accoutrements. Thank goodness Aydan knew better than to review their travel plans with her. They were taking three weeks, a luxurious amount of time in this day and age. They would spend their wedding night on the new sailboat Georgie had ordered over a year ago, a boat Tyler had yet to see. Then Sunday afternoon they were scheduled to fly to New York then on to Rome. They would spend a week in Italy then on to Athens for a few days, followed by Egypt, and then back to Rome to spend the last three days visiting Georgie's grandmother Sophia's relatives in Ceca Castina.

"How is she?" Marnie asked, handing Helen a fresh glass of wine.

"Oh, she's out cold. She's still smart as a whip. I think she knows you two slipped her a Mickey Finn."

That made Marnie laugh. "I think the kids call it a roofie these days."

"Oh, I know and so does she," she teased. "What I can't believe is how much Italian she still speaks. I remember when Georgina was teaching me, little Georgie was my practice buddy. Oh God, we would have your aunt in stitches with our baby Italian. It was adorable."

"I think that had a lot to do with Sophia," Lori explained, "her remembering Italian, I mean. Sophia pretty much stopped speaking English after…you know. Anyway, if Uncle Dan wasn't around, Georgie ended up interpreting. I tell yah, you guys must have rocked as students, even if Aunt Georgie found it hilarious."

"Oh your aunt was nothing but supportive with us and patient," Helen said, "but lord oh lord that woman could be fun!"

"You must have really missed her, and all of us," Marnie asked kindly. "I wish I had known, Helen. I really do. I don't know how we can ever make things up to you."

"Marina, and you too Lori Ann, please don't worry. I've had years to come to terms with my feelings. Yes, I would have given anything to be involved in your lives earlier, but I'm here now and I'm so glad, thankful actually. In many ways I can't help but think this is how it was supposed to be. I'm not sure I would have ever recovered from losing Georgina if I'd remained so close to all of you. Coming back to the family now is like a special gift and I couldn't be more thankful. To see each of you girls all grown, so successful, and each so much in love…that in itself is the gift of a lifetime."

Lori watched Marnie, never good with compliments, shake it off. "It was easy for me. I met Jack in high school and that was it. Georgie was hopeless for years." At Lori's laugh, she amended her statement. "Okay, she was a very bad girl, almost as bad as this one." She tipped her thumb to Lori. "Now all we need to do is find the right woman for numb-nuts here. Of course, I've given up on finding a man for Leslie. I'm starting to think she goes through them faster than sous-chefs."

"Oh God," Helen laughed, "you girls turned out just fine. Even Lou isn't so bad. God knows he was one fussy baby. As for you, Lori Ann, I think maybe love has found its way into your heart?"

"What?" Marnie choked on her drink. "What are you talking about?"

"Oh, I think I'll leave this conversation for you two littermates." And with that and a wide grin she headed back up to the guest room.

"Lori?" Marnie growled her warning. "Since when am I the last one to hear?"

"It's not like that, Marns. Well, it is, but I just figured it out and I didn't want you to freak seeing as how I kinda screwed the pooch on this one." When that solicited only a raised brow, she pushed on, knowing Marnie was the one voice she had been missing in all of this. "So, I kind of fell for this girl, I mean woman, but she works for us so I did the honorable thing and told her boss that I had intentions. Turns out I wasn't the only one. Anyway…"

"Which boss?" Marnie demanded. "I want to know who didn't have the guts to come to me."

"It wasn't like that. I talked to Tyler because this woman works for her and…"

"Don't tell me—"

"Will you cut it out? I'm trying to tell you everything and you keep interrupting."

"Whoa Lor, it's just me. What the hell's got under your skin? Did Tyler warn you off Aydan or something?"

"No, it's not like that. I screwed up."

Then she waited as Marnie swooshed the wine in her glass in a circular motion, thinking, considering, putting the pieces together. "Aydan sent me a Personnel Relationship Declaration, as per cooperate policy and as per policy, she was only required to acknowledge the person she's involved with works in a different division. I just assumed she was interested in Zoe…Oh poor Zoe…oh geez, that stupid bet, the silk scarf…Please tell me you two haven't broken Zoe's heart?"

Lori bristled. "Until recently we didn't even know she had one and for your information she's fine."

It took Lori the better part of an hour to spit out the entire story including the stupid bet and the mounting situation with Peachy. Marnie took that latter part a lot better than Lori had imagined, even praising her and Megan's recovery plans and preparations, and for knowing better than to share that vengeance crap with either Tyler or Georgie.

"You know, I never thought either day would come. Imagine my Lo-Ann in love and our Georgie walking down the aisle…I wish Dad could be here, even in light of all the shit that's come up."

"You know he wasn't a bad guy, just kinda broken. I think that happened to a lot of men back then, you know, Vietnam veterans and such."

Marnie's face showed she was not only unconvinced but in complete disagreement. "That doesn't really cut it. I'm always telling the boys they're one hundred percent responsible for their own actions at all times. I don't know what I would do if either of them ever hit a woman, or worse. The thought just makes me sick. Whenever I hear the stories of nice girls going off to college only to be raped by some little shit who thinks it's some sort of sport—what the fuck is that? My boys are good boys, but sometimes I just can't believe the stupid stuff that comes out of their mouths."

"Like wanting to tell the family lawyers they're gay to up their inheritance?"

Marnie all but snorted out her response.

Getting up and retrieving the wine bottle and topping up both their glasses, Lori gave her cousin's shoulder a consoling pat. "I have to admit I still laugh. Those two are always up to something and don't worry, I wasn't offended. Actually, Georgie and I stuck our heads together and plan to offer them each a building lot for graduating from college. Skippy too and Zoe if she ever gets around to finishing." She qualified, "If you're okay with it?"

Marnie smiled at her over the rim of her wineglass. "You know, life would have been so much simpler if they had actually turned out gay. At least then I wouldn't be worrying if I raised them right. It's always the mother who gets blamed when they turn out all wrong."

"Hey there Marns, no worries. Besides, being gay is no guarantee a guy will be decent. Even gay guys get their share of disgusting little gutter snipes. Anyway, between Jack, me and Georgie, we'll all kick their asses from here to kingdom come if they pull any crap with anyone. Promise, okay?"

Marnie's twin sons turning eighteen meant they would be off to college soon. It was something she worried over nonstop. Standing she waved. "Come on, you. We'll need some sleep if we're ever going to get Georgie dressed and down the aisle in one piece."

"Don't you know it," Lori groaned. "Just one more thing. You've been bustin' my balls about not sharing everything with you. Meanwhile I've been waiting patiently for you to come clean with me."

Marnie looked like she would protest, then, surprisingly, nodded. "I'm okay. I...I thought maybe there was something."

"Something other than ghosts?"

She nodded. "I should have said something, but it wasn't until Georgie was in the hospital that I realized I had to face it or risk the company later on."

"Please tell me you got Margaret O'Shea to look at you. She may be a scheming bitch, but she's a brilliant surgeon scheming bitch."

Marnie nodded her agreement. "She ran a battery of tests and scans. Turns out it's not early onset menopause like my idiot family doctor proposed. That is the last time I see that guy. I swear I am so off dumbass—"

"Marnie! Eyes on the prize. What did old Mags come up with? You're okay, right?"

"Relax, it's just a slow thyroid. She's got me on meds and it's working. These last few weeks I've been feeling like my old self again."

"Thank the sweet baby Jesus! Marn, I gotta tell you. I don't know if I coulda handled another upset, but I would have. You know that, right? I mean, you keeping this from me really freaked me out."

"I know, and I promise, it won't happen again. The truth is I was feeling a little sorry for myself. I guess a part of me has been on the manage Georgie wagon for so long I was feeling a little unwanted. In a way I kind of sympathize with Zoe, her feelings," she said, adding, "not her behavior."

"Me too and in a big way. It's funny but it's Tyler and Aydan who explained a lot to me on that front. I never really understood how unessential the kid must feel. It's crazy, but I kind of understand a bit more why Lou pulls such crap too.

Maybe it was easier for us. It's not like we ever tried to measure ourselves against Georgie, but I think they do."

Marnie groaned, offering her hand to help her up from the couch. "I wish I was as good as Georgie at instilling confidence. It's really all the kid needs, her father too. Although, Lou is doing much better running his own shop. Some days he reminds me of when we were all still at home. The way his eyes would shine when he got to tell a story over dinner or when the whole family would come out for his hockey games. He loved making Georgie proud. As proud as he was at pleasing our dads."

Up on her feet, Lori agreed. "You're right. I never thought about it that way but you're right. Now how do we do that for Zoe? Her ego's been cruisin' for bruisin' for years, but I had no idea the kid had zero self-esteem."

Marnie hooked her arm, leading her one-time nursery mate to the stairs. "Let's get Georgie through this wedding then we can worry about Zoe, not to mention a certain breach of corporate policy, hmm?"

Wrinkling her nose in a look of contrition and amusement, Lori pleaded, "Promise, but I want one in return. No more keeping serious stuff from me. Got it?"

Marnie playfully slapped her arm. "I promise. Now go to bed. I'll go order the sausage party to their bunks and hit the hay myself. I have a feeling tomorrow will be a long day."

Lori agreed. Tomorrow would be a long day, but not as long as the week had been. Since her Monday night discussion with Aydan she had been on pins and needles wanting to know how she felt. She had repeatedly told herself everything would work out while at the same time being absolutely sure she would never earn Aydan's forgiveness again. Aydan had asked for the week to consider everything. She had been kind, even understanding, but the hurt was evident. That was something Lori never wanted to see ever again and it was a promise she had silently made to herself.

CHAPTER TWENTY

Aydan walked the length of the boatyard, tablet in hand, inspecting all the last-minute details. They still had an hour before the wedding and she was determined to make sure everything went off without a hitch. The tents were up, the tables, including the linens, glassware and china, were all set. The flowers and decorations were being finalized as the catering staff buzzed around the reception and buffet tent, making sure everything was in order and serving drinks to the first arriving guests.

As Megan had promised, the guys from the Cattaraugus Reservation had delivered the fresh cedar shavings the day before and had returned today to add a second layer. They had done another solid for the wedding, commandeering the yard tractor and giving the lawn another clipping. Now the heady scent of fresh cut grass comingled with the pleasing aroma of the cedar shavings. As she stopped to take everything in, Sanjit caught up with her.

"Okay," he began, "the cops are telling me everything's been quiet. The valet company is a little put off by the added numbers, but I assured them most would be locals and to just let the little shuttle buses pass through."

"Do you think everyone got the message to just walk over here or flag down the shuttle instead of driving?"

"I think so. Me and Megan pretty much visited everyone living out here. I still can't believe they invited everyone."

She wasn't sure if he meant that as a compliment or not. "I think that was Lori's idea. After all, most of the people out here are retired employees or extended family."

"Well, whoever's idea it was, it's really generous and just like these guys. I think Tyler's marrying into a real awesome family. Sometimes I wish I were a lesbian."

He said it with such sincerity it forced her to smile. "I see why Megan says you're such a good guy."

Making their way to where the sound equipment was being set up, she asked, "So I hear both you and Megan have been accepted into the police academy. Congratulations."

"Oh, I know. I can't believe how lucky I am and I get to go with my best buddy. How awesome is that?"

That tidbit caught her by surprise. Much like everyone else she had imagined he and Megan were dating. "Best buddy? Is that what you two are?" She was about to apologize for invading his privacy, then changed her mind. Personal information sharing seemed quite normal with this group and she believed her friendship with Tyler gave her some excuse for meddling.

"Yeah," he admitted without a second thought. "Lots of people think we we're hooking up but it's not like that. Me and Megs have blue hearts…you know what that means, right?" At her headshake, he explained. "We're just the kind of folks who were born to be cops. So we kinda get each other, you know, like best buds."

"I think I understand. It's very nice that you two can be such good friends and share your life's passion. It's like me and Skip," she said, realizing the truth of it the moment the words were out. "We talk the same language when it comes to engineering. Georgie too but Skip and I are working at the same level, seeing the same things, and we learn from one another."

"Yeah. Like that. Lots of guys don't get why my best friend is a girl, but I don't see her that way. Since I started here, we've been taking these classes and studying together, you know, learning the job. It's so cool to have a friend who gets that."

"I know what you mean," she said sincerely, while clicking back through the checklist. "I can't believe the number of guests has inched up over five hundred!"

"They really wanted everyone to feel welcome. I was kinda shocked too at how many people from around here accepted the invite. I mean..." He colored slightly, suddenly aware of what he was suggesting. "I just mean like they're all pretty old, you know, so I was kinda shocked they would want to go to a wedding."

"A lesbian wedding, you mean?"

Clearly embarrassed, he tried to explain. "I...it's just people are always freaking out about gays and lesbian and gay weddings and then when there's a chance for free booze and a fancy meal and they're all like, me too, me too."

"I don't think it's that bad. At least not around here," she added, hoping it was true. The good folks on the peninsula, at least those south of Cattaraugus Creek, were almost all living on DiNamico/Phipps property, in houses owned and maintained by two out and proud lesbians and all had worked for the family company or were the family of retirees. If they had issues with either Lori or Georgie, or Georgie and Tyler's wedding, she would be shocked or at least disappointed. Of course, there were always those individuals who felt compelled to bite the hand that feeds them. Today though, neither she nor Sanjit would allow it to happen. He too had been briefed on the situation with Sue Ellen Peach. Megan had vouched for his discretion, bringing him into the small circle of those preparing for trouble. "I think everything's ready, or will be. All we have to do now is make sure things don't fall apart between now and when the brides arrive."

"Don't worry, Aydan," he reassured her. "The way we set up security, no one's getting past Erie Street without an invitation, and only the limos will be allowed past Exchange Street. We're ready for anything."

"I'm sure we are," she said kindly, while concern bombarded her every nerve.

And then there's you, Lori Phipps. Just what do I do about my feelings for you?

Just last night she had read the book Lori suggested. She could admit to being particularly attracted to the character with a past, but it was the intensity of the protagonist's attraction to her more innocent partner that had resonated so deeply.

Waving Sanjit off, she watched him head back to the catering tent. He wanted to make sure the truck, rented to transport all the leftover food to several local shelters, would be able to extricate itself from the yard and guests after dinner. Several people had been shocked to learn food would be served all night. The family called it a Newfie supper and couldn't be persuaded otherwise regardless of the estimated waste. Leslie too had championed the plan, even going as far as contacting shelters and arranging for a rental van and volunteers to make deliveries. Aydan had to commend her efforts, considering the number of guests had started at eighty and now topped five hundred. Between the guests and the long night of food service, the catering staff had swelled to the size of a regiment, a sea of uniformed movement buzzing around in packs and fussing to make sure everything was just right. Several paraded around the green lawns, drink trays overhead, greeting the arriving guests. Considering Sanjit's comment about everyone loving a lesbian wedding when the food and booze were free, she eyed the new arrivals looking for some sign of disingenuous intent. Seeing only smiles and glad tidings, she shook off her suspicions. Every family, she was discovering, carried some component of shame no matter how healthy or evolved.

Tyler's family seemed to be the exception. She did rather unkindly ask how perfect things would be once they were forced to face Megan's sexuality. But right now they, like Megan, had just ignored the question. *Much like I did.* She understood where Megan was, still so focused on what she wanted to do with her life and unconcerned for much else. The difference between them was more than being fledgling lesbians; she had been tossed out by her family even though she had been the one to remove herself permanently from their presence. Megan, she knew, would have the support of her sisters and most probably her parents too. She didn't know them well, but they seemed like genuinely good people.

Georgie and Lori's family too were amazing, but learning they hadn't always been so perfect was both hard and encouraging. They had worked through so many demons in these last few months. The results not only saved Tyler and Georgie's relationship, it had opened the whole family to forgive and heal. As witness, and lifted in hope for her own family one day in the future, she finally understood that their opinions were just that. Opinions formed from ignorance and shame.

I was like that—frightened by shame. But I'm not afraid anymore.

A long line of limos made their way up Allegany, pulling into the employee lot. She watched as Sanjit, dressed in what she was sure was a borrowed suit, trotted up to meet them, pointing the lead limo to the bridal party tent. This was Tyler and her family. Buoyed by her own excitement, she headed over to meet them.

The moment she walked in, Tyler's eyes were on her. Aydan assured her, "Everything's fine, I promise. Just stopped in to wish you luck and let you know everything's ready. Most of the guests have arrived too."

Tyler nodded, clearly too hyped to even speak.

"Just breathe, baby!" her mother counseled, then turned to Aydan. "Hello, sweetie. You look so lovely."

"Thank you, Mrs. Marsh."

"Oh no, you know better than that," she said, slipping a willowy arm around her shoulders. "You're family with us, Aydan, and if you don't start calling me Debbie I will put you over my knee. Understood, young lady?"

Aydan grinned. "Yes, Debbie, and thanks. Listen, why don't I get one of the waitstaff to bring in some champagne? I know Leslie ordered several bottles to settle any pre-ceremony jitters."

They were enjoying a knowing chuckle when Tyler stormed over. "My pre-ceremony jitters will settle as soon as my fiancée shows her face. Where the hell is she?"

Carl, resplendent in his tux, wrapped a soothing arm around his daughter. His other arm was full of giggly little Ella and her flower girl frills. "She'll be here, pumpkin. No worries there."

"Yeah," Kira added, pointing to the other bridesmaids, Leslie, Susan and—Zoe who was carefully repacking purple rose petals in Ella's basket. "If she doesn't, we'll kick her arse!"

"Me too," Aydan answered with uncharacteristic confidence, joining in on the family repartee.

"Girls!" Debbie warned them much as if they were all her own. "Now let's not plan Georgie's demise until she's actually late…"

As if in answer they heard a horn blow, and Aydan stepped out in time to watch as the second set of limos pulled up on the other side of the yard, stopping in front of the opposite bridal tent. Stepping back in, she reassured everyone, "She's here. I'll go check on them and report back. Any last wishes or requests?"

Tyler had choked up again and while Debbie worked to calm her down, Carl occupied the flower girl. Zoe, Kira, Leslie and even Susan stuck their heads out hoping for a glimpse of the other team. Herding them back inside first, she finally made her way across the lawn. But before she could check on her charge, Sanjit was back at her side.

"The honor guard is here. What do I do with them?"

Men and women from Georgie's guard unit were standing in a tight group and looking a little lost. Resplendent in their air force blues with white gloves and belts, sheathed swords hung from each one. At the end of the ceremony they would form a long arch of crossed swords for the two brides to traverse under. It was supposed to be good luck or something. The request for the honor hadn't come from Georgie, but the men and women from her Air National Guard unit. *My, how far we have come!* Only a few years ago, Georgie's sexual orientation would have been met with scorn, investigation and even banishment from military service. Today her unit would honor her commitment to live her life honestly.

"Their seats are on the opposite side of the orchestra. Why don't you get them over there and I'll let the catering staff know it's time to hold the drinks and start ushering guests to their seats."

"On it!" he said, and was gone in a flash.

It didn't take her much longer to signal the headwaiter and bartenders to get everyone moving in that direction. It was time. The orchestra, really just a string ensemble, was already in place and would take their cue from the wedding officiant. She, Aydan noted, had arrived and was making her way from Georgie's tent to Tyler's.

Spotting Aydan and knowing her place in the family and business, she stopped, offering a friendly greeting, "Afternoon, Ms. Ferdowsi. I'm just headed in to check on Tyler. Georgina's all ready to go. Is everything set out here?"

"It is. I'm just getting everyone seated," she explained eyeing the padre's colorful vestments. While the brides were wearing traditional white, the wedding party was all decked out in shades of blue. Tyler had chosen the color in respect to Georgie's branch of service and the first flowers she had ever given her. Secretly, Aydan was sure it had more to do with blue being her favorite color, but it did make Georgie happy and kept her from insisting on wearing her uniform. Tyler hadn't been against it but had complained about the general plainness of her air force mess dress uniform. As always, she had gotten her way, simply by asking Georgie to wear a dress. It was like magic to watch how easily Tyler could persuade her. More, though, was Georgie's respect for Tyler. She never took advantage of her influence over her very, very soon to be wife. Earning and keeping Georgie's respect was as important as her love and affection. Knowing her boss, Aydan now understood that for her, love and respect all flowed from the same place. Maybe that was the magic about these two she so envied. They never seemed to waste too much time on the past. They talked, never keeping their feelings suppressed, even when the subject was hard or trying.

Head down and deep in her own thoughts, she was heading the final few yards to Georgie's tent when she spotted a late-arriving limo making its way up Allegany. She was about to pop in when Sanjit's words came back: "Only the limousines of the wedding party and the immediate family would be allowed past the security on Exchange." She was sure she had counted all of Georgie's party arriving and couldn't imagine whom she had missed when an eye-catching redhead, dressed inappropriately in white, was helped from the vehicle.

Sanjit, too, was immediately at Aydan's side. "Is that one of the cousins from Newfoundland? I thought they were all here already. Do you know which one that is?"

"Oh, I know who that is and she's not a cousin."

He blanched at her angry expression. "Should I toss her out? No one was supposed to get this far without an invitation. How did she make it past security? Should I call them?" He reached for his phone.

"No, it's okay, Sanjit, I've got this. You go ahead and get the last of the stragglers seated."

She strolled over to introduce herself to Sue Ellen. "Ms. Peach, I'm Aydan Ferdowsi, Georgina's executive assistant—"

"I know exactly who you are!" she spat. Then she added in an unnervingly jovial tone, "Call me Peachy."

Aydan immediately realized the woman had been drinking. Luckily she wasn't completely drunk. That was all she needed to deal with, especially when the ceremony was minutes from kicking off. "I'm sorry but the wedding is invitation only. I'll have to ask you—"

"Here," she said, shoving an invitation in Aydan's face.

"Where did you get this?" she demanded with as much control as she could muster. She knew the invitation list backward and forward and Sue Ellen Peach was definitely not on it. "Look, Ms. Peach, I understand you're friends with Georgie and Tyler and you probably think that's why you're here. I also suspect you're in pain. I get that, I do, but I'm not going to let you make a scene today. Please, if you care for Georgie and Tyler at all—"

"I do!" she insisted. "I'm not a monster, you know. I wanted to be here. Maybe I was mad for a while but I wouldn't—"

"Really? Then where did you get this?" She held up the invitation.

Looking rather pouty and annoyed, she finally confessed, "I'm Zoe's plus one, but don't blame her, please Aydan. I kind of talked her into it."

The string ensemble began the first song and she knew Georgie and her attendants would begin making their way to the altar in seconds. Giving the woman standing before her the toughest look she could muster, she announced plainly, "*If,* you promise to be on your best behavior, and *if,* you are willing to sit with me, you can stay. After all, Georgie and Tyler said you were a friend. You are, aren't you?"

"Yes, yes I am!" Her antagonism seemed gone. "Aydan, I know I came to cause trouble but…everything's so beautiful and you're right, they've always been real nice to me. Here, let me take your arm. That way you can keep a hand on me and if I get out of sorts feel free to slap me upside the head."

Aydan let her take her arm, saying not unkindly, "I'd rather have your assurances."

"I promise. And if you or Lori want, I'll leave right after the ceremony."

She led them to the rear row of chairs just in time to watch Lori and Marnie lead the procession, listening the whole while to Peachy's oohs and aahs over the music, the dresses, the flowers, and finally the brides. "Oh my God, look at Georgie. She looks like fucking Sophia Loren!"

Aydan gave her arm a nudge, reminding her to rein it in. Peachy settled in to watch the service. She was right, though, Aydan conceded. Georgie did look a lot like the great Italian heartthrob. Tyler too was gorgeous, outstandingly so but as usual it was the pleasure on Georgie's face at seeing her that said everything. If anyone had ever questioned the strength of the love shared between these two women, they would have to be deaf and blind to question it now.

Beside her and still holding her arm, Peachy was in tears. "They're so beautiful," she whispered as they watched as first Henry and Helen at Georgie's side, and then Carl and Debbie with Tyler, handed off their parental responsibility to each other's charges. Unconventionally, both Henry and Helen, and

Tyler's parents too, took a moment to hug each bride, only then taking their seats on opposite sides of the aisle. As the guests sat, the officiant began the service. She spoke of the two brides and their commitment to each other, the importance of family and friends as witness, even commenting on the breathtaking summer day.

Aydan nudged Peachy, whispering, "This is where they say the vows they have written." Aware of the challenge facing Georgie, they held their breath, watching her telltale clues: closing her eyes to see the words she had long since memorized.

"I fell in love with your mind first. I read about you, your work, your ideas, I even read your graduate thesis, and I knew I was in love…Then you walked in. I was sitting at my desk… and yes, I was hiding. It was one of those days. Then you walked down the stairs into old Luigi's grand office, and I knew I was in real trouble. I couldn't for the life of me understand how anyone as brilliant as you could be so stunningly beautiful too. Then it got worse. You opened your mouth and spoke so eloquently of your ideas and expectations. And for a long moment I actually asked myself if someone was playing a masterful practical joke on me…Here you were, like some perfect dream, standing in my office and chastising me for jumping off a perfectly good boat in the middle of winter!" Everyone laughed politely, while Georgie stood transfixed. "In that moment, I knew without a doubt, I would love you forever."

Tyler smiled so sweetly that there could be no doubt those words were cherished. Then she spoke.

"It took me a long time to understand the Georgie DiNamico brand of crazy." And now everyone was having a good laugh. "That first day was like walking into a strange dream. I imagined my life had hit rock bottom, then I almost tripped down the stairs! What an entrance that would have been. Instead of that first day being my worst, it was a day of revelations, or at least the first of many wonderful discoveries to come. You, my love, are an opportunity creator, but more than that you continued to open doors for me even when you believed my interests lay elsewhere. It took time for me to see that, see you for all your complexities and kindness. But love, the love was always there. I just had to look to see it. The moment I did, something changed deep inside me. It was as if you had shared some deep part of you and it brought me to my knees. Never have I fallen so completely and desperately in love. Today I'm standing here, with all our family, and friends, and I can't imagine being anywhere else than with you and loving you the way I do."

That brought tears and applause and more applause as they completed their formal vows, finally exchanging rings.

Aydan took in the wedding tableau. Beyond the dresses, flowers and familiar faces, she saw happiness. She had missed that before, not the love or even the deep respect, but the sheer overwhelming joy. It wasn't a revelation that she wanted that too—who didn't? But wanting it with a certain someone was a breakthrough moment, and Lori, as if sensing her presence, her need, was scanning the guests, stopping and smiling at her, before turning to cheer with everyone else as the brides shared an intense yet tender kiss.

"She loves you," Peachy said, interrupting her thoughts.

"What—"

"She loves you. Lori, I mean," Peachy explained as the honor guard marched into place. They stood with all the guests, listening to a young lieutenant call out commands. Finally, with swords drawn and raised, Tyler and Georgie began their procession under it. Afterward, followed closely by the wedding party, they beat a path along the cedar trail to the area set aside for formal pictures. All around Aydan and Peachy, happy voices built in volume.

Pulling Aydan along with her, Peachy began moving toward the parking lot. "I shouldn't have come, but thank you for letting me stay."

Stopping just short of her limo, she turned to Aydan. "I don't love her," she said. "She's my friend and I got a little crazy, possessive crazy. Besides, seeing the way she looks at you...what kind of friend would I be if I did something to mess with that? I'm so sorry for the way I acted. I hope you won't take it out on her?"

Of all the things she had prepared for this wasn't it. It was hard not to like this vibrant redhead and she could certainly see why Lori would appreciate her friendship. "Do you mean that?"

"Yeah, I do," she affirmed.

"Would you like to stay? I mean, Zoe did invite you…"

Peachy, squeezing her arm, cut off her invitation. Laughing, she noted, "Zoe will be fine. Take a look over there," she said, pointing to the long line of servers, all moving with trays loaded with flutes of champagne. "Talk about a target-rich environment."

While Aydan had never heard the phrase before she supposed it was apt. There did seem to be an abundance of lovely young women among the caterers, not to mention the musicians, and the private security. Grinning at the revelation, she nodded to Peachy. "I see your point. Still, please don't leave on account of me and Lori."

"It's the right thing to do. I saw the ceremony and that's what counts, and I can see how she looks at you and that's all I needed to know."

She climbed into the back of the stretch limo. "And Aydan… I'll be expecting an invitation to your wedding. Promise me you won't forget," she begged with a wink. And then she was gone.

Aydan stood firmly fixed in the vacuum left by Sue Ellen Peach. Moving only when she sensed Lori close by, she turned, seeing her concerned face. She blurted, "She doesn't love you."

"No, she doesn't."

"Do you love her?"

"No, I don't. It was never like that."

"Like that?" Aydan asked, curious to understand what she meant.

"Like the way I feel about you." Lori added quietly, "The way I love you."

How very upside-down, turned around, and utterly curious this whole thing was. Curious, and heady, and completely unfathomable. "Good, because I'm in love with you, and just in case you don't know, I don't play well with others."

She watched as Lori's sweet lopsided grin made its way to her blue eyes. Nodding she offered her hand, leading them back across the lawn to join the other guests.

Surreal and incredible, walking so openly and proud, she couldn't resist the urge to squeeze the hand holding hers. "You know," she teased, "I have expectations."

"I know you do, princess." Turning to take her in her arms, she brushed her lips against Aydan's cheek, delivering just the gentlest of kisses.

Looking up into Lori's striking blue eyes it was so easy to appreciate her confidence. So many people counted on her strength and in that moment, she knew she could too.

"I love you, Aydan, and I promise—I'm all in."

Bella Books, Inc.

Women. Books. Even Better Together.

P.O. Box 10543
Tallahassee, FL 32302

Phone: 800-729-4992
www.bellabooks.com